THIS

MONSTER

OF MINE

THIS MONSTER OF MINE

SHALINI ABEYSEKARA

UNION
SQUARE
& CO.

NEW YORK

UNION SQUARE
SQUARE
& CO.
NEW YORK

To the quiet but dangerous girls who seethe at injustice:
may they never see us coming.

CONTENT WARNING

This romantasy runs quite dark and contains events that may be difficult to read. Please make every decision you must to keep yourself safe, even if that means stopping here. I remain so very grateful for your interest in *This Monster of Mine*.

This book contains the following: alcoholism, bigotry, immolation, amputation, execution, sex, depression, gaslighting, graphic violence, mutilation, PTSD, nonbinaryphobia, and abuse.

PROLOGUE

The girl was still alive when he returned with the tablecloth they'd use to dispose of her.

The material slid between his fingers. Honeybee silk, a shroud suited for bluer blood than hers, though she wouldn't be grateful. A burst of wind swept in from the balcony to dim the sconces ringing the ballroom, but he could still make out the figure on the floor, hear labored breaths quickening as he approached. More corpse than girl, she contorted into a fetal position, clutching what was left of her robes around her thin chest. Lacerations graffitied her breasts and sallow face. Chunks of singed hair littered the floor around her, the remainder melded to her scalp.

His lips pressed together. *Not again.* After a brief, futile search for patience, he fixed the fool across the room with a stare.

"Five minutes," he said through clenched teeth. "I left you for five minutes to cut her up for disposal. What in all the hells is this?"

The oaf fidgeted, clutching his arm. A nasty wound bled through his fingers. "It's a prime piece of flesh."

There was nothing prime about the body bleeding over the floor, but his business partner wasn't known for his intelligence.

He spread out the tablecloth. "How did she cut you?"

"She's a healer," the fool spat. "Ripped at me when I touched her."

"Well, she's weak or she'd have liquefied you, bones and all, wouldn't she? You'd be a screaming shapeless mass of skin." He let the suddenly quiet man consider that image. "Pack her up."

"I didn't even get to enjoy her," the fool said mulishly, crouching to ponder the mess he'd made of her. "Might still be able to make it work, though."

Trying and failing to be surprised that the man could evoke enthusiasm for a half-burnt, half-dead girl, his gaze drifted back to the floor. Her resistance had cost her. The bones of a chair lay fragmented by her skull, a once ornate vase's ceramic shards studding her skin to leak blood over the tiles. By the Elsar, disposing of her was going to be a headache.

"What I don't understand is why she was here." His voice was dangerously quiet. "She's clearly no illusion magus, and this room is well warded. How did she get in?"

The other man rose, color slowly leeching from his face. "In my defense," he mumbled, "I couldn't have known that she was awake."

Alarm spiked sharp through him. *In my defense.* The most useless words in the common tongue.

In two strides, he seized the man by his collar. "Explain."

"I stuffed her in the closet before our meeting, alright? For afterward. I thought she was asleep—" The fool choked, going ruddy as he tightened his grip. "Her wine was drugged! A few sips should have incapacitated her!"

He released him with a barrage of curses. "She pretended to drink it, you *havïd* fool. They're smarter these days. They don't simply swallow what's offered to them."

Which meant that she would have been lucid throughout it all. Could have overheard them. Everything he'd worked for could vanish like lightning, and all for one man's depravity. He'd never liked the fool, but, tonight, he'd happily burn his throat to a crisp. His thoughts must have shown because the other man sidled out of reach.

"By the Elsar, it was a mistake," the fool croaked. "It won't happen again—"

"So don't let it linger," he hissed. "Carve her up. *Now.*"

"But I didn't get to—"

"Do I look like I give a damn about whether or not you got to bed her?"

The fool shrank away. "There's just one other thing."

I should just kill him. He waited.

The man looked everywhere but at him. "She's the one that girl of yours brought."

He stilled as the words sank in, then lunged across the room. The fool darted to one side, a finger sweeping across a rune on his armilla. A shield of lightning hissed and crackled to life, enveloping him.

Within, he crossed his arms, chin jutting out despite the sweat beading on his temples. "She's just some northern girl!"

"Some *northern girl* that my *aide* valued enough to bring here!" he snarled. "Did she see you with her tonight?" He swore when the man nodded. "What happens when she finds her missing and you were the last person seen with her?"

"We're handling it, aren't we?"

We. Of course, it was suddenly his duty to remedy everything. "That's why *you* shouldn't have touched her, you useless fuck!"

Hands fisted, he glowered down at the girl. Her eyes fluttered, consciousness coming in bursts. She had to vanish. She knew too much. But what of his lovely aide? Once the body was found, she would suspect the fool. An unwanted distraction when he had such plans for their future. Throwing her off their trail would—his head snapped up, heartbeat settling back into a placid rhythm.

He smiled. "Drop your shield."

The other man had the gall to eye him warily before complying. The lightning dissipated with a crack, smoke lingering in the aftermath.

He gathered up the tablecloth. At least they'd spare the silk. "Throw her off the balcony."

The fool's jaw dropped. "But that'll draw even more attention."

"Precisely. Is it a murder? Suicide? A lovers' spat gone wrong? Everyone will have a theory. They'll write us a story."

"That girl of yours might not buy it." The man scratched a grizzled cheek. "Is she really that special? She's pretty if you go for the frail type, but—"

"She'll buy it," he said curtly. She always did. Spotting the relief dawning on the man's face, he snaked out a hand and gripped the now-bruised flesh of his neck again. "But pull a stunt like this again, and it'll be you I'm flinging off."

The fool nodded, eyes watering at the grip. Releasing his throat, he ignored the brief flash of anger across the man's face. Resentment was the defining characteristic of their alliance. A master and his brainless but powerful dog. They needed each other and resented that knowledge.

The girl twitched as the fool stalked to her. Gripping what was left of her hair, he pulled her toward the balcony, shaking her by the scalp when she struggled. Ceramic slivers clinked as her body carved a path through the broken vase. He watched the man hesitate and sighed.

"There'll be plenty like her once things get underway, so just throw her off—"

"You're disgusting."

He paused at the rasp of sound. Propped against the balcony's railing, the girl's eyes defiantly bore into his. He saw in them the knowledge that she was going to die, hatred of him and the fool—all predictable—but the sentiment curving her lips gave him pause. Derision.

"You think you're clever," she croaked. "But someone will notice. They'll wonder why I died."

He crouched as close to her as he could stomach. Truly, the smell coming off her was horrendous—burnt flesh, sweat, and the copper tang of blood that always soured his stomach.

"People may wonder," he conceded, inhaling shallowly. "A few might even put it together. But there's still nothing they can do."

"The Elsar will damn you for this." Her voice held pure loathing.

He straightened. "We pray to the same gods, my dear. And given your condition, I'd say they find me more to their liking. But"—he paused consideringly—"we can make certain of that."

The fool perked up. "You mean—"

A pity. He'd actually tried to spare her this. "We've enough time for a little fun. Let's see if the Elsar make an appearance."

The other man's eyes gleamed, one hand already on the hilt of his dagger.

He tilted his head to the girl in farewell as the fool began. Moonlight struck metal. Blood arced over the balcony's stone tiles—he'd have to have them scoured. Her eyes never left his, terror and rage blotting out all light as she pleaded with the gods and the Saints for salvation. Screaming in desperation, then agony.

He shook his head. Really, she should thank him. By next morning, an unremarkable northern girl would be the talk of Edessa. He was giving her a death so spectacular it would live on in legend.

"The Sidran Tower Girl," he mused, and smiled as she fell into the shattered moonlight. "Oh yes. That'll stick."

CHAPTER ONE

Most days, all Sarai saw was blood.

She found it in the crimson wine being tipped into Chieftain Marus's cup, in the setting sun painting Arsamea's snowdrifts scarlet. It lurked in the mahogany countertop where a dozen cups perched for her to polish. And tonight, she wasn't the only one seeing it.

The red-eyed specter of Lord Death seemed to hover in Arsamea's only tavern, turning the villagers' smiles a little too wide and their laughs too forced. Everyone except Chieftain Marus, of course. At the head of the table, he slapped his pelt-covered thighs, guffawing uproariously. She stepped out of his line of sight. The more he drank, the harder he hit.

"Last toast of the night!" He thrust his goblet high, spilling half its contents.

Sarai raised an eyebrow. They had been on that "last toast" for some time now.

"To the assessors that seek out our humble town every year!" Marus pronounced. "And to the Tetrarchy. Long may they rule!"

Cups rose and clinked, and Marus promptly poured the other half of the goblet over his face in an attempt to reach his mouth. She turned her snort into a sneeze when Cretus narrowed his rheumy eyes in her direction. Hands braced on the counter, he returned to examining his tavern with predatory intent. His profits would be high tonight. Ur Dinyé's most remote village had so little to celebrate that the assessors' visits from the capital had become a strange annual festival. Where everyone toasted the misfortune of those assessed as a Petitor Candidate. Where they thanked the gods, High and Dark, that it wasn't their kin being bundled away to Edessa to be trained for four years at exorbitant tuition fees, only to take their lives after graduating.

That was Arsamea. Grateful for what they had and grateful that others lacked the same. And at present, everyone was grateful that they weren't Chieftain Marus.

"Feels like yesterday when Cisuré started at the Academiae, and she's already graduating," Marus boasted to a silver-haired man whose smile looked frozen on. "One month and she'll be a *Tetrarch's* Petitor."

"You aren't . . . worried?" the man ventured, causing several others at the table to stiffen.

Marus waved a hand. "She's mountain bred. None of that city-folk weakness in her. She'll handle the job."

For once, Sarai wanted him to be right. She couldn't lose Cisuré on top of everything else, and their letters, brief and stilted as they could be, were one of her few tethers to hope.

A few years back, this unease around Petitors would have been unheard of. They were highly prized for their rare brand of magic: detecting lies and tunneling into the memories of those accused of crimes to extract evidence during trials for public view. A talent so indispensable to governance that assessors scoured Ur Dinyé for Candidates and trained them at the land's most prestigious school. Graduates all received lifelong posts with government officials, with the very best getting to work for the Tetrarchy, the land's ruling judges. Then, four years ago, the Tetrarchy's Petitors had begun taking their lives. Now, Candidates were highly prized for a different reason.

"Word is that there's only a few Candidates left in the Academiae. The rest all fled Edessa." Ethra, the town's new healer—and Marus's bit on the side—pursed her lips. "Imagine running from serving a Tetrarch."

"The job's cursed," Flavia, Arsamea's oldest resident, pronounced. "Don't the Codices warn of the forbidden realms of the dead and their lust for resurrection? Something haunts the Tetrarchy. On Wisdom, I feel it."

Sarai hid a snort when the table agreed in hushed whispers. *This* was why southern Urds classified everyone from the north as backward, largely magicless mountain swine. Yet, sometimes, she wondered if Flavia had a point. The Tetrarchy had hidden the conditions of their dead Petitors' corpses, but the capital's grapevine had unearthed and passed on murmurs of sliced limbs, self-immolation, and daggers shoved to the hilt in throats, all of which had raised the same questions across the country. Why would a Petitor take their life with such brutality?

And here I am pining for the same job. Sighing, she picked up another cup to polish. *No hope yet*, whispered the meager coins in the pouch around her neck. *Not for a long time.* Because it didn't matter that she possessed the magic the assessors sought. She couldn't afford a year of the Academi-ae's tuition, let alone the requisite four; and until she could, she wasn't a Candidate. She was nothing.

"Must be nice in the capital." Ethra gloomily stared at the snow piling outside. "Imagine all that sun and sand on our—your skin," she corrected, after a glare from Marus's wife.

Sarai warily eyed the two women's tight grip on their utensils. Their last fight had ended in her scrubbing the floor for hours to prize off the deer gizzards they'd thrown at each other.

Oblivious to the fact that he was the root of most of the village's problems, Marus shot Ethra an irritated glance. "Nothing wrong with our life here."

"It can be a little dull," she foolishly persisted, looking around the table for support. "Haven't you wondered if the south might have more to offer?"

The table fell quiet. Clouds gathered on Marus's face. *Now she's done it.*

He rose with the menace of a blackstripe bear. "Run off to Edessa then. Or have you forgotten what happened to the last brainless woman who did that?" He jabbed a finger that, even in his drunken state, unerringly found Sarai.

She stilled. Anger, always so close at hand, welled forth like blood as heads swiveled toward her from across the tavern, sporting matching expressions of glee. Reminding her that she was worse than nothing because *nothing* received merciful indifference. She silently prayed to all seven of the High Elsar that the barb was a one-off. Then again, the gods had never been overly fond of her.

Booted steps approached the countertop. Marus tossed his cup at her, spite on his red-splotched face. Emptying half an amphora into his cup, she returned it to him. *Don't do it, Marus. Leave me alone.*

"That's what stupid ideas get you," he told Ethra, prodding the air by Sarai's face to indicate the ridged scars mapping every inch of her, brown tributaries within golden skin. "Still think the south has anything to offer?"

Sarai's nails formed red crescents in her palms as Ethra shook her head with distaste. *Stupid ideas.* As though her scars were a punishment from the gods. She had no insight into whether the Elsar gave a *havïd* that she'd dared to be orphaned in a town that froze over for nine months of the year, or that she'd been desperate enough for education to leave Arsamea four years ago and follow Cisuré to the capital. But the good townsfolk *certo* did. So when she'd returned as a scarred wreck after only three days in Edessa, they had never let her live it down.

Perhaps the scars were punishment for the day she finally poisoned them all.

Marus snorted when she forced herself to placidly polish another cup. "If Cretus didn't need the help, I wouldn't have allowed you back, scum. So certain you were too good for us, only to crawl back as a patchwork creature. The Academiae didn't want the likes of you, and Cisuré had no use for you at all."

At least the second half wasn't true. *Your daughter writes to me every month, asshole.*

"Four years," Marus told his rapt audience. "Cisuré's soon to be a Petitor, and this one's still a barmaid. Blood will out. The worthy will rise, but the rest? Destined for dirt." He seized her jaw. "Though someone already taught you that lesson, didn't they?"

A shudder ripped through her at his touch. Crimson tainted her vision, bitterly familiar. She bit her cheek as the walls pressed closer, the room tilting and rippling while the warm salt of blood filled her mouth. Just as it had *that* night in Edessa when her body had smashed into the ground, blood pouring from shattered limbs, as *someone* crouched over her and—

Marus released his grip, shoving her head back. She collided with the wall, nearly knocking over a row of amphorae. The cup she had been polishing clattered to the ground as laughter erupted from every corner of the tavern.

"Did you see her face?" someone yelled. "Where'd you go, Sarai? Back to Edessa?"

"Maybe get another new nose while you're there," another hooted.

Trapping her tongue between her teeth, she picked up the fallen cup and braced herself for another blow. Marus's fist rose right as an ear-splitting cheer went up outside. Past the window, a stampede of Arsameans launched themselves onto the snowy streets.

"The assessors are here!" a passerby yelled. "Drag your sotted selves out!"

Thank the High Elsar.

Sparing her an ugly glance, Marus raced out the door. Chairs scraped across stone as the town's fairest and finest elbowed past each other to parade behind the magi. A mismatched assortment of bells chimed in chorus, dull peals mingling with the deep boom of a gong that some enterprising villager must have dug out of the cellar. It was nothing she hadn't seen before, and tonight would be no different. She'd man the tavern, manage the raucous magi and their helpers who showed up expecting Arsamean women to do anything to please them—and wonder if she'd ever have enough coin to leave this glacial hellhole.

Snow swirled through the open doorway, ice clinging to threadlike fissures in the tavern's stone walls. Rubbing the shoulders of her thin tunic, she straightened the chairs and collected the grease-covered plates left on the tables.

"Tunnel rat." Cretus hobbled over, holding out a wrinkled palm. "You still owe a denarius for this month's rent."

She frowned. "I've paid my two denarii."

"Rent's gone up." He stuck a finger in his ear and dug for something. She hoped whatever it was tunneled all the way to his brain.

They'd played this game before. As the only person in Arsamea who'd house and employ her, he meddled with her rent and wages as he saw fit. And every time, he would seek a reaction.

Cretus snapped his fingers, beady eyes slitted. "Deaf now? You paying or moving out? Plenty who'd take your room."

It's a fucking storage shed. She held back the urge to snap his wizened wrist. "I'll pay."

His mouth pulled back in a triumphant smile. "Keep everyone drunk tonight. I want an accounting of every bottle sold. And for the Elsar's sakes, duck your head while serving, or you'll put the assessors off dinner."

With that, he dragged his hood over the wisps of hair valiantly clinging to his scalp, and plodded toward the outhouse. She saluted his back with a middle finger, then sank onto the nearest chair.

Cretus paid her one bronze assarius a day. With rent going up, she'd have to miss meals to maintain her current rate of saving. Sarai quashed the ache in her stomach warning her that she ate too little as is. Four years ago, she had felt life drain from her with every agonized breath. Had barely survived, only to be thrown out of Edessa without justice and left with no recourse but to save coin after coin serving wine, while the man who'd destroyed her body, her hands—her *life*—ran free. Hunger held little weight in comparison.

Unknotting the coin pouch from her neck, she spilled her savings onto the drink-spattered table. Firelight winked off three gold aurei and five silver denarii. *Not enough.* It would take years for her to afford the Academiae's tuition. But only Petitors and Tetrarchs could access sealed case records. And somewhere in sun-drenched Edessa, within the restricted Hall of Records, was a wax-sealed scroll bearing her name. *Victim.* Beside it would be a single charge—attempted murder—and details of the night she couldn't remember four years, three months, and twenty-eight days ago. Details someone had wanted hidden. And somewhere in that same city lurked her assailant. Becoming a Petitor was her best chance at revenge.

Once she could afford the Academiae's tuition at least.

Sighing, Sarai scraped the coins off the table. "I hope at least you're doing well, Cisuré."

For a moment, she could almost see the other girl sitting across from her with a blinding smile, enthusing over a new bit of frippery, or sobbing into her shoulder after Marus had beaten her for yet another imagined show of defiance. But that had all been four years ago, before Cisuré had become a Candidate and the Fall had made vengeance Sarai's master. Before they'd discovered that even friendship couldn't entirely bridge some divides.

Swallowing, she rose and halted at a movement past the snow-streaked window. A figure stealthily emerged from the shadow of Cretus's smoke chamber for wine, lugging an amphora behind her.

Havïd. Sarai snatched her birrus from behind the counter, locked the door, and raced outside into a blast of icy wind. Cursing roundly, she covered the scant yards to the fumarium and shoved both the girl and the amphora into a snowdrift, just as Cretus emerged from the outhouse. She ignored the wine-thief's annoyed squeak, waiting until he'd faded to a thumb-sized speck in the direction of the town square before releasing her grip to scowl at the sputtering girl.

"I thought we'd agreed that you'd stop."

Vela brushed snow from her closely-cropped dark hair. "Coin's got to come from somewhere. Cretus can afford the loss."

"You can't afford being caught. He'll whip the blood out of you."

"The last time Cretus moved faster than an inch a minute was when Marus was in swaddling furs."

Sarai's lips flattened. "He sliced off another tunnel rat's fingers only two weeks ago for pocketing a loaf off the counter." The boy had met her eyes with knowledge of his fate—infection, fever, which would become sepsis without a healer, and a delirious, prolonged end. Before the Fall, she might have been able to heal him. Now, her hands were too ruined to save anyone.

Undaunted, Vela shrugged. "The boy was careless. I'm—"

"Clearly as bad, because I saw you. Wrath and Ruin, if there was a drunk asshole around, he'd break your hands if it meant getting his on this." She took the amphora from her. "There are worse things in life than Cretus's retribution."

"I know." The twin moons lit Vela's wince as her gaze darted away from Sarai's scarred features.

Pretending not to notice, her grip tightened around the amphora, a ruby-red drop leaking past the loosened seal to hit the ground. Blood on ice.

Sarai looked away. "Where are you selling it?"

"Sal Flumen." Vela fell into step beside her.

"You're mad." It was a fifteen-day walk. She'd attempted it once and nearly died of cold.

"I'll survive." The younger girl set her jaw. "I'm staying there for good. *Havïd* to this village."

"Agreed."

A few minutes south of the tavern, they stopped before a depression in the snow. Vela tapped her boot over it in a series of metallic thuds, and the trapdoor to Arsamea's tunnels swung up. Centuries-old relics of Ur Dinyé's wars, they ran under the village and through the mountain, though no one dared venture that deep. A bedraggled girl waited atop the ladder leading down. No more than eight winters, she stared at the amphora, all hollow eyes and cheeks.

"Guard it, and I'll bring you dinner, Elise," Vela promised.

Sarai reluctantly relinquished the amphora when Elise held out her hands, wincing when the girl staggered at the weight. But assisting her would only make Sarai a target. The folk in those tunnels would gladly rip the pouch from her neck and divide her savings just as they had done to many others. She knew their ravenous hunger well. The tunnels were her birthplace, and where her parents had met their end in an *ibez*-smuggling run gone wrong, leaving her with misshapen memories of gaunt faces and what could have been a mother's smile or a drunken grimace. Cretus had plucked her out at seven when searching for exploitable labor, because she'd been small enough to harvest snowgrapes from their thick, brambly vines. She'd been lucky. Those tunnels held more corpses than people.

"Any other children this winter?"

Vela closed the trapdoor with a clang and followed as Sarai turned back to the tavern. "Just Elise. Parents lost everything at a gambling house and crawled down with her. They're long dead."

Damn it. Pretending to adjust her birrus, Sarai discreetly withdrew a silver denarius and shoved it at her. *It's fine.* She was nowhere close to affording the Academiae's tuition anyway. Vela's eyes widened as she took it.

"Take Elise with you." Sarai tamped down all regret as the coin left her fingers. "When are you leaving?"

"Tomorrow morning, while everyone's wasted in bed. Might even steal a horse." Vela's grin faded. "You don't have to keep looking out for any of us, you know. It'll confuse Elise into thinking that people are decent. Still confuses me."

"Tell her that the coin is yours. In Sal Flumen, pretend to be middle-class siblings whose parents were attacked by brigands. Pity and a child in tow might get you far."

"Brilliant." Vela marveled at the denarius, flipping it between her knuckles. "You sure you don't want to leave Cretus to rot and join us?"

The thought was always compelling, like spun sugar on her tongue until reality dissolved it.

She feigned a laugh. "The rent's twice as high, and I can't compete with the fabri. They'll say I'm too old for any profession but pleasure-work." The irony was that Arsamea was the safest place for her until she had enough for tuition. She knew the villagers' habits. In any other northern tavern, she could suffer much worse than Marus's fist.

"Must be warm." Vela stared longingly at the golden glow emanating from the town square at the end of the street. Raucous cheers carried on the wind. "Do you think they ever wonder if we're cold?"

"They don't think about us at all." Sarai eyed the snow-mottled furs strewn on the street in a semblance of a carpet for the assessors, while people froze to death in the tunnels only yards away. "So you shouldn't think about them. If they poisoned us all tomorrow, no one would care."

Wind shoved at their backs. Both moons hovered above, silver Praefa melding with Silun's bluish incandescence to cast the town in a sepulchral glow. A moonbright night—both orbs near full but never full together, ordained by the gods to wax and wane at different intervals. Perhaps her dreams were the same, destined to never intersect with her.

A sharp rap snapped her out of self-pity. Squinting at the tavern, a frisson of worry ran through her at the violet-robed figure silhouetted at the door. *What in* havïd *is an assessor doing away from the square?*

He knocked again. "Anyone inside?"

Sarai sighed. "I'd best go get his drink."

Vela nodded, staring at her feet. "Well . . . goodbye then."

Sarai managed a smile. "I'm glad you're getting out of here. Steal that horse tonight. There's a snowgale in the air."

The younger girl sniffed the wind and scowled. "Damn. I'll leave now then. I'll try to send some fruit on the next merchant wagon."

"Save your coin and eat well instead—" Sarai grunted when Vela threw her arms around her. Letting go just as quickly, the other girl stuffed her hands in her pockets and bobbed her head awkwardly before racing in the direction of the stables.

Live well, Vela. The ache in Sarai's stomach rose to her chest. Envy, yearning, happiness for the other girl. She let it fester, grow tendrils that sank all the way to her threadbare boots. Then, the cold seeped in and killed the roots, the buds, the ache.

Glancing at the annoyed magus banging on the tavern door, she returned to her frozen life.

Sidling in through the back door, Sarai peered at the assessor framed in the window.

"One moment!" she called, crouching behind the counter and fishing in her pockets for her armilla.

Engraved with the user's runes of choice, the white-gold bracelets were a magus's preferred way to access dormant magic—much tidier than the alternative, bloodletting and drawing runes with the blood. She prized out the pin slotted into the bracelet's bulky hinge, pricked a fingertip, and smeared the blood over *nihumb*, the rune for "concealment." Silver flashed in the rune's deep grooves, a corresponding lurch tugging within her chest. The deep brown scars wrapping her blurred, then faded into her skin. An illusion discernible by touch, a secret she'd kept from the townsfolk, and a skill she'd nurtured in the event she ever saved up enough for tuition. She'd never used it in public before. Contrary to Cretus's certainty that her face was bad for business, the assessors were usually too deep in their cups to care about how mangled the barmaid was. But he was early, and she was alone, and despite her features having been altered during reconstruction, her scars were a rarity, evidence that even multiple healers had been unable to fully restore her. They made her recognizable. And there was always the risk that one of these assessors could be *him*.

Unlocking the door, she bowed. "Welcome to Arsamea. I'm Sarai. A pleasure to serve you, Magus . . . ?"

"Telmar." He swept past her in a whirl of violet robes and collapsed into a chair, snow sliding off his shoulders. "Icewine. And shut the gods-damned door before I freeze to death."

Judging by the magus's bloodshot eyes, he was more in danger of pickling himself in drink. Nevertheless, Telmar seemed lucid enough to survey her as she brought out an amphora of Cretus's best icewine.

"Sit." He imperiously gestured at the chair beside him once she'd filled his cup.

"Apologies, Magus Telmar, but my place is behind the counter."

He gave her a disdainful look. "By the Elsar, you hicks bore me to tears. Off to your counter then. Like there's anyone else for you to serve. They're all busy listening to the same speech year after year." He affected a sonorous voice. "Every year, our courts accumulate defendants requiring a Petitor's aid. Some need to be Examined, their truths distinguished from falsehoods, and—"

"Others must be Probed and their memories Materialized in public for assessment," Sarai finished, and the magus snapped his fingers.

"See? You should deliver it next year. I'm tired of shaking hands and being praised like I'm one of the Elsar. You lot *reek*."

He doesn't seem out for lechery. She sat across from him. "How's the search for Candidates going?"

Telmar gave her a look that could have been appraising. His eyes merely twitched in his skull. "What do you think? Like Petitors offing themselves in every godsforsaken way for the past few years wouldn't dampen things."

"What about borrowing some from other cities?"

He snorted. "No chance. No Praetor or Tribune will relinquish them, and Petitors who would've killed to serve a Tetrarch won't go near one now. They'd rather be bound to a no-name town official than turn corpse in Edessa. Only three Candidates from this year's graduating class haven't scarpered, and they're being watched in case they try."

"Cisuré's one of the three, isn't she?" At Telmar's confused squint, Sarai elaborated. "Pale hair, dark eyes. Memory like a bear trap."

"Oh yes. Taught her to handle a sword last year." He chuckled at her unamused stare. "Mind out of the gutter, barmaid. I meant that literally. She was terrible with a blade. Wouldn't be surprised if she's the first to die."

"Don't say that," she grit out.

Telmar flapped a hand in dismissal. "Well, she's graduating. Time for her to be bound to an official, and there are no vacancies anywhere but the Tetrarchy. Her father sounds right proud."

And Sarai had nearly taken refuge in Marus's certainty. But here was an assessor, an instructor at the Academiae, musing that Cisuré was poised to *die*.

The wall enclosing her scant memories of *that night* shuddered. She drew slow lungfuls of air, but it wasn't enough. Every breath brought back a sound, a sliver of memory from her journey to Edessa four years ago. Squeezing into a fruit seller's wagon with only two goals: to follow Cisuré to Edessa and become a healer so renowned that no one could look down on her. Jumping off the wagon, ready to forge forward, and . . . *blood. Rain. A wet crack as her body hit the cobblestones. Splinters of her ribs shoving through her lungs—*

Her fist hit the table. Telmar gave her a wary look. "Do all the Petitors die every year?"

"Depends. When one dies, the rest get spooked and flee. But last year, they all died." He laughed into his cup. "And we still trundle to every corner of Ur Dinyé, seeking more victims."

"But other officials' Petitors are alive and well! Why are only the Tetrarchy's ones killing themselves?"

Telmar's glazed eyes shuttered. "There's nothing we can do." Dipping a finger in his wine, he stirred it and flicked the excess all over the table. "You serve wine, and I hunt for souls to throw into the job. It's on them to survive."

Wait. Her head jerked up. "Throw into the job? What happened to four years of training?"

He scratched his short beard. "By Wisdom, I knew that word came slow up here, but you didn't know that the Tetrarchy waived that requirement? Better an untrained Petitor than none at all."

She stared. "You're joking. The Tetrarchy can't be that desperate."

"They are." He shrugged at her dropped jaw. "Telling truth from lie is the only standard that matters on the job, and every untrained Candidate can do that much. The Academiae teaches refinement and theory, but if a Candidate lasts long enough, the job'll whip them into shape better than schooling could. Take me." He jabbed a finger at his face, nearly poking out an eye. "Six years of study and all I learned was some tosh on the Borderland Wars. Nearly died during my first stormfall, because I hadn't been taught how to handle . . ."

Sarai stopped listening. A foreign weightlessness expanded in her chest. It took her a moment to place the emotion; it had been so long since she'd last known it. Hope.

She wrapped trembling fingers around her coin pouch. *Three aurei, four denarii*. Not enough for tuition. But it would get her to Edessa.

Her pulse pounded in her ears. "Anyone you find becomes a Candidate? No training or payment necessary?"

"The Tetrarchy decreed it. But why—"

"I'm a Candidate." Her hands trembled as the words *finally* left.

Telmar squinted. "You're what now?"

"You came to find someone who can Examine, Probe, and Materialize, yes? You've got one."

He nearly spat out his wine. "Drink's gone to your head, barmaid."

In two strides, she rounded the table. "Assess me. You'll know if I'm lying."

"You don't even have an armilla!" He indicated her bare wrist. "Will you draw runes in blood? Blame all the grease on this table when they don't work?"

In response, she dug out the bracelet and slapped it down, positioning *nihumb* away from his line of sight.

Telmar blinked, then shoved his cup aside. "That's of Edessan make."

"I was at the capital. Four years ago."

He peered through a fog of drink like he was seeing her for the first time. "Why leave?"

Because I was thrown off a tower at the Academiae, and I have no memory of who did it.

"Does it matter?" She reopened the cut she'd made earlier.

Telmar's brows rose when she pressed the blood over *zosta*, the rune for "Examination" and the simplest of what was known as the Petitor's Trio. No one fully understood the merging of magical bloodlines that produced a Candidate, but only they could use *zosta*, *herar*, and *astomand*, and after the night that had ruined her life and ended her career as a healer, she'd mastered the Trio out of rage.

Blood filled *zosta*'s deep grooves, and silver blazed within, power flooding her in a heady rush not unlike adrenaline. Telmar's eyes widened.

Sarai took a steadying breath. "Try me."

Eyes on the gleaming rune, he didn't move for a moment. "I, Magus Telmar, born in Edessa, graduated from the four hundred and seventy-third class of the Academiae," he began slowly. "It's my sixth year coming to this frozen hell you call a village."

She closed her eyes, evaluating the cadence of each syllable as they thrummed through her. Some of it rang clear, true. "This is your sixth year as an assessor here. The rest is all true." Her eyes flew open. "But you aren't originally from Edessa."

Alertness pushed past Telmar's wine-induced languor. "Let's see you Probe."

She pressed a dot of blood into *herar*, the rune for "Probing." Another silver glow joined the two on her wrist. At his short nod, she placed her fingertips on either side of his head. Between one heartbeat and the next, she plunged into his mind.

Probing was technically a punishment, a violation of the mind in retaliation for prisoners going tight-lipped. But it was only as unpleasant an experience as the Petitor or Candidate made it. Every mind unconsciously reflected its owner's temperament. Some, like Cisuré, had their memories in pristine bookshelves. The sotted tavern patrons she'd tested her skills on—only after they'd been nasty first—had arranged their lives as tapestries, wine casks, or harp strings.

Telmar's mind was a hall of paintings. The recent ones were thin sketches, precariously insubstantial. Only some would remain after tonight, alcohol returning them to blank canvases. The intricate works of depth and color were memories he revisited often. His hometown had to be among them. She reached for a painting of a field and let go upon glimpsing the first time he rode a horse. She went deeper into the hallway before finding her answer in a scene of the Kaycakh Mountains.

She dropped her hands from his head and opened her eyes. "You're from Kirtule."

Telmar gaped. "Why in the Elsar's names have you been rotting away here?"

"Couldn't afford the Academiae's tuition." Darting behind the counter, Sarai retrieved her satchel. "Well? Am I worthy of being sent to Edessa?"

"Wisdom alive, it isn't a matter of being *worthy*. You're riding off into death."

Wouldn't be the first time. "And?"

"You'll be bound to a *Tetrarch*." He shook his head. "Your peers have gone through years of training in diplomacy and politics. You haven't."

"What happened to the job teaching me everything?"

"*If* you last long enough. You can't handle the stress."

"Stress is serving drunkards every night." She rolled up her only spare tunic and packed it. "Pursuing justice is an honor."

Telmar's eyes bugged slightly. "You're mad."

"Desperate." Without an ounce of guilt, she stuffed some of Cretus's bread rolls in her pack. "I'd have saved you the trip if I'd known the Tetrarchy had waived training."

"I almost wish I'd never told you." He sighed, fishing out a crumpled bit of parchment and a half-snapped reed pen from his pockets. Wetting the tip with his wine, he scrawled a few lines, poured some wax off a nearby taper, and impressed his seal. "Go with the High Elsar, if you insist. I'll send word ahead to the Academiae. The Robing is on the first equinox, the fifth day of the Month of Moons. Reach Edessa by then."

She nodded, pulse drumming. Hefting another amphora from Cretus's finest stock, she plunked it on the table. "Help yourself. I owe you."

"It may be the chance of a lifetime, barmaid." Telmar's voice was quiet. "But it isn't worth your life."

"Just as well then." Sarai shoved open the door, tying her birrus around her to face the cold. Her lips formed their first real smile in years. "I have no intention of dying."

She stepped into a sea of snow. There was no further thought, no looking back. Adrenaline pushed her down the deserted street, feet kicking up icy clouds.

The broad logs that formed the town gates swayed under the press of wind. She veered toward the thatched stables on the left, tugging at the stiff door until it swung outward in a rush. She stumbled in to find a group of confused equine faces. But no stable hand. Arsameans were a miserly people, but this night—and this night alone—was when they lost their minds to drink and left their goods unguarded.

Sarai grinned. "Which one of you wants to get out of here with me?"

A glossy chestnut poked its head over a stall door bearing the name "Caelum." She unlatched the stall, the empty one beside it telling her that Vela had left. The mare trotted out. Whispering a quick thanks to the Elsar, she patted its velvety nose.

"We're going to Edessa, Caelum."

The mare whickered, holding still as Sarai tacked her with the only halfway decent saddle available—and climbed on. Her heart pounded so loudly she wondered if the horse heard it too. Wind stabbed at her skin as she left the stables, but none of it mattered. She was finally leaving. Finally able to hunt *him* down.

23

Silhouetted between the main gates, she turned. Snow billowed down an empty street of ice-capped houses, devoid of life and warmth. A fitting final image.

"Goodbye, Arsamea," she whispered. For all its evils, it was the only home she'd known.

Four years ago, she hadn't looked back as she left, believing that a greater destiny awaited her. She was no longer that naïve. This was no trade of the High Elsar's Bright Realms for the Dark Elsar's ten hells, but of one vise for another. Poverty and Marus's fist exchanged for a deathtrap of a job and vengeance.

Sarai faced the winding road through the Arsamean mountains. Somewhere, hundreds of miles away, was the monster who had thrown her off a tower.

"I'm coming for you," she whispered.

The wind took the words and flung them into the abyss down the sheer drop on her right. And as she wound her way down, she could have sworn that the abyss laughed back.

CHAPTER TWO

Rain pounded the cobblestones, sliding off her broken body at the base of Sidran Tower. Pain had long since become a part of her. It ebbed and burned, every drop of rain igniting another cataclysm on shredded skin.

She didn't know why she was here. Tugging on the weak threads of her memory had only made them snap, faces and voices leeching like blood from her skull. All she knew was that the half of her that had met the ground was pulp, and the rest of her wasn't much different.

A man loomed over with a horrified curse. "What have you done?" Revulsion filled his voice. "Her face is gone."

Another pair of boots joined him. "Get her another." The newcomer had the most beautiful voice she'd ever heard. Smooth, mellifluous, unforgettable. A sliver of sound escaped her lips, a plea. The two men didn't seem to notice.

"You surely don't think she can be rebuilt after this! Anyone who sees her—"

"Can be bought," the beautiful voice noted.

"This is the last time I'll cover for you," the other man roared. "Never again!"

A dry chuckle. The scrape of boots against stone. "If only that were true."

Sarai started awake with a scream, clutching handfuls of Caelum's mane. The mare halted its pace with a disgruntled snort. Having experienced more than one such outburst over the past twenty-five days, it waited patiently as she dragged air in through her cupped hands.

Terror bled from her along with the echoes of her only memory after the Fall. Forcing her assailant's voice from her head, she slumped over the horse until her pulse eased. *Lord Fortune, please tell me we've stayed on course.*

The mountain road from Arsamea's gates had led down into the port of Sal Flumen, where she'd sent a letter to Cisuré to say that she was coming and purchased a waterskin.

"Another one succumbing to the south," the vendor had groused when she'd made the mistake of mentioning where she was going. "What's wrong with a quiet life?"

"Nothing," she'd answered honestly, which earned her a glower and mutterings about girls with fanciful ideas who didn't know what they were getting into.

"You'll find out soon enough." The vendor had relented somewhat after Sarai had purchased her sturdiest—and most expensive—waterskin. "Southerners, they only care about themselves. The Guilds send less goods up every year. We can starve as far as they're concerned." The woman's eyes were bitter. "Don't tell them you're a northern girl. You might still be able to get a job that way."

Sarai had thanked her for the advice and set off. After a week, snow gave way to chalky soil. The stretches of northern villages, with their smoking forges and grim populace, red-cheeked with cold, petered out. Dust-coated towns became infrequent splotches on the horizon, all of them bustling with activity, because the south had the bulk of Ur Dinyé's sunshine and dry but arable soil, and made the most of it. Upon hitting desert country and its notorious stormfall, she'd sheltered in towns at night, where the best rates were often found at xanns, inns run by brothel madams where female travelers were often guaranteed better safety than they'd find in reputable lodgings. She'd followed the sinuous Chaboras River for hundreds of miles, with everyone she'd asked for directions telling her that she'd know the capital when she saw it.

Rising from her prone position on Caelum, Sarai stilled at the mass on the inky horizon. They'd been right.

Massive sculptures of ancient Qases and Qasses protruded from the russet marble of Edessa's city walls—a homage to Ur Dinyé's monarchical past. Its present and future lay in the motto etched above the gates in all three languages: the ancient tongue of nobles, the common tongue, and Urdish, Ur Dinyé's native language and that of its runes.

Tetrarchia nos protegit. The Tetrarchy Protects Us. *Cahar srayidan zhar.*

Magnificent. She released an awed breath. It was all magnificent.

And entirely unfamiliar.

Havïd. She'd hoped for a spark of recognition or some sign that her missing memories would return with the right stimulus. Sighing, she steered Caelum toward the obsidian-and-gold city gates and peered at the battlements higher still where magi patrolled the capital's perimeter. Four years ago, she must have taken all this in with utter elation. She reached for those memories and found only a blood-soaked hole between jumping off the fruit seller's wagon and waking to the nightmare that had haunted her since. The three days she'd spent in Edessa were gone.

Tamping down her bitterness, she halted at the gates. A group of robed figures lounged there, short swords marking them as vigiles, soldiers who served one of the four Tetrarchs.

One raised a hand, torchlight glinting off the gold accents in his black robes. "Name and business."

She slipped off Caelum, the illusion hiding her scars in place. "Sarai of Arsamea. The new Candidate." Telmar had promised to send word ahead, but in case wine had obliterated his memory that night, she withdrew his letter.

The guard's tan features had gone slack at her name. Breaking the seal, he skimmed the letter, other vigiles clustering around him. One by one, their heads swiveled from her patched-up tunic to her worn saddle. She chafed under the scrutiny until the first vigile nodded. Two men drew open the city gates in a rumble of metal.

"You came." The first vigile still looked rattled, but his subtext rang loud and clear: What manner of *havïd* fool willingly stepped into this job?

He indicated the entrance to Edessa. "First time here?"

No. Her polite smile didn't falter. "Yes."

"Then welcome to Tetrarch Kadra's Quarter. I'm Gaius, head of his vigiles." He bowed. "All Candidates stay at the Academiae. It's the citadel at the center of the Quarters, about an hour away." Gaius nodded to two men who jumped to attention. "They'll make sure you don't get lost."

Two minders. "I'll be fine," she insisted, but he shook his head.

"We wouldn't want you getting lost." His voice was firm.

She wanted to point out that she wouldn't have bothered coming all this way just to run away now, but the tension in his shoulders halted her. For some reason, Gaius really was worried.

Frowning, she mounted Caelum, her guides behind her. The other vigiles' gazes never left her, pity on each face as she passed through the parted gates. She fought a shudder. *How many dead Petitors have they seen to think I'm already doomed?*

The city hummed with life despite the late hour. Guildspeople clustered around braziers, their blazeleaf pipes wreathing them in smoke. Grimfaced vigiles in black and gold robes dined outside taverns, their skewers of meat dripping fat onto colorful tablecloths. Her stomach growled, but she refused to part with the single gold aureus left of her savings.

Insulae dotted Edessa, each home stacked on top of the other like salt blocks. Night markets bustled with merchants still luring buyers to their wares. She glanced at a few armilla sellers, trying to recall where she had purchased hers. Her memory remained blank.

The most striking thing, however, was the rune-covered metal rods marking the corners of every dwelling. *Fulgur scuta*, lightning shields, invented by Head Tetrarch Aelius. Several assessors had spoken of them.

If Arsamea and its neighboring mountain towns were notorious for snow and sludge, Ur Dinyé's lower south was beset by stormfall. Every city would have been flattened by lightning had Magus Supreme Priscus of some eight centuries back not come up with a system for rotating groups of magi to patrol the city's battlements and redirect lightning strikes into the surrounding terracotta desert—if a few travelers perished as a result, they could only blame the gods.

Yet, diverting lightning took great power, forcing magi to make devastating decisions when multiple bolts approached the city at once. Every stormfall had seen casualties until Tetrarch Aelius had found a solution four years ago: a steel rod carved with runes repelling lightning to be placed outside every structure. A miracle for the south for which Aelius's name was rightfully revered. Even a few of the wagons passing her sported the four-foot rods.

The citadel that housed the Academiae stood on a plateau, overlooking the city. Her guides followed her up one of the well-traversed roads snaking up the incline before taking their leave. And she was finally there.

Reining Caelum to a halt, she dismounted before the Academiae's gates. Ur Dinyé's most prestigious school rose from the heart of Edessa, a spider at the center of a web, waiting to bleed its next unwary victim dry. As it had her.

Icy bands tightened around Sarai's chest. The palatial complex of orange-red limestone sneered down at her like a haughty lord, its moonlit towers, assorted spires, and domes bristling that she had dared return. Asking if she hadn't learned her lesson.

"I'm back," she whispered. "You won't get rid of me so easily this time."

Sconces bracketed the metal doors before her, casting a flickering glow on the letters engraved at the top. *Lisran Tower Gate.* According to a map Cisuré had drawn in an old letter, this was the Academiae's northwestern tower.

And Sidran Tower rose to the north.

Her jaw clenched. Eight towers at cardinal directions around the Academiae. Eight Tower Gates beside each, guarded by magi. Sneaking in was

29

impossible, but somehow, at fourteen, she'd done it and fallen into Death's arms. And she couldn't remember *why*.

"Speak your business," came a stentorian roar.

Her eyes flew up to the sentry in the Tower Gate's watchtower. She lowered her hood. "I'm Sarai, the new Candidate. I was told to come here."

The man raised an eyebrow, before the latch locks crowning the doors snapped down. The Gate creaked open with a screech of hinges, revealing a violet-robed magus who gave her a scathing perusal.

"The mountain girl arrives at last." Taking Caelum's reins, he rapped on the ladder leading up to the watchtower. "Hand over that aureus. Told you she'd come. No sense in these northerners. Petitors dying on the job, and they're walking in."

Asshole. She tamped down her irritation as the sentry tossed down a gold coin with a resentful grunt. Patting Caelum farewell, she made to enter the Academiae when the magus blocked her path.

"Not so fast." He smirked. "Confirm your identity first, or we'll have every northern barmaid racing here and calling themselves a Candidate."

Sarai pricked her finger, smearing blood across *zosta* before forcing a smile. "Yes?"

A nasty gleam lit his eyes. "I think you're a looker. Truth or lie?"

Her nails bit into her palms when the syllables reverberated in jarring echoes. "That's a lie." While he guffawed, she wiped her blood over *zosta* again, turning the rune dark. "Can I enter now?"

"Wait over there. Someone'll come for you."

Another guard. "I really didn't come all this way just to flee before the Robing."

"Like I care." He rolled his eyes. "Wait in the courtyard, mountain girl."

Biting her tongue, she took her first steps into the Academiae in four years. Snatches of conversation reached her as the magus called up to the sentry.

"Can't believe she came. Ten aurei says she'll be the first to kill herself..."

A muscle twitched in her jaw. He wouldn't be the only one with that opinion. Pacing the courtyard, she waited for her newest minder. *Gods, they're being ridiculous.* She could understand their vigilance if she'd been dragged here kicking and screaming, but she'd walked in. An unsettling suspicion pricked at her. *Unless this isn't about me.* From Gaius to the magi here, no one had acted like *she* was the problem but like they'd been shielding her from one. *But that doesn't make sense.*

Stowing the puzzle away for later examination, she took in the view. Eight towers encircled the Academiae, tens of miles apart. A maze of walkways, colonnades, and ramparts bridged instructional buildings scattered across the grounds, magi of various disciplines still training in courtyards despite the late hour.

Magic was like coin. Some Urds had more than others, and you could only blame the gods if you weren't born with much. Every country had an element that most of its people could manipulate, Ur Dinyé's being lightning. Its formation, redirection, and use in combat was the land's most common magic—albeit one she didn't possess—followed by agriculture, healing, and the odd Petitor and illusionist. Some people had a strong talent in only one branch. Those, like her, with ability in multiple branches had limits. In addition to a Petitor's abilities, she could only use one illusion rune, *nihumb*. Her only attempt at a more powerful illusion—hair color—had failed, drained her of magic, and left her feeling like she'd been beaten to a pulp.

Talent aside, the biggest hurdle for many was training. Schools offered tutelage at hefty prices, resulting in people going into debt for the prospect of a better future. Others sought work as fabri, tradesmen in the north, or apprenticeship in the southern Guilds, which didn't require coin for entry but assigned exploitative, backbreaking hours. Entering the Academiae, Ur Dinyé's best school, was a dream for most. As it had been for her.

Sarai stared at the sconce-lined courtyard. *What did you think?* she asked her fourteen-year-old self. *What did you see here?*

Rain, whispered the hole in her mind. *Splinters of ribs shoving through lungs with each breath. One eye ruptured upon impact*—Sarai slammed a hand into the wall, cutting off the memory.

Breathing hard, she focused on the banners draping the courtyard's walls until their letters swam into view. *All citizens capable of Probing, meet with an assessor now!* one demanded. *Join with a Tetrarch and earn four thousand aurei every year!*

Join with a Tetrarch. Sarai snorted. *Now there's a turn of phrase.* But gods, that salary! Clutching the gold coin left in her pouch, she imagined four thousand of them. She could eat three meals a day, feed Arsamea's poor for years. Could toss Marus into the tunnels and kick his face until—

A bright bolt danced jagged across the sky. Her head whipped up to the black-edged horizon just as thunder rent the air. *Shit.* If the lightning bristling under those clouds was any indication, Edessa was about to get one of its infamous storms. And she was outside.

Sarai didn't pause to think. The rules for surviving stormfall were the same as for an Arsamean snowgale: get indoors and stay indoors. She raced under an arch and out of the courtyard, searching for shelter. Similar frantic footsteps came from the surrounding courtyards, but given how quickly they faded, everyone else knew where to go.

Light flashed in the distance, the thick air starting to pick up speed. Storm clouds churned above, blotting out both moons. With mounting panic, she spun in a circle in search of refuge when a hand locked around her wrist.

What in havïd? She fought the hold before the hand's owner pointed at an enclosed garden folly barely visible some yards away.

Thank the Elsar. The world narrowed to the air scraping the back of her throat and the blood rushing in her ears as they ran. By some miracle, she and her rescuer managed to drag the garden folly's door open and squeeze in right as the storm hit. She peered through the windows in horrified awe as the sky cracked open as though one of the hells had opened above Edessa. Rain pounded down in heavy sheets, granules of cobblestone flying at the impact. The Academiae's sconces sputtered out. She could barely see her hands.

"Thank you." She turned to the man who'd just saved her from death by deluge. "I owe you, Magus . . . ?"

"Drenevan." The stranger's baritone was a caress. Butter smooth, every word richly, impeccably enunciated.

Her jaw dropped. *Gods alive.* She stared at the patch of darkness where he sat as unease slid down her spine. Inhaling sharply, she quelled the memories of the Fall. Just because the man had a stunning voice didn't mean he was *him*.

"I'm Sarai." Realizing that she hadn't properly thanked him, she reached for her coin pouch. "I'm sorry. I only have an aureus. If you'd like it."

Part of her hoped he didn't. It was her last coin.

A long pause. "You don't owe me."

"You had my life in your hands. It's hard to believe that you don't want something for it."

Gods, please don't let it be sex. Her fingers slid to her armilla, seeking out *beshaz*'s ridges. The rune allowed rudimentary access to a body's organs to those with any healing ability and was equally useful as a weapon. Despite her ruined hands, she could still mangle a tendon or two.

More silence. Then, "Have you always seen life as transactional?"

"It *is*, even if those in gilded places like this think otherwise. Coin trumps common sense, decency, law. We're all borrowers or lenders, chasing it—" She bit her tongue, realizing that she was inches from a tirade and had indirectly insulted him to boot.

"Is that so?" He sounded amused. A flash of lightning seared his silhouette into her eyes. He was taller than she'd first glimpsed. "Which one are you? Borrower or lender?"

Odd. She normally didn't do well with strange men and confined spaces. "You first."

The magus didn't move, and she had the strange sensation of being assessed through the dark. "I'm a debt collector."

"So, law enforcement?"

"Yes." Again, that sense of him staring at her. "Your turn." His voice slipped down her spine, sliding to a part of her that she'd long ignored.

She swallowed, grateful for the dark enclosing them. *I bet his bed's never empty.* The storm made the world fall away, took her to a realm where she wasn't a woman whose face had once made a child cry, but a Candidate talking to a man with a voice like the smoothest icewine. And it was all so foolishly peaceful, a cocoon of quiet outside time itself, that she gave him the truth.

"I just want to give," she said quietly, watching rain punch the ground. "Taking is inevitable in life. But I'd like to give more than I receive."

He was quiet again. Outside, the Academiae blanched as a bolt of lightning arced above, halting its downward progress to ricochet in the sky instead. The magi on the battlements must be hard at work.

Hold on. "Aren't you supposed to be aiding with the storm?"

"I always do." A wry note entered his velvet note.

"Until you had to stop me from being roasted alive." She winced. Not showing up for duty would get him severely reprimanded, if not worse. "Gods, I'm sorry. I'll vouch for you if you get in trouble. You were still saving lives—well, *a* life. Is it too late for you to get to a Tower Gate or up on the ramparts? How can I help?"

A pause. "What if that means entering the storm?"

She glanced at the madness outside the window and sighed. "I owe you. I'd prefer not to." Debt seemed more dangerous than stormfall in this city. "What do you need?"

This silence was the longest yet. She'd begun to wonder if he regretted helping her when he finally spoke.

"Stay here." A rustle of clothing indicated that he'd stood. "I can get there."

"Oh," she faltered. *Then why did you stay with me in the first place?*

Booted footsteps crossed the distance to the door and paused. Lightning streaked above just as he inclined his head.

Knife-sharp eyes cut into hers. "A pleasure to meet you, Sarai of Arsamea." The door swung open, clattering in the howling wind. She'd barely started to her feet when it slammed shut.

She'd never told him where she was from.

Perhaps all the Academiae's magi had been told to watch for her arrival. That was the most logical explanation, because if not, then . . . *he was waiting for me.*

A chill ran through her. *Don't be paranoid.* There was no reason for a magus to do that.

Outside, the storm raged, streaks of lightning painting the sky for what felt like hours before dwindling to a few stray flashes. Rain pattered to a stop. A wave of humidity slammed into her the second she opened the door. The ground not covered by cobblestones was sodden, little more than mud.

So this is what stormfall leaves in its wake. She couldn't imagine life before Aelius's fulgur scuta. At least they protected the populace from lightning strikes, even if not the deluge.

Avoiding the muck, she tried to figure out how to get back to the Lisran Tower Gate when a yell sounded behind her.

"Sarai!" A blurry figure raced toward her. She barely had time to take in the girl's familiar features before she found herself enfolded in a hug. "It's so good to see you!"

A rusty grin stretched Sarai's cheeks as she hugged her oldest friend back just as tightly. Time blurred and for a moment, she was fourteen, unscarred.

"I was on my way to get you, but the storm—" Cisuré pulled back, grasping her shoulders. "How are you? I was so worried that you didn't make it inside."

"A magus helped." Sarai grinned, taking her in. There was a new maturity to Cisuré's eyes, a tautening of her impish features, but the pale-haired girl still radiated the same sunniness. Four years. It felt like a lifetime. "He already knew I was from Arsamea, though."

"That'll be Telmar's fault. He's been regaling everyone about how you went from pouring wine to Probing him like a seasoned Petitor. At this rate, we'll have assessors scouring taverns for Candidates."

"They can search the outhouses if they'd like. Deaths aside, tuition is the issue. I thought I'd be fifty before I saved up enough."

"That's the price of prestige." Linking their arms, Cisuré steered her past an obscenely ornate fountain. "If everyone can come here, then no one will want to come."

"It's an education, not passage to the Bright Realms," Sarai said wryly, sighing when the other girl wrinkled her nose and shrugged. Cisuré had wanted for much in life, but not wealth. Sometimes, it showed. "So, you're my minder!"

Cisuré winked. "The magi know I won't run, so they let me show you around. You look great by the way. Your skin . . ." she trailed off with a flinch. "It must have been a relief, getting the scars removed."

Sarai's brow furrowed. "I didn't."

There had never been any hope of that. The healers who'd knit her back together had warned afterward that the scars would never fade. No magic could do more for her than what had been done, short of Summoning a god and begging for mercy. Perhaps Cisuré had forgotten.

The other girl faltered. Something dimmed in her eyes as she traced the invisible ridges of the scars over Sarai's hands. "Was this the illusion rune you were talking about after . . ."

Sarai nodded. She'd gone more than a little mad in the months after the Fall, drawing rune after rune in blood, praying that one of them would light up, that she had something left now that healing had been stolen from her. Only *nihumb* and the Trio had shown promise.

"It'll last about a day, even through sleep, so I should be safe."

Releasing her hand, Cisuré bit her lip. "Well, that's . . . good."

Havïd. Perhaps starting their reunion with her most glaring remnants of the Fall hadn't been the best idea. Glancing around, Sarai tapped one of the banners.

"Any reason why these make the job sound like we're being paid to sleep with a Tetrarch?"

"Right?" Cisuré's good humor returned. "Still, it's a marriage of careers, and a bargain. A husband wouldn't pay half as well."

Sarai winced in agreement. Marriage in Arsamea had meant rearing children, and slaving over cooking fires while men like Marus slept their way through the surrounding villages. Neither she nor Cisuré had thought highly of that future. And after the Fall, she'd barely thought of men at all.

"I still can't believe it." Cisuré squeezed her arm like she thought Sarai would vanish. "You, *here*. Just like—" She looked uncomfortable again.

"Like we'd initially planned," Sarai finished tightly.

A protracted silence fell. Cisuré's grip loosened. "That day we returned to Arsamea . . . I thought that was the end."

So did I. "Never! We wrote to each other every month."

"But it wasn't the same."

No. The hollow in her chest where that particular pain lived reopened, echoes pouring out of the day a few vigiles had unceremoniously tossed her on a wagon out of Edessa. Of Cisuré's pale face wreathed in tears as the wagon hit every ditch on the road up into Arsamea. Of the devastating words she'd uttered: *"You need to stay here from now on. Recover."*

Sarai had argued that Arsamea was the last place she should be when her face—when *she*—was no longer the same. When everyone would hold it over her. There had only been a pause and the painful loosening of the other girl's hands from hers.

That day, Cisuré and the wagon had left after depositing her in Arsamea. They never came back. And something had altered between them in the four empty years since. At times, Sarai thought she could see everything they were avoiding in the gaps in their carefully worded letters, in their every hesitant "it's been so long." Some days, she thought the parchment would bleed if she dared set it all down.

"Did you blame me back then for leaving you there?" Cisuré's voice shook.

There it is. The question they'd avoided for four years. A rush of icy wind parted them as though some vestige of Arsamea had followed her all the way here.

"No." The lie plowed past years of loneliness. "You were trying to help."

Cisuré gave her a pinched smile, but the tension didn't leave her shoulders. They passed a series of columns framing another courtyard when she took a deep breath. "Why did you come? You must have heard about the deaths."

"Who'd turn down being a Tetrarch's right hand? Or four thousand aurei?"

"Nearly all my classmates did, or the Tetrarchy wouldn't be desperate enough to axe training. But you still volunteered to walk into danger. Again."

"To be fair, I don't think I knew that the first time around—"

"Sarai!" Cisuré rounded on her.

Sarai stiffened at her taut features. "I—"

"You nearly died last time! Do you know what it was like for me to see you in pieces?"

No. "Cisuré—"

"Your face was shredded! Every limb snapped—"

"Stop!" Sarai shouted. Jerking her arm from Cisuré's grip, she hunched over, drawing deep lungfuls of too-humid air. *Don't think about it. Do. Not. Think. About. It.* A lifetime of shoving away her emotions reared to the surface, reflexively obeying.

"I'm so sorry," came Cisuré's anguished voice above her. "I didn't mean to . . ."

"I know." Straightening, Sarai squeezed her hand. "I know."

Her gaze drifted to the east, to the spire just barely visible behind Lisran Tower. *Northwest.* Disquiet slithered up her spine. *North.*

Cisuré followed her gaze and swallowed. "Do you still dream of it?"

Every night. "No."

The other girl's lips pressed together. Taking Sarai's hand, she dragged her out of the courtyard and down a hallway until she halted in front of an alcove and pressed them in.

"I need you to promise me something." Her trepidation sent an answering ripple through Sarai. "Stay away from Sidran Tower."

The name hung in their cramped quarters for a few awful seconds. "Why?"

"No one knows you survived," Cisuré whispered. "The vigiles kept it quiet. So your fall became Edessa's most infamous mystery. Sarai, they call you the Sidran Tower Girl! Conspiracy mongers still pop up every year claiming that you were an assassin or a spy!"

"If you're telling me to be careful—"

"I'm telling you that I'm scared. This isn't Arsamea. Edessa will have you for a mouthful and spit your bones outside the gates. The Sidran Tower Girl is *dead*. She needs to stay that way."

"I know—"

"And I know *you*. You were always so angry about the injustice of practically everything. I can't imagine that's changed. You still look back and wonder, instead of letting the past *rest*."

Her throat constricted. *How?* How was she to move forward when the past wrapped around her body in a thousand scars? When she didn't have so much as a face or a name to curse?

"You will find no friends here," Cisuré said grimly. "You're an unknown who waltzed in from the north. People won't be kind."

"Then Arsamea's prepared me well. I'm here for the job."

"Which demands impartiality and delivering the law's verdict at *any* cost, neither of which you're good at! You're going in blind! Sidran Tower's a distraction you don't need, so just swear to me that you'll leave the past where it belongs." Cisuré held out an unblemished hand, delicate joints and fingers enclosed in supple skin. Everything a hand should look like. "*Please*."

Damn it. If she refused, Cisuré would know that Sarai intended to dig into the Fall, go into paroxysms of panic over her safety, and almost definitely try to stop her.

Sighing, Sarai dropped her illusion, pretending not to notice Cisuré's wince at the return of her real appearance. Matching her palm to the other girl's, she hid a flinch when Cisuré gazed at it in horror, taking in the crooked joints, the parchment-thin scars feathering her skin, the perpetual, incurable trembling of her fingers.

"Your hands." Cisuré interlocked their fingers, gripping them tight as though she could halt the shaking. "When you said you couldn't be a healer anymore, I didn't realize . . . I'm so sorry. It was all you ever wanted—"

"It's fine," Sarai broke in tonelessly. A skill honed for years, lost in a night. "I can still heal cuts and the like. Just . . . nothing further."

Tears pooled in Cisuré's eyes. She bowed over their hands. Their subsequent silence was weighted with the memories of years of healing both their wounds from Marus. Sarai wanted to mourn too. But she'd spent too long burying the hurt. She didn't know where to start digging.

"The gods give and take away." Cisuré wiped her face. "If you hadn't lost healing, you wouldn't have thought to look for *nihumb* or gotten proficient with the Trio. You're *here*," she said fiercely. "Don't lose what you have by looking back." Their clasped hands shook. "Promise me. On the Elsar."

Sarai closed her eyes. *I can't,* she told the gods. "I swear," she lied. *I'm sorry.*

Cisuré released her hand after a long moment and watched her reestablish the illusion. "Let's get you settled in."

Leaving the alcove, they entered the shadow of Lisran Tower. An enormous statue of Lady Wisdom, patron goddess of Petitors, hugged the base of the red limestone building, brandishing a pen in one hand, a hammer in the other, and a sword at her hip. *Poet, artisan, and warrior.* From the buildup of candle wax at its base, the tower's jewel-and-marble protector had seen at least a century of fervent prayer.

"Beautiful, isn't it?" Cisuré said with awe.

Try ostentatious. Even the smallest of the rubies set into the pommel of the goddess's sword could have fed Sarai for a couple years.

"Beautiful," she echoed a smidgen too late, and Cisuré's eyes narrowed.

"Try to sound genuine, will you? You're too blunt."

She had heard the same in Arsamea. Cisuré was expressivity itself. But the words used for Sarai had been different. Too quiet, *bitter.* They weren't wrong. Slaving for coin had taught her that emotion was best concealed, opinions were a liability, and that dreams were for the wealthy.

She smiled wryly. "I've mostly said '*certo*' and 'thank you' for the last few years."

"*Tibi gratias ago,*" Cisuré corrected. "Tetrarchs and their Petitors use the ancient tongue whenever possible. Commoner speech isn't becoming of our stations."

Sarai blinked. "But we serve those commoners."

"Doesn't mean that we should emulate them." Cisuré's face brightened. "And you're going to meet the Tetrarchy so soon! You'll love the Robing."

Sarai winced. The Robing wasn't just a Petitor receiving their Tetrarch's robes. Held in the Amphitheatrum Aequitas, the highest court in the land, it was an opportunity for citizens and gossip rags alike to sketch a first impression of each new Petitor.

"Guess I'll be practicing the *havïd* ancient tong–" She yelped when Cisuré smacked her.

"Watch your language! You'll be a Petitor soon. Act like it." Her hair lit up like a halo under a nearby sconce, and Sarai couldn't help laughing. Always the saintly sun to Sarai's dour moon.

"Surely even the Tetrarchs curse. What's life without a sporadic 'shit' or 'fu–' Ow!" She rubbed at where Cisuré had dug her elbow into her side.

"Perhaps Kadra curses, but the rest keep their words lily-white and so shall we." Cisuré pursed her lips, daring her to argue.

"Yes, my lady," Sarai groused. "Is there a Tetrarch you've got your eye on?"

"Oh, we don't get a choice." Her laugh held a nervous edge. "Let's get your uniform from the Night Office. I'll show you around Edessa if we get a moment after the Robing."

Sarai nudged her. "I thought you said I'd find no friends here."

"You'll always have me." Cisuré grinned. "Here we are. Lisran Tower."

Northwest. Sarai's steps slowed. *North.*

Slowly, her gaze slid to the right, to the spire-topped column miles away glowering down in recognition. For a moment, she was fourteen again, lying in her own blood, rain pounding from above. Her eyes lifted to the balcony at the top. *A hundred-and eighty-seven-foot drop.* She shouldn't have survived. She shouldn't remember any of it.

But she remembered enough. Agony as healers knit her back together. Despair when the vigiles had ended their investigation after three days, sealed her case records, and tossed her out of Edessa.

Resolve burned in her chest. Four years ago, someone in this city had wanted her dead.

And by all the gods, she was going to make him pay.

CHAPTER THREE

A dry chuckle. The scrape of boots against stone. "If only that were true." The man with the beautiful voice stepped away from her.

Don't go. Her lips soundlessly shaped the words. She didn't know why she was begging, only that she believed he would listen.

She willed her fingers to move from where they rested inches from his boots. Her knuckles twitched, and pain ignited along her hand, shooting up to her skull. Her functioning eye rolled back as blood filled her nostrils, seeped from her open mouth—

Sarai's eyes flew open. Stumbling off the bed, she grasped the vanity, breathing hard until her vision cleared. The face in the mirror was gaunt, eyes feverish, thin, brown scars standing out in relief, as if someone had glued together a thousand pieces and hadn't bothered to hide the seams. She numbly traced features that still felt unfamiliar. The healer who'd reconstructed her face hadn't bothered with faithfulness to the original—a fact that had given Arsamea much fodder for abuse. Even her eyes were an unnatural gold from their original black.

It could have been worse. Scarring aside, her face was normal enough. But she'd endured enough flinches in Cretus's tavern to prove that most people saw only the scars.

If only that were true. Her teeth ground together at the memory of that beautiful voice. The outline of Sidran Tower peered through the dirt-flecked window, a ghost at the edge of her vision. She averted her gaze and cursed before forcing herself to look back at it. From now on, she had to act the part of a normal person. And normal people did not panic at the sight of Sidran Tower.

Morning air teased her hair as she stepped onto the balcony. Ironically, she'd been given the highest room in Lisran Tower. Sarai gripped the railing as the tiles seemed to sway beneath her feet. Heights. The first fear she'd gained after the Fall.

Pulling her gaze up, she drank in the Academiae's sun-drenched halls, stone walkways, and green courtyards that spoke to talented agro-magi working around the clock to keep the grounds thriving. Fifty-foot walls separated the central citadel from Edessa, punctuated by the Tower Gates. Below them lay wide central roads, weaving through the city's four Quarters, each named for the Tetrarch who governed them: Aelius, Tullus, Cassandane, and Kadra. Sarai couldn't believe she'd be meeting them soon.

She poured power into *nihumb*, scars vanishing as a thread of red entering the gleaming rune. The illusion would hold until the rune went fully crimson, warning her that she'd depleted herself of magic. Sloughing off layers of travel dust and what felt like a good amount of skin in the bathing room, she donned the genderless uniform worn by Candidates over which her Tetrarch's robes would go after the Robing: inky black and starkly cut, with buttons that extended from the uniform's collar to her waist where the skirt flared out to brush her trousered ankles. Weaving her hair into a braid, she stared at the unrecognizable figure in the mirror. Hollow-eyed, yet dignified. *Not a barmaid. Not a victim. A Petitor.*

A lump built in her throat. "Petitor Sarai," she whispered, and her reflection stood taller.

She descended Lisran Tower's spiral staircase, firmly ignoring the wretched tower to the north. Cisuré had said that a raeda would take her to the Aequitas. She'd also mentioned something about breakfast in the Academiae's dining hall, but Sarai knew her nervous stomach would do worse with ammunition.

Outside, the raeda waited by the Lisran Tower Gate as promised along with a few magi who looked relieved that she hadn't run away.

"Petitor Candidate Sarai." The coachman bowed. "An honor to escort you."

A month ago, no one would have said that. She wondered if he was pulling her leg, but his weather-beaten face held only curiosity.

"Thank you," she said and paused at the narrow-eyed look a passing magus shot her.

She stifled a sigh. *Right. No "commoner speech" from Petitors.* And the south wondered why northerners found them pretentious.

Climbing in, she gaped. All burnished oak and violet cushions, the carriage would have made Cretus weep. She sat gingerly, half expecting it to turn to smoke. The gate opened, and the carriage started forward, cobblestone blurring as it sped onto the road leading down the citadel.

Edessa lay below, resplendent under the sun, its sprawling streets lined with shops, bare patches denoting public squares, and the oblong domii of the wealthy. Years ago, atop a tall snowgrape vine, she'd looked down at Arsamea and spanned it with a hand, an uncaring fist in the distance. But Edessa could swallow her.

They joined a many-laned road, competing with other raeda heading to the Aequitas in the south. The coachman called back to her, pointing out various landmarks: domii of famous people she'd never heard of, Guilds, the Grand Elsarian Temple.

"The Hall of Records," he said, and she nearly pulled a muscle twisting to spot a series of marble structures. *Soon*, she vowed.

Like the Academiae, Edessa's major establishments were situated at the center of the city. Neutral territory.

"Best that no one Tetrarch controls it all," the coachman confided. "Imagine if a Tetrarch could halt access to a Guild during a feud!"

"Do they feud often?" Four heads probably didn't agree on everything.

"Might be because they care in different ways. You'll help too. This is your city now."

Warmth rose in her. Propping an elbow on the window, she smiled at the bustling world beyond. The road flattened into a public square the size of Arsamea. Their pace slowed.

Clusters of people poured out into a field, competing for entry into a gargantuan structure. *The Amphitheatrum Aequitas.* Craning her neck, she counted the amphitheater's five tiers of flawless white marble and intricate arches and smirked. *Guess I'm not destined for dirt after all, Marus.*

Sentry posts dotted the perimeter of the Aequitas. Hard-eyed vigiles in colorful robes squinted suspiciously at everyone, barking orders to confiscate weapons or large items. An elderly man belligerently objected to a wineskin being taken, to no avail.

"They wear their Tetrarch's colors," the coachman explained. "Black and gold for Tetrarch Kadra, ivory and silver for Tetrarch Aelius, and so on. Almost every vigile is here. Can't be too careful with the Tetrarchy and Guildmasters gathered for the Robing. *Certo,* with you too . . ." he trailed off with an awkward glance.

That's why we're transported separately, she realized. *To make it hard for us to flee.*

Evading the mob, he steered into a fenced-off side of the Aequitas, halting before a massive statue of a regal man, almost as tall as the courthouse. The coachman indicated a door into the court, partially hidden by the statue's base.

"The horn is your cue to enter." He bowed. "Take care, Petitor Candidate Sarai."

She responded in kind, Petitor language conventions be damned, then turned to the sculpture. The marble man wore a benevolent smile, stretching a hand to the sky, a rune-studded rod clutched within. *Which of the seven High Elsar is this? Lord Fortune? Harvest?* She squinted at the rod.

"Tetrarch Aelius and his first fulgur scutum," a low voice commented in her ear.

She jumped, goosebumps pebbling her skin.

The lanky young man behind her grinned unrepentantly. "Incredible, right?"

She could think of other words, but she supposed that the Head Tetrarch, the most powerful magus in the land and inventor of the south's beloved lightning shields, had the right to erect ludicrously large replicas of himself.

"Harion of Dídtan." The newcomer's black hair stuck up at the ends, skin as golden as hers, but there was no missing the condescension in his eyes. "You must be the barmaid."

"Sarai of Arsamea," she corrected politely.

"Pleasure." He took his time looking her over. "You northern girls are usually meatier."

"Sorry to disappoint."

"She has a tongue." Harion's eyes narrowed speculatively. "You've put it to good use to get this far. Which Tetrarch did you sleep with?"

Here we go. "Excuse me?"

"I mean, the Tetrarchy needs Petitors, but I doubt we're desperate enough for *you*. Unless you offered *other* incentive." He circled her. "Can't be Aelius. You were gawping at his statue like a tourist. Can't be Kadra either, he's a block of ice. That leaves"—Harion made a face—"Tullus? Really? Unless you swing the other way for Cassandane—"

"It's my *first* time meeting the Tetrarchy."

He wrinkled his nose. "Suit yourself, but whoever you're fucking won't choose you. They've lined you up for *him*. Someone's going to be the odd one out."

"There are four of us and four Tetrarchs," she pointed out.

"Oh, you *really* don't know." He looked positively gleeful. "There's only ever been three Petitors for the past few Robings. Kadra has never taken one."

Odd. All she knew of Kadra was that he'd been elected the newest—and youngest—Tetrarch in a landslide victory a few years back. No one in Arsamea had bothered to journey to the capital to vote, and as the Tetrarchy left the north to its devices, the election had been largely ignored. But she was surprised that Kadra's lack of a Petitor hadn't come up.

Becoming a Tetrarch was a daydream for all but the wealthiest Edessans. Hopefuls began as Tribunes in the military, or iudices, lower court judges, and worked to amass power until they could run for office. Even then, they had to be powerful lightning magi, popular with the masses, and shrewd politicians with spotless reputations. Aspirants relied heavily on their Petitors to ferret out unscrupulous friends and con men. For Kadra to have never had one was unheard of.

Harion stooped so they were eye to eye. "It isn't too late to leave. You won't last a day with Kadra."

He clamped a hand on her shoulder, and she flinched. Panic bubbled to the surface, bringing with it unanchored echoes of *fingers digging into her skin. Something sharp cracking over her head. Screams echoing in a black space—*

Shoving Harion's hand off, she willed herself to breathe. Men. Another fear born that night.

"Don't touch me."

He made a show of backing away. "Like I've any interest, barmaid. No one does in someone so green that you don't even know *why* you're here. Edessa nicknames each year's Petitors, you know. To keep them straight, given how many we've gone through. Cisuré is 'the Saint.' Anek is 'the neutralis.'" He smirked. "And I'm 'the lover.' But you're just the northerner the betting books have already marked as a dead girl walking."

Her hands balled into fists, when a low voice spoke behind them.

"I wouldn't buy that. Several magi were calling him 'the lecher' just last night."

She snorted at Harion's indignant sputtering as a genderless neutralis descended from a raeda, fiery spirals of hair spilling over their forehead.

"Anek of Edessa." Razor-sharp brown eyes swept over her for barely a second, but she had the discomfiting sense of being thoroughly assessed. "You must be Sarai."

"Pleasure."

Another raeda halted to release Cisuré, who hugged her in greeting. Harion immediately began pestering the other girl on which Tetrarch Sarai had slept with. Sarai started toward him with a curse when Anek raised a hand.

"Enough, Harion. Look, we may as well put our cards on the table. Who does everyone want?"

"Anyone but *him*," Harion pronounced.

"Cassandane for me." Anek folded their arms, uniform stretching tight over impressive biceps. They turned to Cisuré. "Tetrarch Aelius for you, yes?"

A trick of the light seemed to paint Cisuré with a sudden pallor. "No preference."

"No preference? Please. You've been wild for *years*—"

"We don't get a choice." Cisuré flashed a nervous smile. "Let's just hope for the best."

They rolled their eyes. "So, Aelius for you, Saint. And Sarai?"

Glancing at a red-faced Cisuré, Sarai wondered what that was about. "I—"

"She's getting Kadra." Harion shrugged. "Everyone knows it."

"No, we don't," Anek snapped. "It could just as easily be one of us."

Unease crawled up Sarai's spine. "Is there something wrong with Tetrarch Kadra?"

"Something wrong?" Harion whistled, leaning against Aelius's statue with breathtaking insolence. "Besides him being a bloodthirsty madman? Let's see. How about that every one of our dead colleagues were last seen in Kadra's Quarter before their untimely ends?"

The implication dashed over her like icy water. *There it is.* The missing piece of information that explained everyone's paranoia last night.

"My congratulations on being a human sacrifice for Kadra. Youngest Tetrarch in a century but the man's mad." Harion snickered at her blood-less face. "Gods, Saint. Didn't you warn her?"

"I didn't want you to worry." Cisuré gave her a pleading look. "There are . . . rumors about Kadra."

Rumors that had never reached Arsamea, because the assessors had never discussed *why* the Petitor deaths had begun. Had it been a murderer at the top all along?

Anek made a sound of exasperation "You lot are worse than the gossips. If there was a shred of evidence, he would've been put on trial. *No one—* not even Kadra—can talk someone into killing themselves. We've plenty of reasons to be wary of him without resorting to gossip."

Harion smirked, and Sarai couldn't help wondering if Anek was wrong. She'd heard of kings in the far western wastelands commanding ice, and the Kashyalin people beyond the ocean opening portals between countries. If she could read lies, then who was to say that there wasn't some equally rare talent where someone could induce another to die?

The dull boom of a horn cut through her panic. Long and low, the note rippled to a close, and Sarai's heart thudded. It was time.

They clustered by the side door into the Aequitas. Anek gripped the handle. "Ready?"

They exchanged grim nods, and the door swung open. Soil yielded to a pristine marble hallway, the crowd's roars growing with every step. A shaft of sunlight pierced the ground ahead, and the corridor gave way to the Aequitas's stage. Tens of thousands of voices swelled in an explosive roar across the tiered, open-air amphitheater. Sweat gathered on her hairline, trepidation clasping her heart instead of triumph, as she wondered just how many Petitors the crowd had seen come and go.

Opulent seating boxes graced the front row, filled with extravagantly attired Guildmasters and nobles. Everyday folk clustered in the higher rows, straining for a glimpse of their soon-to-be Petitors. Catching her gaze, Anek inclined their head toward the long dais at the other end of the stage where the four people who held Ur Dinyé in their palms watched and waited.

A beautiful, dark-haired woman occupied the far left of the dais, crimson robes buttoned to the throat. Sighting Sarai's wide-eyed stare, she wiggled her fingers in a cheerful wave. *Cassandane.* Beside her was a stern-faced man in indigo robes, gray threading his temples. Tullus, the oldest and longest-running Tetrarch. He looked more like a cleric than a statesman. Drawing her gaze from him, she found Harion staring at her with a knowing smirk.

"Whore," he mouthed.

Pretending to smooth a wayward lock, Sarai presented him with her middle finger.

On the middle right of the dais, a handsome man in ivory robes beamed at the crowd, all gold skin and brown eyes, dark curls wreathing his boyish face. Head Tetrarch Aelius looked exactly like his statue. Statesman, inventor, magus, and the most powerful man in Ur Dinyé. Sarai followed his gaze to Cisuré, who bowed her head in greeting. *Like they're acquainted.* But that was impossible. Cisuré would have mentioned something that momentous.

Sarai turned to the only remaining Tetrarch. Her gaze rose to the man directly across from her and stuck there.

Impeccable was the first word that came to mind. Every line of him was crisp, precise—from the sculpted planes of his face to the tanned hand resting on the arm of his seat. Gold-trimmed black robes clung to broad shoulders, a baldric running crosswise over them. A smile somewhere between amusement and boredom played on his lips as he gazed at the crowd, a cruel-eyed god surveying his pitiful subjects. His black hair was swept back from his forehead, dark eyebrows drawing over even darker eyes.

Her breath stuttered. She didn't realize she was staring until one of those eyebrows rose a fraction.

Shit. Tearing her gaze away, she wiped her clammy palms on her uniform. So this was Kadra. Not *him*, she silently prayed to the High Elsar. *Anyone but him.*

Smiling widely, Aelius raised a hand, and the applause quieted. "Welcome, everyone, to this year's Robing." The amplification runes on the arms of his seat flared golden, projecting his voice across the Aequitas. "Many of you have traveled far to witness these defenders of law take their vows and join the hardest battle of our time: the fight for justice. Today, we have four Candidates ready to commit themselves to this challenge. Please, step forward."

Sarai nervously followed the others, stopping before the steps to the dais. Draped over the backs of each Tetrarch's chair were identical robes in their colors: crimson and bronze for Cassandane, ivory and silver for Aelius, indigo and sky blue for Tullus, and—Sarai blinked. There was nothing on the back of Kadra's chair.

"The Tetrarchy will address what is, no doubt, foremost in your minds," Tullus took over, crisp diction betraying his military background. "Today, we at last robe four Petitors instead of the three that were custom of late because our fourth Quarter cannot go any longer without a Petitor's helping hand." He slanted a sly look at Kadra. "Thus, the decision was made to provide my fellow Tetrarch with the aid he evidently requires."

Well, then. But Kadra didn't seem offended at the barb. A corner of his mouth twitched.

"It'll be you," Harion murmured under his breath. "They won't give him a trained Petitor, but you're fair game."

Her glare was at odds with the hammering in her chest. "We'll see."

Tullus raised a hand. "Please rise as the Petitors take their vows."

The amphitheater filled with the sound of thousands getting to their feet, and vying for space. Four vigiles stepped before the dais, each unfurling a scroll. Every Tetrarch save Kadra raised an ink pen, the sharp tips dripping ink onto the marble floor.

"Petitors!" Aelius took over as orator. "Do you vow to be as pure as the law you uphold?"

Imitating the other Candidates, Sarai clenched her right hand into a fist, drumming it thrice against her chest. "I do," she echoed.

Every Tetrarch save Kadra made a mark on the parchment before them.

"Do you vow to be unbending in your service of justice?" Aelius asked.

One. Two. Three. Her fist struck her chest. "I do!"

Another mark. Kadra didn't move. The vigile holding his scroll shifted nervously.

"Do you vow to be bound in life and mind to this land and your Tetrarch until the gods take you?"

"I do." She stiffened as Kadra's gaze brushed her.

"Then, as of this day, so you are and so you shall be." Aelius turned to the crowd, exultant. "Ur Dinyé! Your new Petitors!"

A deafening cheer accompanied the proclamation. Sarai saw Aelius's gaze drift back to Cisuré, not even pausing on the other Candidates. *Has he already made his choice?*

"May the High Elsar watch over this new chapter of your lives," he intoned.

Sarai prepared to bow but Anek shot her a warning glance. "Not yet," they muttered.

"May Wisdom and Truth guide you through every Probe. May Temperance calm you in moments of doubt. May Radiance heal your fears, Harvest bless your hearth, and Fortune fill your purses." Aelius stretched both hands to the sky. "May Wrath banish from your days the Dark Elsar: Avarice, Discord, Famine, Indolence, Pestilence, Deceit, and Ruin. And may the Wretched who follow them never darken your door."

Her eyebrows rose. "As the Elsar will it," she chorused with the crowd.

She'd heard that the southern cities were fanatically devoted to the gods, but she hadn't expected the Head Tetrarch to end with a prayer. *Proximity to repeated natural disaster, I suppose.* When the heavens tried to burn everything down every week, the gods probably seemed especially near. And angry.

"Now begins our choosing. Cassandane, if you will?" Aelius gave the other Tetrarch a winsome smile.

Cassandane descended the dais in a graceful swirl of crimson. Hoping her nerves weren't showing, Sarai met her gaze as it rested on each of them. *Is there a method to this?* She held her breath when Cassandane smiled.

"Anek of Edessa, please join me."

Sarai's heart sank as a broad grin broke across Anek's face. Bowing low, they followed the Tetrarch up the dais, where Cassandane draped a set of bronze-edged crimson robes over them. The Tetrarch signed the bottom of the lifelong contract and presented it to Anek, who did the same.

Sarai clenched her trembling fingers. *Three Tetrarchs left.*

Tullus was next. Striding down, he made short work of his selection, glossing over her with a disdainful sniff. "You." He pointed at Harion.

Shooting her a mocking smile, he strode up the dais for his Robing. And suddenly, she had the horrible feeling that he was right. There was only one way this selection was going to end, and everyone in the Aequitas, save Cisuré, had known it. Her heart sank. When Aelius stood, Sarai didn't even try to meet his gaze. Squaring her shoulders, she sought the cruel-eyed god who still hadn't touched the contract before him. Black eyes rose to hers and narrowed, as though he hadn't expected to be the object of her scrutiny. His expression hardened.

Air rushed out of her as though she'd fallen from a snowgrape vine. Depthless black filled her vision, his eyes boring deep as though he were peeling her apart, layer by layer. Cheers sounded in the background. *Aelius must have chosen Cisuré.* But she refused to look away, to break their silent battle. Kadra's sharp focus altered into something almost startled. Then, he turned away.

She drew in a long, shuddering breath, knowing that she was alone onstage. Kadra whispered to the vigile still holding the scroll before him, who looked like the same one who'd let her into the city last night–Gaius. He turned, confirming her suspicions. *No wonder he was so startled.* He had probably known that she'd be Kadra's Petitor from the beginning.

Aelius cleared his throat. "That leaves one. Tetrarch Kadra, if you'd be so kind."

Sarai swallowed her bitterness, holding her head high. Without looking at her, Kadra raised a hand. She jumped at the squeal of stone on stone. A door to the left of the dais grated open to reveal a hulking man flanked by vigiles. Steel chains dragged on the floor as he was shoved toward the wooden post at the center of the stage and tied there.

This can't be good. A glance at Cisuré's pale face confirmed as much. Yet, the Aequitas was buzzing with excitement, the crowd hooting their delight.

Aelius's brow pinched. "Tetrarch Kadra, this is no time for a trial. You can't object now."

"This isn't an objection." Kadra's voice swept over the Aequitas, gloriously low, wine smooth, and *familiar.*

She went stock-still. *The magus last night.* Raising her head, her stomach dropped when he inclined his head toward her, an amused gleam in those tar-like eyes. *A debt collector,* he'd said. Pulse pounding, she revisited their meeting and found an uglier answer for his presence. *He was waiting for me, knowing I'd be assigned to him.* And she had been so foolishly, utterly unguarded with a man who could be a murderer.

"Look here, Kadra," Tullus growled. "You—"

"People of Ur Dinyé, many of you know that I have never taken a Petitor." Kadra didn't spare Tullus a glance. "Nevertheless, you came here for a spectacle. And I desire a test of the woman who is to be my right hand. What do you say? Is that a fair trade for your time?"

The crowd paused, muttering as they considered the offer.

SHIT. Sweat trickled down her jaw. A test? Was she supposed to prosecute the furious behemoth tied onstage? Giving up on decorum, she undid her topmost button and stilled when the Aequitas erupted in cheers.

"Trial! Trial!" the crowd chanted. The other Tetrarchs' faces turned to stone.

Kadra looked unsurprised at the victory. "Far be it from me to deny the people."

Her limbs felt like lead when the Aequitas gave her its undivided attention. *Don't freeze. Think.* Like every town in Ur Dinyé, Arsamea had owned a copy of the Corpus Juris Totus, the laws of the land. She'd memorized it years ago.

"First, bow before whom you serve," trial etiquette demanded. *"Follow their every command throughout the trial."*

She gritted her teeth and folded forward in a stilted bow of respect. A sardonic glint lit Kadra's eyes, and she itched to slap it off. To think she'd offered to vouch for him last night.

"Ennius of Edessa." Kadra indicated the prisoner straining at his bonds. "Held under suspicion for *homicidium* of his wife and son. He vows he was at a tavern at the time of the murder, sleeping off the previous night's drink. But no one has vouched for him."

Simple enough. Get the truth out of Ennius. Sarai took a deep breath, pricking her finger and spreading the blood over *zosta* when Kadra spoke again.

"We'll start with a single log." He sat back.

She stilled. Where was she to find a log, and why in *havïd* did she need one?

"To the right." He tilted his head as though he'd read her mind. The crowd fell silent.

A log pile waited to the right of the stage. Her steps echoed as she walked toward it, eerily loud. Bewildered, she placed a log at Ennius's feet.

"Light it," Kadra commanded.

Her blood turned to ice. She saw her horror reflected in Cisuré's tight features.

Kadra raised an eyebrow. "Is this too difficult for you?"

Beside Tullus, Harion snickered, the sound echoed by a few in the crowd. She stared at Kadra's stone-cold face, emptying her mind of the magus who'd helped her and to whom she'd given a rare bit of honesty. *He doesn't want me here.* Swallowing, she glanced at the rest of the

Tetrarchy who stared straight ahead. *They won't intervene.* This was between her and Kadra.

She had no choice.

Pricking a shaking finger, she drew *yaris,* the rune for "fire," on the log by Ennius's feet. The wood burst into flames, and he shouted in fear. Her breath came fast. The onlookers roared their approval.

Kadra leaned forward, eyes cold. "Ennius, did you kill your wife and child?"

"Fuck you," the prisoner snarled.

Kadra considered that, before inclining his head at Sarai. "Another log."

The world shrank to the midnight pools of his eyes. *A test,* he'd said. Of whether she would adhere to his commands. Of whether her allegiance lay with him. To balk was to fail. And if she didn't leave this Robing as his Petitor, she had no hope of accessing her records.

Gritting her teeth, Sarai added a log to the growing pyre. A snap echoed as the flames cradled its new fodder.

"Did you kill your wife and child?" Kadra's silky voice asked once more.

"I didn't!" Ennius screamed.

The words thrummed through her, a grating chord. Meeting Kadra's gaze, Sarai shook her head. He gracefully gestured to the right.

Sweat ran down her temples. He didn't have to keep asking the same question—he could have her Probe Ennius and pluck the answer from his head. *It's like he wants me to torture him.* Fighting nausea, she ran to the pile and back, tossing logs on the fire. The crowd watched with bated breath when it flared even higher. Ennius's jaw worked, his gaze trained on his feet.

This isn't a trial, she realized. *It's an execution.* Bile rose to the back of her throat. She caught Ennius's eye, silently pleading. *Just give me the truth, and this ends.* His gaze shuttered.

Kadra's eyes never left her. "You know what to do."

Her heart thudded. Flames greedily swallowed the distance to Ennius's heels. If she brought another log, he would begin burning before Kadra's next question. She could obey Kadra and let the man burn to death, but that wasn't the justice she had just sworn to uphold. Yet, to disobey Kadra was to fail his test.

Time stopped. The clamoring crowd blurred into a sea of gnats. This was the chance of a lifetime, the only way to get into her sealed records. But if Ennius was innocent, could she live with letting him die? With doing to someone what had nearly been done to her?

Sarai's teeth ground together. On the dais, Kadra tapped a finger against the arm of his seat with utter detachment. *Damn you.* Her gaze rose to the cloudless sky in condemnation of the gods. Four years in Arsamea, yearning for justice.

But she couldn't condemn an innocent man.

"Let me Probe him." Despite not being amplified, her voice rang out. "Please."

The crowd gasped. Head held high, she waited for Kadra's response. There would be time for mourning later. Right now, she'd do what had to be done. What Kadra *should* have done.

Not a twitch in his gaze. "Another log."

Fuck that. Pressing her bleeding finger into *herar,* she reached across the low flames and gripped Ennius's skull. The world went black, the crowd's surprised yells fading as a knotted ball of wool bloomed before her. She grasped at frayed memories, skimming through Ennius's life while smoke choked her. Gambling, theft, habitual drunken assault. The man was garbage. *But if he isn't a murderer, then he shouldn't die.*

A scream shattered her concentration. She resurfaced to find fire licking at Ennius's feet. Frantic, she plunged back in, hands shaking as his yells intensified. Grasping a barely visible thread, she froze.

The burn of wine . . . scarlet on his knuckles after a fight . . . a woman berating him . . . blood raining in a thick arc. A child's agonized whimpers. The memory frayed further as Ennius went insensate with pain. She gripped it, sweat running down her temples, and pressed her bleeding finger into the last rune on her armilla, *astomand,* the rune for "Materialization." With a burst of power, she wrenched the memory loose.

Transparent figures flickered to life on the Aequitas's stage. Ennius brandishing a weapon, drunk out of his mind. His wife dropping to her knees and covering a child with her body. Sarai inhaled sharply when Ennius brought his knife down once, twice. She lost count. By the time he was done, there was nothing left to stab.

Nauseous, Sarai dropped his head. "He did it!" she yelled to Kadra. "He's guilty!"

A strange glint lit the Tetrarch's eyes. "So, he is."

He gestured lazily at the blaze. She jumped back as the fire soared, engulfing its victim as he shrieked, pleading for life until the fire took his voice. And with a garbled gasp, Ennius of Edessa left the world.

The Aequitas went still. One heartbeat, two. Thunder crashed into their midst. She started, knees buckling to hit the stage only to realize it was the crowd *clapping. What the fuck?* She stared at the rows of people standing in a wave to gleefully celebrate the charred corpse beside her. On the dais, Cisuré and Cassandane were pale. Tullus looked disgusted, and Harion's eyebrows were level with his hairline. Only Anek and Aelius were blank-faced.

"Why?" Kadra's beautiful, wretched voice asked.

Anger vibrated down to her clenched fists. "If I'd gotten another log, Ennius would've caught on fire. He wouldn't have answered you after that."

"So you abandoned the trial." Kadra sounded amused.

This was no trial. He'd ordered her to burn Ennius before asking a single question. He'd already decided that the man was guilty.

"I knew I'd be abandoning this *spectacle*, Tetrarch Kadra, but I wasn't going to ignore my duty to give the accused justice. The vows I just took demand that much."

"You're aware that you were being tested on more than those vows."

That was the last straw. Her furious gaze cut to his. "Then I have had an impossible choice. Follow your orders and abandon my vows, or follow my vows and abandon this trial. But I want to *give* more than I *take*, Tetrarch Kadra." She bitterly reminded him of her answer the previous night. "I don't regret my decision."

A predatory spark flared in his eyes. "Very well."

She waited for his wrath, his dismissal.

"Come up."

Sarai froze. Stared wordlessly at his cruel face. The audience quieted. Her body moved before she could make any sense of him, climbing up to where Kadra stood, freshly inked contract in hand. Accepting the proffered ink pen, she signed her name, then eyed the robe-less back of his chair. He clearly hadn't wanted a Petitor. *Guess I won't get Robed—*

Fabric slid over her shoulders, warm and smelling faintly of citrus. The robes were too big, spilling onto the marble. He'd given her the ones he'd been wearing. She flinched when he helped her into the armholes, conscious of the material's warmth from his body. Kadra registered the motion with a humorless smile, buttoning the collar at her throat. Air left her in a rush when he stepped away.

"Well, that concludes our Robing." Aelius shot an exhausted glance at Kadra, brow smoothing when he turned to Sarai. "It's been a difficult half hour for our newest Petitor, but she's joined us now. Sarai, everyone!"

The world spun as pinpricks of people chanted her name. Still in shock, her heart pulsed in rhythm with the cheers. The Tetrarchy descended the dais to tumultuous applause, forming a line across the stage with their Petitors. She stiffened as Kadra stood beside her.

"Always thank them when the trial is done," the final chapter on trial etiquette in the Corpus Juris Totus had insisted.

"Tibi gratias ago," Sarai muttered. "I appreciated your guidance."

A sardonic gleam lit his black eyes. "If only that were true."

Her heart stopped.

If only that were true, a beautiful voice from another night repeated. Past and present converged. Sarai tottered, drawing a concerned glance from Cisuré as they bowed as a group.

It can't be. When they rose, Kadra swept past her without a backward glance. The crowd began to flood out.

I must have it wrong, she thought as Cisuré enveloped her in a hug, asking if she was alright. But there was no denying that voice, *his voice.*

"If only that were true."

It was *him.*

CHAPTER FOUR

Sarai stared at her plate. Roast meat—when was the last time she'd even had meat?—and vegetables glistened in a golden sauce. She wanted to scream.

Cisuré nudged her, looking worried. "You should eat."

"She just watched a man burn." Anek reached for the soup ladle. "It's enough to turn anyone's stomach."

But not yours. They'd taken Ennius's death the same way they apparently took everything else. With equanimity.

Magi bustled about the Academiae's candlelit dining hall, long tables bursting with food and chatter. The Petitors had their own round table. Students nudged each other, pointing at them, before speeding off when Harion waved back.

Sarai numbly speared a chunk of beef and brought it to her lips. It didn't smell like human flesh. She almost laughed. Yesterday, she hadn't known what a roasting man smelled like. She chewed, barely registering the flavor. The tightness that had built in her chest throughout her journey back from the Aequitas grew a little sharper with every breath.

Not now. She couldn't panic in front of everyone.

A few magi-in-training sidled up to the table, bashfully extending their congratulations. She took the chance to shovel down food, her plate nearing empty by the time Harion resurfaced from the compliments with an even larger head.

"Gods, to be that young." He laughed.

Anek rolled their eyes. "You're only nineteen."

"In a few days, we age out of the Academiae. Then, it's on to purchasing a domus. We aren't measly Candidates anymore."

"Measly Candidates get to eat here. Petitors have to fend for their meals." They bit into a skewer of spiced beef. "By Harvest, I'm going to miss this spread. Taverns just aren't the same."

"Try getting your name on a waitlist for a scutum," he muttered. "The Metals Guild said it'd be *three months*. What the fuck do I do if lightning hits my home?"

Anek shrugged. "Wish you were a measly Candidate safely cloistered in Lisran Tower."

Sarai made a mental note to join the waitlist. If it hadn't been for the garden folly last night, her fate wouldn't have been dissimilar from Ennius's. Her stomach soured, recalling who'd led her to that folly.

She forced down a final bite. "Is Kadra always like that? It was like he knew that Ennius was guilty."

"He probably did," Anek confirmed. "That man is uncannily accurate at reading people."

"He's vile." Cisuré set down her glass with a thud. "It's a travesty that he was elected."

"Well, people love him." Harion swiped some beef off Cisuré's plate. "He speaks to their, ah, bloodthirstiness. Get used to it, Saint. As of today, we control all those people."

"We *serve* them," Sarai said coldly, blocking his fork as it attempted to thieve from her plate. Anek's gaze flickered to her as Harion snorted.

"This from the girl who just burned a man alive on Kadra's orders." He rapped his fork against the table. "Climb off that self-righteous horse."

Years of practice kept her face blank. "You're on a pretty high horse yourself, lecher. I could help you dismount."

"Sarai." Cisuré gripped her wrist, eyes pleading.

"Oh, Sarai," he mimicked. "I'd make your goodbyes now, Saint. Your friend won't last long."

Sarai arched an eyebrow. "Harion, you're wasted as a Petitor. There's a future for you in shoddy soothsaying."

His smile was pure spite. "Listen here, barmaid. Your vows were to your Tetrarch first, and everything else second. It's in the fucking wording. But you, on your little self-righteous crusade, just showed *everyone* that your loyalty is to your own judgment. Now, Kadra is the most popular Tetrarch we've seen in decades. What do you think people will do to you for slighting him? Between them and him, you won't last a month with the impression you've made."

Havïd, *he has a point.* Determined to wipe off his smirk, she shrugged. "Bet on it if you're so sure, then. A hundred aurei if I survive *three* months."

Anek choked on their drink. Squeezing Cisuré's shoulder when she made to protest, Sarai held out a hand. Harion gaped, then seized it with greasy fingers. Holding back a flinch, she withdrew quickly.

"A hundred aurei it is." His eyes gleamed. "I'll see your corpse soon."

A crimson veil slammed over her vision. Reining in the memory, she pasted on a pitying look. "If only—" She froze.

If only that were true. Her fork clattered on her plate. Gold winked from her sleeves, and she almost screamed at the realization that she was still wearing Kadra's robes.

"Sarai?" Cisuré whispered.

Her lungs constricted, bright spots filling her vision. The dining hall went hazy, the sharp tightness in her chest, warning her that she'd put the panic attack off for too long.

She stood quickly. "Just tired. Goodnight."

Ignoring Harion's jibes, she wove past throngs of students to the hall's main doors, breaking into a run once outside. Preoccupied with steadying her breathing, she barely noticed at first when the cobblestones below her boots grew speckled. Then, she did.

She raised her head. Silhouetted against the night sky, Sidran Tower's spire leered in greeting.

No. Backing away like it was a blackstripe bear, she took off toward Lisran Tower, not stopping until she'd raced up the spiral staircase and bolted the door to her room. Tearing off Kadra's robes, she collapsed on the carpet. Ugly sounds tore from her, sobs mingled with stifled screams. Pulling her knees to her chest, she rocked back and forth, wiping at her cheeks.

Anyone who sees her. Can be bought. When the vigiles had abruptly ended their investigation and thrown her out of Edessa, she'd guessed that her assailant must have been someone powerful. But plotting revenge had kept her sane, and after a couple years, she'd started to believe the mad consolatory tale she'd spun. Where she saved up for tuition, attended the Academiae, and became such an exceptional Petitor that when she inevitably found her assailant, no one doubted her word.

Sarai laughed bitterly. *I've been a fool.* How was she to take down a Tetrarch? This was Marus all over again. Wealthy men who sat above the law, spilling blood because they *could*. What chance did she have against a monster?

"The law needs to change," she'd once bitterly told Cisuré before the Fall, when they'd witnessed Marus drunkenly beat a tunnel rat to death in the tavern. Frozen behind the counter, she'd clutched the cup she was polishing like a shield as Marus had pounded him into the table. Cisuré had stared at her plate, eyes glazed over as she retreated into an inner world that violence couldn't touch. The man's neck had snapped like a twig. He'd slid off the table onto the floor. Marus hadn't even remembered doing it the next day, but everyone had immediately and fearfully agreed that the tunnel rat deserved it.

"Why does the Corpus even exist?" she'd spat, scouring the man's blood off the tiles. *"Why not have Marus write his own laws at this rate?"*

Dead-eyed, Cisuré had shrugged. *"Without established order, people have no incentive to behave."*

"Then what incentive does Marus need?"

"There's no changing him." Cisuré had looked defeated. *"This man should've just gotten himself out of poverty. You did. He had the chance for a good life too. If he hadn't been a tunnel rat, he'd be alive."*

At the time, Sarai had thought it ungrateful to argue that a good life shouldn't involve her risking her neck on snowgrape vines, so she'd simply accepted a teary-eyed Cisuré's hug. But something within her had gained consciousness that day, morphing over the years into a force she'd caged and shoved into slumber. But now, she wanted nothing more than to allow it free rein. To hold a blade against the column of Kadra's throat and ask him *why*.

Because there was more than one explanation for what he could have done. She'd considered an alternate theory over the years—that the voice's owner had been trying to protect her by healing her, giving her a new identity, a new face. Yet, he still hadn't intervened when she'd been hastily thrown out of the city.

Sarai breathed into her cupped hands as her body calmed. *Friend or foe, he was there that night.* And she would extract what he knew if it meant tunneling into his head and shattering it.

Someone knocked on her door. Tottering to her feet, she glanced in the mirror, wincing at the puffy-eyed creature within. *Havïd.* Opening the door, she feigned a lengthy yawn.

On the other side, a familiar face waved. "I expected you to make a splash, barmaid," he slurred. "But I didn't think you'd go that far."

"Magus Telmar?" Sarai gaped. "Are you drunk?"

"Not really." He attempted a bow and nearly face-planted into the doorjamb.

Sarai took in the wineskin in one hand, the other on the banister to prevent a tumble down the stairs.

He looked about shiftily, then dropped his voice. *"Ibez."* He held out the wineskin in encouragement. "Nine-tenths pure."

By Ruin. Aside from her parents having met their end smuggling the stuff, she'd heard enough of the potent brew of fruit, spice, and wheat to know that it was a bad idea diluted, let alone pure.

"Telmar, I'm pretty sure that's illegal."

He chortled. "Mighty fine, though."

Right. She darted a glance at the landings below, rife with students. The last thing she needed was for a gossip like Harion to see her with a drunk magus.

She stepped out of the doorway. "Is there a reason you're here?"

"Yes, yes." He patted himself and fished out a crumpled scroll. "Brought you a present." His features went eerily blank. "Not sure it's a present. There's a raeda downstairs for you. The . . . coachman told me to give you this."

Frowning, she took the scroll. "Thank you. Did the coachman mention the sender?"

Something flickered in his glazed eyes. "Oh, you'll know."

Foreboding skittered down Sarai's spine. Her gaze dropped to the seal, and she nearly slid to the floor at the "K" imprinted in black wax. Snapping the seal, she scanned the sharp, bold handwriting.

Stay at my tower until you purchase a domus in my Quarter.

At least he got straight to the point.

"I'm to help bring your things down." Telmar stared at the ground.

So Kadra thought she'd immediately ride off to his home, did he? Her mouth formed a grim line. *Then again, what better place to begin investigating the Fall?*

"I'll handle it," she said quietly.

"Can you?" A tinge of lucidity entered Telmar's voice. "After this morning?"

"I didn't want Ennius's blood on my hands if he was innocent."

"At what cost? You just made yourself a target."

"To whom?" she whispered. "In Arsamea, you said every Petitor from last year's Robing died. Was it the same for the years before? What's *really* been happening to them?"

He pressed a finger to his lips. Laughter sounded below them and he spoke quickly, words slurred with the drink.

"When one died, the others fled. If they didn't, they joined them. That hasn't changed for four years, so someone *will* die this year. If you mean to survive, barmaid, then keep that stubborn chin of yours *down*. Don't look farther than the end of your nose—" Awareness left his eyes.

"Why?" Forcing herself to grip his shoulders, she shook him, trying to stop the *ibez* from taking him under. "Did the Petitors really commit suicide? Who should I be watching for?"

Telmar squinted. "Barmaid!" He patted his pockets. "Did I give you your present?"

Shit. Releasing him, she nodded. "Thank you for the scroll."

Looking on the verge of tears, he flashed a watery smile and stumbled downstairs, nearly careening into Anek. They moved out of the way, shooting Sarai a curious look. She cursed as Harion's gleeful face emerged behind them, followed by Cisuré.

"Late-night visitors already?" Harion eyed her. "Elsar only knows what they see in you, though Telmar isn't much of a prize. Never sober—"

She threw the scroll at his head. "He was here for *this*."

Catching it, Anek stared at the message. Cisuré read over their shoulder and blanched.

"Well," Harion pronounced. "You've made *quite* an impression."

Sarai's eyes narrowed. "Don't Petitors usually reside near their Tetrarch?"

"The point being 'near.' Kadra's telling you to live *with* him."

"This isn't right." Cisuré stared at the parchment like it had grown fangs. "New Petitors get a few days to pack our things, make our farewells. You've only just had dinner, and he's summoning you this late—" She crumpled the scroll. "This is an abuse of power."

"Looks like you'll be losing the bet." Harion raised his hands when Anek shot him a withering glance. "There's a chance."

"Don't go." Cisuré tossed the letter in the fireplace. "In addition to never taking a Petitor, Kadra has *never* allowed anyone into his tower. Who knows what he could do to you there?"

"Wisdom alive, he won't eat her." Anek gave Sarai a meaningful look. "The choice is yours."

I'll be staying at his home. It could have *answers*, evidence. Granted, she'd probably join Ennius on a pyre if Kadra caught her snooping, and she was in grave danger if he had the suicide-inducing ability Harion thought he did. *But I could ruin him.*

"I'll go." She shook her head when Cisuré protested. "For better or worse, I'm his Petitor."

"Finally, a decision," Harion groused. "You women *certo* take your time."

"Probably because we're surrounded by men waiting for us to stumble so they can find purpose," Sarai muttered. He glowered.

Anek and Cisuré helped her pack her few possessions, while Harion ran a blood-boiling commentary on the unfashionability of her two tunics. When he finally left, Sarai let out a barrage of curses that earned her a dig in the ribs from Cisuré.

"Harion's mostly all bark," Anek said. "It's well known that any woman who spends an hour in his company regrets it."

Sarai snorted, shoving Kadra's robes into her satchel. "What about the Tetrarchs? Cassandane looks like she'd be highly sought after."

Anek chuckled. "She prefers the company of women. Nothing unsavory about her."

"No, that would be Kadra," Cisuré muttered. "Everyone knows that he accompanies his vigiles when they cavort at pleasure houses."

Lovely. "Harion called him a 'block of ice.'"

"Because despite going with his people, he never engages in their activities," Anek added. "Hasn't touched a pleasure worker or had romantic liaisons even before he took office."

"Who'd want to sleep with that?" Cisuré laughed scornfully.

Who indeed. Sarai thought back to her first real glimpse of Kadra on the dais. Hard-eyed, untouchable. Exuding power without so much as lifting a finger. This was a man more interested in blood than any other sport.

She locked the door with quiet finality, Cisuré promising to return her key to the Night Office. Outside, the moons hung low.

Tension rippled through her. "Where do the Tetrarchs live?"

"Here." Anek gestured at the grounds. "In the four tallest towers. They double as vantage points from which to control stormfall when it strikes."

Cisuré still looked grim. "Kadra resides in Aoran Tower to the west. Every Tetrarch's tower is heavily warded, but his has the strongest, fully cloaked in illusion magic. No one knows where the entrance is."

So why let me in? The question followed them to the Lisran Tower Gate where her third raeda of the day waited, painted in the black and gold of Kadra's colors. She shivered. It looked like a gilded hearse.

Inclining her head to the coachman, she turned to Cisuré, sighing at the deep furrows between her eyes. "I'm not going off to war."

"You may as well be." The other girl hugged her fiercely. "Don't be reckless. Send word if you need *any* help, and for the Elsar's sakes, don't—"

"Lose my temper, I know," Sarai said wryly, the warning drilled into her over many years.

"Kadra has a way of getting into people's heads. Keep him out."

"My head's always been a hard nut." She patted Cisuré's shoulder. "I'll be fine."

"You will," Anek said dryly. "Kadra is many things but offing a Petitor who publicly defied him is too on the nose. Even for him."

Somehow that didn't make her feel better.

With a parting nod to Anek, Sarai climbed into the carriage, feeling like her last tether to normalcy had died along with Ennius. Then again, perhaps that was best—to lack all illusions as she entered a monster's lair. Drawing the raeda's curtain aside, she waved as the coachman clicked his tongue and hooves clattered to life.

I'm sorry, Cisuré. She watched her friend's pinched face fade to a flesh-colored blur. *But I'm going to have to get very reckless.*

CHAPTER FIVE

Her first thought was that Kadra's tower resembled him.

Sarai's eyes widened as she alighted from the raeda. Obsidian pillars framed the cavernous doorway of a structure easily a fifth of the Aequitas's breadth. Fire danced in a single sconce, casting shadows swallowed by the ebony door. Behind her, an ornate gate swung shut. Neither door nor gate had been visible until the raeda had passed through Kadra's wards.

Sarai apprehensively eyed the entrance. The night breeze carried the scent of citrus. Too gentle for lemon, too sweet to be lime. *He must have an orange grove.*

"Tetrarch Kadra awaits within." Firelight illuminated the coachman's gray hair and the deep smile lines around his mouth.

She wondered what anyone working for Kadra would have to smile about. "*Tibi gratias ago.* I'm Sarai, by the way."

"Cato." He tilted his head toward the door, amused. "He doesn't bite."

No, he only burns people alive. With a steadying breath, Sarai stepped into a terrazzo-tiled atrium. Here, too, a single sconce was lit. The open-air roof typical of southern domii was conspicuously absent.

"Does Tetrarch Kadra have no use for light?"

Cato smiled. "An open roof is an invitation to his enemies. No matter how many people say otherwise, at the end of the day, Tetrarch Kadra's only a man."

She had a hard time believing that.

"That's the tablinum." Cato indicated the rightmost of two doors at the back of the atrium. "He wishes to speak to you alone."

She could only imagine what conversation Kadra had in mind. Wiping clammy hands on her tunic, she discreetly reached for her armilla. Under the guise of taking a calming breath, she pricked her finger and pressed the dot of blood into *zosta*. *Let's see how often he lies.* Steeling herself, she knocked.

"Come in," called an all-too-familiar baritone.

With a deep breath, she pushed the handle down and stepped inside. Kadra's study was less ostentatious than she'd expected. Floor-to-ceiling bookshelves covered the walls, framing two reading couches. At the back, a winding staircase paused at a mezzanine before curving to the upper levels of the tower. On the right side of the study stood a stately desk littered with scrolls. And behind the desk sat the man himself.

Sarai met Kadra's stare and froze. His hair was damp. Dark strands hung over his forehead, softening the harsh planes of his face. A loosely knotted robe gaped half-open down to his waist. She dragged her gaze up, trying and failing to ignore the expanse of tanned, hair-sprinkled muscle laid bare by the gap.

"Welcome." The man she was doing her best not to stare at lazily tipped a wineglass in her direction.

Damn him. Approaching the desk, she bowed so low her head almost hit the wood.

"*Tibi gratias ago* for the kind invitation, Tetrarch Kadra." She managed to look everywhere but his chest.

A spark of amusement in his depthless stare. "It wasn't kind, and it certainly wasn't an invitation."

"My thanks stands, nonetheless."

He rose, the robe gaping wider at the movement. She fixated on his face. He was striking but lacked Aelius's roguish beauty, a stamp of ruthlessness having hardened features that could have been classically beautiful.

"Sarai of Arsamea." His voice was velvet, but there was nothing seductive in his cruel eyes. "Stormfall aside, how are you finding Edessa?"

Shivering despite her birrus, she crossed her arms. "Warm."

"And the Aequitas?" He rounded the desk and placed his glass by her hand. The sweet haze of wine filled her nostrils.

"Loud."

"And the Tetrarchy?"

"I've hardly met everyone."

A brow rose. "So you don't have an opinion?"

"I didn't say that—" She froze upon realizing that he was barely a foot away. *Too close.* Why hadn't she noticed? Normally, her body would have panicked by now.

Inhaling sharply, she took a step back. Kadra shot her an assessing glance, topping up his glass with half the contents of a wine bottle, before pouring the rest into another glass and holding it out to her.

It can't be poisoned if he's drinking it. She cautiously accepted. "Tetrarch Kadra, I'm not sure what response you're looking for."

"An honest one. Like you gave me last night."

Damn you for bringing that up. But his answer rang clear. *Truth.* "Are you asking me about the Tetrarchy? Or the trial?"

"Both."

She swallowed. "I thought it was monstrous. The trial." *You.*

His eyes flickered with humor, as if he'd heard her unspoken verdict. Every hair on her body rose as he drew closer. And then he did the strangest thing. Raising a hand by her neck, he paused, as though awaiting permission.

Sarai waited for her body to protest his nearness, but it seemed to be in shock. Why was he asking for permission? Confused, she inclined her head. If he hurt her, she'd break his wrist, consequences be damned.

Something flickered across Kadra's face. Long fingers brushed her neck, unpinning her birrus where it fastened at her throat. The fabric slid off her shoulders in a rustle that felt too loud. His eyes never left hers, amusement fading the longer he held her gaze. Her mouth went dry.

Then, he drew away.

She fought the urge to gasp for air as he hung her birrus by the entrance to his study. A frisson of heat uncurled within her, sliding through her limbs until her skin felt too tight.

Havïd. No. Absolutely not. His voice was bad enough but *this*? She smothered the wayward feeling, almost flinching when Kadra turned back to her.

"Are you afraid of me?" he asked matter-of-factly.

Visions bloomed in her head of Ennius shrouded in flame, shrieking. Of the monster leaning close and asking for permission before touching her.

"No."

She flinched as a warm hand closed around her wrist. He raised it to her face, showing her the goosebumps on her skin.

"Really?" he asked dryly.

"I'm not afraid of you."

"But?" He lowered her wrist before letting go.

"A bit unsettled, perhaps," she whispered.

"Hmm." He took a sip of wine, eyes boring into hers. "That's a damn sight more useful than fear."

Truth. She fought to maintain a calm exterior. Reaching for her glass, she gulped the wine. It slid down warm. Heady.

"Slowly now." There was no mockery in his gaze, only cool assessment.

She wondered what had gone through his mind when he'd beheld her body. When he'd walked away. There hadn't been any emotion in his beautiful voice while she'd been dying. And she was all aquiver simply because he'd touched—

Sarai set down the glass. "Thank you for the wine, Tetrarch Kadra. I should—"

"Why did you become a Petitor?"

To find you. "To do some good in the world." At his raised eyebrow, her jaw clenched. "To uphold the law, and see that justice is done."

He digested that for a moment. "What sort of justice?"

"Fair and transparent."

"Seen a lot of that, have you?"

"Not enough. But I intend to give as much as I can."

A harsh burst of sound. Sarai started, only to realize that he was laughing. For a man with such a beautiful voice, the sound was ugly. Empty.

He smothered it with a sip of wine. "I take it that you don't think highly of burning people alive."

He was goading her. She clenched her jaw, refusing to answer.

"What of mutilation, then? Castration? Beheading?"

"Those all sound like the same thing," she said through gritted teeth.

"And if I told you that was justice?"

Don't say it. "I would say that you're a Tetrarch, and I'm your Petitor of one day, so who am I to question your opinion?"

A corner of that hard mouth rose. "At least you know that trials aren't won on sentiment."

Her eyes narrowed. "No, they're decided using the jurisprudence you didn't consider at trial. The Corpus Juris Totus provides that the penalty for *homicidium* is death by *hanging*. Not by vaporizing in an inferno—" She halted at the predatory look entering Kadra's eyes.

"Is that so?"

Havïd. He'd provoked her. Made that crack about sentiment to force a response. And it had worked.

"Have you ever seen a hanging?" Kadra sounded curious.

She cleared her throat, cursing herself for taking the bait. "I've heard of one." Some years back, a rapist had been hanged in Sal Flumen. A pull of a lever and a snap of the neck, they'd said. A scarce dent in the hour and it was over.

"What do you think of it?"

She cast around for a response. "As a punishment, it seems"–she struggled with the word–"humane."

"And you believe in a humane response to what Ennius did?"

"You don't have to become a monster in order to punish one."

"Ah." He smiled laconically. "You're morally superior."

"Like hells I–" Sarai's lips pressed into a tight line. She'd come here for vengeance. Not to debate with this–her eyes made a wary ascent–six-foot lunatic. "My beliefs are unimportant. I was just surprised that the Tetrarchy condoned veering from established law."

"There's little the Tetrarchy doesn't condone. Despite what I did today, I remain one of the most powerful people in Ur Dinyé." He paused. "How does that reconcile with your beliefs?"

"The Tetrarchy didn't give you power. The people did by electing you."

"You disagree with their decision, then."

She exhaled in a bid for composure. "Tetrarch Kadra, I'm in no position to make that assessment. As long as you serve the people in the manner they wish–which you're doing excellently, if today's cheering was any indication–my opinion is irrelevant."

"And if I told you that your opinion is paramount?"

She threw up her hands. "By all the gods, why?"

"Because you're going to have to choose."

"Between?"

His face had never looked crueler. "The Tetrarchy. And me."

Truth. She gaped for all of a second before a laugh burst out of her. Loud and incredulous. Her eyes watered as she clutched his desk for support.

"I can give you that answer now," she managed between chuckles.

"Sleep on it." Kadra's gaze was inscrutable.

"It won't change," she informed him.

"Then you don't have to give it now." He didn't even sound bothered.

"Why do I need to choose anyone?" she dared to ask. "You're part of the Tetrarchy."

"I plan on tearing it apart." There was something disturbing in his eyes. Not mockery or cruelty, something infinitely more worrying for its namelessness. "And you don't want to stand in my way."

True. Her good humor vanished. She didn't realize she'd taken a step back until she nearly tripped over his reading couch.

"Why?" *And why tell me?*

"Because the law of this land is wrong," he said quietly, watching her, every word ringing with truth. "And you know it."

Her heart halted. A long-suppressed part of her snapped awake, rattling its cage, all hunger and sharp teeth, like it had been waiting for this very second. She shoved the ugliness back under, watching Kadra with the sinking realization that it had woken for *him.*

Kadra has a way of getting into people's heads, Cisuré had warned.

How did you know? How did you see into me?

He looked even more amused at her silence. Reaching into his robe, he tossed her a key. "Upstairs. Left bedroom." His gaze never left her. "Goodnight, Sarai of Arsamea."

Too disconcerted to respond, she gave him a faint nod and headed up the stairs at the back of his study, tracing over the unfamiliar runes in the key as if they would ground her. This must be a key through his wards. She'd be able to enter Aoran Tower as she pleased.

Reaching the mezzanine overlooking Kadra's tablinum, Sarai looked over the railing. She bit back a curse as the layout of Aoran Tower became clear. The tower's only staircase began from Kadra's study, baring the upper levels to his view. The moment she left her room, he would know. There would be no snooping around this tower unless it was empty.

The mezzanine held two rooms. Hers, and a door to the right that was probably his. Unlocking her quarters, she drew the bolt behind her and dropped her illusion, wincing as fatigue sank in from her prolonged use of magic. She could make no mistakes in Kadra's tower and having *nihumb* and *zosta* active was going to drain her faster than the one-day estimate she had given Cisuré.

Threading the key onto a cord around her neck, she sank onto the four-poster bed, taking stock of an oak vanity, washbasin, wardrobe, and curtain-shielded window. She'd never had so much *space*. This room was palatial compared to Cretus's shed. *Even if I'm sharing walls with my assailant.*

He had disarmed her tonight, all damp hair and open robes, but he was sorely mistaken if he thought that his muscled chest would make her lose sense. She had no trouble building a wall between her eyes and her mind.

Still, her unease persisted as she settled under the covers. He hadn't lied once the entire night.

She blew out the candle atop the nightstand. Between one breath and the next, she fell into a turbulent sleep, where she fell and fell and fell.

And each time, it was Kadra who pushed her.

CHAPTER SIX

The man who'd conversed with the beautiful voice brushed a lock of hair from her face, and sprang back with a scream.

She could guess at how she looked. A bubble of blood burst from her mouth. Cold settled on her broken fingers, moving inward as her life leeched away. The red-eyed god robed in midnight would come soon, a scale in one hand to weigh a soul's deeds. The few who had managed to Summon Lord Death had written of a sight immeasurable in words, and a voice icier than winter. She wondered if he would be kind. If he'd understand that she had tried so hard—

"Tetrarch Kadra requests your presence."

Sarai fell out of slumber, slamming her head into the headboard. Disoriented, she scrabbled at the bedposts for purchase, before hitting the ground.

"Is everything alright?" the voice outside inquired. Cato. The coachman. Or Kadra's manservant. Whatever he was.

"One moment!" Getting *nihumb* and *zosta* active, she waited for her scars to disappear before opening the door.

Sarai forced a smile. "Good"—she glanced at the pitch-black sky outside her window—"evening, Cato?" How long had she slept?

Tray in hand, he inclined his head. "Congratulations on your first day as a Petitor. I thought you might prefer to take breakfast in your room."

She shot another glance at the window. "What time is it?"

"A little past two."

"In the morning?"

"Tetrarch Kadra prefers to work while it's dark," Cato answered matter-of-factly. "Daylight affords too many opportunities for assassination."

"I imagine burning people alive probably doesn't help that."

"But then who would eradicate the Enniuses of this world?"

"It isn't a binary choice." The Tetrarchy made the law. If Kadra disliked it so much, it was well within his power to change it.

Cato's smile didn't waver. "Of course." Taking the robes Kadra had lent her—which stank of Ennius's pyre—he gave her a new set and a bathrobe. "The bath is to the left of the tablinum. Tetrarch Kadra is outside when you're ready."

Once he left, Sarai sank onto the bed, head in her hands. She'd dreamt of the Fall for years, but there'd been something more vivid about these memories, as though Sidran Tower's proximity had begun returning them to her. Eyes closed, she tried to recall the face of the second man that night and grimaced at the blurry outline her head yielded. *I need to see that case record.* Perhaps it had his name. Depending on Kadra's idea of a workday, she might even be able to visit the Hall of Records today.

A long breath whistled through her teeth. *By Fortune, I'm so close.* Brimming with determination, she scarfed down her breakfast: a roast chicken leg, sizzling in herbs and butter, accompanied with root vegetables and a cup of lemon-honey brew. A far cry from the stale bread she'd filched from Cretus. Wrapping herself in the bathrobe—trying to ignore its similarity to the one Kadra had worn earlier—she crept downstairs and out of his blessedly empty study.

Her jaw dropped when she entered the bath. Gold-speckled tiles encased a pit above which a metal pipe stuck out of the wall, studded with runes for scouring and heat. Reluctantly impressed, she scrubbed herself under a warm jet of water, and donned her robes, tracing the gilded vines twining around the cuffs and branching up to the shoulders.

They could be her attacker's robes.

Nothing felt real—the job, the comfort, the Hall of Records containing her answers only some tens of miles away. Everything she'd yearned for, and it felt unnatural. Trepidation weighed her steps toward Kadra, and not just because of the Fall. In Arsamea, she'd been guarded, unwilling to show much of herself to anyone who could use it against her. But she'd faltered three times now, as though one look from those penetrating eyes made every bitter word she'd trapped behind her teeth strain to break free.

Approaching the front door, she took a steadying breath. *He's just a man.* She gripped the handle and prepared to push.

"I didn't think you'd be smiling with a Petitor shackled to you." Cato's voice was muffled. Her fingers faltered. She pressed herself against the door to hear better.

"The shackle runs both ways," came Kadra's mellifluous voice.

"What I and everyone else at the Aequitas saw begs to differ." The mild-mannered coachman had shed his skin. Whoever Cato really was, he spoke to Kadra as an equal. "She disobeyed you. People are saying that you only accepted her as your Petitor to make her pay for it. And those aren't even the more unsavory theories."

Please don't tell me they think—

"A few fools think you're interested in her." Cato confirmed her fears.

"Interesting." Kadra sounded unperturbed.

"Drenevan, why is she here? Weren't you going to run her off before the Robing?"

I was right. But then why hadn't he gone through with it? Hells, he could have easily let her perish in the storm.

Kadra seemed to be mulling over his answer. Moments passed before he spoke. "I changed my mind."

What?

"Why the hells did you do that?" Cato's reply echoed her bewilderment.

"She's dangerous." Her pulse surged at the dark menace in his response.

"*Certo*, to us!" Frustration edged Cato's voice.

"She'll be useful."

"She despises you," Cato said firmly. "You have to admit that your nature won't convince anyone to choose you."

"If not, we'll leave her to the wolves. Her decisions are her own."

The hairs at the nape of her neck stood on end. Cisuré's fears were well founded. Whatever these men had planned for her wasn't anything as benign as doing her job. She retreated inside Kadra's tablinum, wondering if it was too late to flee.

She waited for the front door to open before exiting, pretending she'd been about to leave. She forced a placid smile at Cato as she passed.

Who is he? Either Kadra allowed his coachman to berate him, or the rumors of him never having taken a lover weren't true. She grimaced. *Wisdom and Wrath, Cato's over twice his age.*

Icy wind ribboned around her when she stepped outside. The two moons painted swaths of cloud in blue and iron gray, highlighting Kadra's profile as he saddled a horse. *Her* horse. Caelum looked quite pleased to be nibbling on Kadra's grass as he made short work of securing the black-and-gold saddle.

"Good morning." Kadra glanced over his shoulder, dark hair brushing his collar.

Her breath stuttered. "Good morning." She kept her tone curt. Politesse was all he'd get from her. "*Tibi gratias ago* for bringing Caelum. And for the saddle."

Black eyes roved over her before he extended a hand. Her heart pounded as she realized he was offering to help her into the saddle.

"I can manage." She quickly put some distance between herself and that callused palm.

Settling onto the new saddle, her eyes widened at the sleek leather stretched over a sturdy frame, a far cry from the Arsamean contraption that had rubbed her tailbone raw on the journey to Edessa.

"I take it you like it." Kadra mounted his horse with a faint smile, and she suddenly wished she could burn him and the saddle.

She'll be useful, he'd said, as though she were a knife he planned on wielding. Fishing out her last aureus from her coin pouch, she tossed it at his back. He caught it without looking and turned to her with a raised eyebrow.

"Like I said," she said with her most insincere smile, "I don't like being in debt."

A glint in his eyes before he pocketed the aureus. "As you wish."

There goes my last coin. Telling herself it was for the best, she followed him out of Aoran Tower and watched as the gate and the tower's front door vanished.

So these were his infamous wards. She patted the air and came up against an impenetrable, invisible wall. *That's a complex bit of illusion magic. Nihumb* provided a blanket concealment of her scars but didn't prevent anyone from feeling them. Kadra's wards blocked even touch. She reached for her key, and the gates and Aoran Tower's door reappeared when she gripped it. *How powerful is he?*

She eyed him warily as they followed the cobblestone path. "Are you an illusion magus?"

He didn't seem to mind the question. "No."

"But Cato is," she guessed. "He isn't your coachman." She waited for him to lie, but Kadra pulled in a satisfied breath as if he were pleased that she'd seen through the act.

"He was married to this quarter's previous Tetrarch. He prefers to keep it a secret that he lives here and," a wry note entered his voice, "he's a good cook."

Truth. So Cato was the real talent here. Kadra was only powerful in title. *Ha!*

Kadra's lips twitched like he'd read her mind. "Cato forms the wards, but I sustain them."

Her smirk vanished. "Magic pooling?"

Only extraordinarily powerful magi could siphon off some of their power for another magus to use. Even then, the subsequent drain was said to feel like being hit by several sacks of grain.

"Naturally." Kadra raised a hand, sleeve falling back to reveal an obsidian armilla with *every* rune alight. Her skin crawled. She recognized *yaris* for fire and a few other runes for lightning formation and manipulation, but the rest were a terrifying mystery.

Wrath and Ruin. Just how powerful is he to sustain those wards every single day without keeling over? Lips pressing shut, she followed him to the Aoran Tower Gate. Every brush of his gaze sent shivers down her limbs. Her attacker, a *Tetrarch*. And there wasn't a *havïd* thing she could do about it.

Steel scraped against stone, punctuating her bitterness, as the Gate drew open. The bleary-eyed vigiles stationed there bowed low to him and eyed her with disapproval.

"Morning, Tetrarch Kadra. Will she be accompanying you?"

"At all times."

Her head snapped to him. Biting her tongue, she waited until they were out of earshot before turning to him.

He cocked an eyebrow. "Is there a problem?"

There havïd *well is!* How was she to search his home or visit the Hall of Records? "I may be from the north, Tetrarch Kadra, but I doubt that Petitors here are normally glued at the hip to their Tetrarchs."

He dropped his voice to a conspiratorial rumble. "Perhaps that's why the previous ones are largely dead."

Her pulse jumped to the speed of lightning. *He's already given himself an alibi.* If she died, he merely had to point out that he'd accompanied her on the job and done everything in his power to help her. Any suspicion directed at him would evaporate before her corpse was cold.

"I see," she whispered. "Because their deaths were a matter of oversight, and you would undoubtedly be innocent if I died."

A slow smile spread across Kadra's face. He leaned across the scant distance between their mounts, his lips to her ear.

"Naturally." The word brushed her cheek. "Because if I wanted to kill you, Sarai of Arsamea, you'd already be dead."

Truth. Air stuck in her throat when he drew away, and she had to bite her tongue to keep from yelling that he'd failed four years ago. Without a backward glance, Kadra spurred his horse to a gallop. And as Sarai followed, she could only wonder what torture he had in mind for her this time that was worse than death.

An hour later, Sarai reluctantly concluded that Kadra's Quarter wasn't the cesspool of violence that she'd expected. She'd taken brief stock of it the night before the Robing, but they ventured deeper, where raucous whoops sounded from bazaars in full swing, their entrances draped in jeweled fabrics and signs dictating that mounts, pets, and, occasionally, children, weren't allowed entrance. Laughing women clung to inebriated men, their artfully lined eyes hard.

Most bowed as Kadra passed, eyes averted in respect—or fear? Others waved, some drunkenly raising a bottle, all to which he inclined his head. *The people love him*, Harion had said. The Elsar only knew why.

Clouds blanketed the capital, Praefa and Silun all but obscured. She shot the sky a glower at the memory of her dash for safety with Kadra scarcely over a night ago.

"We won't see stormfall for a few days yet," his voice broke in.

She jumped. By Ruin, how did the wretched man know exactly what she was thinking? "I'll be prepared this time."

"Garden follies aren't so easily found in Edessa," he said blandly, and she, once again, debated the merits of strangling him. "The storms tend to arrive at night."

"Sounds like quite the wrench in your regimen."

"Mine?"

"Working from two in the morning to noon," she said coolly. "Most people fear the dark for what it hides. It's a rare man who avoids daylight."

A glimmer of laughter in his eyes. "It's easier to see my enemies at night. As you said, it's a rare person who skulks in the dark."

Damn him. He had an uncanny ability to turn words on themselves, to invert and recenter meaning. *As befitting a politician.* Unable to think of a retort, she lapsed into sullen silence.

The domii and storefronts on either side grew smaller the farther they got from the Academiae, shifting from opulent marble to cement. A wall began on one side of the road, sloping up to end in a parted gate. Moonlight glinted off the stately buildings beyond, mercifully not liveried in Kadra's colors, unlike the vigiles dashing across the grounds, eyes heavy with fatigue. At the center of it all rose an oblong structure forming a three-sided square: the vigile compound, a central hub in every Tetrarch's Quarter to which their vigiles reported. The soldiers oversaw prisons, manned patrols, and coordinated disaster efforts during stormfall. They also didn't like her much, if their scowls were any indication.

Dismounting, Kadra tilted his head toward a smattering of smaller structures across the grounds. She wrinkled her nose at a pungent odor that worsened as they neared a domed building. Acrid, it sat somewhere between a rotting animal and a spoiled batch of Cretus's wine.

"What in all the Elsar's names is that stench?" she finally spluttered.

"The morgue." Kadra swept past her, unaffected. The door scraped open, unleashing a blast of putrid air. Sarai clapped a hand to her mouth as her breakfast rose to her throat.

"Tetrarch Kadra, why are we at a morgue?"

"For Jovian of Edessa."

She tried not to gag. "What about him?"

"Four months ago, he was found dead in his study, pinned under several bookcases."

"What piques your interest after *all* this time?"

Her emphasis prompted a dark smile. "Jovian was one of last year's Petitors."

She halted. "What?"

"The very last to kill himself." A sconce backlit his face in washes of umber. "Pulverized so badly, his own brother barely recognized him."

He could have been discussing the weather for all the emotion he showed. Trepidation wrapped bony fingers around her ribs. Why was he starting off her first day by showing her a Petitor's corpse? *Is this a threat?*

With great effort, she kept her voice from shaking. "If he killed himself, then why are we here?"

Kadra didn't elaborate, striding past several corpses perched atop medical tables. Lugens pored over the disarrayed maps of the bodies, trying to intuit the cause of their demise. On the fringes of the room, young healers-in-training carefully cut into organs, rinsing their hands to make notes on their structures. Quashing the ache of her younger self's dreams, she followed Kadra.

A hard-nosed woman with salt-and-pepper hair rose at his approach. "Tetrarch Kadra." She bowed low. "Whom did you come to see today?"

"Jovian."

Surprise flickered across her face. "Of course." She turned frosty eyes on Sarai. "Lugen Geena."

"A pleasure to—" Sarai blinked when Geena walked past her.

Well, then. She could almost hear Harion snickering that he'd told her so. Irritated, she followed Geena and Kadra down a flight of stairs at the back.

The bustle and clatter of Lugens and metal implements faded, replaced by the quiet of death. A chill hung in the air, ice sealing the cracks in the stonework. The stairs culminated in a short hallway leading to a snow-crusted door, which Geena unlocked.

"He was placed on ice as requested," she said. "The body is exactly as we received him, which is to say, there isn't much."

The door scraped open, a glacial blast rushing out from the gap. Ice encased the narrow chamber within, massive blocks rising from the ground like frozen coffins. She focused on a shapeless form atop one, and her heart dropped. *Jovian.*

The first thing she saw was a finger, severed at the second knuckle. Bone peeked through the nail, pointing toward the remnants of a hand. Trying not to vomit, she followed the hand up to Jovian's shattered upper arms, the fragments of ribs hanging from a broken chest. *Gods.* What had happened to ruin his hands so horribly? If she didn't know better, she would have thought this was— She froze.

Slowly, she dragged her gaze to Jovian's face. The eyes shoved into their sockets, the chin buried somewhere in his neck, lower jaw unhinged in a scream that had ended violently. Her breath fanned out shakily. Because there was only one explanation for the mangled hands and missing face, while the back of his skull was in one piece. Because people always threw their hands out at the end, in the vain hope of easing their collision with the ground.

"Four oak bookcases and a dagger to the chest." Geena's voice seemed distant. "Why would he choose to die this way?"

This wasn't the work of any bookcase. Sarai's hands shook. *This is . . .*

"A fall," a beautiful voice pronounced.

Kadra was staring at the corpse, face grim. The air in her lungs was suddenly scalding as a single realization crystallized.

He did it.

Her. Jovian. And very likely all the other Petitors. Harion was right. It wasn't suicide. Kadra had killed them all.

"But he was found in his study." Geena looked bewildered.

"He didn't die there." Kadra examined Jovian's broken legs. "He fell to his death."

"Tetrarch Kadra, I beg your pardon, but a body has to fall at least a hundred feet to look like this," Geena stammered. "No building in this Quarter is that high—"

"Aoran Tower," Sarai whispered. A prickling at the back of her neck told her that she had Kadra's full attention. "Sidran Tower. Lisran Tower. From what I've seen, the Academiae's towers are the highest points in Edessa. Well over a hundred and fifty feet."

"And not one magus noticed a Petitor falling off?" The Lugen scoffed.

Sarai steeled herself. "No one saw the Sidran Tower Girl fall either."

"Don't bring that dead guttersnipe from gods only know where into this," Geena snapped. "Petitor Jovian was someone of *standing*. He mattered."

Sarai was suddenly the temperature of erupting lava. "I don't think *standing* determines if someone matters."

Geena snorted. "Look, I understand that you northerners don't know how things work, but we Lugens investigate the dead, and Petitors handle the living. And it's my *professional* opinion that Jovian was crushed to death under four bookcases . . ."

A dull buzzing filled Sarai's ears. *You're wrong.* Clenching her shaking hands into fists, she tried to breathe, failing which she searched for a blade nearby, anything sharp to impale the man who'd brought her here to show off a *kill*. She found only ice.

What if it isn't him? hissed the black part of her Kadra had roused. *Why would he throw you off and have you healed afterward? If he's been killing Petitors and disguising it as suicide, then why leave only you alive?*

Because no one would believe me, she retorted. But her fury faltered. Kadra was too wily to risk a loose end. Especially when a Petitor could drag out her scant memories of that night and identify his voice.

It doesn't make sense. She stared at Jovian's ruptured eyes, realizing what had made Kadra's companion retch at the sight of her. How had the healers even put her back together?

"Why do you think that he fell from a tower?" Kadra cut in.

"Because . . ." Her voice dwindled to a croak.

The ground teetered. Jovian's corpse elongated into shadows that fled to every corner of the room. Kadra's voice was a dulcet blur. She dug her nails into her arms. *Not here. Not now. Not in front of them.*

"He . . ." she tried again, only for the word to end in a wheeze.

Something clamped onto her wrist, firmly propelling her forward and out of the room. Warmth returned to her fingers in a painful rush as the door swung shut. She released a tight breath. Her vision cleared.

The grip on her wrist registered first. She followed the large hand circling it until the shape before her settled into the harsh planes of Kadra's face. *Shit.*

Before he could speak, she cleared her throat. "His hands."

He raised an eyebrow. She kept her face blank as his eyes dug into hers. Finally, he let go. "Explain."

Rubbing her frigid skin, she temporarily forced her suspicions aside. "If Jovian was crushed to death by those bookcases, he would have faced a short distance to the ground. There'd be evidence of internal bleeding or asphyxiation, bruising on his back from the bookcase's weight, not this"— she swallowed—"pulverization. That requires height and gravity. Like he . . . splintered on impact. Someone would have noticed if that happened in public—everyone probably saw his face at last year's Robing. But his body could go unnoticed for much longer in the Academiae. It's less busy there, and I haven't seen any building that rivals the towers for height."

Kadra leaned against the icy walls. "And how is it that a man who fell from a tower was found in his study under four bookcases?"

You know why. She dared meet his gaze and found steel within. *Careful.* She still had no proof of his involvement. Yet, fire crawled up her throat when she glanced at the door behind which Jovian rotted.

Pretend it's a theory. It's just a theory. She unfettered her tongue. "I imagine that a death on the Academiae's grounds would be . . . undesirable."

"Meaning someone concealed his suicide to preserve the Academiae's reputation?"

"I never said his death was a suicide," she whispered.

A stillness graced Kadra's face, as though she'd surprised him, and he was perturbed by it. Withdrawing from the opposite wall, he approached her, bending until their faces were level.

"Petitor Sarai." His voice was silk. "That's a dangerous theory."

She didn't move. "Danger doesn't change the truth. I used to climb snowgrape vines for a living. I . . . know what a fall looks like. And I don't think he wanted to die."

His face tightened. "Agreed," he said softly.

The door to the ice room with Jovian's corpse scraped open. She hurriedly stepped away from Kadra as Geena emerged.

"I thought Arsameans slept in snowdrifts. Didn't think the cold would be too much for you," she scoffed. "How would you like me to record the death, Tetrarch Kadra?"

"A fall. The suicide was staged." His tone brooked no refusal.

"*Homicidium?* But—" Geena halted when Kadra glanced in her direction. "*Certo.* Should I do the same for the other one?"

Other one? Sarai's heart halted. "There's another corpse like Jovian's?"

"Tullus's Petitor two years ago." Kadra started up the stairs. "He apparently walked into a bull pen and was trampled to death."

Truth. Another mangled corpse. Another method of disguising a fall. But if Petitors were falling off the Academiae's towers, then . . . *what happened to me never stopped.*

It wasn't just her and Jovian. Someone was killing the Tetrarchy's Petitors.

"Why?" she whispered. The question echoed up the stairwell to Kadra, who gave her an inquiring glance. She ran up to him. "Why are you only investigating this *now?* If there's another body like Jovian's, then there's been a killer behind some of these supposed Petitor suicides for years! And you only formed a theory of death for Jovian *today.*"

"I didn't."

"We agreed that it was a fall just *minutes* ago." Inches from the main landing, the stench of death choked her. "Wasn't that the purpose of this little jaunt?"

Geena's eyes nervously darted between them as he drew an inch closer.

"No, Petitor Sarai." His voice sank low, and she swallowed. "I've visited this corpse on nine occasions to hear the same explanation of death by bookcase from nine different Lugens." The barest smile brushed his lips. "No one has shared *my* hypothesis. Until today."

Truth. Frozen, she stared numbly as he straightened and vanished upstairs.

"And I kept saying it wasn't a fall!" Geena covered her mouth in horror. "Do you think I offended him?"

"I doubt it," Sarai muttered. Kadra evidently didn't take offense to much. Ungluing herself from the stairs, she paused when Geena caught her elbow.

The Lugen looked uncomfortable. "How did you know it was a fall?"

She flinched. "The hands." She stuffed hers in her pockets, hiding joints doomed to eternally tremble. "There's no hiding the hands."

Departing the morgue, she drew deep gulps of fresh air. At the entrance to the vigile station, Kadra mounted his horse and steered it to face her.

"Ready?" The strange stillness she'd glimpsed in the morgue was back in his eyes.

Her gut tightened. *Kadra's just a man,* Cato had said, but she couldn't afford to believe it. Ur Dinyé's most notorious Tetrarch was a formidable strategist, a powerful magus, and, above all, a manipulator who could warp a situation to his advantage in a blink.

But he must have a weakness. She'd keep her head down and her guard up throughout this investigation or whatever charade he was conducting. She'd arm herself with his secrets. And he wouldn't see her coming when she ruined him.

Mounting Caelum, Sarai faced the monster who could be her assailant. "Ready."

CHAPTER SEVEN

Reading hadn't been her strongest suit growing up. There'd been too much that Cretus needed done for her to learn, and when she'd once made the mistake of staring longingly at booksellers from Sal Flumen in the town square, Cretus had spread word that the tunnel rat was getting aspirations.

She'd resorted to eavesdropping behind Arsamea's only schoolhouse, memorizing organs, blood vessels, which herbs, roots, and fungi could be used as anesthetics and which would induce pain—the town's healer had limited that discussion to a disappointing "if you don't recognize it, don't eat it," and her dreams of giving Cretus laxatives had died early. But healing had come easily to her, while her reading had been limited to *Violet Snowgrape Delight, bottled in the Month of Seas, Year 548 of the Tetrarchy*—Cretus's worst wine, though no one dared say it—until Cisuré.

The first time she'd spoken with Marus's daughter had been upon finding her crying outside the schoolhouse, clutching the ends of her newly chin-length hair.

"It looked so pretty on Instructor Flavia," she'd wailed, tugging up her hood when other children leaving their lessons snickered.

"It looks nice," Sarai had ventured. Her own hair kept snagging on barbs when she climbed for snowgrapes. Cisuré's shorn locks made a good deal of sense.

She withdrew her small harvesting knife and took it to her braid. Dropping the hair, she shook her much lighter head and found Cisuré gaping at her like she'd gone mad.

"You really like it?"

Sarai thought her hair spoke for itself but nodded anyway. A few girls had halted, looking from Cisuré's hair to Sarai's. She fidgeted, conscious of her grimy face from pressing too close to the window to listen, and quickly left. The next day, no less than four other girls showed up with short hair, much to the dismay of their mothers.

She hadn't thought much of it until Cisuré sat at the back of the schoolhouse. She'd wondered if the other girl had gotten in trouble. Then, Cisuré had angled her slate to show Sarai the paragraph she was copying down as their instructor read aloud from *An Accurate History of Ur Dinyé*. Their eyes had met with identical grins. And at the age of ten, she'd acquired three great gifts: Cisuré's friendship, every book the other girl had, and literacy.

She'd never been more thankful for it than now.

Sarai reached down to massage a cramp in her legs and immediately adjusted herself at Kadra's searching look.

"Tired?" Behind his desk, he sat across from her without a hair out of place, as though reading a hundred petitions took no more energy than pouring a glass of wine. Meanwhile, her head was swimming, and she could feel the hollows under her eyes growing deeper.

"No." She forced her sagging back to impeccable posture. His faint huff of laughter proved that she wasn't fooling anyone. *Damned man.*

She hadn't had a lick of time to visit the Hall of Records. Departing the morgue, they had returned to Aoran Tower, much to her bewilderment.

"Shouldn't I be helping adjudicate cases?" she'd asked upon entering his tablinum.

He'd sat at his desk, and she'd prepared to firmly inform him that she wouldn't be frozen out of the job simply because he hadn't wanted a Petitor. Then, he'd shifted half the scrolls on his desk toward her. And he had a *large* desk.

"Start with those." He'd tilted his head expectantly at the pile.

She'd been swimming in ink and parchment since.

Petitions were preludes to a trial, setting down the parties, grievances, and witnesses, and infrequently accompanied by statements given by the defendants. Scribes across Ur Dinyé recorded both and referred them to iudices, the closest town's judges, for trial. Where matters involved complex issues of law or where the iudex saw no reasonable path to resolution, the petitions were brought to a Tetrarch. From every corner of the country.

She rested her head in one hand, dazed after hours of going over *homicidium*, *calumnia*—malicious prosecution—and crimes that just kept coming. No wonder the Tetrarchy didn't decide the outcome of every case together. They'd never get anything done.

She returned her last scroll to Kadra's desk and fought the urge to collapse onto it. Beyond his windows, Edessa's rosy dawn had given way to noon. *Nihumb* and *zosta* blazed scarlet on her armilla, warning that she'd be out of magic in a couple hours. *So this is the infamous workload of a Tetrarch's Petitor.* But she hadn't expected for Kadra to work just as hard.

Cretus had been a lazy taskmaster, but Kadra seemed to demand as much of himself as he did of her. In the few hours of their reading, he'd worked his way through his half of the pile of scrolls and then started on hers, focus unwavering for so much as a second.

Sarai risked a glance at him in the sunlight. Faint lines hardened his temples and bracketed the grim set of his jaw. Yet there was a grace to his features, unyielding in the way of a sculpture. As she stared, one of his brows rose.

"Yes?"

She cleared her throat. "Do the other Tetrarchs get this many petitions?"

"Every day." He set down the one he'd finished. "Not what you expected the job to be?"

"I expected more writing than reading."

"That'll come in two days." He rolled up the scroll, large hands securing the tie around it. "We'll be adjudicating these over the week."

"This week," she echoed weakly. A hundred cases in a week, and she was the poor sod who'd be determining who was lying. She turned to the remaining half of the petitions with the painful realization that she was going to have to read them, too.

As if he'd read her mind, Kadra indicated the small mountain of parchment. "When you can," he said pleasantly. "Is five hours enough?"

Now you're just mocking me. "Plenty." She ignored the fact that it was going to take her at least eight. "I won't slow you down."

Kadra looked as though he were fighting a laugh. "Of course." He made a notation in the margins of a scroll.

She watched the sharp strokes of his pen with a sinking feeling. *Might as well get it over with.* He'd notice the second she started writing.

"Do you require good penmanship?" she asked in a rush.

"Why?"

Taking a scrap of parchment, she dipped her pen in the inkwell and, with a deep breath, wrote her name, acutely aware of him tracking the wobble of the letters, how some sat slightly higher than the rest. Every flaw, magnified.

She set the pen down and splayed her fingers on the desk, which quivered even worse under the attention. "It's a . . . condition I can't control," she reluctantly admitted. "I know judgments need to be legible. If this is unacceptable, I'll train myself to do better."

He rounded the desk to extend a hand into the tense space between them. After a moment's hesitation, she gave him the parchment.

"I don't see a problem." His scrutiny went from the letters to her. "Your writing suits you."

The swell of pride that had foolishly rushed into her chest at the first half of his pronouncement immediately disappeared.

"Because it's irregular and imprecise?" It came out grimmer than she intended, and his face turned thoughtful. He flipped the scrap to reveal dark wounds on the back where she'd dug the pen too deep in an effort to steady her hand. Embarrassed, she winced, but he looked unsurprised.

"I only see determination." His voice was a low rumble, surely calculated with the effect of undoing her because every word sank into her bloodstream, potent as wine.

She would have let herself be swept off to a world where men like him were kind without reason, if it weren't for the way his gaze tracked her, studying her response. *Manipulator.* He'd say anything to make her choose him over the Tetrarchy. And yet, her body didn't panic despite the scant inches separating them. Her shortness of breath seemed less a product of anxiety than . . . anticipation.

Absolutely not. Crumpling the parchment, she stood just as he leaned down and collided into his shoulder. She instinctively gripped him to steady herself. The second her fingers clutched the front of his robes, she knew it was a mistake. She stilled. Whatever she'd been about to say died in her throat. And for a moment, they simply stared at each other.

Why you? she wondered bitterly. She'd resigned herself to the fact that a normal life wasn't possible, that no man would want her when she flinched away all the time. So what cruel joke of the gods was it that only *he* didn't trigger the panic?

After a breath, the indifference on Kadra's face gave way to faint surprise. His stern jaw tightened, guard visibly going up. Sarai couldn't tell if she was relieved that he was taken aback as she was. She released her grip, palms up to convey that she hadn't meant to touch him and hid her embarrassment by brandishing the long-forgotten bit of parchment with her writing.

"I don't need pity," she muttered.

"I have none." His voice held no softness. "But I won't hold you to the standards you hold yourself. I will ask many things of you, Petitor Sarai, but I will not ask for perfection."

Damn you. For an awful second, she felt utterly exposed before him. Before she could snap that not everyone could flout the world's unwritten rules the way he did, the tablinum door swung open.

"Tetrarch Kadra, there's a—" Cato halted in the doorway. "Visitor."

Breathing fast, she stepped away from Kadra, searching for something to occupy her hands. She'd barely begun gathering the remaining petitions when Cato cleared his throat.

"The visitor's for you, Petitor Sarai. It's Petitor Cisuré."

Juggling an armful of parchment, she turned in time to see Kadra's face harden. She raced upstairs and dumped the scrolls on her bed before joining him outside.

Beyond the gate, Cisuré waited in ivory and silver robes. Evidently unable to see them through Kadra's wards, she squinted at Aoran Tower, then jumped at the sound of him unlocking the gate.

Her face lit up with relief upon sighting Sarai. "There you are—" Cisuré's eyes went flat as Kadra emerged. "Tetrarch Kadra," she spat. "May I borrow Petitor Sarai if she's done for the day?"

What in havïd? Sarai stared. She'd never seen the other girl so furious.

"What business do you have with *my* Petitor?" Kadra asked softly.

Her mouth fell open at his emphasis. As thunderclouds gathered on Cisuré's face, Sarai had the strangest feeling of being the rope in a tug-of-war contest.

"Tetrarch Aelius would like to meet her. With your consent." Cisuré sounded as though the bit of politesse had cost her a limb.

"Of course." Kadra barely acknowledged her, eyes still on Sarai. Her pulse jumped when he dipped his head toward her. "Come back in one piece."

"Naturally," she muttered, turning to Cisuré. She halted.

All color had drained from the other girl at Kadra's parting comment. Face pinched and pale, an ugly light roiled in her eyes, looking unnervingly like hatred. Without a word, she gripped Sarai's wrist and stalked away, pulling her along.

Sarai struggled to keep up. "What, by all the High Elsar, was that about?"

"What do you mean?" Cisuré walked faster.

"You! Spitting at Kadra like he was your sworn enemy. I thought you were terrified of him— Oof!"

Cisuré seized her in a tight hug. "By Temperance, I was so worried! Did he try anything last night? They say he's ice, but he's a man . . ."

Memory returned unbidden of the brush of Kadra's fingers across her neck when he'd removed her birrus. An uncomfortable heat crawled up Sarai's cheeks.

"I'm fine. Kadra has no interest in me."

"It's just odd." Cisuré took a cobblestone path going east. "Tetrarch Aelius only asked me this morning to move into the domus by his tower. I'm close by and retain my privacy. Why did Kadra rush you into living with him? It's not like he wanted a Petitor."

True. In her determination to enter his stronghold, she hadn't thought about why he'd invited her there. What part of him tearing down the Tetrarchy required her to stay at Aoran Tower?

She couldn't ask Cisuré. One mention of Kadra demolishing the Tetrarchy and the other girl would likely have an aneurysm.

Sarai shrugged. "Who can tell what goes through his head?"

"Ugh, who wants to? . . . So, what's Aoran Tower like?"

An image flashed in her head of Kadra's half-open robe, of firm muscles rising and falling with each breath. "It's nothing special," she bit out without thinking. "It's just been a while since . . ." *I've felt anything substantial beyond anger. Since—*

"Since you've seen anything outside Cretus's tavern, yes?" Cisuré drew her through a series of corridors. Students parted for them, nervously eyeing their robes. "So he doesn't have any heads on pikes? Hasn't imposed a curfew?"

"No, and no." Sarai tossed out the unnecessarily detailed portrait of Kadra's chest her brain had chosen to capture. For a notoriously private man, he hadn't laid down any ground rules for how their cohabitation was to work. "What do you know about Kadra? People seem to love him, but you and Harion act like he'll kill us all."

Cisuré cast a glance around them before pulling her behind a pillar. "Everyone knows Kadra's history. They just don't talk about it openly."

"Why not?"

"Kadra's adopted. Rumor says he was a street rat, found in an alley as an adolescent. Probably why he's always been barbaric." Her lips formed a moue of distaste. "That tower of his used to belong to Tetrarch Othus, his foster father. The relationship was reportedly quite poor, what with Kadra being Kadra."

Cato must be Othus's husband, she realized. No wonder he'd been taking Kadra to task that morning.

Sarai snorted. "So Kadra became Tetrarch via his father pulling strings."

"If only. Kadra's a . . . talented magus," Cisuré admitted with distaste. "Everyone at the Academiae thought he was slated to be the next Magus Supreme. Instead, he graduated early and began working as an iudex. At fifteen. At first, he followed the letter of the law and rose rapidly through the judiciary. Then it began. The spectacles of violence, the bloodshed."

"Why would people vote for him?"

"His devotees are as rabid as he is," Cisuré said darkly. "And here's something very few know about why that election was called. Four years ago, Tetrarch Othus was found butchered in an alley in his own Quarter—what's now Kadra's Quarter. Who do you think got his wealth, his tower, and his seat as Tetrarch?"

Four years ago. Sarai froze. "When did Othus die?"

Cisuré's eyes widened, following Sarai's train of thought. "It has nothing to do with the Fall," she insisted.

"When?"

"Three days later." She averted her gaze. "But he was a Tetrarch. There's no connection."

Isn't there? Could Othus have been the other man with Kadra that night, who'd been reluctant to cover for him? Was that why he'd been killed?

Cisuré sighed. "You worry me, you know?" She pulled back Sarai's sleeve to display *nihumb* and *zosta*'s crimson glow on her armilla. "A rune used to alter appearances is suspect as is, and you're using it in *his* tower." Her eyes took on a familiar dullness, some splinter of memory resurfacing. "He has more blood on his hands than Marus. One slip and he'll kill you. I wouldn't even know how to retrieve your body."

Sarai slung an arm around Cisuré's shoulders. "I'll be careful. He won't see it."

"You need to get out of there. I'll help."

Not yet. Not until she got the answers she'd entered it for. Pricking her finger, she wiped the blood over *zosta,* turning it dark to conserve magic. "Well, I'll need some of this four-thousand-aureus salary if I'm to purchase a domus. The journey here emptied my purse."

"Oh, that won't be difficult." Cisuré launched into an explanation, which slipped past Sarai's ears as her mind wandered back to Aoran Tower's enigmatic master.

Vicious. Sadistic. Cold eyes cutting into whomever was fool enough to meet them. A man who'd apparently killed his foster father and pushed her off Sidran Tower.

Yet the pieces didn't fit. The humor that wove in and out of his face was empty, like he'd long ceased to find the world interesting. Harion would've delighted in her shoddy writing, but Kadra hadn't mocked her, or made any reference to her being a northern barmaid. And he'd wanted her opinion on Jovian's corpse. *Why? Does my opinion actually matter to him?*

She swallowed a laugh at that thought. Like a man who lounged about elbow-deep in blood and wine and poorly knotted robes had any interest in what she thought. His chest resurfaced in her head and she bit back a curse. *Gods, if that appears again, I'm jumping off Sidran Tower on purpose this time.*

Its black spire loomed ahead, as though the gods wanted her to try. The single balcony at the tower's top taunted her. Had Jovian fallen over that railing too? Had he smashed into the same cobblestones and bled out before Kadra? Her bitterness was a nocked arrow. By Wrath, she should spend all that focus on his chest determining how best to pierce it.

Forcing her gaze toward Aoran Tower didn't help. It couldn't be Jovian's place of death. In keeping with his paranoid protection of his home, Kadra's abode had only two egresses on the upper floors: her window and his. Even then it was a short drop, barely enough to break a leg. *Two out of eight towers down.* And Sidran Tower remained the most likely suspect.

Cisuré pointed at something, and Sarai nodded without comprehension. Sometimes she wondered if it was for the best that she couldn't remember what had raced through her head as she'd hurtled toward the ground. Some days, she wished she could do as Cisuré said and leave it all behind. But all it took was a flinch away from a man or pained understanding of the years she'd lost while others fell in love and saw themselves as lovable. She couldn't. The rage was part of her now.

"Sarai, are you even listening?" Cisuré waved a hand in front of her face. She blinked. "Yes."

Cisuré squinted at her suspiciously. "As I was saying, that's Tetrarch Aelius's tower. He's been there for nine years, since election."

Sarai eyed the elegant structure in the east, its walls the same blinding white as Aelius's robes. Like Aoran Tower, it had no exits higher than fifteen feet. Unlike Aoran Tower, the main doors were visible, an intricate twist of birchwood and silver. To her surprise, not one fulgur scutum was erected near the structure. Then again, Aelius could probably fend off any bolt.

Apprehension struck her. *I'm meeting the Magus Supreme of Ur Dinyé.* "What does Aelius want me for?"

"*Tetrarch* Aelius. We may fraternize with them, but they're our rulers." Cisuré's voice softened. "Don't be nervous. He's a humble man and, unlike Kadra, he's done much for the country."

Her brows rose at her friend's pink cheeks. "Fond of him, are we?" Vengeance had become Sarai's master, but Cisuré seemed to have chosen a worthier contender for her heart. No wonder Anek had teased her at the Robing.

"I'm not *fond*. He's a decade older! I admire him."

"Right." Sarai grinned, remembering how Aelius had watched Cisuré at the Robing. "Did you two know each other before yesterday? He looked at you like he knew you."

"Before?" Cisuré flushed. "No, he reads people in seconds. He was probably confirming that I was a worthy Petitor."

Makes sense. There had been something equally familiar in Kadra's gaze at the Robing. As though he'd seen right through her . . . and found it amusing. Sarai scowled.

Cisuré laughed. "You thought of Kadra, didn't you? Cheer up, you're meeting a proper Tetrarch now."

"Don't you mean *Tetrarch* Kadra?"

"Like he deserves the respect! What he does is ungodly."

Ungodly? Four years had evidently introduced more than Aelius to Cisuré. She hadn't placed much stock in the gods back in Arsamea.

At Cobhran Tower's gates, Cisuré raised her armilla. A half-sphere of golden filaments materialized around the structure, tendrils of sizzling light racing across it in jagged patterns. *Lightning.* So these were Aelius's wards. Her skin crawled. Anyone who ventured too close would be fried alive.

Cisuré pressed blood into a rune on her armilla, and the barrier split down the center, a rush of cool air filling the gap so they could enter. She knocked on the birchwood double doors.

"Ready?"

"*Havïd*," Sarai muttered, earning her an elbow in her side, as the doors noiselessly parted to reveal an airy, white-walled atrium.

Unlike Kadra's midnight mansion, Aelius embraced light. It streamed through wide windows and an expansive glass roof, bouncing off the reflective tiles. At the atrium's center rose an ethereal tree, laden with white-petaled blossoms. A breeze from an open window spread their scent across the room.

"Magnolia," Cisuré breathed. "Beautiful, isn't it?"

Astounded, Sarai nodded. A short hallway stretched ahead, so pristine that she felt her worn boots were committing a crime with each step. Beyond it she could make out the faint outline of a banquet table and . . .

"Is that a dais?" she whispered. "You'd think this was a trial."

The other girl's smile froze. "He's a fair man. You'll see."

Sarai's magnolia-induced daze faltered. Unease skittered across the back of her neck. "Is there something you aren't—"

"Ah, she's here," a voice called.

Her stomach plummeted. They had reached the end of the hallway, which opened into a receiving room. The banquet table she'd spotted earlier rose front and center. Towering vases hugged the walls, vivid splashes of flora within, but her gaze stuck on the figure—figures—seated at one end of the table.

Aelius. Tullus. Cassandane. Three calculating gazes met her as she tottered forward, with all the grace of a deer wandering into a hunter's gathering.

Ambush, her intuition screamed in warning. At the edge of her vision, Cisuré melted into a corner, a guilty flush across her cheeks.

Betrayal rose sharp in Sarai's chest. *Why didn't you tell me?*

Aelius's brown eyes crinkled as he gave her a wide grin. "Welcome to Cobhran Tower."

Unlocking her frozen knees, she bowed low. "Tetrarch Aelius, Tetrarch Tullus, Tetrarch Cassandane. I'm honored."

"Please sit." Aelius indicated the high back chair across from them.

It screeched as Sarai pulled it out, the seat leaving her legs dangling above the ground. Feeling ridiculous, she clasped her hands in her lap and attempted a smile. The men immediately reflected one back at her.

A frisson of tension slid down her spine. *Mirroring.* A social trick she had employed with many a drunk in Cretus's tavern. But these were powerful people, busy ones, if Kadra's workload was any indication. They wouldn't fritter their time away with people like her unless they wanted something.

"I hear Kadra's putting you through the wringer." Aelius gave her a commiserating smile.

How had he heard that when she'd been reading in Kadra's tower all day? "I expected the job to be hard work," she said carefully.

"Of course. This must all be very new to you. But you performed extraordinarily well at the Robing."

"I just . . . did my job."

"Oh, we all saw it." On Aelius's right, Tullus popped a grape in his mouth, eyeing her chest with interest as he chewed. "How is Aoran Tower? Not a patch on Cobhran, I imagine."

She cringed internally. The Robing had proved there was no love lost between Kadra and Tullus. "I've spent my entire life in Arsamea, Tetrarch Tullus. Compared to it, both towers look magnificent to me."

"A born diplomat." He seemed to be trying to see through her robes. "Wouldn't have thought a hick town possessed any of those."

"And yet, Arsamea has yielded two Petitors." Cassandane broke in. She looked ill at ease. Sarai had the strange feeling that the other woman didn't want to be at this gathering either. "You must have had a thorough schooling."

"I taught myself. Runes, Probing, and all." She'd be damned if Arsamea received any credit for her labor. Aelius's eyebrows rose, but he thankfully didn't ask for the specifics. She couldn't very well admit to practicing on sotted tavern patrons.

Taking the grape bowl from Tullus, he peered at her over the lip. "Now, Sarai, are you gods-fearing?"

She recalled his lengthy prayer at the Robing. She wouldn't call herself devout, but she believed in the Elsar. Despite the Fall and her miserable life.

She nodded. "I'll be making a visit to the Grand Elsarian Temple soon." She named the largest house of worship in Ur Dinyé.

"Good." Aelius beamed. "We're a humble people here. Our lives are at the gods' mercy, so we rely on their every kindness."

"I've heard much of your scuta keeping people safe as well," she ventured.

"Well, many do call me the Naaduir of invention." He grinned, referencing the minor pantheon of humans who had achieved deification through devotion to the gods. Those Naaduir who served the High Elsar were known as Saints, while devotees of the Dark Elsar had a different appellation—the Wretched.

"The Temple has been asking Aelius to consider being formalized as a Saint." Tullus turned to her. "What do you think? Should he take them seriously?"

What in havïd *do I say to that?* She stammered, "Yes, I—"

"You really should, Tetrarch Aelius," Cisuré piped up from her corner. "Ur Dinyé hasn't formalized a Saint in centuries. The monarchs back then lazed in their palaces without doing half as much as you have. You deserve the honor."

Torn between awe and bewilderment as Cisuré's speech continued, Sarai glanced at Tullus and nearly choked to find him nodding sagely. Only Cassandane looked like she was searching for a hole to swallow her.

"You've made your case." Aelius raised his hands with a smile, sleeves falling back to reveal a silver armilla blazing with lit runes like Kadra's. "I'll speak with the Temple."

At Cisuré's flush, Sarai slid her a reproving glance. *What were you saying about not being fond again?* Avoiding her eyes, the other girl began fanning herself.

Aelius returned to Sarai. "Pardon our distraction. You must be wondering why we invited you. And why Tetrarch Kadra did yesterday." He steepled his fingers. "Strange, isn't it? Calling a young woman over in the dead of night."

Havïd. Cato was right about the rumor mill being busy. *Best to nip this in the bud.*

"I'm sure he thought it necessary, seeing as I work with—for him now," she corrected when Tullus's eyes narrowed. He clearly didn't consider Tetrarchs and Petitors as equals on the job.

"What's his tower like?" Tullus demanded. "It's been ages since I was last there."

Why is he so focused on Aoran Tower? "It's"—Sarai cast around for a neutral answer—"quite dark. I'm afraid I didn't see much of it last night."

"Really?" His brow creased in irritation. "You saw *nothing*?"

"I—"

"She probably only had a few hours of rest before beginning work with him," Cassandane interjected, sending Sarai a reassuring glance.

Tullus looked like he couldn't care less if Sarai slept or not. "I knew Kadra's predecessor well, Tetrarch Othus. We were in and out of each other's homes. Then, Kadra takes the throne, and suddenly no one's allowed in. That's suspect, being so paranoid about visitors."

Well, we're in a tower with lightning around it.

"It's like he's hiding something dangerous there. Could be treasonous correspondence, forbidden magic, even bodies." Tullus's eyes finally moved up to her face. "And you're the only person in Ur Dinyé with access to it all."

The ensuing silence had a dangerous weight to it. Anticipation. Insistence. Her spine stiffened in understanding.

She folded her hands in her lap before daring to speak. "Are you asking me to spy on Tetrarch Kadra?" Behind her, Cisuré sucked in an audible breath.

Aelius gaped. A wide grin broke across his face. "Now, there's an idea! You're a bright one. We all saw it at the Robing, didn't we?"

Tullus gnawed on a grape. "Splendid idea. Will you start tomorrow?"

Wait, what? Why were they acting like this was her idea when she'd only said what they'd kept beating about the bush at?

Sarai realized her jaw had fallen open and wrenched it shut. "I was only—"

"You've seen how dangerous Kadra is." Tullus talked to her chest, scratching his grizzled chin. Sarai itched to whack him with his grape bowl. "The man delights in gory spectacle. It's a travesty that he was even able to ascend to the position."

She squirmed in her too-high seat. Granted, in two days, Kadra had proven himself to have no regard for the law, no qualms with making her burn a man alive, and, even under her most benign interpretation, had hidden that Jovian and the other Petitors had been murdered. But to spy on him? She may as well ring her own death knell.

"And there's the eerie coincidence of our Petitors vanishing in his Quarter." A cloud passed over Aelius's handsome features. "Poor Jovian. Such a hard worker."

Every coherent thought slipped through her fingers like water. *Jovian was Aelius's Petitor?* The corpse's crushed features returned to haunt her.

"If you do this, you'll go down in history," Aelius vowed. "I will ensure it."

Her head spun. She could see it now. The tale of a daring Petitor who'd betrayed her sadistic Tetrarch.

And gotten murdered for the trouble. Oh yes, she could see it.

In the periphery, Cisuré widened her eyes, urging her to agree. There was no denying that this was an honor. *So why am I hesitating?*

"What must I do?" she whispered.

"You stood up to Kadra at the Robing," Aelius said gently. "How about giving us a little more? Inform Cisuré if he's acting suspicious. The rest of his business is his own."

She took a deep breath. "By 'suspicious,' do you mean anything involving the Petitor deaths?"

"Exactly that." Tullus snapped his fingers. "If there's anything that ties him to the suicides, or if he seems out to get someone, you will let us know, yes?"

Fear lanced through her at the question's knife-sharp undercurrent. She should agree. She had every intention of tearing down Kadra herself. Why not earn the favor of three Tetrarchs while she was at it?

Cassandane looked oddly pale. "You're the best-situated person for this task. The decision is yours." *But so are the consequences*, her eyes seemed to say.

Sarai's throat locked. *This is mad.* Kadra could kill her for this. But she couldn't stop thinking of Jovian's broken body. Of Kadra's voice in her nightmares for four *havïd* years. What did it matter to her why the Tetrarchy seemed so hellsbent on tearing each other down? Joining with Kadra's enemies would give her vengeance faster than she could alone before a court. With three Tetrarchs behind her, there would be nowhere for him to run.

"I'll do it." The words reverberated in the sunlit hall. She swallowed.

Aelius's answering smile held respect. "You're a rare bird, Petitor Sarai. That took courage." Rising from his seat, he came around the table to grip her hand. "Welcome to our little alliance."

Dazed, she quickly eased away, hoping he hadn't felt any scars in the process. Dropping Tullus's grape-sticky palm after a few interminable seconds, she turned to Cassandane, who simply inclined her head, watching her with strangely sad eyes.

"We'll reconvene in a month or so. If you find anything urgent sooner, let us know. But be careful," Aelius urged.

"Ignore anything Kadra says," Tullus added. "That man doesn't need magic or a Petitor to tunnel into a mind."

Believe me, I know. Bowing low upon their dismissal, she fled Cobhran Tower, Cisuré behind her. The second Aelius's doors drew shut, the other girl seized her in a hug.

"I'm. So. Proud. Of. You!" Cisuré punctuated each word with a squeeze. "I know that wasn't easy. You love hiding in the periphery too much to have enjoyed it."

Sarai paused. "I don't." She'd done it in Arsamea because attention had invited mockery. This ordeal had been equally discomfiting. "Why didn't you warn me that they were all there?"

Cisuré winced. "He's my Tetrarch. I can't usurp his authority."

"Usurp?" Sarai halted, utterly thrown. "I'm your friend!"

"*Always.* But he's my Tetrarch." Cisuré searched her eyes. "You understand, don't you? I can't have any secrets from him."

Sarai thought of the banners still covering the Academiae. "It really is a marriage then."

Cisuré turned pink. "Not in *that* way."

"Gods, I hope not. He's a decade older than us, so just . . . don't fall too deep." Sarai blew out a breath. *A Petitor one day and a spy the next.* "It's a lot to take in."

"You won't regret it," Cisuré insisted. "Tetrarch Aelius is nothing like the monster you're stuck with."

True. Sarai stared at Kadra's black tower several miles away. But as she journeyed back, she couldn't shake the strange feeling that the rest of the Tetrarchy wasn't quite as placid as they seemed.

CHAPTER EIGHT

Red was one of the few colors that hadn't vanished from her vision. It ran from her pulverized limbs to form puddles with the rain and coated her throat when she tried to speak.

The man who'd argued with the owner of the beautiful voice was still retching. He stopped when footsteps drew near. Apparently having recovered his composure, he then began yelling instructions at the newcomers that made no sense.

"I want every limb mended!" he roared. "Put her back together."

A chorus of gasps rose as the others reached her, but no one questioned his directive. Hands gingerly slid under her, lifting portions of her body.

"Tetrarch Othus?" someone called through the rain. "We need a name for the records."

"Mark her as dead," the man ordered.

"But—"

"She is dead." This time his voice rang like steel. "Do you understand?"

But why? Sarai wondered as people pulled her onto what felt like a cloth-bound frame. Why did she have to be dead and nameless? Agony spiked when someone gripped the back of her broken scalp. The world went dark before she could find an answer.

Sarai jolted awake, clapping a hand over her mouth before the scream building in her throat could come free. Breathing hard, she hunched over her writing desk.

This flash of memory was new, unmarred by repetitive terror as the others were. She parted the curtain and closed it just as quickly at the sight of Sidran Tower's spire in the distance. *You're bringing it all back, aren't you?* She wanted to remember. But the place made her seize in a way that went beyond whispers of a faintly remembered terror. Something shifted in the ravines of her mind whenever she dug too deep, and part of her feared she already knew. After all, her clothing had been torn that night.

She dragged her mind away from that path. *Tetrarch Othus.* She'd been right about the other man's identity. *But why did I have to be dead, Othus? Why were you killed when you covered for Kadra?*

Stumped, she rolled up the pile of petitions she'd finally finished reading before bed. A few sported annotations in Kadra's sharp script—clearly for her benefit as they detailed Guild customs and business practices.

She sent an accusing glance at the Elsar, wherever they were. *Wisdom and Wrath, make him make sense.* Everything pointed to Kadra's involvement in the Fall from the Petitor deaths beginning around the time of his election to the fact that he was an unapologetic madman. And said madman had left her helpful notes on Edessa's Guilds. *Gods, why can't evil be simple?*

Groaning, she jumped at the sound of a door close to hers unlocking. *Speak of the Wretched, he's awake.* Footsteps rang on the slim stretch of tile between their rooms, and she sprang into motion. *Clothes. Decency!* She'd barely gotten *nihumb* active when he knocked.

Giving up on putting on a robe, she undid the bolt. "Good morning, Tetrarch Kadra. Will we—" She froze.

Kadra's bare chest was less than a foot away, unmissable even in the dark. Her head shot to the left fast enough to pull a neck muscle, but the sight of water dripping from his hair, sluicing through the light trail on his muscled abdomen, had already carved itself into her brain.

She stared at a point beyond his shoulder. "Will we be heading out?" she asked icily.

His eyes dropped to the sweat-soaked neckline of her tunic and returned to her face. He raised a finger. The candle stump on her desk sputtered to life, illuminating the stack of petitions.

"You've been busy."

"I said I wouldn't slow you down." She crossed her arms, horribly aware of how close his bathrobe was to slipping off his shoulder. "I gather we're heading out a little early?"

"Jovian's brother, Decimus, has agreed to meet with us. Will half an hour be enough for you to get ready?"

"Less. I'll meet you downstairs." She watched his gaze almost imperceptibly return to the sweat trailing from her temples. The lines in his brow deepened for a second before he nodded and left.

Closing the door, she exhaled. *It's just a chest.* She could name every blood vessel weaving through it, could fracture his sternum with a touch.

Stripping off her tunic, she dropped the illusion and regarded the mess of scars circling her ribcage, bisecting her breasts. No one would lust over this. He'd robbed her of even that.

Dressed, she went downstairs and found Cato lounging on a couch in Kadra's tablinum. She didn't understand him either. Why would Othus's husband share walls with the man suspected of killing him? A thought shook her. *Were they in on it together?*

She'd barely begun considering the horrifying possibility that she lived with not one but *two* murderers when Cato raised his cup of tea.

"Drenevan's outside. Watch your step, Petitor Sarai. Stormfall hit us a few hours ago."

So that's why Kadra was wet. "Tibi gratias ago."

At the stilted response, Cato looked uncomfortable. "I hear that you know I'm no coachman. It was a precautionary measure, for Kadra's safety. Nothing personal."

It never is. At best, she was currently a tool to both sides of the Tetrarchy. Neither saw her as a person.

"I understand." She mustered a smile. "I keep hearing that it's no small thing that I get to see this tower."

"It isn't," he said cryptically. She left him to his tea.

Muggy air hit her when she stepped outside, the slippery mud making walking difficult. Worse was the hint of smoke in the oppressive damp, uncomfortably like the stench of Ennius's pyre. She trod carefully to where the source of all her problems waited by their horses.

Kadra lazily wiped a finger over his armilla, setting the few runes that weren't lit aglow. Silhouetted against the indigo heavens, he seemed otherworldly. How odd that Aelius was so close to formalization as a Saint, and she felt nothing in his presence. Yet, she could easily believe that the monster before her was one of the Wretched.

They journeyed down the citadel in silence. It was still hours away from sunrise, the sky vast and clear. There was a softness after stormfall, the same quiet that had warmed her three nights ago in a garden folly with this man. Wind teased her cheeks and brushed through Kadra's damp hair. She'd never hated him or herself more.

"The night before the Robing, why didn't you get rid of me?"

He shot her a sidelong glance. "You already know."

You're going to have to choose. She would have rolled her eyes if she weren't painfully aware that he was probably keeping her alive because of that ridiculous question.

She dropped the subject. "What happens now that Jovian's death has been noted as a murder?"

"His brother was notified after we left the morgue. The investigation is kept from the public until we have definitive proof and a suspect."

The more secretive, the better it is for you. Meanwhile, Jovian's brother had believed that his death was a suicide for months. He would likely have blamed himself for not somehow preventing it. She couldn't imagine having to grieve again, knowing that it was murder and that the investigative trail was at least four months old.

"Why let his brother believe a lie for so long?" she bit out. "If you'd always suspected that Jovian fell to his death, why not announce the truth from the start?"

He inclined his head. "A commendable idea, but tell me, then or now, what do you think would happen if I did?"

"The job would cease to exist." Not only would Candidates studying at the Academiae flee, but unassessed potential Candidates like her would eschew assessment. Her anger burgeoned. "So you'd rather pretend nothing's wrong and have more victims offer themselves up. When you're the only one who knows there's a killer."

"What makes you think I'm the only one?"

Her retort collapsed into a sharp inhale, because he was *right*. Aelius, Tullus, Harion, Cisuré, and even Cassandane had seemed to suspect Kadra yesterday. Only the public had bought into the tales of supposed suicide.

He gave her a half-smile. "As heartwarming as it is that you consider my intellect head and shoulders above the rest of the Tetrarchy, I'm not the only one who's noticed."

Then I can't trust the other Tetrarchs either. One of their own could be a murderer, and despite their suspicion, they'd been covering for him for years, bringing more unwary Petitors to their deaths. Ice solidified through her. Everyone here had an agenda.

Kadra veered off onto a side street, venturing into the northern edge of his Quarter, toward the border that divided it from Aelius's. The paved road vanished after several miles, their mounts kicking up clods of mud as the houses around them grew dilapidated. An hour later, they dismounted outside a single-storey dwelling. The cracked stone exterior had seen better days, as had the soot-blackened roof tiles clinging desperately to the eaves.

She wiped a layer of dust from the iron nameplate over the door while Kadra secured their mounts to a post. "Decimus of Edessa."

Jovian's name had been etched below his, but a line ran through it now. She glanced at the unsmiling man beside her. Moonlight glanced off the taut peaks of his cheekbones, and she swallowed a ball of rage. *I'll find out what he did to both of us, Jovian.*

"Something on your mind?" Kadra reached past her to knock.

Her face went blank. "No."

His chuckle told her that he knew she was lying. *Gods, how?* Was he a Petitor himself? Was that how he'd gone so long without one?

"Lies have non-magical tells," he informed her, still somehow reading her mind. "People have patterns, conditions under which they reach for a lie."

Truth. She cocked her head to one side. "Then what are mine?"

"Whenever you're angry." A strange tension crossed his face. "Whenever I find you watching me."

Her mouth opened. Closed. She nearly collapsed against the door. He opted to watch as she struggled with a retort. She'd nearly come up with something when they heard footsteps inside the house.

The door cracked open and a maid poked her head out. Mousy, unkempt hair framed a worn face that squinted at them in irritation. "It's three in the *havïd* morning. What do you want—" Her eyes widened.

"Is your master home?" Kadra asked pleasantly.

"Y-yes. My apologies. Please come in, Tetrarch Kadra."

Wood squeaked as she flung the door open and waved them in. Or Kadra, rather. Sarai nearly walked into the door when the maid tried to slam it shut after him.

"Pardon me, Petitor Sarai." The maid's hand jumped to her mouth. "I didn't see you. You're *so* much shorter than you looked at the Robing."

Lovely. At this rate, it didn't matter if Kadra was behind the Petitor murders. His devotees would kill her themselves.

Following the maid inside, she took in a cozy atrium, fabric-draped armchairs and cushions stuffed to bursting. At one corner was a door with the largest lock she'd ever seen.

"I'll fetch Master Decimus right away," the woman stammered, already halfway up the stairs.

"*Tibi gratias ago*," Sarai said politely, examining the overlarge lock. A shadow fell over her shoulder.

"You use the ancient tongue often," Kadra noted.

She shrugged. "I was told that Petitors must avoid the common tongue where possible."

"Don't we serve those commoners?" His voice brushed the back of her neck.

She swallowed. *Wrath take him.* "Be that as it may, Tetrarch Kadra, the world is quick to indulge a *man* who flouts convention, but it isn't as kind to the rest of us."

"Doesn't convention demand flouting if it uses language to elevate some above others?"

"Then it's the Tetrarchy's duty to correct that," she shot back. "In the meantime, us beggars have no choice. Take me. I'd rather not have our every conversation turn into a moral or political debate, and yet, here we are."

An unholy sound broke into their battleground. Part shriek, part death rattle, it had her swiveling to search for a weapon. A balding man fell at Kadra's feet.

"Tetrarch Kadra! You honor my humble home!" he wailed, clutching Kadra's hem.

Sarai sighed. *Yes, yes. Why don't you just formalize him at this point?* Aelius could become a Saint, and Kadra could take his place among the Wretched. Granted, the latter did have better titles. Take Perfidia, Wretched Countess of Conspiracy. Her eyebrows rose as Kadra reached for the man's hands, a stern god before a member of his flock. *Kadra, Wretched Prince of Punishment.* She smirked. It had a ring to it.

"Forgive me. It's been a trying day." Decimus wiped his eyes, tugging the flaps of a dressing gown close. "How can I help find the killer?"

"We'd like to examine Jovian's belongings," Kadra said smoothly.

"*Certo,* yes! They're in his study." Indicating the locked room, Decimus fished for the key.

"Why did Jovian live in Tetrarch Kadra's Quarter?" she broke in. "Doesn't Tetrarch Aelius give his Petitors a domus?"

"Petitor Sarai, a pleasure to meet you." Decimus sketched a bow. "Truthfully, my brother didn't care much for fancy domii. His true home was the Hall of Records. Practically lived there until about two weeks before his death. That's when he suddenly insisted on staying with me. Never said why. Even procured a scutum for us when it's so much coin." He indicated the steel rod outside. "But he kept acting furtive, like he knew something bad was coming." Decimus's voice choked. "I thought he was stressed."

He reached for the lock. Metal snapped loose, and the door parted. Motes of dust greeted them, forming lazy spirals in the air.

"Tetrarch Aelius's vigiles searched it brick by brick, but didn't find anything," Decimus said sadly.

Taking the study in, Sarai winced.

Books lay in pieces, their innards spilling out. An oak desk was overturned on one side, long fingers of dried ink spreading from a pulverized inkwell. The fireplace sat lifeless, chair legs jutting from it. The rest of the chair, scrolls, and cushions were strewn about in varying states of ruin. But what struck her most was the rune painted repeatedly across the walls. Sharp lines met and diverged at perpendicular angles, dribbles of hardened ink running from them.

Sarai blanched. There was a manic freneticism to the runes, the fingerprint ridges indicating that Jovian had daubed it.

"*Modrai.*" Kadra's expression darkened.

She went very still. "The rune for 'death'?"

"And more." He turned to Decimus. "This study wasn't searched after Jovian's death. When did Aelius's vigiles really come here?"

She was about to ask how he'd come to that conclusion when Decimus crumpled.

"They came the day before he died. But my brother was no criminal. I swear it!"

"Was Jovian being accused of something?" she asked, surprised.

Decimus's lip quivered. "They never gave me the details. Just that Jovian had done something awful and to alert them when he returned. I thought I heard something at night, but the lock was intact, so I shrugged it off. Next morning, the walls were covered in *modrai* and I found him under all that wood—" The tears that had been gathering in his eyes spilled. "I still see it every time I come here."

Sarai winced, wondering if it had been as hard for Cisuré to pass Sidran Tower for four years. She thought back to the promise the other girl had begged from her before the Robing, and a fissure of guilt cracked her chest.

"Once he passed, Tetrarch Aelius sealed the records. Said nothing good comes from speaking ill of the dead. But all I can think of now is that I doubted him to the end. And he was murdered!" He fell to his knees again, sobs wracking his body. "Please give him justice, Tetrarch Kadra. I need to know what happened!"

Her eyes burned. *You could be begging your brother's killer.*

"You won't find justice in the courts. Not when coin trumps everything." She stiffened as Kadra repeated her words from their first meeting. "But I'll find those responsible, and I promise you this: They'll pay in kind."

"*Certo.*" Decimus nodded fiercely. "*Certo!* Kill them all."

Sarai's jaw tightened. So this was how Kadra indoctrinated everyone to his brand of violence. He took their broken hearts and reshaped the fragments into daggers. Yet, despite the picture of solicitude he made, Kadra's eyes were empty. When Decimus's sniffling subsided, he dropped the consoling hand. "We'll need the room to ourselves while we search."

And just like that, the compassion's gone. How no one saw it was beyond her.

"*Certo.*" Decimus paused. "If I may ask, Tetrarch Kadra, why are you reinvestigating this? I imagine Ur Dinyé doesn't lack for cases."

"But it lacks Petitors." Black eyes found hers. "And I've one of my own to watch out for now."

Damn him to every one of the ten hells. Sarai shot Kadra a look of pure disgust while Decimus and his maid gaped as if he'd proposed marriage. Before they could start writing hymns to Kadra, she ushered them out of the tablinum and shut the door.

Back against the wood, her lips pressed in a thin line. "Kindly leave me out of your games. Those two would do anything you ask. You don't need to use me to get a few seconds of goodwill."

He looked curious. "Was that what I was doing?"

"We're investigating a murder. None of this is because you—" *Care for my safety.* Breaking off, she picked her way around the room, stopping at Jovian's fallen desk. "Is there anything I should be looking for? Correspondence with the killer?"

A wall sconce flickered to life with the barest motion of Kadra's hand. "Correspondence," he repeated thoughtfully. "Do you have a suspect in mind?"

"I didn't say that," she muttered quickly. Too quickly. Avoiding his narrow-eyed look, she wedged her fingers under a corner of Jovian's desk and tilted it up.

"Interesting." His voice sank low. "Is there someone you think pushed Jovian to his death?"

Turning, she froze at Kadra's dark smile. "No."

He stepped closer. "He would have bled out. Unable to beg for help. Lying in the ruins of his body."

Stop. Chest tight, she struggled to breathe evenly.

He crouched at the opposite end of the desk she still held. "Is your suspect in this room?"

Her hands went nerveless. The desk crashed down, splinters breaking off at the impact. She held herself still, breath coming in short bursts.

Gripping an unfragmented corner, Kadra righted it in a swift motion. "And you said you weren't afraid of me."

"I'm not," she snapped.

"Hmm." There was a wealth of disbelief in the syllable.

Don't lose your temper. "If that was a test of my"—she couldn't bring herself to say *loyalty*—"intelligence, it was in poor taste."

"A Petitor must consider all avenues."

Sarai clenched her fists to keep from strangling him. "By all means, then. If there's something here that implicates you, do let me know."

Storming to the other end of the room, she began sifting through the skeletons of torn books. After an unreadable glance in her direction, Kadra examined the desk, large hands pressing the surface at corners to search for hidden drawers. The sky lightened as they scoured the study, tidying where they went. She kept to the opposite end of whatever corner Kadra inhabited as chairs were righted, books recompiled, and letters sorted. Morning rose when Sarai shelved the last tome.

"I don't understand," she admitted. "There isn't anything here that could remotely sustain a criminal charge. What was Jovian found guilty of for Tetrarch Aelius to seal in the Hall of Records?"

"Treason."

She gaped. "How can you possibly know that?"

"The walls." Kadra tilted his head to the rune scrawled everywhere.

"Some people worship Lord Death."

"*Modrai* is also a Summoning rune."

Her jaw dropped. "He was trying to *summon* Death?"

There was a slim chance of summoning one of the Elsar, High or Dark, if one knew the proper sequence of runes and had the power to channel into them. Aside from the benefit to clerics hoping to ascend to prophets, the gods granted a wish to whomever summoned them—a life-changing prize for the desperate. But the sheer expenditure of power required killed almost all who attempted a Summoning. There hadn't been a successful one in decades.

He set a scroll down. "What do you know of the worst punishment in the Corpus?"

"Being flogged to death, isn't it?"

"Performing a Summoning at the Aequitas."

121

She spun toward him, agape. "You can't be serious."

Kadra's grim face didn't seem capable of joking. "Every Summoning sequence ends in *modrai*. A bit of irony on the gods' part making hopefuls court death in order to see them. The rune has a notorious reputation as a traitor's mark."

"But that's madness!" She examined the closest rune. What she'd thought was ink was a mottled brown, patches of it flaking off the walls. *Blood.* Her stomach roiled. "It's suicide, not justice! And you passed this law?"

"Absolution for the worst crimes can only come from the Elsar. If the gods refuse to intervene, then the defendant must be guilty." He smiled faintly at her incredulous snort. "That was the rationale Aelius provided when he created the law eight years ago. Quite a religious man, the Head Tetrarch. But"—his eyes cut to her—"you saw that for yourself yesterday."

Her stomach twisted. She had the awful feeling that he knew what the Tetrarchy had asked of her. That he'd known even as he agreed to the meeting.

Sarai forced a neutral expression. "Aelius's beliefs are his own."

"Are they?" Kadra flipped through a stack of letters. "He'll be devastated to hear it. He's been trying to make them everyone else's for quite some time."

"What he does is none of my concern. At the end of the day, *you're* my Tetrarch, and I answer to you," she muttered.

At the sudden stillness behind her, she turned to find Kadra watching her as though she'd done something unaccountably strange. It struck her that she'd just said something that smacked of . . . loyalty. *Shit.* Her mouth went dry when his gaze dropped to the pounding pulse at the base of her neck.

Cursing herself for unbuttoning her collar, she fumbled to do it up. "Well . . . this can't be all Jovian's correspondence. Is the rest of it in his old domus?"

Kadra still looked perturbed. "Decimus will know." He left the study, giving her the first blessed bit of space she'd had in hours.

Sarai threw herself into an armchair missing half its upholstery. *Temperance save me, he's nerve-wracking.* She scanned the room.

"What happened to you, Jovian?"

The ugly runes on the walls called to her, something eerily hypnotic about their repetition. *Jovian came back just to paint these.* After Aelius's vigiles searched the study, but before his death. *But why?* An admission of guilt or treason? Or did the rune mean exactly as it said. But if Jovian had been predicting his death, then who had he suspected?

A movement in the fireplace caught her eye. She peered down at the fragment of parchment swaying in the breeze leaking in. Wiggling it free, she dusted off the soot. It appeared to be the remnants of a letter written in Urdish. *Odd.* She hadn't thought Petitors would learn a language now largely used by northern fishing villages. Some of the words had been obliterated by flame, but enough remained to turn her legs to cotton wool.

. . . were right. The answer lies with her. The Sidran Tower Girl must have seen . . .

The words knotted in her head. *Why am I mentioned here?* She read it over and over until Jovian's cramped writing had imprinted itself behind her eyelids, barely noticing the study door grate open as Kadra returned with Decimus. His eyes narrowed at her white-knuckled grip on the fireplace's mantelpiece. When he strode over and took the scrap of parchment, she let go without protest.

No one could accuse Kadra of being an expressive man. His features could have been carved from stone as he read, evidently proficient in Urdish. Then, she saw it. A tightening of his temples. She waited for a sardonic smile, some tell of amusement at the mention of her, at the fact that no one still knew it was him. Then he looked up.

Her breath caught. A horrible coldness filled his eyes, swallowing all emotion until the man staring out from them barely seemed human. Her grip on the mantelpiece went slack. *Why aren't you pleased?* He'd walked away from her body. *This doesn't make sense.* But if she'd been a more foolish woman, she'd have called the look in his eyes almost . . . bleak.

Taking the scrap from Kadra, Decimus stared at it, perplexed. "Is this a code, Tetrarch Kadra?"

"It's Urdish," Sarai said at the same time Kadra asked, "Was Jovian interested in the Sidran Tower Girl?"

Decimus's tear-ravaged face pulled tight with misery and affection. "On Truth, he was obsessed with her. He was a first-year Candidate the night it happened, and he never got it out of his head that there was more to the story. Swore he'd be the first to crack why she died."

"Did he have any theories?" Sarai asked hoarsely.

"Plenty, all stemming from the same premise. Everyone wondered how the girl snuck past all the magi guarding the Academiae, but he was convinced that was a misdirection."

Her hands shook. "Why?"

"He spent so much time in the Hall of Records. Said an old plan of the Academiae detailed an ancient passageway built into the foundations for the wealthy to flee in the event of attack. He theorized that the Sidran Tower Girl must have entered that way. But the fact that she knew of the passage led him to the same premise every time." Decimus wiped his eyes. "She didn't sneak in. She was invited."

A bolt of pain slammed into her, so sharp she wondered if her head had cleaved in two. Flashes of a storm and the slow build of rain threatened the weakened barriers of her mind. She tried to speak, but air just wouldn't come. *She was invited.* Her lungs strained. *Invited.* She dimly heard Kadra asking Decimus if Jovian had shared his theories with others.

"He was thick as thieves with Tetrarch Cassandane's former Petitor, Livia." A pause. "Awful what happened to her. Her mother never recovered. Wanders on the outskirts of Cassandane's Quarter last I heard."

Another dead Petitor. Black consumed Sarai's sight, nails cutting into her palms as she tried to stave off the panic attack. *She was invited.* But she hadn't been a fool at fourteen. If Kadra had invited her anywhere, she'd have run in the opposite direction. The only person in Edessa whose invitation she'd have accepted would have been . . . But *that's impossible.* Cisuré hadn't known the Sidran Tower Girl's identity until Othus's vigiles had brought her in after Sarai kept calling for her.

"Who were his suspects?" Kadra asked, and she wanted to scream—to throw everything in the open and wrench out the truth of why he'd been there that night and what he'd done.

"I don't know, he—" Decimus's breath caught. "He and Livia always whispered about the Metals Guild. This letter, it would have been to her. She even helped pay for our scutum when he was short on coin. He was on that waitlist for months—" He broke off, wiping his eyes.

The Metals Guild? She couldn't make sense of it, the locus of her being centered on oxygen. *Aren't they only known for manufacturing scuta and weapons?* She could only vaguely make out Kadra's voice as he thanked Decimus for his assistance. Drawing on every ounce of strength, she did the same as Decimus left the study, and then leaned against a wall, discreetly counting her breaths. The tightness in her chest slowly dissipated.

"What do you think?" Eyebrows drawn low and broad shoulders limned in sunlight, Kadra seemed ethereal. One of the Wretched in human form. And she simply couldn't hold back any further.

"Why are we really investigating this?" she asked quietly. "If you want me to choose you over the Tetrarchy, I think I deserve some answers. Jovian, and now Cassandane's former Petitor, why dig all this back up?"

"Do you want the dead to have justice?"

"Of course I do, damn it! But why wait this long? It isn't like you needed me to start."

He finally looked at her, and she was suddenly in the middle of storm-fall, lightning striking on every side.

"I did."

True, her magic informed her, but she already knew. Alongside the cruelty and cunning on his face was a gravity that shook her to the core. Like he saw something in her. Like she was crucial to whatever he was planning.

The room seemed to rise and spin with them as the unmoving center and then eased back down, everything sharper, harder, murkier. She understood none of it.

And as they returned to Aoran Tower for another day of petition-reading, all she could think about was what he could see in her, and what she and Jovian had witnessed to warrant death.

CHAPTER
NINE

Sarai's first day of trials began with stormfall.

She kept to herself on the journey to the vigile station, unsure of how to act around Kadra after his pronouncement at Decimus, and stayed out of the way while Kadra's people loaded their mounts with pens, inkwells, and parchment in between shooting her the occasional glower. By the time they were done, Edessa was roaring to life with the sun, bright-eyed tradesfolk preparing to hawk their wares under a lightening sky.

Following Kadra out of the station, she stared when he dismounted at a bazaar where—to her bewilderment—he drew up a seat at a shopkeeper's table. Queues wriggled to life within seconds, and Sarai suddenly found herself the focus of every Urd in the vicinity as Kadra quite literally prepared to hold court.

Here? Lost, she watched his vigiles clear the center of the market to place two chairs there, rudimentary seats for the plaintiff and the defendant. She'd heard of fancier goings-on in Sal Flumen.

"Petitor Sarai, you'll sit at the other end." A familiar vigile with deep lines marring his forehead indicated a chair at the opposite corner of the table from Kadra's.

The one at the main gates when I arrived. He'd also been at the Robing. "Thank you. Gaius, isn't it?"

He gave her a stiff nod, and her smile drooped. *Harion was right.* These people would never forgive her for publicly disobeying Kadra. Sighting the disapproval souring many a face in the audience, she sat down, feeling small without anger to buoy her.

Kadra unrolled a petition. The crowd fell quiet as he read out the plaintiff's name. An irritated man elbowed his way to the front and sat in the plaintiff's chair. And the strangest court session she'd ever heard of began.

With *zosta* active, she focused on the plaintiff and outraged defendant as they made their cases. At the plaintiff's first lie, she turned to Kadra, unsure of how to bring it to his attention. She found him already watching her, silently asking how she wanted to do this.

She steeled her nerves and spoke to the crowd. "He's lying."

Some spectators gave her dubious looks but most gasped, riveted. She released a breath. At least they weren't throwing tomatoes.

When it came time for judgment, she was a bundle of nerves. The plaintiff, guilty of theft of an astronomical sum of denarii, and now perjury, fell to his knees before Kadra, pleading for mercy.

She winced. *Dear Lord Fortune, please let him take a finger.* She couldn't stomach a repeat of Ennius's pyre.

"A year in the mines," Kadra announced pleasantly.

What? She stared when two vigiles seized the struggling man and dragged him away. Turning back to Kadra, she stiffened at the cruel edge to his smile, like a knife catching sunlight, telling her that he knew what she'd expected. Swallowing, she reached for the next petition, feeling rather like he'd taken a knife to her insides.

She kept up with the first ten trials, transcribing judgments as quickly and legibly as she could. Then, they started to blur. Plaintiff, defendant, her Examination of both while they spoke, Kadra's verdict, repeat. Barely registering the hundreds squeezed into the bazaar, she only broke focus from writing to interject when she'd caught a lie. But that didn't stop the whispers.

"That's the northerner who defied Tetrarch Kadra," she caught a particularly loud one. But even more concerning than the dirty looks and tsking were the sly glances flicking quickly from her to Kadra as though manifesting some sort of . . . *connection*. Every time she caught Kadra's gaze and gave her answer, a buzz ran through the crowd like she'd committed a crime.

Impervious to it all, Kadra threw her for a loop with every judgment. Be it estate management or negligence, he was suddenly following the very letter of the Corpus. Shaking her head as he handed out yet another reasonable verdict, Sarai wondered if two souls inhabited his body, one being Ruin's spawn, and the other the soul of justice.

By noon, she'd Examined so many people that she had half-forgotten who she was and had a splitting headache to boot. A quick check of *nihumb* and *zosta* explained the latter. They glowed an ugly crimson, warning her that she was running low on magic. Passing Kadra a completed judgment, she closed her eyes in relief at the empty expanse of table between them. *Praise the Elsar, we're done.*

"Wait!" A man stumbled out of the crowd, covered in bruises. An cut on his forehead bled down the side of his face. "Tetrarch Kadra! Please hear one more!"

Without thinking, she started to her feet when two well-dressed men emerged from the hubbub and seized the wounded man. Blood marred their knuckles.

"Ignore him," one in a red tunic called to Kadra. "This is a private matter."

"And this is *my* Quarter," Kadra said in the too-calm tone she'd come to recognize meant danger.

The audience knew it too, because the bazaar fell silent. Seemingly realizing that he was out of luck, Red Tunic let the plaintiff go. Kadra nodded to a vigile who retrieved the man's petition just as someone cleared their throat pointedly.

Behind her, Gaius groaned. "Fortune's ass, not again."

The onlookers parted for a stocky, pale-haired man in robes that made her suddenly very grateful that Kadra's colors made them look like Death's ferrymen. Gold, green, and blue, with bejeweled rings coagulated on every finger, the newcomer was the human embodiment of wealth.

"Why is he dressed like a bruise?" she muttered under her breath.

Gaius snorted, looking less antagonistic. "That's Helvus, Metals Guildmaster. They're Ur Dinyé's most prominent Guild. A bit of a criminal group, too, the past few years."

The Metals Guild again. Squinting at Helvus, she couldn't imagine her younger self agreeing to go anywhere with him. "I thought people waited months for a scutum. Why would a Guild producing Ur Dinyé's most in-demand commodity resort to crime?"

"Because they can. Forging scuta is slow, precise work, so supply is scarce. But need is always high, so the Guild sets what prices they want. They have the south at their mercy, so they're untouchable."

"Even by Ka–Tetrarch Kadra?"

"Without a Petitor, Tetrarch Kadra wasn't allowed to hear any case against a favored Guild." Gaius sounded outraged. "Helvus accused him of jailing people on baseless assumptions in other Guild cases."

So there's no love lost here. "Who are the favored Guilds favored by?"

Gaius began to respond when Helvus cleared his throat again.

"Tetrarch Kadra," he drawled. "I'd recommend against hearing this now."

"Recommendation noted." Kadra unrolled the plaintiff's petition. "Reason being?"

Helvus raised an imperious eyebrow. "This is your first matter involving my Guild, and my Guildsman has had no chance to prepare a defense." Red Tunic crossed his arms, smug.

Kadra showed no signs of caring. "He can do so now." He tilted his head at her in silent question, and at her nod, sent the petition rolling down the table's distance to her.

"This is unwise–" Helvus stopped upon receiving the full weight of Kadra's gaze.

"Step back, Guildmaster. Unless you're including yourself as a defendant."

She skimmed the petition while Helvus stormed to the forefront of the crowd. Her breath caught at the charges. *Praeripio*, kidnapping, and wrongful detention, *plagium*.

"Sit," Kadra ordered the plaintiff, who collapsed onto the chair. "Why do you accuse a Metals Guildsman of kidnapping?"

The man's knobbly fingers gripped his knees. "I'm an engraver, my Tetrarch. A year ago, I borrowed fifty denarii from the Guild to purchase a chisel. I was ambitious. I thought I could pay it back. But when the time came a month later, I couldn't even make the interest. After that, everything my family earned went toward the debt, but it grew and grew. So my son agreed to work it off at the Guild. We were told it would be paid in three months." The plaintiff shot Red Tunic a bitter look. "It's been six, and I haven't seen him. I've begged. But they say I'm harassing him and that he doesn't want to see me." His voice broke.

"What are we to do if he's better off without a useless father?" Red Tunic snarled. "The boy came to *us*, because you didn't return our coin."

Sarai bit her lip. *Neither is lying. But that can't be right.* Red Tunic wouldn't have beaten up the plaintiff or tried to stop the petition being heard if he was innocent.

Kadra tapped his pen against the table. "And the boy's well?"

"He's well and working, damn it! Who'd would want to return to a life of debt?"

He's well. The remark stuck in her chest, vibrating disharmoniously. *Shit.*

Red Tunic threw up his hands. "See? No lies. What a fucking waste of time. And *you*"—he stalked over to the plaintiff—"you're going to pay for accusing *me* of—"

"You're lying."

A thousand pairs of eyes turned toward her. She swallowed.

Red Tunic looked like the dirt on his boots had started talking. "The northerner thinks she's a Petitor. Look here, you've been announcing that this person and that are lying all day, but how do we know if *you* aren't? Not like you've been properly trained."

A few onlookers tittered, and for a second, she smiled. Because *this*, this was familiar. The *eyes,* the mockery. Instincts of over eighteen years reared their head, telling her to make herself small, to nod, and smile, and agree with all they said to save herself pain. But this wasn't Arsamea. And she wasn't a barmaid anymore.

"I have no reason to lie," she said calmly. "Can you tell me that the boy's well? That he doesn't want to see his father?"

"He's eating well, drinking well, and shitting well. Going to say I'm lying?"

A cacophony of sound thrummed through her. "You are," she whispered. "Is he alive?"

"I don't need to answer this," Red Tunic sneered. "Not to some jumped-up northerner hiding behind a table. This is a private *Guild* matter."

Biting her tongue before she could spit out a retort, she turned to Kadra, hating that she was going to have to ask him for help. Then, she saw where he was looking. Hunched over in his seat, the plaintiff stared at the ground, arms wrapped around himself, all hope gone. And this, too, was familiar. Hadn't she done the same in Cretus's shed? Holding herself together, weary of knowing she couldn't win, wondering if she could simply sit and never get up again.

"I'll ask you again." She came out from behind the table to face Red Tunic. "Is he alive?"

He mimed locking his mouth. "What now? Will you Probe me? I won't consent, so that'll be assault. The likes of you . . ."

His voice dulled to make way for the sustained scream in her head. *Think*. If he wouldn't answer, she needed an excuse to Probe him. But that was reserved for serious crimes, like *homicidium* or . . . assault. She looked at Kadra, still watching the plaintiff, at the rapt audience, at Red Tunic, now shoving his index finger in her face. She took a deep breath.

Lose your temper. Just a fraction.

Sarai laughed. "That's a lot of big words from a man who tried to prevent this trial. Were you scared?" She scrunched her face in mock pity as he swelled. "Was that why you ran to your Guildmaster with your tail between your legs? And you call yourself a man—"

"You bitch!" In one step, he was before her, fist at the ready.

The irony. She'd taken his abuse for long minutes, and it had taken four sentences to enrage him. Dodging his first punch, she watched the second approach, bracing herself and slowing her movements so it would land. *One hit and we've an assault charge.* He threw his body behind the blow, and every second of it was all too familiar. North or south, cruel men were cruel men.

A rustle of fabric. The slap of flesh and a violent thud. But no pain.

She opened her eyes, bewildered at the absence of impact. Her mouth fell open. Kadra stood in front of her, one hand on Red Tunic's wrist, having slammed it into the table hard enough to embed it within. The man screamed at his shattered knuckles as Kadra turned to her, his hard face frozen in what looked oddly like shock. Reeling, she stared back, completely lost on why he'd stopped the blow. Silence spread between them and hung among the stunned crowd, before she found her tongue.

"Is the boy alive?" she stammered.

Kadra glanced at a still-screaming Red Tunic. Whatever the man saw in those eyes immediately loosened his lips.

"He's alive, damn it."

True. She nodded at Kadra, muttering a prayer of thanks to the Elsar.

"You'll return him." Kadra leaned against the table, ignoring Red Tunic's attempts to dislodge his broken fingers. "Any others like him?"

A familiar throat cleared itself. Looking furious, Helvus stalked over to Kadra. "That's irrelevant. This trial has only one plaintiff."

Her heart sank. *True.* The Corpus only allowed for a victim or their families to petition for relief. If the other debt-slaves' families didn't know that they were being held prisoner, then there was no rescuing them. The law needed a plaintiff, a defendant, and a well-attested crime to rouse itself from slumber. Feeling hollow, Sarai returned to her seat to transcribe.

"The boy shouldn't have agreed to work if he wasn't up to the rigor," Helvus argued. "Or his father would have done well to pay his debts. Tetrarch Tullus *will* hear about this if we're punished for abiding by the laws of business."

"Profit above all, yes." Kadra looked bored. "Debt-slaves are still illegal, Guildmaster."

"The boy agreed! And any harm is superficial!"

Glancing at the now-sobbing plaintiff, she tightened her fingers around her pen. But there wasn't much more that even Kadra could do. The Corpus dictated that punishment for wrongful detention was *damnatio ad metalla*, time in Ur Dinyé's notoriously harsh mines. That time would be whittled down by the mitigating factors here: the initial debt, the boy's gender, that he'd come willingly, even that he hadn't died. The plaintiff would be lucky if Red Tunic got six months.

At the end of Helvus's tirade, Kadra nodded. "He's going to the mines for a year."

"The Metals Guild is the lifeblood of—"

"Without an arm."

She dropped her pen as chaos exploded across the bazaar, cheers clashing with the Metals Guildspeople's outraged yells. A primal shudder shot through her when Kadra smiled, pondering a terrified Red Tunic—who'd ripped his hand from the table—with terrible anticipation.

Helvus's thick knuckles clenched. "This has gone on long enough." He snapped his fingers at a Guildsman. "Inform Head Tetrarch Aelius that this man needs to be reined in. Your nonsense may fly in this Quarter, Kadra, but I will not have my men mutilated for—"

"Assault," Kadra supplied mildly.

Assault?

"Whom did I assault?" Red Tunic yelled, above the Guildspeople's furor. His gaze snagged on her, and he sneered. "Her? I didn't strike her!"

"No," Kadra agreed. "You struck me."

The man went stock-still with an almost piteous gasp of horror. Sarai's jaw dropped.

He's brilliant. "Anyone who inflicts harm upon a Tetrarch loses the offending limb," she recited from the Corpus, "be it hand, eye, or tongue."

How many steps ahead had Kadra been plotting when she'd set her plan into action?

Red Tunic fell to his knees. "Forgive me, Tetrarch Kadra. I'll pay in lieu of my arm. As much as you want! The Guild will assist!" He turned pleading eyes to Helvus, who huffed and turned on his heel, pushing through the crowd.

"Cold," Gaius remarked, then rolled his eyes. "A moment, Petitor Sarai."

He strode to where Red Tunic had managed to free his hand from the table. The Guildsman sprung toward the crowd, attempting to make a run for it, just as Gaius gripped his tunic and dragged him back to the table, right between her and Kadra.

Bile flooded her mouth at the song of metal being unsheathed. Kadra's sword gleamed in the sunlight, as another vigile came to Red Tunic's side to hold his arm widthways across the wood.

"I beg you, please not my hands." Red Tunic—gods, she still didn't know his name—clawed at the vigiles. "Don't take my livelihood! It'll never happen again!"

Kadra's teeth flashed. "That's what I'm ensuring."

He brought the sword down before she could look away.

An ugly crack. Blood sprayed across the table and into her inkwell. The arm hit the ground, lopped off below the shoulder, bone flashing white. She couldn't breathe.

Screaming, the man scrabbled in the dirt, gripping the limb and pressing it to the gaping wound as though the seam would mend itself. "I need a healer! Bring me a healer!"

Kadra raised a hand. The limb burst into flame, withering quickly as Red Tunic howled.

And the quiet, monstrous part of her smiled.

She stood so quickly the world spun and stumbled over to the plaintiff. He stared blankly at the proceedings. Her eyes burned. All this bloodshed, and no one had asked what *he'd* wanted.

She knelt beside him. "Are you alright?"

"Yes." She stilled when a bloodthirsty grin split his face. "Yes, Wrath be praised. The bastard deserved it." He gripped her hands in his worn palms, and she halted a flinch. "Feels good, doesn't it? Seeing justice."

The heat behind her eyes spread like a stain. She looked away, looked inside to the black force caged in her head, grinning wide. Something she didn't want to name clogged her throat.

"Yes," she whispered. *Gods forgive me.* "It feels good."

The crowd dispersed as Kadra called an end to court and discussed Red Tunic's transport to the mines with his vigiles. Numbly returning to her now-blood-spattered judgment, Sarai blotted it with her sleeve, watching red vanish into the fabric. She sighted a figure watching them from the bazaar's gate. Helvus's eyes darted from her to Kadra in the slow manner of a blackstripe bear surveying its prey before launching an attack.

The most prominent Guild in Ur Dinyé and I made an enemy of them. Her hands shook worse than ever as she smoothed out the scroll and began writing out Kadra's verdict. She gripped her wrist with her left hand to steady it when a shadow fell over the parchment.

"I'll finish it." Kadra's voice brushed the shell of her ear.

Her breath hitched. "Don't make allowances for me. I need to get used to this if I'm to earn anyone's respect." She paused. *"Tibi gratias ago* for stopping him earlier."

A wrinkle formed between his eyebrows. "You would have dealt with him anyway."

"And gotten my cheekbone broken. I know you didn't do it for me, but thank you."

The wrinkle deepened. "You're my Petitor," Kadra said softly, like he hadn't tried to make her leave the job at the Robing. "No hand can strike you."

Does that include yours? She couldn't move when he took the parchment from her. Suddenly, it was all too much. The harsh sunlight, the buzzing of people in the bazaar, the bloodstains on the table. *Him.*

"Am I . . ." Her voice came out ragged, and she tried again. "Are we done today?"

Studying her, he nodded. "Gaius will accompany you back."

She bowed stiffly, not insisting on finishing the damned judgment or asking why he wasn't coming with her. She'd only taken one step away when he spoke again.

"You did well."

Her guard cracked. Storming off to her horse with Gaius trailing after her, she dug in her heels, fighting tears all the way to Aoran Tower. A single realization tormented her throughout.

Kadra hadn't lied once all day.

This time, when the knock came at her door, she was ready.

Sleep had eluded her for hours. Upon her return to Aoran Tower, Cato had taken one look at her and made a lovely orange and honey brew in what seemed to be a never-ending apology for a minor bit of deception. But the nightmares had still found her, garish visions of Jovian's mangled body coming to life on the ice block, pleading for justice.

Staring at the ceiling, she'd tried to rationalize Kadra's actions that day. Even evil men performed a few decent deeds, didn't they? Nothing changed the fact that Kadra had been present the night of the Fall and hadn't mentioned that pertinent fact even with the discovery of Jovian's letter. *He isn't after justice*, she reminded herself. *He just likes blood.*

So when the knock came again, her shield was firmly in place. Scars hidden, she drew the bolt open. "I'm ready."

Mercifully clothed, but entirely in black instead of his customary robes, Kadra gave her a rapid but piercing assessment, stern mouth pulling into a line. "You haven't slept."

"I've enough magic for another day of trials. That's all you need, isn't it?"

"Not today." He handed her a tunic and trousers exactly like his own. "I'll be outside."

Her eyes narrowed at the clothing. *Black. Nondescript.* "What's this for?" she called, but he'd left.

Dressing quickly, she found Kadra saddling two unfamiliar horses.

"Wherever we're going, you don't want to be recognized," she accused.

A sliver of a smile. "On the contrary, I probably *will* be recognized. But this creates plausible deniability."

Dread seized her. "Where are we going?"

"To the remaining debt-slaves." He inspected a vicious-looking knife before tucking it into her saddlebag.

"But we don't have a petition! Do we even have a warrant?"

His ferocious smile was confirmation enough. She took a step back in disbelief. *Is there ever a day when he doesn't abuse his power?*

"The Metals Guild is a piece of work, but shouldn't we, at least, try to play by the law?"

"The law is a game the powerless play and lose." Having mounted his horse, Kadra stared down at her with perilous intensity. "Coming?"

This is illegal. She only had to hop on that horse and ride east to Cobhran Tower to bring Aelius's wrath down on Kadra's head.

"Fine," she heard herself mutter instead.

Following him out of Aoran Tower, she told herself that this wasn't a mistake. She could just as easily inform Aelius later. Better to observe how he operated and let the bodies he left in his wake shatter her ridiculous awareness of him. Perhaps there'd be a clue about the Fall in this Guild establishment they were sneaking into. *Perhaps.*

Out of the Academiae and down the citadel, they rode to the north of Kadra's Quarter, where the cobblestone roads petered off into dirt trails by the city's outer ring of farmland. Kadra dismounted several yards from a shabby domus, unremarkable but for the Guildsmen guarding it.

"Here." He passed her a thick strip of black cloth.

Resigned, Sarai tied it around her nose and mouth, pocketing the knife he'd packed her. "I gather we're taking every precaution except the legal ones." *Wrath's cursed blade, am I a bandit or a Petitor?*

"Both decide who lives and who doesn't," Kadra said mildly, and she realized she'd said it aloud. "It comes down to if you prefer the robes."

Sarai gave him a withering look and paused. Masked, his eyes held an enigmatic sort of mischief that struck her silent. *Evil men joke, too*, she told herself, extinguishing the part of her that wanted to chuckle. *He was there the night of the Fall.*

She crossed her arms. "How are we doing this?"

"Uncomplicatedly." Leaving their horses, he walked toward the front door. The two burly Guildsmen dropped their hands to their swords the moment he entered their line of vision.

"Halt!" one roared. "Identify your—"

Fire engulfed the door behind them and both men sprang away, shrieking. Her head swiveled from the door to Kadra's raised index finger.

"How many debt-slaves do you have inside?" he asked pleasantly, and her jaw dropped.

I thought we were keeping a low profile! There was no one within city limits who wouldn't recognize that voice.

"Who the hells are you?" the first man demanded. She stared. Apparently, she was wrong.

The man charged, blade aloft. Unconcerned, Kadra sidestepped the slash, hooked an arm around the man's throat and squeezed. A sickening crack filled the night air. The man fell, unmoving.

Her pulse halted. *There's the monster.* She forced herself to take in the Guildsman's open eyes and sagging mouth, death so new that he hadn't registered it. Perhaps he hadn't been involved in the debt-slave ring beyond serving as a sentry. He could have been a father, a husband. *Or you're writing epitaphs to justify that he tried to protect the ring even after it was clear why Kadra was here,* the vicious part of her hissed.

Meanwhile, the other guard had fallen to his knees, arms raised in surrender. "There're ten slaves inside," he blurted out. "And two more guards."

Knocking him out, Kadra moved his hand in a tugging motion, and the fire spreading across the front door trailed toward a stockpile of logs to crackle there merrily. Still shaken, Sarai followed him through the charred door. He hugged the shadows, glancing back occasionally to see if she was floundering. She gave him an exasperated look after the second time. Sneaking was a skill embedded in every tunnel rat.

The domus was built on a single level. Past the vestibule, the atrium's courtyard was populated with stone ovens, hammers, anvils, and all manner of tools, the square roof opening allowing for rainwater to drain into a pit of black water, likely used for smithing. The courtyard walls were lined with barred cells where huddled figures stared through the gaps in the metal, looking lost.

Fury boiled in her. She nearly started toward the cells when a shadow crossed the courtyard. *The two remaining Guildsmen.* Beside her, Kadra was one with the dark, a blade to its sheath. Alert, yet unruffled. He was clearly no stranger to nights like this.

"They're on either side of us." His breath brushed her hair.

Shivering, she followed his gaze to a pair of oblong shadows at the far back of the courtyard.

"Stay here."

Before she could hiss her outrage, he strolled out of their vantage point and raised a palm in the direction of the Guildsman on the left. She saw the second his tunic caught fire. Batting frantically at the blaze, the man ran across the courtyard and threw himself into the water pit, and right into Kadra's grasp.

While they fought, Sarai spotted a flicker of movement on her left. The inky spot where the previous man had been hiding separated into two.

Each figure slunk behind a pillar. Her breath seized. The Guildsman outside had lied about there being two men inside.

On the other side of the courtyard, Kadra had dispatched Burnt Tunic and engaged what he probably thought was the last guard. He ducked a wild swing that placed his back to the two hidden Guildsmen. Moonlight winked off their blades as they flanked him, creeping closer.

She moved without thinking. Gripping the knife Kadra had given her, she slipped out of her hiding place, melting into the dark. Her breath came fast.

Steel rang in the courtyard. Kadra's sword pierced the chest of the guard he was fighting. The Guildsman behind him raised his knife at the same time she did.

"Watch out!" She let her knife fly right as the Guildsman jerked at the realization that Kadra wasn't alone.

It hit him square in the shoulder. Pivoting, she grabbed a discarded board and jumped in front of Kadra just in time for the other guard's blade to thud into the wood. The impact sent her stumbling back into Kadra, who regarded her as if she'd done something utterly baffling.

"I—" her breath cut off when he locked an arm around her waist and thrust her behind him. His sword rose, dripping crimson. Halting it at one of their necks, he traced a thin line.

"The keys to the cells," he said, his tone soft and lethal.

"You're trespassing," blustered the Guildsman with Kadra's sword to his jugular. "Our scout's already on the way to inform the Guild."

"Even if that were true, the mines will have you before your Guild arrives."

The man chuckled. "Do you know who I am? Every Minewarden knows my name. I'll be out in minutes."

Kadra's teeth gleamed. She'd seen Arsamean wolves grin like that before they tore into rabbits.

"Then I'll just have to ensure that no one knows your names." He moved like lightning, a black storm cloud gliding behind them to slam their heads on the closest anvil. Ripping the knife from the first man's shoulder, he cracked the hilt into his mouth and gripped the man's tongue when he screamed. Then, the blade descended.

In two breaths, both men's tongues dropped to the dirt. Their fingers joined them several screams later. Torn between revulsion and awe, she could only watch the blood trickle through gaps in the stone, indelible.

Metal glinted from the pocket of a guard Kadra had killed earlier. Sarai stooped to grab the keys and halted at the sight of a glass-paned door that provided a perfect view of the courtyard behind her. She laughed, a miserable ghostly thing. He hadn't needed her help earlier. He'd seen the hidden men coming and let them think they had the upper hand.

Catching his sidelong glance, she busied herself unlocking the cells. The captives had pressed away from the walls during the fighting, but now eyed her with desperation, stumbling out when she pulled the doors open. Most were able-bodied adolescents, only a few years younger than her.

"They worked us like animals," a girl raged, stretching out hands toughened with calluses and burns.

"There's nothing they didn't do to us here," another rasped. His first move upon leaving his cell had been to bludgeon every piece of equipment in the courtyard. He spat on the now-tongueless Guildsmen. "Elsar be praised for you both."

Hollow, she shook her head. "I did nothing."

She repeated the refrain through every tearful thanks and nod of gratitude. By the time Gaius showed up to help the children return to their families—or renounce them—and cart the men off to the mines, she was wrung out. Sitting on an upturned bucket, she cleaned and oiled Kadra's knife while he instructed his vigiles on where to dispose of the bodies. When the hushed voices came to a stop, she knew her reprieve was over.

Odd how she could tell his footsteps at a distance now, the eerie pad of a predator. She held out the blade when he loomed over her. "I know. I shouldn't have jumped in earlier. Like you'd ever be in danger."

The stern line of his mouth quirked. "It's happened."

The fool's probably fifteen feet below ground. Dismembered. "They didn't recognize you."

"Not everyone knows what their politicians look like." A breath. "You did more than 'nothing.'"

Her every muscle went still. "No." She raised her eyes to his. "No, I didn't have *zosta* active, so I didn't know that Guildsman had lied about the number of guards inside. I didn't survey the landscape to note the glass door and interfered when you knew what you were doing. I struck that Guildsman's shoulder when I should have gone for his neck for what he put these children through. And if it had been up to me, I may not have come here at all. I'd have waited for a fucking petition and a warrant and let *everyone* here suffer while I stuck to the formalities, because even though I care *nothing* for the law, I thought I was duty bound to adhere to it." Her voice had risen steadily until she realized she was shouting. She took a deep breath, shame coursing through her. "I did *nothing*."

The irony was that she wouldn't have thought twice about aiding anyone in Arsamea. But in the six days she'd been a Petitor, the weight of that mantle had grown. In the bazaar with everyone watching, at Cobhran Tower with Tullus eyeing her like a cut of meat, and at the Robing with Kadra waiting for her to fail. Every instinct had screamed caution. But her hesitation hadn't helped anyone. And the man she'd condemned had.

Dark eyes roved over her face. "You came."

She stood, squaring her shoulders. "Not for the right reasons."

A pause. Then he bent toward her, and her pulse jumped. "Was taking measure of me the only reason you came?"

He knew. Frozen in dejected horror, she gave him the truth. "No."

"There." That glorious voice wrapped around her heart like a fist. "I've little use for perfection, Petitor Sarai. I won't hold you to it."

This was manipulation. He was watching her even now to gauge his effect. But by all the gods, how she foolishly wanted to believe him.

She stared at her feet. "I'm still not choosing you."

"Of course." Amusement back in his eyes, he returned the knife to her. "Keep it. That was a precise throw earlier."

"Every snowgrape harvester learns to throw a knife. It was—"

"Nothing?" he finished dryly, tilting his head outside. "Come, Petitor Sarai. Adjudication awaits. We've a great deal more nothing to complete before noon."

She stared at the curve of his lips, at the spray of blood across one cheekbone. And it all came together with devastating silence. The caged force in her head ceased to rattle its bars because she finally *understood*.

Perhaps, just perhaps, it didn't matter if he was after justice or just wanted a reason to kill. And perhaps the gods despised her more than she'd fathomed. Because the madman she'd set out to ruin was everything the most desperate, anguished parts of her had always craved.

And he was still hiding that he'd been there the night of her Fall.

CHAPTER TEN

Why was he there that night?

The question plagued Sarai over two weeks of trials as she pushed herself to the brink of exhaustion, keeping *nihumb* and *zosta* glowing on her armilla while trying to reconcile a man who seemed to viciously, violently give a shit about his Quarter with the one who'd ordered that she be given a new face. But Kadra remained terrifyingly inscrutable.

Because he simply didn't lie.

Over two weeks, he'd removed a man's hands for domestic violence, branded the face of a slaver who'd been mutilating young girls for sale to a pleasure house—before castrating him for good measure—and ensured that a noble scion was whipped until gouges marked his back for abusing an elderly servant. But throughout it all, he'd never used any of the white lies or embellishments that littered conversation. He sent men to Death in the blink of an eye, but a simple lie was apparently anathema.

Not that he had similar trouble reading her. Every day after court, his eyes narrowed when she packed up her things and dashed off to Aoran Tower before *nihumb* could falter. She had no doubt that his otherworldly intuition sensed that she was hiding something, but by some suspicious benevolence of the gods, he hadn't raised the issue.

Nihumb was also making visiting the Hall of Records impossible. Maintaining the illusion and *zosta* throughout hundreds of trials had her too low on magic to go at the end of the day, and archivists forbade removing sealed records for later reading. Progress on Jovian's death and the treasonous crime he could have committed was at a standstill while Kadra's vigiles combed the outer edges of Edessa for Livia's mother. All of which left her with no suspects beyond Kadra and the Metals Guild, no proof or motives for either, no way of confiding in Cisuré without her panicking, and no Tetrarch she could trust.

Out of the corner of her eye, Sarai watched Kadra pronounce that the plaintiff's neighbor—who'd been poisoning her well—was to immediately drink several cups from it. The onlookers roared their agreement. She sighed as part of her did as well. Four years of obsessing over revenge really had blackened her soul. *By Temperance, I sound like Cisuré.*

She vaguely registered the screaming neighbor being force-fed bowls of poisoned water. *Why were you there that night, Kadra?* She'd been soldered to him long enough to glean that he didn't act without justification. Even if he was a bloodthirsty sadist.

"Petitor Sarai?" Gaius interrupted, drawing her attention to the puddle of ink growing around the inkwell as she dipped her pen for the umpteenth time. "The verdict?"

Havïd. She printed the last line and waited for the ink to dry. "Why are we ending early?"

He cleared his throat. Despite still being stilted with her, he was less standoffish than the other vigiles. "The Tetrarchy will be meeting in six hours. Even Tetrarch Kadra needs his rest."

She rolled up the judgment. "Has something happened?"

"No, no. Every three weeks, the Tetrarchy meets to determine which cases constitute matters of national importance and schedules them for trial with all four of them at the Aequitas. But, if you ask me, that takes up the first hour," Gaius confided. "They spend the rest digging into the goings-on in each other's Quarters."

"So it's cutthroat, not cooperative."

Gaius shrugged. "If they agreed on everything, we'd have a dictatorship."

She raised the inkwell in agreement.

"I've also been asked to deliver this." He hesitated before withdrawing an ivory-and-silver square of parchment. "I'm told that the other Petitors will be at a tavern near the Tetrarchy's place of meeting, if you'd care to join them."

Unfolding the square, Sarai grinned at Cisuré's neatly printed invitation. *Come drink!*

"Gods, yes."

It was strange being on the receiving end in a tavern.

Sarai thanked the overworked barmaid when she deposited an amphora of wine at their table. The woman's eyes widened, sweeping over the array of robes—Harion's varying shades of blue and Anek's crimson and bronze were draped over the backs of their chairs. Cisuré still wore her ivory and silver, as Sarai did her black and gold, albeit only because she was so low on magic that her illusion only covered her hands, face, and neck. She probably shouldn't have come, but, by Radiance, she needed a break.

"Temperance's tits, at last," Harion groused, emptying the amphora into his cup. Taking a gulp, he sighed in bliss. "Now, all I need is a woman."

"Good luck." Anek moved their cup when he tried to fill it. "I'll need my senses tomorrow."

"Like Cassandane doesn't get sotted. The Tetrarchs probably cut loose at these meetings." Harion gnawed at a chicken leg. "On Wisdom, these cases have been stupid as shit. The parties lie to my face and start sobbing when I reveal it. Not a brain between them."

But they don't question your findings. There hadn't been a day when someone hadn't raised her lack of education or made pointed comments about her sex. The words rolled off her for the most part. It was the gossip she couldn't stand.

Kadra's Quarter had come up with many a reason for her residing at Aoran Tower, *all* of which involved sex. Willing, unwilling—of which *he* was the victim—and just plain disgusting—the theory had involved entrails.

That she worked over fifteen hours a day, reading petitions and jotting notes for when trials began at dawn, was apparently irrelevant.

"The letters are *so* boring." Cisuré groaned. "Tetrarch Aelius says I should read his to understand what Ur Dinyé wants, but they're so dry."

Sarai shrugged. "I like them."

In addition to petitions, Tetrarchs received questions of law and policy from across the country. After she'd argued in favor of pardoning a deserter who had been forced into the military, Kadra had handed her a stack.

"Tetrarch Kadra, they don't want an answer from me."

"They want a response. How to raise taxes. How to exempt themselves from those taxes," he'd said laconically. *"You'll be fair."*

"I'll be excoriated," she'd muttered but had reluctantly answered a few. No one had complained. Yet.

Cisuré nudged her playfully. "You *would* like them. It's like traveling for you, isn't it? I keep forgetting how little you've seen of Ur Dinyé."

"We haven't either." Anek sliced at a steak of venison with mesmerizing precision. "Our trip to Miduz in second year wasn't exactly a tour of the country."

"But it provided perspective," Cisuré said earnestly. "Tetrarch Aelius often speaks of the value of broadening our horizons. It helps us know our place in the world. Serving the gods and guiding people."

"People don't want to be guided, Saint." Harion waved his cup. "They need a whipping."

Cisuré scowled. "They need to trust in the Elsar. Their problems would vanish if they looked to the gods, but they aspire to grand positions instead of being happy with their lot and descend into anger and entitlement when their path doesn't intersect with wealth. Then, they resent the rich." She shook her head. "I wish they'd see it."

Realizing that her jaw had descended, Sarai snapped it shut. *So much for only looking up to Aelius.*

"My family must be doomed then," Anek noted. "We don't care much for the gods."

Cisuré's face drooped. "You still haven't given the Temple a try? Just once, Anek!"

"Don't force it."

"It's for your own sake!"

Sarai drank more soup. Now *this*, she understood. Cisuré's religiosity, Harion's condescension, Anek getting straight to the point. It was only Kadra she couldn't pinpoint.

Anek looked pained. "Cisuré, my parents' souls and mine are our concern. It isn't like we've ever seen a god."

Harion seized a chicken thigh. "Regardless, we'll all have to make our rounds of the Temple if we're to keep ourselves in the public's graces." He wiggled the thigh at Sarai. "You too, if no one's knocked you off."

She gave him the finger, and he bowed, sauntering off to demand another amphora of wine. Anek fled the table when Cisuré continued proselytizing, and the other girl inched her chair closer to Sarai.

Cisuré dropped her voice. "No rush, but have you found anything?"

Sarai's spoon froze halfway to her mouth. Visions swam before her of dead Guildsmen and freed debt-slaves. Tongues lying in dirt. Sunlight arcing off the blade coming down on Red Tunic's arm.

"He's been the same as usual," she whispered.

"What about in his tower?"

Searching it was impossible with Cato there. She shook her head. "I don't know what wards he could have placed around his room, so I need to be careful."

Cisuré drummed her fingers on the table. "You could always pretend you're ill. Wander around the tower and pretend you're sleepwalking if you happen to trigger one of his wards."

Kadra's raised eyebrows flashed in Sarai's mind. She shook her head. "He'd know." The man really didn't need her. During trials, he seemed to know who was lying before she spoke.

"Well, it wouldn't be a lie." Cisuré reached out and surreptitiously adjusted Sarai's cuffs. The worry in her eyes said she'd seen that *nihumb* was covering only the visible portions of Sarai's skin. "You've been draining yourself every day."

"I'm managing." Her head throbbed with exhaustion. "The past two weeks have been a whirlwind."

"I'll say." Amphora in hand, Harion plunked himself down. "I hear you royally pissed off the Metals Guild."

"What?" Cisuré bolted upright, shooting Sarai an accusatory look. "You never mentioned that."

"Come now, Saint. If you're going to mingle at the top, you need to have ears across Edessa." He gave her a worldly smile. "Honestly, the Metals Guild reigns supreme as the magically–poor man's greatest ally, so sending one of their own to the mines was a *terrible* idea."

"Then he shouldn't have forced children into servitude. Debt-slaves were abolished centuries ago."

"Tell that to the everyday Urd working themself to the bone for coin." Harion waved a hand. "Irrelevant. What I want to know is whether Kadra really swept in to rescue you from the ignominy of a punch to the face."

Shit. Her eyes flew to his in surprise, and he choked on his wine.

"He did?" Sputtering, Harion wiped his chin. "I thought my man was lying."

His sources are good. A look at Anek's unruffled features confirmed that they'd also heard about Red Tunic's case. A few sidelong glances told her that at least half the tavern was following the conversation.

"Well, tell us the secret." Harion's stupefied look melted into an ugly smirk. "How'd you get the ice man besotted?"

She snorted. "It wouldn't reflect well on him to allow his Petitor to get walloped. He was protecting his reputation. I benefited. That's all."

"What, so nothing goes on in that tower? A man and a woman *alone.*"

"Enough, Harion. We're in public," Anek interjected coolly. "I'd rather not have us be the talk of the city tomorrow."

"The voice of reason, our *neutralis.* She's got a point." At Anek's glower, Harion snickered. "He's got a point?"

Their features tautened.

"We've known each other for four years, and you're still acting like what you've got between your legs is some big secret. Are you ashamed of being a woman or something?" He tipped his head back with a squint. "Or a man?"

Red climbed up Anek's cheekbones, flags of fury risen to full mast. "I said. Enough."

"We're all thinking it. You don't get to pronounce that you're something unnatural and whine when you're questioned on it."

Cisuré examined the table with interest. Sarai glanced at the rest of the tavern, her skin crawling at the curious, gleeful eyes watching. *I'm back in Arsamea*. But tonight, she wasn't the target.

She thought about it for all of a second. Then, snagging Harion's amphora with practiced ease, she dashed the contents in his face.

"What the fuck?" He jumped to his feet, crimson darkening the robes on his chair.

Cisuré clapped her hands to her mouth. Anek looked like their wages had come early.

"Sorry," Sarai said without an ounce of sincerity. "You're drunk. Spewing nonsense. Thought this might snap you out of it. Really, Harion. We've a workday tomorrow."

"It's on my fucking robes!" he spat.

"It'll stain," Anek noted gravely. "Tullus won't be pleased."

"Fuck!" Harion stormed out of the tavern. Seconds later, everyone heard the splash of him throwing his robes in the horses' water trough and starting to scrub.

Anek shook with silent laughter, clinking their cup with Sarai's.

She grinned. "I know you can handle him, but I *really* can't stand him."

Cisuré looked like she'd gained Sarai's headache. "What were you thinking?" She leveled a look of such disappointment that a knot formed in Sarai's throat. "You're a Petitor, not a common drunk! No—don't tell me. You got angry, and you thought assaulting a colleague was the right choice."

"He was being an ass—" Sarai raised a placating hand and froze when the illusion over it wavered. *Shit, I'm almost at my limit.* Cisuré's gasp said she'd seen it too. Thankfully, Anek hadn't. "At any rate, probably best if I leave. Good seeing you, Anek, Cisuré."

Grabbing her birrus, she apologized to the barmaid for the mess, tipping her with one of the shiny new aurei she'd received as wages, and ran outside. She'd barely gotten a foot in the stirrup when a figure blocked her horse.

"Get out of my way, Harion."

The tinny whistle of an object through the air was her only warning. She ducked right as a knife thudded into a post by her head. Caelum jumped in fright, and she stumbled off, catching herself on her knees. *An inch to the right and I'd have lost an ear.*

"You—" She struggled to keep her voice calm. "What the fuck was that?"

"What?" Harion spread his arms. "I didn't see anything."

She had to get out of here before she ran out of magic. "I'm not doing this. You're drunker than I thought if you're trying to assault a *havïd* Petitor."

"Are you one, though?" In two steps, he bracketed her against the wall. Fear slipped down her spine like ice. "My family saved for *years* to get me into the Academiae. Worked themselves half-dead and used decades of savings for four years of tuition. And *you* just sauntered in from the middle of fucking nowhere to act like you're one of us."

Insecurity pricked at her. "This isn't going to solve—" She flinched when his hand balled into a fist by her head. "Harion, take it up with your Tetrarch. They agreed to abolish training. The dead Petitors left a vacancy."

"They didn't *leave*," he hissed. "The man you're fucking killed them."

I don't know. Blood hummed in her ears. "Is it that hard for you to understand that some men don't get their rocks off by forcing colleagues to sleep with them?"

"Keep defending him. He'll still kill you."

"I'm defending *myself*, damn it!"

A familiar glint lit his unfocused eyes that she'd seen many a time on Marus. "So am I."

Shit. She reached for her armilla when he wrenched her head by her braid, throwing her against the tavern's outer wall. One hand seized one of her wrists, the other gripped the back of her head and dunked it into the water trough. Liquid burned up her nostrils. Her vision was black. She struggled uselessly, elbowing his side with her free hand, trying to find purchase on the trough to rear back and slam into him.

"Maybe now you'll respect your betters," he panted, lifting her head. "Or maybe I'll just keep you here." He shoved her back in.

Squirming to reach her pockets, she found the knife Kadra had given her and slammed the hilt into the wrist on her head. Harion yelped, releasing her. She swiveled, gritting her teeth when the other wrist he still held wrenched at the motion, and slammed her fist into his face. She took vicious pleasure in the snap of bone.

He collapsed, howling. "Bitch!"

"Don't fuck with a tunnel rat." She wiped her knuckles with a feral smile. The blood vanished into her robes. Perhaps this was why Kadra liked black so much.

"Sarai? What are you doing?"

Damn it. She closed her eyes with a wince and turned to face a white-lipped Cisuré. "I was just . . . leaving."

Horror and distaste warred for prominence on the other girl's face. "Harion, I apologize on her behalf. She's just sensitive—"

"Shove it," he spat, with a look so spiteful she was nearly impressed, before running for his horse—undoubtedly to find a healer.

Cisuré was ashen-faced. "I thought you'd finally learned to control yourself."

"I had to! He—"

"Do you think the gods want us to lash out at the first sign of disrespect?" She examined the swelling on Sarai's wrist and flinched. "Rage and violence are ugly tools used by people who don't know how to resolve conflict without resorting to bloodshed. This was unnecessary. You're better than that."

"Look at me! I'm sopping wet for a *reason*. He would've drowned me."

Cisuré stared at her, disbelieving. "I've known him for four years. He has his flaws, *certo*, but he was just angry after your stunt with the wine. He'd never behave like—"

"A self-absorbed man who took a blow to his ego? He can, and he did. Should I have drowned and returned from the Bright Realms to tell you that I stayed kind and true to the waterlogged end? Do you think he'd have stopped if I asked *nicely*?" She realized she was yelling when Cisuré's face crumpled, eyes taking on a hunted look.

Gods. She needed to leave, but not with Cisuré like this. Marus had been happy to bruise and wound Sarai in public, but Cisuré's scars had occurred in darker places.

She took Cisuré's hands. "I'm sorry. I am. I tried to hold it in."

"There's something in you at times. I saw it earlier. You enjoyed hurting him." Cisuré squeezed her hands, and Sarai winced as her sprain throbbed. "I don't want Kadra to rub off on you. Take this matter with the Metals Guild. Why antagonize them? We'd be done for without their scuta. Do you know what it was like without the scuta four years ago? *Nothing* was certain. All it took was more lightning than the magi protecting the area could control and homes would go up in flames. The Metals Guild hold the *safety* of our country."

"Debt-slaves are illegal!"

"What if the Guild just meant to give them a job like Cretus did for you? The children just misunderstood the rigors of work, and started complaining." Cisuré shook her head. "You're a Petitor. Try to see both sides instead of only your own. Please."

Sarai dropped her chin to her chest. "I have to go."

"You don't have to like what I'm saying," Cisuré said ruefully. "Just try to believe me."

She swallowed a glum sigh. Sometimes, Cisuré could be a little too ignorant of the real world. "I'll see you soon."

Balling up her soaked birrus, Sarai led Caelum to the front of the tavern and stilled at the figure waiting by the door. Kadra considered her wet hair, then made a sweep of her bedraggled frame. She sighed.

"First assassination attempt." She climbed onto Caelum, shrugging when he suddenly looked murderous. "I sent him to the healers. I'm tired. Goodnight, Tetrarch Kadra."

She spurred the mare on. Glancing back, she froze at the faint smile forming on his face. And the question returned. *Why was he there the night of the Fall?*

CHAPTER
ELEVEN

It was still black when she opened her eyes. She wondered why her head hurt. Then, memory returned and terror with it. He'd drugged her drink. She'd taken a sip only because he was watching, and it had doomed her.

Whisper-soft legs skittered across her skin. She jumped with a muffled shriek and froze. There was a weight over her mouth. Thick and tight.

Panicking, she reached out to claw at the dark, but restraints knotted her hands and ankles. Wood pressed against her knees, softened by cloth. A wardrobe. She threw herself at the walls, silently pleading for a crack that she could prize wider. Finding a hinge, she leveraged her feet to push harder. The door wobbled but stayed put. He must have tied the door handles together on the outside.

Sounds penetrated her struggling. She shrank back as a door creaked open. Footsteps entered the room, a group of men judging by their voices. One approached the closet, purposeful strides ticking like seconds on a water clock. He stopped before the doors.

Gods save me.

Sarai's eyes flew open to utter black. *Not again.* She struggled against the sheets, throwing them off to sit on the edge of the bed, her head in her hands, blinking back tears.

Another one. Too vivid to be a dream, laced with the same sharp panic that characterized her memories of the Fall.

Wiping her eyes, Sarai snatched a piece of parchment and jotted down everything she remembered. *A wardrobe, a man, a drugged drink.* She paused. *Restraints.* She grimly glanced at her swollen wrist from Harion's attack hours earlier and sucked her lower lip between her teeth, her theory solidifying. The healer who'd repaired her skull had snippily informed her that severe head trauma often resulted in permanent amnesia, but perhaps that wasn't a rule. The rest of her memories could be waiting for the right key.

The walls of her room seemed to draw closer, darkness caging her in. She unlocked the door and walked along the mezzanine.

Below, the tablinum was dark—a rarity, seeing as Kadra seemed to work every hour of the day. The robes hung by the door indicated that he was home. Elbows propped on the railing, she inhaled low and slow, finding peace in the silence. In the knowledge that he was only a few yards away and that nothing could touch her within Aoran Tower without his say-so. *Nothing but him.*

Neither the drugging nor the restraining seemed like something Kadra would do. Which left the Metals Guild, who had means, opportunity, and power. The only questions left were why—and how the hells she was to get more information when their investigation was at a standstill given that Livia's mother's whereabouts were still unknown. The trail of evidence for older Petitor deaths had long grown cold. *I can't hold the illusion long enough to visit the Hall of Records.*

Several yards away, a bed creaked. She glanced toward Kadra's bedroom and silently bolted toward hers. Going to shut the door, she halted on impulse and left a gap, peering through.

He emerged knotting a dressing robe over that godsforsaken muscular chest. Instead of heading downstairs, however, he sat on the uppermost step. The dull thunk of glass meeting ground, and he raised a wine bottle to his mouth, drinking deep, staring ahead.

He can't sleep, she realized. It was strange seeing him like this, man not monster, roughly carved out in the moonlight. She hated that she found his too-stern features beautiful. That she wanted to know where else he could touch her when her body had proven that it wouldn't panic if he did.

She hated that she wanted him.

For weeks, she'd held on with iron will whenever they argued, whenever he dipped his head toward her, eyes alight with amusement or cunning, and whenever the rich timbre of his voice had shaped her name. But the desire frothed within her, as hungry as vengeance and far more foolish. He was a Tetrarch and a killer. And she was a patchwork creature.

She withdrew from the door, ignoring the burn in her throat. Sitting at her desk, she lit a candle and read petition after petition for hours. And when the man she shouldn't crave knocked at her door, she could almost convince herself that she felt nothing.

Half a day later, she tottered out of the marketplace and wondered if this was all there was to her life now. Court, a blur of names and accusations, and more petition-reading. Harion, Anek, and Cisuré hadn't detailed the minutiae of their workdays, but the former two seemed to have significantly more free time than she did if they'd been gathering information on her to boot.

After the previous night's fiasco with her illusion, she'd reduced it to cover only visible skin instead of her entire body. A quick look at her armilla showed that she had a couple hours left before her magic sank low. *Not enough to visit the Hall of Records, but perhaps enough to see another Quarter.*

Glancing over to where Kadra was giving his vigiles some directive or the other, she hopped on Caelum. Gaius spotted her and frowned. Miming that he should tell Kadra that she was leaving, she raced off before he could protest.

Kadra's Quarter bordered Tullus's to the north and Cassandane's to the west. The marketplace they'd just adjudicated in had been in the north, so she went farther that way, until she entered an ivory-bannered public square. Dismounting, she tied Caelum to a post.

Coin pouch pleasantly full from her wages, she took a turn about the shops, examining bejeweled fabrics, ribbons for the end of her braid, polished leather boots, and a place that had her halting before the doors, grinning from ear to ear. A bookseller.

She stepped inside, the day's stresses falling away at the mix of aromas: cedar-scented leather tomes, pinewood, cinnabar, burnt resin from the ink bottles lining the back of the shop, and the clean sweetness of linen thread. Cross-legged by one of the shelves, the proprietor glanced at her and smiled.

"Here's a surprise," the woman said, setting aside the books she'd been shelving. "Been a good while since I last had a Petitor visit. What can I do for you?"

She didn't have a clue. "I'm open to anything. I haven't seen so many books before."

"Well, this is going to be a treat." Before Sarai could think, the bookseller was steering her by the shoulders. "I've a bit of everything. The history annals are here." She indicated books as wide as their combined heads. "The city's in no shortage of poets. We have more than we know what to do with. The religious texts and annotated editions of the Codices are toward the back. If it's politics and philosophy you're after, they're over by the inkwells. And the romances"—she stopped before a bookshelf that, at first glance, was pure chaos—"are here."

Sarai studied the sea of volumes, their fabrics every shade under the sun. At thirteen, Cisuré had managed to sneak enough coin from Marus to purchase a romance. They'd giggled all night over the swaggering pirate lord and his very exasperated but willing captive-turned-wife and tried to understand the mechanics of the very graphic sex within.

Seeing her hesitation, the bookseller nodded. "It's overwhelming. Of course. If you'd rather get to know Edessa better, there's plenty in the contemporary section. I've everything from betting books to *The Alternate Histories of the Sidran Tower Girl*."

Sarai started. "The what?"

"Excellent stuff. Well-researched accounts of who the Sidran Tower Girl could have been as written by magi and vigiles." Showing her a set of books with numbers etched on their spine, the woman plucked one off the shelves. "This one says she was a spy sent to assassinate the Tetrarchy by the last known heir to the royal bloodline. Compelling evidence. But this one has some promising points that *she* was actually the heir. Oh, and there's the romance in the fifth volume!"

Wrath and Ruin. The woman snapped open a crimson volume to reveal an illustration of someone who looked nothing like her ferociously kissing a magus-in-training. Sarai sagged against a pile of books, almost toppling them over. Perhaps Othus had been onto something by having her recorded as dead. The Elsar only knew what these southerners would have come up with if they'd known she was alive.

At the other woman's expectant glance, she coughed weakly. "I think I'll just take this."

She snatched the largest volume off a shelf and thrust it in the bookseller's hands.

"Excellent choice." The woman happily accepted two aurei in payment.

Departing in a daze, Sarai cracked open the novel and immediately snapped it shut, face burning after a few filthy lines. *Well, then. Something to look forward to later.*

Heading back to Caelum, she pulled back when the crowd surged in the square, people running to catch sight of two figures on white horses. Fighting panic from the press of bodies, she wriggled out at first opportunity and spotted Cisuré and Aelius making a round through the square. Judging by the throng, this was a social visit.

As she watched them, an ache spread inside her. There wasn't a face in the crowd that didn't smile at Cisuré, people approaching her on all sides. Despite coming from the north, her elevated parentage granted her the same respect as her southern peers. She was just as popular as Aelius, glowing in the afternoon light and, smiling up at him, all soft eyes and adoration. It was odd. She'd seen Cisuré besotted before, but this crush had none of the wide-eyed girlhood she remembered.

For his part, Aelius was nothing but congenial, smiling genuinely as he gripped every hand and waved at children. And there were tells here too. A softening of his gaze when it rested on Cisuré, an acquiescence to her directing him toward vendors. Off-kilter, she turned away, squeezing past several spectators in search of Caelum. She paused when she heard her name above the square's chatter. Within minutes, Cisuré appeared at her side.

"I thought I saw you!" she panted. "What are you doing here?" Before Sarai could answer, her eyes went to the book in her hands and widened. She grinned wickedly and slung an arm around her shoulders. "I didn't think you had it in you."

"Apparently, I've a lot more than I thought. *The Alternate Histories of the Sidran Tower Girl*? Really?"

Cisuré shrugged sheepishly. "The fifth volume was a massive success."

"I wonder why." Finding her horse, Sarai stuffed the book into her saddlebag right as Aelius joined them.

"There you are, Cisuré. Petitor Sarai, a pleasure." He smoothly escorted them out of the square. "How have you been?"

"Very well," she stammered. It still boggled her mind that the Head Tetrarch of Ur Dinyé knew her name. "And you?"

"I'm well taken care of." He chuckled with a smile at a blushing Cisuré. Sarai suddenly wanted to bury herself in a hole. "I hear that your searches haven't been proving fruitful."

She nearly choked. "Unfortunately not."

"Well, I didn't think it would be easy." He sighed. "Tullus has received several inquiries from the Metals Guild about missing Guildsmen in Kadra's Quarter. You wouldn't happen to have heard anything about that, would you?"

Her instincts kicked in. "Missing?" She furrowed her brow. "I'm sorry, Tetrarch Aelius. We haven't received any petitions regarding them."

It wasn't a lie. *Damn it to hell. I'll turn into Kadra at this rate.* A slight shift in the parameters of an answer was his favorite tactic.

"That's quite alright." The lines under Aelius's eyes deepened, and for a second, he looked far older than his age. "I wish he wouldn't make things so difficult. We're all on the same side, and what's best for Ur Dinyé is all that matters." He exchanged a rueful look with Cisuré. "Incidentally, we're having a little gathering in a week and a half, on the moonbright night. Would you care to come?"

"Oh, I don—yes," she amended at Cisuré's vehement nod. "*Tibi gratias ago*, Tetrarch Aelius. It would be an honor."

"It'll be our pleasure to have you." Making his farewells, he merged back into the spectators.

"Alright, I'll concede that I'm a little fond." Cisuré sighed.

"A *little*?"

"He won't take it seriously. I think he thinks I'm too young."

"Ten years is a *difference* at our age."

Cisuré pouted. "Don't remind me. Anyway, I keep hearing that Kadra's tied you up in cases. You'll enjoy the convivium—party," she amended at Sarai's confused look. "Everyone who's anyone will be there."

"Should I get something to wear?"

"No need! You don't have to dress up. Just look good."

Most days, she doubted she could. "I'll try."

"You'll love it. You know the city, the job, and the commoners now. Time to meet some people of value."

Value. "Will the Guilds be there?"

"Without a doubt. You *will* come, won't you? It's on the eighth day of the Month of Wind at Delran Tower."

Sarai smiled grimly. Perhaps an audience with Helvus would trigger another memory.

"Wouldn't miss it for the world."

The Month of Moons ended with a plethora of gossip about Harion's new nose—a distraction for which she'd thanked the Elsar daily. Kadra hadn't pried about her attacker's identity at the tavern, but judging by his faint smile at the topic of the nose, he knew. A week into the Month of Wind, the second moonbright night of the year arrived quietly, marking over a month that she'd been a Petitor. Dressing, she marveled at the thought. On the first moonbright night, she'd been assessed by Telmar in Arsamea. And here she was, readying herself for a gathering with Ur Dinyé's most influential people.

Her spirits lifted at the mirror's now familiar reflection of her in Petitor's robes, hair piled on top of her head in a bit of architecture that had taken hours. She couldn't paint her skin or lips when *nihumb*'s illusion would just cover it all, but she could do this much.

Cato looked surprised when she came downstairs. "That's beautifully done, Petitor Sarai. Any reason?"

"Tetrarch Aelius's convivium," she said, and could have sworn that his eyes narrowed for a moment. "I won't be staying until the end. I'll be back before two."

He considered her. "I'll take you. Delran Tower, I imagine?"

"Yes, but you don't have to—"

"You'll be in elevated circles tonight, Petitor Sarai. It wouldn't do for you to arrive smelling of horse," he pointed out, a smile softening his words. "I'll be only a moment."

Which was how she found herself arriving at Delran Tower in Kadra's ornate raeda. Dismounting, she realized that Cato was right. She would have been a joke if she'd arrived on horseback.

Situated between Cobhran Tower and Cassandane's Favran Tower, Delran Tower was an architectural masterpiece. It looked to have been carved from a piece of limestone so large the gods themselves must have dropped it in position. A semicircular decorative wall rose above the entrance, featuring detailed sculptures of the High and Dark Elsar. Magi, nobles, and people in expensive fabrics that rippled like water stepped out of raedae around her, sauntering through the main doors with barely a nod to the magi vetting them.

She looked down at herself. Kadra's robes were well cut, and opulent enough that she wasn't out of place, but they were clearly still Kadra's robes and not a gown from Edessa's best dressmakers.

Can't back out now. She needed to meet Helvus. Thanking Cato profusely, she straightened her back and entered, following the other attendees as they would their way up a spiral staircase.

A glass ceiling wrapped around the top of the tower to bare the heavens to the attendees' gazes. Every star seemed inches away, the sparse sconces keeping the room in a state of perpetual twilight for better viewing.

"Incredible," she whispered. A sharp pain jabbed the inside of her skull. She scrunched her eyes with a low hiss and blinked at a brightly lit ballroom with frescoes tiling the walls, sweeping up to the cavernous ceiling. Jewels dripped from the party's wealthy attendees, winking from ears, necks, and rings. Platters of meat occupied a long table at the center of the room, people popping a few morsels into their mouths as they sized up their peers.

"Told you you'd love it." An arm looped through hers. Startled, Sarai gasped and the luminous ballroom winked out. Breathing hard, she took in the darker, *different* ballroom she was in.

Another memory. And she'd been *awake.* Sweat beaded on her forehead. *Calm down. Make sense of it later. Gather information now.*

"Alright there, Sarai?" Cisuré peered at her. "It takes your breath away, doesn't it?" The other girl had never looked more stunning, golden curls cascading down her back. Her silver shift was liquid moonlight, hugging her waist before billowing at her ankles. "Your hair! Oh, it's lovely, but your . . . robes." She sighed.

Sarai inhaled raggedly. "I thought we didn't have to dress up."

"Which meant that you should at least wash your face, barmaid." Harion sauntered over from the wine table, glass in hand. His new nose still looked raw.

She feigned sympathy. "Does it still hurt to wash yours?"

"Let's not speak of it," Cisuré interjected. "It was a little tiff that got out of—"

"She got lucky." Harion drained his glass, unconcerned. "Another minute, and I'd have had her."

Sarai gave Cisuré a meaningful look. With a waspish look in Harion's direction, the other girl dragged her across the room, introducing her to a slew of people. They passed a resplendent Aelius, Cassandane looking stunning in a crimson gown, and Tullus's roving eyes. Helvus was conspicuously absent, much to her frustration, but there was no shortage of influential faces. Tribunes from military camps on the borders, Praetors of southern towns, charming playwrights and more noble families than she'd known existed clustered around tables packed high with unusual dishes.

After an hour of faces and names and no further triggered memories, a pattern emerged. Almost no one was from the north. She'd only run into one other person, an elderly Tribune. Ur Dinyé's north-south divide was on full display tonight. *If these are the country's most renowned businesspeople and talents, then no wonder the north's upset.*

"And they sent in petitions for weeks." An older iudex chatted with Cisuré about the northern towns who'd complained after the latest hike in Grains Guild taxes. "You'd think they'd have some sense. Why bring a claim against the Guild you rely on for bread?"

Because they aren't getting any regardless. Staying silent through sheer force of will, she popped a tart into her mouth, wondering how many in Arsamea would kill for a morsel from this table.

When Tullus joined their conversation, she immediately feigned rapt attention in the iudex's chatter. After many attempts to get a word alone with her, he slunk away when Cisuré pulled her to meet yet another person of import.

"Grains Guildmaster Admia." Cisuré waved down a sharp-faced woman in emerald robes, who eyed Sarai with mild distaste. "Such a pleasure to see you again."

You've met before? Sarai looked askance at Cisuré and pasted on a smile as the Guildmaster assessed her clothing.

"We just heard about the tax increase." Cisuré wrinkled her nose. "It can't be easy weathering that criticism."

Admia made a dismissive gesture. "They can complain all they want. It changes nothing. If they want grain, they'll pay the coin on it."

Sarai's hand curled tighter around her wineglass. "What do the extra taxes go toward?"

"Well, growth and seizing opportunity are crucial to our operations. Rising profits dictate a healthy economy, and Guilds are the backbone of that."

A lot of words to say nothing. "Do the profits go to wages, equipment, expansion?"

Admia's eyebrows arched. "You're very interested in how I allocate *my* coin."

So, the money goes to you. It had probably paid for her dazzling emerald robes. She recalled those winters where grain had run dry. Cretus had ceased serving flatbread, and there hadn't been so much as a crust to steal. So this was one of the people behind those hard months. A well-fed viper.

Cisuré shot her a warning glance. "No! She's curious about how you're *expanding* operations. Have you considered bringing Urd farming techniques to other countries with arid soil? I hear that Kashyal is facing drought."

Admia tsked. "Their rulers won't hear of it, but there's coin in the venture, *certo.*"

The tarts Sarai had been shoveling in her mouth were starting to taste like dirt. She'd assumed that Kadra's rebuffing of the law was asinine, because surely, as a Tetrarch, he could change everything with a few words on a scroll. Yet, the Tetrarchy's hands were largely fettered when it came to economic matters—the leveraging of Guild taxes, rent, or the price of goods—where Guilds and nobles held more power and less responsibility. And their greed ran too deep for words on parchment to accomplish anything.

Stomach leaden, she gave her empty plate to an attendant collecting them with a whispered thanks, and realized that she'd lost Cisuré. Squinting in search of her, she jumped at a tap on her shoulder. An inebriated group of what looked to be siblings eyed her with curiosity.

"Good evening." She glanced at the signet ring on a man's hands. *Nobles.*

"You're Kadra's Petitor, right?" The ring's owner clapped clumsily when she nodded. "Perfect. See, he never comes, and my sister's tired of putting up with this bore in the hope that he'll arrive." He nudged his sister who rolled her eyes.

"I asked where he was *once*," she grumbled. "But really, why doesn't he come?"

Sarai was at a loss. "Well, I wouldn't know." She assumed he'd been invited. Aelius wasn't the sort to scorn him. "He's quite busy."

"Aren't we all?" Signet Ring chuckled. "He was always off somewhere before, and he's still at it." He dropped his voice. "We were magi-in-training at the Academiae, you know. Different years, but he was *known*."

She couldn't resist probing further. "Was he a difficult student?"

"Difficult?" Signet Ring whistled. "He was a genius. Spun lightning in circles around us, literally. Tetrarch Aelius had just become Head Tetrarch, and everyone was already putting Kadra's name forward as his replacement. His old man was furious."

"He was furious every day," another chimed in. "Wasn't a day when he wouldn't chew him out in public."

"Entertaining as shit," his sister guffawed. "In class, Kadra was untouchable, and outside, Othus was boxing his ears behind Safsher Hall." She mimicked a harsh, male voice. "I wanted the best, and I got you!"

Oh. Sarai quieted. So Kadra had known it too. The awful feeling of being watched through one's denigration.

"So you've lived with him a month, right?" Signet Ring's sister began speculatively.

"I barely see him," Sarai said shortly, before the group could start prying. Politely excusing herself, she wandered about the room deep in thought until a familiar man entered her path, wineskin in hand.

"Evening, barmaid. You couldn't look more lost if you tried. Here." Telmar passed her a wineglass.

"Good to see you, too, Magus Telmar. But I've already had—"

"Just hold it. It helps you look less confused. See? You aren't alone and friendless. You're on your way to a drink."

Sarai cracked a smile, and he looked pleased.

"You'll get used to this." He grinned cheerfully, well on his way to sotted. "Just a lot of hob . . ." He paused in search of the word. "Cob?"

"Hobnobbing?" Sarai offered.

"Precisely!" He smacked his thigh and tottered. Sarai caught his elbow with a wince and gently ushered him over to the sidelines where he proceeded to inform several attendees that he'd "discovered her."

Anek joined her, a vision in scarlet, fiery hair in lustrous, tight curls. "Gods only know why he's always like that." They shook their head sadly. "But this business is something else. More uncomfortable than the Robing."

"I'll drink to that." Sarai sighed. "I'm out of place."

"I doubt I belong here either." They shrugged. "But I'll show up until I do. They can make the space for me."

She envied their confidence. "I keep thinking that they won't."

"We're already past the hardest part. Not everyone gets an invitation to one of these, only big names. I believe Tetrarch Kadra was invited a few years ago when he was a iudex, and never went after the first."

Disquiet crawled through her at the memory of the luminous ballroom she'd glimpsed earlier. "These conviviums, are they always at Delran Tower?"

"They used to be at Sidran Tower." Sarai's heart plummeted. "The space was rented to Guildmasters and so forth for their escapades, but the practice was discontinued after the Sidran Tower Girl." Mistaking her frozen face for surprise, Anek explained. "Apparently, there was a convivium up there the night the girl fell. No word on who the organizer was, but everyone in attendance swore they didn't know the girl."

She almost couldn't speak. "Can the average person obtain an invitation to a convivium?"

"They'd have to be very talented or very desperate."

I know which one I was. Jovian's theory that she'd been invited to Sidran Tower was looking increasingly plausible. She clutched her empty glass like an anchor.

An invitation. A secret passage into the Academiae that took me inside. A party with Edessa's wealthiest. A man who'd drugged my drink. And stormfall after I fell. But who had brought her there?

A commotion at the entrance diverted her attention. Exchanging a look with Anek, they both rose on tiptoe, trying to make out who was causing all the fuss. She fell back on her heels at her first glimpse of a pair of piercing eyes.

Anek's jaw dropped. "But Cassandane said he *never* comes."

Kadra emerged from the darkness of the hallway, passing by curious conversants with disinterest. *He's wearing his robes.* And suddenly, she couldn't be gladder that she'd done the same.

"Would you look at that?" Harion popped up by her elbow with a sneer. "You match. He wears it better."

She dug an elbow in his ribs, right as Kadra turned and spotted her. The world stopped for a moment as the lines bracketing his mouth relaxed. The broad line of his shoulders grew less rigid. *He was looking for me.* She made to go to him when Signet Ring's sister stepped into Kadra's path, looking excited.

Ice built in Sarai's chest. *What am I doing?* Hating herself, she veered to where Cisuré stood by a pillar instead. "Doing alright?"

"Much worse now that he's here," the other girl slurred with a glower at Kadra. Her eyes looked a little too glassy for Sarai's comfort.

She plucked the wineglass from her hand, holding it out of reach when Cisuré reached for it. "Isn't there a dance later on? Imagine stepping all over Tetrarch Aelius's feet."

That quieted Cisuré. She slumped against a wall, fanning herself. "Quite the night, isn't it? Though I don't know why *he* had to come."

"I wish you'd tell me why you hate him."

"He's Marus. Don't you see?" Cisuré's face sobered. "It's all there."

Is it? She knew the flat of Marus's hand and the violent eruptions of his temper too. She hadn't found either in Kadra.

Across them, Signet Ring's sister gave Kadra a coquettish smile, angling her impressive cleavage into his line of sight. The ice in Sarai's gut cracked. *Enough of this.* She raised her head, forcing herself to see Kadra's reaction. She nearly choked.

He looked right through the woman, features perfectly polite but so utterly devoid of expression that the woman began to falter. After a few more minutes of chatter, Kadra met her eyes and held them. The woman froze, blanched, then turned on her heel and raced for the wine table.

Sarai stifled a snort. Mood much improved, she turned to Cisuré only to find her regaling a group of nobles with stories of the north.

"And that's how snowgrapes are harvested, but Sarai would really know best. She's done it for years."

Sarai shrank back at the dawning curiosity and derision on the listeners' faces.

Not seeming to notice, Cisuré slung an arm around her. "And that's not all she could do with a harvesting knife, if you'll believe it. I pitied whoever faced her down in Arsamea."

A dark figure at the edge of her vision paused at the words. *Of course he passes by now.*

Sarai determinedly avoided Kadra's curious glance. "Cisuré, I really don't think—"

"If anyone dared trouble her, she'd find a way to get revenge. Once, a few girls decided to break into her little shed while she was working at the tavern. They turned the whole place upside down. Over the next few days, she drugged their meals, crept into their homes and shaved their heads as they slept!" Cisuré choked, wiping a tear. "The girls knew it was her, of course, but they couldn't never understand how they'd slept through it."

Kadra was looking more amused than she'd ever seen him. Awkwardly clearing her throat, Sarai nudged her friend.

"You'll have everyone thinking I'm deranged," she said through gritted teeth.

"Never." Cisuré waved a hand airily, knocking a wineglass out of a passing Guildmaster's hands and onto his robes.

"What the *fuck*?" His roar cracked through the ballroom. Everyone fell quiet.

Oh no.

Cisuré's smile slid off her face, a familiar panic in her eyes. "I'm so sorry!" Her voice was high. "Here, let me."

Before Sarai could stop her, she batted at the man's robes, smearing the drink. He shoved her aside. A broken sound left her. On the other side of the ballroom, Aelius abandoned a group of nobles and strode over. Aware of all the eyes on them, Sarai dragged Cisuré behind her, but the Guildmaster wasn't done.

"Why don't you watch where you're going? Disgraceful behavior, flailing about like that, like a drunk—"

"Petitor," Sarai interjected. "Like a drunk Head Tetrarch's Petitor. Happens to the best of us, doesn't it?"

A loud "Hear, hear!" from Signet Ring's group shattered the predatory quiet. Several people tittered, and the crowd moved on.

Sarai led Cisuré off to the sidelines, an arm firmly around her shoulders. "Breathe. You don't have to say anything."

Aelius caught Sarai's eye on their way past him and gave her a grateful look, inserting himself to soothe the ego of the irate Guildsman. Spotting the balconies overlooking the ballroom, she pulled Cisuré toward one of the curtain-covered stairways leading up to them.

Behind the curtain, Cisuré planted herself on a step, chin wobbling. "I ruined everything." Tears threatened to spoil her artful eyepaint, and Sarai shook her head, kneeling beside her.

"It's alright. It was an accident, and he overreacted. Everyone thought so." She repeated variations of the phrase, patting Cisuré's back until she'd calmed down enough to laugh at the whole thing.

"The next time I have more than two drinks at one of these, stop me."

"The next time I come to one of these will be too soon," Sarai said with a groan. "Now, go out and dance." She could hear instruments picking up. "I'm happy where I am."

Cisuré left after giving her a hug. Sarai resolved to stay behind the curtain until it was time for her workday to begin. She'd had enough excitement.

Music soon filled her quiet hiding place, stringed and wind instruments vibrating in notes of such joy that she could understand why the Naaduir of music had been elevated to one of the Elsar in many cultures. She tapped her feet to the tune when voices drew close to her curtain.

"I can't imagine what he's doing here. He knows he isn't wanted. At least two-thirds of us have lost coin because of him," a woman sniped. "Not like we don't know what he's done."

"There's no proof he killed Othus," a man noted.

"Oh, isn't there? Who hasn't heard Othus roaring at him? Kadra had motive, opportunity, and gained everything. I can't believe he wasn't jailed."

"And those eyes." Another woman made a sound of disgust. "He looks like a blackstripe bear, you know? Just craving blood."

Sarai doubted the woman had ever come within a hundred feet of a blackstripe bear.

"What about that new Petitor of his? The one who's fucking him," a second man asked. "Anything we can do with her?"

"If he's fucking her, then I'm a Saint. I saw her earlier, and she's the homeliest thing."

Sarai stared at her hands. *Fair enough.* She wished they'd leave. She could barely hear the music.

"He kills all his lovers," a second man insisted. "That's why you never hear of them. He's using this northern girl as a shield. I bet you the bodies are in his tower. If we use the girl, we could break in, obtain proof, and get rid of him."

Alright, that's enough. She pushed aside the curtain and smiled blandly when the group of assorted nobles and Guildmasters jumped.

"I haven't seen any bodies yet, but I'll be sure to keep you informed." She gave each of them a scathing once-over. "Now if you'll excuse me, I need to inform the Tetrarch I'm fucking about a very sinister plot to storm his tower."

They watched her with complete indifference. One opened his mouth when a quiet footfall sounded, a figure emerging to stand at her shoulder. She didn't have to look. The frozen expressions on the group's faces gave his identity away.

Kadras's tar-black eyes, unnerving on the best of the days, held enough muted violence to reduce them to stammers and rumbles of discontent. But when he turned to her, he wore only the same surprise and perturbation as when she'd goaded Red Tunic into throwing a punch. Like he hadn't expected her to defend him and didn't know what to do with her now that she had.

Feeling just as awkward, she gave them both an out. Ducking behind the curtain, she went up the stairway and onto the narrow balcony to which it led. Moments later, she heard footsteps behind her. Kadra faced her, one hand braced against the railing. A banked fire encompassed her so slowly she couldn't tell if she was aflame. She was all at once a mortal before one of the Wretched. Transfixed, foolishly eager to approach.

People danced below. Cisuré and Aelius led everyone, silver-clad stars twinkling in the ballroom's gloaming. Harion had managed to wrangle some poor girl into joining him, while the girl Anek was spinning looked half in love with them already.

"Not dancing?" At the edge of her vision, Kadra studied her profile.

"I'd rather observe." After a second, she offered the rest of the truth. "And I don't know how."

"And if you did?"

"I don't know. I think I'd be rather particular about my partner."

He would be a magnificent dancer, she guessed. Just as elegant outside of combat as in it. Theirs was a strange dance around a ballroom of their own. Avoiding, intersecting, joining each other's paths intentionally. Always watching.

Glancing down at the giddy dancers, she looked away when the floor teetered. He moved like lightning, gripping her elbow as she swayed. Warmth radiated where his palm met the fabric. Sucking in a breath, she withdrew. His gaze dropped to the wineglass in her hands, and she scowled.

"I'm perfectly fine, Tetrarch Kadra. I've only had a glass this entire evening. I . . . don't do well with heights."

He considered her thoughtfully. "Yet, here you are."

They were no longer talking about heights. "I wanted to see if it would help."

He seemed to move a fraction closer. The balcony shrank. "Did it?"

"No." They were mirror images now. A hand on the railing in a cursory nod to the entertainment but angled toward each other. She hated it. She wanted to step closer. "I see why you don't come to these now. Walking in elevated circles doesn't mean you can change them."

A slow smile. "We can't all drug and shave the heads of our offenders."

Her cheeks burned. *Fucking Cisuré.* "I was much younger, and it didn't end up being all that clever. I scrubbed out the latrines for a year as punishment."

"Was that when you stopped standing up for yourself?"

She looked up. "What—" She broke off, the dark indulgence in his eyes rattling her even more. "What does that matter?"

"Ennius, court, tonight, you throw yourself forward in everyone's defense. But not in yours."

"Because it's irrelevant."

"Why would it be irrelevant?"

"Why do you care?" she snapped, and realized she'd given herself away when his smile widened.

The quiet that bloomed between them was soft and knowing. After a moment, she lowered her head and sighed.

"It is difficult to have to convince others of your humanity." She stared at her shaking fingers on the railing, inches from his. "Not just being human but being . . . worthy of all the accoutrements of humanity. A roof over your head, fair compensation for your labor, and justice when a wrong is committed." Heat licked behind her eyes. "But so many don't believe that. And they've spent their entire lives proselytizing that people are tools to be exploited. Advocating for myself before these people"—she indicated the jewel-decked attendees and shook her head—"it's impossible. You're the plaintiff, defendant, and Petitor rolled into one. They're the iudices. They conclude that you're biased, envious, and they won't believe a word. So why lose my temper and pay the price when I could keep my head down?"

She barely kept her voice steady. "But it's easier to defend someone else. Because at least *they* don't have to feel like everyone is arrayed against their existence. At least they know they've someone on their side." In Arsamea, it was all she'd hoped for. These days, she didn't bother. "There you are. Will that be all, Tetrarch Kadra?"

She blinked until her vision was no longer blurry and looked up. A roaring began in her ears. Because she'd somehow set Kadra ablaze.

Something quiet and lethal burned in his eyes. "Choose me." His voice was rough, jaw tensed like he hadn't wanted to say it. As if she hadn't given him a choice but to say it.

Her silence stretched, raw and taut. A tendril of hair fell into her face. His brow furrowed, fingers reaching out, waiting for her dazed nod before tucking the lock back in place. An aching warmth hummed where his fingers brushed her skin.

"Can you say that tearing the Tetrarchy apart will fix this?" she whispered. "If it's gone, will you change everything for the better?"

The electrifying emotion faded from his face. "I can't." The words were empty. "But others can."

True. "Who?"

"That knowledge has a price. Do you want me after all?" There was a disconcerting sensuality in his slight smile.

She crossed her arms. "Where's that group of Guildmasters again? I should let them into your tower."

His shoulders shook with a low huff of laughter. And for the first time, she allowed herself to grin back, to fool herself that they weren't enemies, that Sidran Tower had been a bad dream. They stayed atop the balcony watching the partygoers congregate and part like waves. Watching as they danced far above the lives they ruined.

CHAPTER
TWELVE

Sleep came and went. Brightly lit ballrooms and men who'd drugged her abounded in her dreams to the tune of stormfall pounding against the window. Nursing a headache, Sarai came downstairs to find an equally tired-looking Cato.

"This storm was an ugly one." He stifled a yawn. "Kadra will be at the Aoran Tower Gate. He wanted you to know that he's found Petitor Livia's mother."

Her appetite vanished, dread and anticipation taking its place. "I see."

If there was any evidence incriminating Kadra in Livia's death, then this dance of theirs would end. She'd go to Aelius, and her vengeance would be complete. It was everything she'd hoped for only a month ago before entering this tower. So why couldn't she summon any joy?

Feeling unanchored, she barely noticed the reek of smoke and mud in the air on her walk to the Aoran Tower Gate, where Kadra conversed with his vigiles. Faint lines of weariness bracketed his mouth, and she took a deep breath, emptiness sweeping her at the thought of this solid, malevolent man rotting away in the mines.

She hid her perturbation throughout their journey, but couldn't mask it upon reaching the outskirts of Edessa. Left to fend for themselves, the poor clustered in makeshift structures—brick walls and roofs of corrugated metal—or rickety apartments, ill-maintained by the landowners.

"This is Arsamea all over again," she said, dismayed. An hour and a half's ride back into the Quarter and she'd be among the lavish domii of last night's partygoers.

"Edessa has many faces." Kadra dismounted, leading his horse onto a narrow road between insulae. "You won't find a town without poverty."

Spotting a glint of gold some yards away, she squinted. His vigiles hefted steaming pots toward an insula, ladling soup to a group of exhausted people.

The emptiness she'd felt earlier intensified. "You do what you can."

His mouth curved cynically. "I do what my coffers allow."

They approached the border of Kadra's Quarter with Cassandane's, an outward line of crimson-painted cobblestone with an inner line of black stone. Scores of people darted across, making a beeline for Kadra's vigiles, faces hopeful for soup. She wondered if Cassandane knew. The Corpus provided that the Tetrarchy couldn't interfere with each other's governance of their Quarters, a law evidently set in place to impede the creation of a dictatorship, unimpeachable on its face. Yet, in effect, it had discouraged cooperation as much as it had tyranny.

Kadra tilted his head toward a rocky trail tucked behind a hut. It ended in a brick shelter, tiny even by the outskirts' standards. A white-haired woman shifted open the planks that served as a door and moved them back when she saw him.

"Get lost," she snarled. "I don't need another lying Tetrarch."

Another? Sarai edged past him. "We're here to talk about Livia."

"You're here *now*, are you? Didn't bother a year ago when I needed help. I *begged* you lot to avenge my girl, and you gave me excuses." She spat in the dirt.

Sarai glanced at Kadra, who shook his head. She believed him. Kadra was many things, but she'd never seen him turn away a petitioner.

"We think Petitor Jovian may have been murdered," she said tentatively. "Are you saying your daughter was as well?"

The old woman went quiet. She shuffled the boards and emerged, stooped over. "You won't do anything, just like the others. But I'll give you the damn story if you want it so bad."

"What happened to her?" Kadra kept the doorway in his line of sight. Sarai tracked his focus to an oblong shape within the cramped dwelling, wrapped in cloth.

"Death." Her mother shrugged. "One day, she'd stopped by for a meal. The next, she'd fallen into a vat in one of the Metals Guild's forges."

The Metals Guild again. Her heart sank. "How?"

"That's what I asked." The woman crossed her arms. "Apparently, the Guildsmen came in to work and found her arm sticking out of the molten metal. Of course, she'd been murdered! But Guildmaster Helvus denied everything, offered his condolences, then slapped me with a bill for the metal she ruined by dying in it." She laughed bitterly. "Cassandane paid but said there was no way of telling if a Guildsman was involved or which one. Only Jovian knew that something was wrong. Came to Livia's wake and kept muttering that he saw something he shouldn't have. Died a week later too."

Sarai's blood turned to ice. *The Sidran Tower Girl must have seen . . .* Jovian's burnt letter had said. "Did Livia seem afraid before her death?"

"I barely saw her." Livia's mother snarled. "She was worked to the bone. Only came home twice in those last weeks. For a final meal and to get rid of all our scuta. I don't know why," she added when Sarai made to ask just that. "But if Livia wanted it gone, then I'd toss the house itself. I just figured it was because she didn't like the Metals Guild."

Odd. "Forgive me," Sarai began hesitantly, "but did you happen to see Livia's body?"

"See it?" The woman's laugh went eerily off-kilter. "She's always with me."

Sarai's head whipped toward the shape within the hut. Still laughing, the woman plodded inside and returned with it. She drew the cloth away with a flourish.

Sarai's stomach curdled. An arm lay within a wooden box, runes etched all over the wood to prevent its decay. Livia's mother must have paid a Lugen well for such preservation. Fear coiled around her at the familiar shattered fingers, the elbow joint facing the wrong way. Two bodies disfigured in death. And at the center of it all, the Metals Guild.

Her hands shook. "Another fall," she whispered for Kadra's ears alone.

"It was the only piece of her that wasn't coated in metal." Livia's mother hugged it to her. "I don't have anything else for you."

Barely able to breathe, Sarai struggled for words.

"We appreciate your assistance," Kadra said smoothly, after a quick glance at her. "I'll see that her killers pay."

"Ha! You won't do anything either," Livia's mother said scornfully. "I went to Tullus, too, you know. He told me that anger was unbecoming, that the gods decreed Livia's fate and that I should pray for her rest in the Bright Realms instead of conjuring culprits."

Damn him. She took in Livia's mother's ragged clothes, the box she so fiercely clung to, the spark of hope in her eyes that she extinguished every time it flared up. A mother who loved beyond death, whom the world had ignored, just as it had Jovian and Livia. Eyes burning, she hugged her, feeling the bony hills of her shoulders when she patted her back.

"I'm sorry." It was all she could say to this woman who'd been failed in every way. "I'm so sorry."

She was quiet on the way back. Kadra rode ahead, acknowledging her silence but not prying into it. She wished he would. None of this made sense.

The Metals Guild was involved, but how did Kadra fit into this? Jovian and Livia had no ties to him beyond their corpses being found in his Quarter, and all she had was a memory of his voice, which she was starting to wonder if her cracked skull had made up that night.

By the time they reached the vigiles who'd been distributing soup earlier, she had a splitting headache. One set down his pot when he saw them and ran over.

"There's been a strike, Tetrarch Kadra. Eighteen streets north."

Kadra turned to her. "How fast can you ride?"

Her adrenaline surged. "As fast as you need."

"Stay close."

With a white-knuckled grip on the reins, she spurred Caelum on. Their mounts picked their way across the widening streets, breathing hard. Smoke hung in the air, worsening with every mile, scratching her throat. Thinking of the storm she'd been caught in with Kadra, she sent a fervent plea to the gods, her dread burgeoning when the dwellings grew larger. They rounded a cluster of trees, and Kadra drew to a halt. She froze.

Fortune, have mercy.

An insula rose ahead, obliterated. Embers still bloomed on the upper floors, Kadra's vigiles perched on ladders to throw buckets of water at them. People clustered outside, sobbing and screaming in pain, burns lacing their skin. Her breath hitched when two of Kadra's vigiles emerged from the rubble, carrying a blackened corpse between them. At the sight of their Tetrarch, they set the body down and came over.

"How many?" Kadra's features were grim.

"Twelve dead, Tetrarch Kadra." One of the vigiles wiped his sweaty forehead, smearing it with ash. "The rest are either getting there or burned enough to wish they were."

"Get them to the healers and find a few brick Guildsmen who'll help rebuild." Kadra indicated the people clustering around the corpse, wailing. "Ask them where they want the bodies buried and join them in finding shelter. The air's thick. This storm isn't over."

Both vigiles nodded and vanished back inside the charred building. Dismounting, she coughed at the smoke, gaze fixed on the scutum lying on its side at the front of the home. Crouching, she gingerly touched the rod, finding it cool to the touch.

"I don't understand." She turned to Kadra. "Why didn't it work?"

Kadra grimly surveyed the dead. "What do you know of the scuta?"

"They're steel rods, engraved with protective runes that Tetrarch Aelius found in an ancient annal." Her chest tightened when the vigiles brought out another body. "Don't they shield against lightning?"

Kadra's laugh was ugly, humorless. "Do you know what the runes say?"

She shook her head, frustrated. "I can only read a few."

His shadow fell over her shoulder. "May I?" He offered his hand.

The heat from the fire receded as a different rush of warmth hummed over her skin. *I shouldn't.* He might feel her scars. They were at the scene of a disaster.

Yet, she still nodded. His large hand covered hers, another coming to rest on her shoulder in a steadying hold. That had always troubled her. That a man so entrenched in violence was capable of gentleness. She nearly choked when he interlocked their fingers and pressed them to the scutum, tracing each rune to show her their meaning.

"'The strength of the shield cast by this fulgur scutum,'" he read, "'depends on how fervently those who dwell under its protection believe in the Elsar. A prayer will save you. But doubt, that stealthy poison, will doom you.'"

Staring at her shaking fingers gentled by large, callused ones, it took a moment for the words to penetrate. Her jaw dropped. "The shields work on *faith*?"

He released her. "That's what the runes say."

"So if the scutum doesn't work . . ." She broke off. "You can't be serious."

"If it doesn't work, then the inhabitants must not have had faith," he said sardonically.

"Something as nebulous as faith can't govern *this*." She gestured at the catastrophe around them. "Everyone would be better off erecting a monument to Lord Fortune on their roofs. How can *belief* power a hunk of metal?"

"How indeed." The strange gleam she'd seen in Kadra's eyes by Jovian's corpse resurfaced. He turned his mount back to the path. "Come."

"You're going to just walk away? Won't you offer a word of comfort?"

Something bitter tautened his face. "There is no comfort for the living after this. No platitudes that will ease the burn of everyone saying that these people deserved it for lacking faith. The dead will die again by public opinion, and the living will never live it down." He indicated the spectators keeping their distance from the carnage as though it were contagious. "You can't change that."

Without thinking, she gripped his reins. "Don't." Her voice wobbled, aware that his vigiles were watching them, and that she was being insubordinate again. "Don't do what Cassandane and Tullus did to Livia's mother and walk away, thinking that coin alone will help."

"Words won't aid them." His features were hard.

"They will aid *some*. You may never have lost anything, Kadra, but I have, and if even one person had bothered to tell me that it wasn't my fault, I would have appreciated it a great godsdamned deal." She realized that she'd addressed him without his title.

Something shifted in his eyes. After a moment, he dismounted and stalked over to the survivors with her. A few tearstained faces turned at their approach.

Sarai bowed low. "I'm sorry for your losses tonight," she said awkwardly. "And for what it's worth, I don't think that a lack of faith caused this."

"Then why?" a woman cried, clutching her mangled arm. "Who did this then?"

A lump built in Sarai's throat. "I know it's no comfort, but sometimes, there's no one to blame," she whispered. "Perhaps the gods are cruel. Or perhaps they want to take us where it's safe. At the very least, there is no stormfall in the Bright Realms."

Some shrugged, deep in grief. Others lined up to where Kadra was offering his condolences so compellingly, it was like she'd hadn't talked him into it.

Returning to their mounts, she snuck a glance at him. *Why listen to me? Do you care about these people or are they just useful to you? Why were you at Sidran Tower that night?*

Eyes still holding that fierce light, Kadra turned to the road. "This way."

She let the questions turn to ash in her mouth.

They made rounds of the other farms to see if they'd been struck. A city like Edessa didn't have the capacity for much arable farmland, but livestock farmers were always necessary, and littered the outskirts. Leaving a dwelling, Sarai stiffened when Kadra cast a sharp look at the sky.

"Get down." He indicated a nearby holm oak.

She didn't think twice. Dismounting, she'd just finished tethering their mounts when blinding light ripped through the sky followed by a scream of thunder.

A drop of rain hit her shoulder. Then another. And the sky opened above without any garden folly to save them.

Rain spitefully bit into her skin, her robes doubling under the weight. The ground softened into sludge, and she cursed when her worn Arsamean boots began rapidly sinking in. Eyeing Kadra's sturdier footwear, she tried to keep her balance, searching for something to grip. The wide tree trunk behind her had no purchase, and Caelum was too skittish for Sarai to grab her reins.

"You'll have to excuse me," Kadra said quietly.

A warm hand gripped her waist, pulling her against him. The scent of oranges enveloped her. Her boots squelched, ruined. Yet, she only had eyes for the face a foot above hers.

"I would have asked," he said with amusement. "But you were about to fall."

Blood throbbed in her ears. The side of her body touching his sighed at the heat, as if she'd never known she was cold until this very instant. *He's a mass murderer*, she reminded herself fiercely. *He was at Sidran Tower.* Her pulse cooled.

"Thank you," she said stiffly.

Kadra's humor faded, his eyes returning to knifelike sharpness. He surveyed her boots. "I'll have a pair made."

The words held no condescension, but she still bristled. "Thank you, but I can afford it."

"Hmm." Not a change in his expression, but she had the feeling that he'd seen too much in her response.

She hated this. The attraction, the fear, the contradictory directions her body and mind fled in around him. The way she watched for the wry curve of his mouth and how she'd replayed the night he'd removed her birrus a thousand times. A bolt of lightning hissed above, and she wished it would strike her, so she would stop thinking. An angry roar of thunder followed, and she couldn't halt a shudder.

Kadra looked down, raising an eyebrow, and she flushed.

"We're under a *tree*," she said through gritted teeth. It may as well be a lightning rod.

Looking like he was fighting a laugh, he raised a hand. Tension thrummed through him. Her eyes widened when a shimmering lattice unfolded beyond the tree's cover, curving high around them to form a dome. It hovered above the ground, sparking and hissing when rain struck it. Not one drop made it through.

"I didn't think lightning could be used this way," she breathed.

"Every element can." Kadra dropped his hand, and the shield vanished, rain returning to pile on them. The rigid line of his shoulders eased. "I'd keep it up, but I need to see if a bolt gets too close. After all, we are under a *tree*."

If he wasn't all that was keeping her standing, she'd have throttled him. She settled for a scowl, painfully conscious of his arm around her waist. The man who might have destroyed her body, holding it. The gods must be cackling.

"Take tomorrow to rest," he murmured.

She looked up at him. "Why? I'm well."

He directed a meaningful glance at her hands, which seemed to be performing an interpretive dance.

She clenched them into fists. "It happens."

"When you're overworked."

How often had he been staring at her hands to figure that out? "I don't shirk my duties."

"In which case, you should take tomorrow to go over next week's petitions. The Hall of Records will have them."

For a second, she thought she'd been struck by lightning. *The Hall of Records.* Her records of the Fall. Her answers would arrive tomorrow. She waited for elation, but the deep-seated ache she'd battled hours earlier resurfaced. She hated that she knew why. *Kadra, will I find your name in those records?*

"Very well," she muttered.

A dull hum suddenly filled the air, throbbing in an eerie rhythm. Kadra's arm around her turned to steel.

"Close your eyes," he ordered and raised a hand, sparks flying at his fingertips.

She'd barely complied when blinding light flashed beyond her shut eyelids. Kadra's hand moved from her waist to the back of her head, pressing her into his chest. A terrifying snap of sound followed. The mud beneath their feet trembled in response. She snuck a glance in time to witness the lightning bolt that had tried to strike them fly back up to the sky and crack it open, branching into a thousand filaments.

Dropping his hand, Kadra exhaled heavily. *Kadra's a talented magus,* Cisuré had said. But this was beyond talent. *What monstrous power.*

A tinny noise started, similar in vibration to the buzz they'd just heard. *Another bolt.* But farther away, she realized, eyeing the blurred shape of a thick oak in the distance. She stiffened in preparation for the tree to go up in flames when Kadra's hand rose again. Lightning arrowed down, ready to claim its victim when it warped and fled upstream to strike the clouds.

Another low breath left him. His sleeve fell back, the runes on his armilla blazing in the rain. Red had entered a few, and she realized that he must have drained himself controlling the first storm, before they'd gone to see Livia's mother, and was doing so again. How he wasn't comatose was beyond her.

As she stared, the hand gripping the back of her head returned to her waist. She withdrew, pretending she hadn't just been face-first in his chest.

"You're safe." His hand found the taut line of her spine and settled there. "That'll be it for some time."

Safe. The simple word struck her with the weight of a sledgehammer. Conflicted, she stared at him. *When have I ever been safe?*

In the downpour, Kadra's features looked crueller than ever, watchful gaze trained on the sky. *Magnificent.* The realization clenched around her heart like a fist. If she were a bolder woman, she'd have risen on her toes, pressed her mouth to his and lost herself entirely.

But she wasn't. She was a Petitor out of her depth, under an illusion. Her face, her reasons for being near him, none of them were real.

At her silence, he gave her a quizzical look. "I didn't think this would frighten you."

It took her a second to find her tongue. "I'm not frightened, just—"

"A little unnerved?" He quoted her response from her first night in his study.

"And of course, you aren't." He was stormfall itself. More exhilarating and terrifying than lightning. He probably didn't have even a passing acquaintance with fear.

"Sarai." His voice went lower, softer. Her name hung between them, transformed to music. Pulse ricocheting, she raised her head, and it felt like jumping from a cliff.

His gaze singed her. "Are you afraid of me?"

Rain slicked them both, but whereas she probably resembled a drowned rat, he exuded power, control. Safety. Just as he had the night they'd met when she'd believed him to be a mere magus. And she gave him the truth as she had then.

"I should be." It was a relief to finally admit it. "I keep having to remind myself that I should be terrified."

"Why?" The question sounded almost stark.

"Because I don't really know you," she whispered. "I don't know whether you treat me as an equal because you want to use me or because you see me as one." A stray droplet glided down his cheekbone, and she cursed her yearning to trace its path.

"What if I told you that you were safe with me?" His voice was a low rasp. "What if I said no harm would come to you at my hands?"

A shaky laugh left her. "You're too late, Kadra."

Glancing up as his features closed, she laid out the worst part of it all in weary capitulation. She had no reason to trust him, and a thousand to fear him. And yet . . .

"I already believe you," she said bitterly.

A fierce spark lit his face. When she shivered under the weight of her sodden robes, she found herself tucked closer, under his cloak, which he curled around her. Gritting her teeth, she hated herself and hated him as a host of unwanted emotions swelled. Weariness. Comfort. Safety.

You're safe. She felt the truth of those words, because he wasn't just stormfall. He was a tree with roots that extended far below the water-logged soil. Secure, unshakable. Ur Dinyé's homicidal son and its fiercest protector.

Tomorrow, she might remind herself to fear him once more, outside the shelter of this tree and his arms. But perhaps it wasn't so wrong for her to take his safety today.

Her last ounce of resistance vanished. She relaxed against him, watching the sky unleash its fury. And an aching warmth that felt almost like peace filled her when he seemed to do the same.

CHAPTER
THIRTEEN

Situated in the ring of neutral ground around the Academiae's citadel, the Hall of Records was a walled complex of white limestone. An elaborate statue of Lord Time greeted her past the front gates, a young man with three faces: the youthful sweetness of the past, the hardened resignation of the present, and the grim exhaustion of the future. Commiserating with the latter, Sarai waited for Gaius, mind still on the previous day's storm.

Insane. The path of her pacing grew longer. A mass murderer—how many kills had she witnessed?—possibly her assailant, the man who'd made her burn Ennius alive at the Robing. And she'd *relaxed* into him? *I'm going mad.* Slumping against a post, she jumped upon finding it occupied.

Sprawled at the base, Magus Telmar waved. "Petitor Sarai. You look *awful.*"

The stench of *ibez* hit her nostrils with brute force and she coughed. "Why are you on the ground?"

"It's warm." His breath misted into the windchill when he spoke.

Gods. Trying to figure out how to lug a man twice her size upright, she started when he gripped her ankle.

"I'm well." He indicated his thick robes with jerky hands. "You, however, are not."

"I'm fine. Honestly, Telmar, that stuff will kill you. There are better wines."

"Had more life as a barmaid than you do now," Telmar noted, before his bloodshot eyes widened. "Kadra suck the life from you? You look used up."

A few passing magi passing by tittered. Her fragile hold on her temper fractured.

"No one is sucking *anything* from anyone!" she snapped at her audience, before crouching beside Telmar. "Please don't feed the rumor mill."

He doubled over in laughter, spluttering *ibez*. Sighing, she slapped her palm between his shoulder blades. "Are you keeping quiet and still, Petitor Sarai?"

"Mostly."

"Good. Nothing changes, because *they* don't change. They don't answer to anyone, but we bow to them. We're afraid so we bow and force everyone else to bow." Leaning against the column, he closed his eyes. "Damn them all." Within seconds, he was asleep.

She pressed two fingers to his pulse to confirm that he wasn't unconscious before dragging him up the steps into the Hall of Records. Placing him in the closest building, she turned him on his side in case he vomited. Gaius showed up as she was done.

Glancing at Telmar, he groaned. "Hells, he's still sotted? There's a decent magus under there, but drink has ruined him."

"Did something happen to him?"

"The Elsar only know." Gaius shrugged. "Leave him be. He'll wake soon and head to teach as though nothing were wrong."

With a final, worried glance, she followed Gaius. Adrenaline and elation accelerated her pulse with every step into the records repository. Gaius kept up a stream of information about each building, from the Archive of Homicidium to the Archive of Mines. But the one she was the most interested in was the tall, chapel-like structure at the center: the Archive of Sealed Records.

Printing her name in the entry book under an archivist's watchful eye, she peered at the hundreds of scrolls piled on shelves of every height just past the entryway.

"After national secrets, I see." Gaius grinned at her excitement. "Unfortunately, I can't accompany you past this point. Only Petitors get to view sealed records."

"I'll be in and out," she promised. "I've heard so much about it."

"Take your time. You're joining a long tradition." He beamed. "It's the first archive every Petitor visits."

Sarai held her breath as she crossed the threshold, absorbing the gravity of the moment and yearning to reach through time to the frightened, bitter girl she'd been and tell her that they'd made it. That their answers were within reach. No matter how unsavory the crime, it was all here, sealed away to keep the public unaware, but future Tetrarchs and their Petitors informed. And she would finally *know*.

"Good morning, Petitor Sarai. What records would you like to see? Or would you prefer to examine the indexes first?" The archivist, a muscled, balding man, who looked like he could carry the entire archive on his shoulders, indicated a series of leather-bound volumes.

"I"—she took a deep breath—"I'd like to see the records on the Sidran Tower Girl."

He chuckled. "You aren't the first curious Petitor, but I'm afraid that's impossible."

Her smile guttered. She must have heard wrong. "Are they located elsewhere?"

"The records were accidentally burnt," he said apologetically. "One of Tetrarch Othus's—that's Tetrarch Kadra's predecessor—men brought a signed command from him demanding their release, and my predecessor was foolish enough to make an exception. The vigile dropped them in a brazier." He sighed. "All that knowledge lost."

Her shaking hands knotted. This couldn't be real. Any second now, she'd wake. But the pain of her nails scoring her skin flared sharp.

"When were they removed?" She heard her voice, fractured and thin like the crack of ice over Cretus's windows.

"I believe it was three days after the incident."

Something snapped in her. Broke. Died. She thought it might have been hope.

Gone. It's all gone. "Tetrarch Othus's vigile . . ." She desperately tried to keep her smile on, but it must have faltered because the archivist looked curious. "How was he able to enter? What about Tetrarch Othus's Petitor?"

"He'd died only a day prior," the archivist said with a wince. "A riding accident. We allow Tetrarchs to use a trusted vigile to deposit records until a new Petitor is appointed. But Tetrarch Othus died the next day, though that was almost certainly murder." He shook his head. "And Martinus left the vigiles to bear the blame for having destroyed a sealed record. Quite the shuffle in personnel."

It's gone. "Do you know if Martinus left Edessa?"

He seemed to register the numbness in her voice because he chuckled. "Don't worry, you'll get your details. He's still around in the taverns. Hairy as a northerner with the tall tales to boot. You can't miss him." He eyed her thoughtfully. "I see you're one of the conspiracy theorists."

Tears flooded her vision. "I . . ." She nodded to keep from speaking.

"It must be an occupational hazard, Petitors and finding the truth. You aren't the first curious one to come here for answers."

"Was . . ." She swallowed when her voice cracked. "Was Jovian one of the curious Petitors?"

"By Truth, yes. He was in here every night. Utterly inconsolable when he learned the records were gone. You'd have thought I'd told him someone died."

Someone did. He had. Livia had. She nearly had. And it was all futile. There were no answers. There was no proof. Their deaths had faded into legend and conjecture and conspiracy. Everything she'd fought for, hoped for over four years of hell, had been for nothing.

Her records were gone.

CHAPTER FOURTEEN

A booted footstep by her head pulled her back to consciousness.

She cringed, fearing the return of the agony that had taken her under. But she felt . . . nothing. Opening her eyes, she stared at the armored man looming over the healers working on her. Another visitor, and, by the look of his burnished armor, an important one.

She frowned when he brought out an ornate pair of cuffs and fastened them around her wrists. Like she could go anywhere. She didn't realize that she'd said it aloud, until the man crouched beside her in a disharmonious scrape of metal.

"Everyone wants to go somewhere at the end," an ice-cold whisper entered her mind.

Her breath caught in recognition at his red irises. "Not me," she said softly, surprised when her voice worked. Part of her understood why. "I've had enough. I'm happy to go."

Death's outline went hazy. "Your healers don't want that."

She gripped the cuff. "I want to go. There's nothing waiting for me back there."

Death looked curious. "How would you know?" His outline blurred once more. After a long look at the healers, he unbuckled the cuff from her. "Perhaps another day."

"No," she whispered, but his figure melted into the rain until it was only her and the healers. And the pain when they woke her.

Sarai dressed, utterly devoid of emotion. She didn't care about the dream. She didn't care if it was a memory—if so, it was a useless one without a single clue. She stayed wordless on the journey to another bazaar, ignored Kadra's searching glances, and sat through a dozen trials, then a dozen more. She didn't care about any of it. She had nothing.

After the Fall, she'd woken to a team of healers putting her back together, and a few vigiles she'd believed equally interested in her welfare. Fury, pain, fear, she'd cycled through it all, but the vigiles had promised that her assailant would pay. Until the third day.

They'd suddenly stopped allowing her food. The queries directed at her had grown blunt.

"Look, we don't care how many you slept with, but this matter could besmirch the Academiae's reputation so we'd like it settled. Did anyone push you off? Or did you jump?"

"Why would I jump?" Her voice had quavered.

He snorted. *"A life like yours, on your back for everyone. Who wouldn't jump? Who were you involved with? Why is he paying for your recovery?"*

"Who's paying for my recovery?" she'd asked only to be met with silence.

That day, the investigation had ended, and she'd been thrown on a wagon back to Arsamea. Had the plan she'd concocted back then worked, she'd have saved coin after coin, entered the Academiae at the likely age of thirty, spent four years training as a Petitor. And found that her records were gone. Playing by the system had gotten her *nothing*. The best part was that if it weren't for her damned attacker having moved on to killing Petitors, she wouldn't have gotten here this quickly. Life was a joke.

The climbing sun marked noon. She rubbed her aching temples, debating asking a vigile for a drink of water. To her left, Kadra's eyes narrowed at the motion, lingering upon her features. After delivering his verdict, he raised a hand.

"We're done," he announced to the crowd, who groaned their disappointment.

She'd started packing when a sweat-streaked vigile shoved past her to bow before Kadra.

"I've just gotten word," he gasped. "It's Metals Guildmaster Helvus."

She rubbed at where the vigile's elbow had dug into her side. If only Kadra's admirers had a fraction of regard for her. Feeling empty, she finished the judgment, squeezed through the crowd, and leaned against Caelum, wondering if it was fate or choice that she always ended up on the outside looking in.

It was a problem Kadra wouldn't understand. His constituents adored him, and his vigiles clustered around him like a wolf pack daily. She couldn't even mock their loyalty when she'd felt that icy strength. He radiated a charisma devoid of emotion that could still suck anyone into his orbit. People *wanted* Kadra as their leader. What right did she have to suspect him when her only proof of his evil was a half-formed memory from the same mind that had conjured her meeting with Death himself?

"Sarai." The word, perfectly formed, brushed the back of her neck.

She started, clutching handfuls of Caelum's mane. The horse gave her a baleful look as she spun to face Kadra.

"What?" she muttered. *Wisdom and Wrath.* To hear her name in that voice was enough to drive a Saint to lust.

"We've an incident at Decimus's. I'll need you."

Truth. "I wouldn't have thought you'd *need* anyone, Tetrarch Kadra. Least of all, me. Over a month ago, you were contesting my appointment at the Aequitas."

"And we've been bound ever since."

"Right," she scoffed, trying to clip her bag to the saddle. "Bound to a Petitor all of Ur Dinyé knows you didn't want."

A breath. Then, his arms bracketed her, taking the saddlebag and buckling it in place. The air filled with the scent of oranges and road dust, ink and crisp parchment.

"I didn't want a Petitor," he said slowly, and the words didn't cut. Not when she'd already lost so much. "I wanted you."

Her numb shield fractured. Trapped between a horse and a man whose very being seemed to be granite, she swallowed a thousand variations of the same question and nodded.

"If you say so."

Kadra's brow creased, sharp eyes staying on her for a long moment before he got on his mount. She followed him onto the road, the question reverberating with every hoofbeat. *Why?*

Dismounting at Decimus's home, Sarai took in the scene with wary eyes. The dilapidated but cozy domus she remembered was in shambles. The front door had met a quick death at someone's boot, the nameplate wrenched off. Half the roof tiles were shattered. She counted the horses tethered around the perimeter with disquiet. *Five visitors.*

"What happened here?"

"My people have been monitoring Decimus since our visit." Kadra secured their mounts.

"To see if he was in danger, or see if he was dangerous?"

"Both. Initially, he showed no sign of either."

A crash sounded from within the home. She jumped, realization dawning. Despite Jovian's death five months ago, no one had sought to harm Decimus. Trouble wouldn't have come to him without being prompted.

Dread gripped her. "What did he do?"

"Got deep in his cups and accused the Metals Guild of murder," he said dryly, looking amused when she cursed. "They'll have found a pretext to make him regret it. Our presence will limit the damage."

Shit. They didn't even have a petition. She raked a hand through her knotted braid. "So what you're saying is that our powers are limited."

The look he gave her was equal parts sardonic and grim. "The law says so."

At the sound of a scream within, she exchanged a look with Kadra and darted inside. The house was in disarray, the furniture sliced and shattered in an ugly show of temper. She'd believed nothing could top Marus's drunken rampages, but this was far worse.

A Guildsman in the middle of smashing a vase sighted them and sneered. "Looks like you've friends in high places, Decimus."

Kneeling by another Guildsman's feet, a bruised Decimus lifted his head, features ravaged by tears. "Tetrarch Kadra," he sobbed.

"Tetrarch Kadra," a familiar voice echoed. Leaning against a wall, Helvus raised a hand covered in rings, at least ten necklaces glowing around his neck.

"Helvus." A cold gleam lit Kadra's eyes. "I heard you were harassing a citizen."

"Of course not." Helvus didn't sound fazed. "This is a misunderstanding. Decimus, here, has misunderstood his rights. We're rectifying the issue."

"What sort of misunderstanding involves destroying his home to rectify it?" she demanded.

Helvus raised an eyebrow. "Not the girl who told you off before the Aequitas. Tetrarch Kadra, you're more forgiving than I thought, letting her putter about."

"Am I?" Kadra's smile had every hair on her body rising on end.

"Well, she's living with you." Helvus whistled. "I suppose we all have our *preferences*."

Kadra gave her a cursory glance as if just registering her gender, and something in her chest crumpled. "Some of us more than others."

She deflated, numbness creeping back in. *Of course he doesn't care.* She hadn't expected anything. He was ice through and through. But today, her veneer of stability was thin. There was an abyss below her feet, and she was clinging to the precipice. Because none of it mattered. She spent over fifteen hours every damned day delivering a one-woman performance of a competent Petitor only for people like this embodiment of greed to treat her as if she were still a tunnel rat.

Time slowed as she took in Decimus's crumpled form, pleading for mercy within the ruins of his home, because the law allowed *everything* but justice. And she stopped caring.

She faced Helvus. "If you're operating within Decimus's rights, then you shouldn't have any trouble telling us why you're here."

"Have you never seen a bankruptcy proceeding?" Helvus chuckled. "Perfectly legal."

"On what basis?"

"It recently came to my attention that the dearly departed brother of our Decimus here owed my men a little sum. We're taking the house in repayment."

Every word was a harsh jangle of sound. "Did it come to your attention before or after Decimus made accusations of murder in a tavern?"

He smirked. "I don't know what you mean."

Another discordant burst in her chest. "And I know that you're lying. Do you have any proof of this 'debt'? Anything beyond your word?"

Helvus gave her an incredulous look before turning to Kadra. "Can you please inform your Petitor that she's interfering with my legal rights?"

"You don't have any," she snapped. "Jovian never owed you anything."

Helvus sighed. "Please tell your Petitor that this isn't a trial and that she can't Examine citizens at will."

She turned to Kadra whose gaze had remained trained on her through-out, a line forming between his eyebrows. "Please inform the Guildmaster that a Petitor isn't limited to Examining only during trial, and that he doesn't need to wear every ring he owns. It's an eyesore."

Helvus's lips thinned. "Examine all you want, but it's a waste of magic. There's no petition here, is there, Decimus?" Wrenching him to his feet by the back of his tunic, he slung an arm around the cowering man. Her heart sank when Decimus shook his head.

Helvus shot her a triumphant grin. "Your services aren't required. Decimus knows he owes me."

A crash sounded from the vicinity of Jovian's study, and Decimus sobbed harder.

"The house is yours," he said between gasps. "Please stop destroying it."

"There we are." Helvus rubbed his hands together. "Now, *that* is a binding business agreement. Tetrarch Kadra, my men, to whom the debt was owed, have the documents, if you'd be so kind as to witness them."

She knew it was foolish. This wasn't a house of debt-slaves Kadra could sneak into and spray with blood. It was midday. They were up against four Guildsmen and a Guildmaster, and had no grounds for interference as Decimus hadn't asked for help. But she still turned to Kadra with a silent plea.

His severe expression seemed to soften before he gave an imperceptible shake of his head. Then he vanished into the study, leaving her with a supremely smug Helvus.

He considered her for a moment. "I think I like you." Stepping closer, he gripped her chin, looking annoyed at her flinch. "Stay put. Let me see. Yes, I think you'll do quite well."

Goosebumps pebbled her skin at his touch, the hairs on the back of her neck rising to attention. "The feeling isn't mutual."

"It doesn't have to be." His grip tightened. She forced back a shudder. "Let me make this easier."

His other hand slid into her pocket. Weight settled, coins clinking as he withdrew.

She froze at the handful of gold aurei he'd given her. "I don't want this."

"You can quibble over the amount later. You've a mouth on you, but I'll let it pass, seeing as you're new. You've got something to prove. Good. There are a few cases coming up that I need taken care of. Do well, and I'll give you more."

She stared at his weak chin, shrewd eyes, at the absence of anything resembling humanity on his face. This man could have butchered Jovian and Livia, and thrown her from Sidran Tower. Was this how the deal for their lives had been made? A few coins and everyone had looked the other way? Her records ash, her vengeance hopeless. Because a man with power had decided that her life didn't matter.

Her rage boiled over. The locks to the cage in her head sprung open. *I'd just like to give,* she'd told Kadra her first night in Edessa. But she'd been wrong. The only people who thrived were those who *took*. She glanced at her shaking hands. *Then I can take too.*

She gave Helvus a brilliant smile. "Why not?"

"I knew we could come to an agreement." His voice slickened. "I have to say your performance for Tetrarch Kadra was something."

"Well, I perform every day." She laughed. Her voice hardened. "Let me show you."

She gripped the hand on her shoulder and wrenched it sideways. Before Helvus could yelp, she pressed his face into a torn cushion and gripped his head. One heartbeat and she stuck her thumb on the edge of a broken vase. Another and she wiped it over *herar.*

Then, she plunged into his head.

Opening her eyes to a meticulously organized library, she grinned. *Why, thank you, Helvus.* Sifting through tomes from five months past, she pulled out one simply titled "Jovian." The world dissolved.

He could never get used to seeing these corpses shatter. Helvus picked his teeth in front of Sidran Tower, watching rain sweep away the blood leaking from Jovian's body.

"Pack him up."

The two goons who'd volunteered shuffled forward, looking frightened. At his impatient glare, they wrapped the corpse in sackcloth, then stood there, fidgeting.

"Are you waiting for me to carry it?" he demanded. "You wanted to be trusted. This is a crucial task. We'll have others like it, and I'll enlist better people if you're incapable."

After much gagging, the fools hefted the body between them. Thunder rumbled, and one of them cast an apprehensive look at the sky.

"We're fine. They'll ensure it." He held the door open for the men to enter Sidran Tower, leading them toward the broom closet on the first floor. Squeezing inside, he prized open the trapdoor that supposedly led to the cellar.

"Seventeen steps to the bottom, so count carefully," he warned.

Angling, the body downward, the men descended, counting in whispers. He shut the trapdoor behind him. An hour later they emerged in an alley outside the Academiae with no vigile or magus the wiser.

"Bury the body under a few bookcases. Be quiet about it, so the brother doesn't wake."

"Guildmaster," one of the goons stammered. *"How does this help the Guild?"*

"Anything that threatens the scuta threatens us and threatens our clients."

The men nodded, evidently not understanding. Pity, but he'd still have to kill them. He wiped his hands. One night and three bodies.

She withdrew from Helvus's head with a gasp. *I knew it.*

Her fingers trembled violently, the memory of Jovian splattered across the cobblestones as vivid as Helvus's assertion. *Anything that threatens the scuta threatens us and threatens our clients.* The scuta that made no sense, the Metals Guild that manufactured them, Helvus staging the suicides of Petitors, and his mysterious clients. *They're the killers.*

"You fucking bitch!" Helvus roared.

She stepped back in time to dodge his wide swing, right as the study door burst open. Kadra stalked out, eyes going to her.

Helvus pointed at him, breathing hard. "I won't let this go. She dared— you *dared* to Probe me." His finger stabbed the air by her face. "Make no mistake, I'm bringing a petition. You're going to the mines, you northern, ill-bred—"

"Guildmaster Helvus, I don't know what you mean." Sarai's face was a picture of distress. "I only caught you when you tripped, so your head wouldn't hit the floor. Probing without consent is a serious accusation." She turned to the Guildsmen, all of who'd been in the study. "Did any of you see me Probe him?" she asked earnestly.

They looked stupefied. She let the silence linger, watching Helvus turn more purple than his robes. She had to stop him from bringing a petition. She was doomed if she was Examined.

"See? You've no proof." She feigned indignation. Dropping her voice for his ears alone, she added, "So how many Petitors' corpses have you smuggled out via Sidran Tower?"

He froze. She fought a laugh. Reaching into her pockets, she emptied out the coin he'd offered. It clattered on the floor, where his men eyed it eagerly.

"I appreciate the offer, but I don't need this. Perhaps your men do." She smiled pleasantly. "Now, about this house, Guildmaster, is there any way we can change your mind?"

"You're playing a dangerous game," Helvus hissed.

"I'm actually hoping for a binding business agreement," she quoted. "What do think of forgiving the debt? It would do wonders for your reputation. Helvus the Benevolent." She spoke quietly. "Helvus the Petitor-Killer."

He paled. "You don't know what you've done. You think that knowledge gives you power? It's killed better people than you. Now you're next."

He stormed out, yelling for his Guildsmen to follow. The men stared at the aurei on the floor and each other. In a few seconds, both were gone.

Her strength drained out, leaving only bone-deep awareness of what she'd done. *Gods save me.* This was why she'd locked up her rage. There was always a cost to unleashing it.

Numb, she endured Decimus's gratitude, refusing when he offered her Jovian's scutum in recompense. "I couldn't, your brother must have waited months for this."

A long while later, she excused herself to head outside. Untethering Caelum, she realized she was shaking. To enter the sanctum of another's head was a dangerous talent that demanded prudence. Its abuse carried severe punishment. If Helvus brought a petition—which he still might—she'd go to the mines. *I really fucked up.*

Quiet footsteps drew close. She hadn't been able to face Kadra since his reappearance from the study. Now, she had no choice. Turning, she stared at the ground, silent.

She spoke first. "I shouldn't have done it. I don't have any excuses. And, believe me, I'm aware of what I'm facing." She squared her shoulders. "If you're going to dismiss me from office before Helvus brings a petition, I don't blame you."

"Why would I do that when you're doing so well?"

Truth. She finally looked at him. His hard face didn't look the least bit angry. "I dug into Helvus's head against his will!"

"Unorthodox, but I'm the last person who'd take issue with you flouting the law."

"This isn't breaking out debt-slaves! I abused my power!"

"Or should it always have been used this way?" He tipped his head toward a tearful Decimus in the doorway. "Would Helvus have listened if you'd asked nicely?"

She recognized the echo of her own retort to Cisuré after Harion's assault. *So you were listening.* "If everyone did as I just did—" She broke off with a sound of frustration, realizing he had her cornered. "Damn it, Kadra!"

"*There* you are." Triumph laced the gravel of his voice.

She stared as lines crinkled at the corners of his eyes, cruelty vanishing in favor of what looked startlingly like delight. Kadra had always been stunning to her in the way of an Arsamean wolf, and just as dangerous. But *this* man was devastating.

"This is why I chose you." He was so close; she could see the splash of ink on his jaw. "*This* is who I saw at the Robing."

"Someone with more anger than brains?"

"Someone who could tear down a country."

She withdrew. "It all comes back to what I can do for you, doesn't it? Well, Kadra, I'm inches from being sent to the mines. That's what trying to tear anything down gets you."

"You won't." From his lips, it was a foregone conclusion.

"I just saw Helvus and his men drag Jovian through a passage in Sidran Tower! He's up to his eyes in the Petitor murders. Even you might be out of your league."

Kadra didn't look surprised. "Helvus is powerful. So am I."

"Is that what I'm supposed to do?" she asked bitterly. "Hide behind powerful men?"

"Use me." His voice was hypnotic. "I'll shield you."

Her heart hummed fiercely. "Why?"

He spoke with quiet gravity. "You have power here too. Use mine until you find yours. Give everyone no choice but to hear you."

She couldn't help laughing. "That must be so easy for a man to say. Powerful people like you have always made people like me lace ourselves into subservient personalities in order to survive. Then you blame us when they become a second skin."

"I'm not blaming you." The words caressed her cheek, prompting an involuntary shiver. "I'm saying that there is nothing wrong with your rage. And I will stand behind you when you choose to exercise it."

Stunned, she searched for words and failed. Something dangerous and powerful beat in her chest, a trapped bird begging to be set free. She'd yearned to hear *those* words for eighteen wretched years.

Her breath wreathed her face in shaky exhales. "Does this mean I'm choosing you?"

His smile widened. "Not unless you say so."

Inches from his too-hard, cruel face, she realized she wasn't as stoic as she'd thought. Arsamea had frozen her emotions, but this city and this man made them blaze, and she *yearned* to knot her hands in his black hair and pull him to her and grit out that he haunted her head, had stalked her nightmares, and that she'd do anything to know who he was, so she could decide whether to rip his heart out of his chest or give him hers.

Instead, she held out her hand and watched his larger one enclose it. "You have a deal."

CHAPTER
FIFTEEN

Sarai had joined hands with one of the Wretched.

Helvus hadn't come knocking in the five days since she'd Probed him, either because he didn't want her talking about what she'd seen, or because Kadra was looming over her shoulder more than ever.

Temples throbbing under the noonday sun, she transcribed their last case of the day: two street rats accused of stealing bread. In a test of their bargain that he'd shield her, she'd lied to the irate baker's face that the girls hadn't taken the bread and witnessed Kadra's rare smile once again as he'd sided with her, breaking his thus-far ironclad rule of not lying as if their bargain mattered more.

As the bazaar emptied, she snuck glances at him smoothly offering the baker an aurei's recompense for his lost loaves. Walking past the young bread-thieves, something fell from his hands with a pickpocket's stealth. The younger one examined the pouch of aurei that had materialized in her hands with bafflement. The other gaped as Kadra angled his head toward the bazaar's exit. Her grip on her pen slackened, ink blotting the verdict at the realization that Kadra had just slipped the children enough aurei to buy bread for years with no one else the wiser.

Rumor says he was a street rat, found in an alley as an adolescent. Her heart twisted at the memory of Cisuré's comments. *Tetrarch. Murderer. Street rat.* None of the titles fit.

The urge to clear her mind was so strong that upon Cisuré's invitation to grab a drink while their Tetrarchs conferred—without any broken noses this time, she'd specified—Sarai accepted.

Dinner was a lively affair. Anek shared tales of a bizarre case that week—a man who'd insisted that he was one of the Naaduir reborn—Cisuré shuddered after having visited Edessa's outskirts for the first time—"it's *filthy*"— and Harion cracked lewd jokes the deeper he got into his amphora. Sarai was the issue.

"You've been scowling at your soup for an hour." Cisuré touched her elbow when Anek went to refill their plate. "Is something wrong? Has Kadra been piling work on you?"

Harion let out a drunken chuckle. "Is that all he's doing?"

Sarai set down her spoon. "It's just a case." Relating the morning's encounter with the bread thieves, she omitted her lying and focused on Kadra's donation. "Just thinking of the children."

Cisuré stared at her plate, features tight.

A serpentine smile played on Harion's lips. "Are you sure it's the *children* you're thinking of and not our national madman?"

A muscle below her eye twitched. "Yes."

"If you say so. Now, calm down and don't cause another scene," he added when her jaw tightened. "Gods, you can take the barmaid out of the bar, but she'll bring the bar with her."

She was seconds from dousing him in soup when Anek sat down, effortlessly projecting their voice.

"By the way, lecher, I've just run into three women who each insist that you're sleeping with them and that the others are lying. They're locked in a squabble outside, if you'd care to sort it out. There's a crowd gathering."

Sarai snorted as Harion turned a becoming shade of green and raced outside. She mouthed her thanks to Anek when Cisuré spoke, looking serious.

"There's no reason to be conflicted. Kadra didn't help those children." Ice seeped into her voice. "He bought their goodwill, and everyone else's."

"No one saw him do it. It was a fluke that I—" She jumped when Cisuré's fist hit the table.

"Kadra deprived those children of proper, soul-building work. Like you had. Now they'll blow through that money and always expect a handout. *That's* who he is."

A cool silence descended over their corner table. Sarai stared at her oldest friend in stupefaction. Anek contemplated their throwing knife, brow furrowed. Surprise flickered on Cisuré's features like she hadn't expected the reaction.

"It may sound harsh," she added hastily. "But Tetrarch Aelius says—"

Anek groaned. "Please stop there. You can pontificate on Tetrarch Aelius another night."

Cisuré reddened. "You say that, but you'd be kneeling at his feet, if he were here."

"I would. But because he's a Tetrarch, not a god."

Cisuré's chest swelled. Before she could launch into a tirade, Anek placed a few denarii on the table and patted her shoulder in farewell, nodding to Sarai as they left. Cisuré's features flushed in anger.

Sarai expelled a long breath. She hadn't expected Cisuré to stay the same after four years, but her diminished empathy was a bitter surprise. Time truly was the cruelest of the gods.

"You know Kadra's insane, right?" Cisuré whispered after a moment.

"Of course."

"I just thought . . . for a moment, you seemed intrigued. He didn't give *you* that coin, you know. There's no need to identify with those girls."

"That was the furthest thing from my mind!"

Cisuré's lips formed a thin line. "I know how you get about these things—"

"Don't."

"He's not the sort of man who would have rescued you in Arsamea, and he won't now!" At Sarai's look, Cisuré took her hands. "Tossing money at a street rat doesn't make him a Saint."

"I'm *havïd* well aware of that!" She struggled to keep the anger from her voice, and Cisuré flinched. "Do you really think I'd paint him as a Saint after *one* deed? You—"

"It's so easy for him to manipulate you. A show of righteous anger or—"

"Please, just don't."

"*Listen,* I—"

"Don't say it," Sarai snapped. "If you think I'm gullible, fine. But don't announce it to the tavern."

"You keep getting angry." Tears welled in Cisuré's eyes. "It's such a destructive emotion."

Sarai rested her head in her hands. "I'm sorry. I'll go."

"No! Just listen to me." Cisuré sniffed. "Four years ago, seeing you . . . like that, you can't imagine how hard it was for me. I could have chosen anger then, but I didn't. And I . . . attended one of Tetrarch Aelius's trials. The plaintiff was awful, accusing the Tetrarchy of all sorts of crimes. He even pulled out a blade. Kadra would have burned him alive, but Tetrarch Aelius didn't respond to the provocation. He simply ordered him to be removed from the court. And I knew that this was a good man, a *safe* man. But you can't say the same about Kadra. His legacy is blood and ugliness. You shouldn't forget that."

"I haven't." The trouble was that she didn't care.

Perhaps she and Cisuré weren't so different. In some small way, she did see Kadra as the embodiment of the sort of justice she'd hoped for growing up, while painfully aware that he was a powerful manipulator. Cisuré saw safety in Aelius because he was the very opposite of Marus. She stifled a groan. *Gods, we're nutcases.*

"Have you found anything?" Cisuré ventured timidly.

Helvus and Jovian flashed to mind. She shook her head.

The other girl winced. "It's been a month and a half."

"I'm trying. Temperance and Time, I feel like I've aged a year since I came here."

"You'll be fine. You've always been strong." Cisuré hugged her. "Find something to throw Kadra in the mines, and we'll toil away at this job until we're old and gray."

Disquiet crept down her spine. "Do you still think he's involved in the Petitor deaths?"

"He's a monster." Cisuré looked like she couldn't believe Sarai had asked the question. "That's what monsters do."

After she'd left, Sarai stared at her plate, wondering if she'd fallen into an age-old trap in thinking that this monster might be different. A thousand different glimpses of him swam behind her eyes. Sardonic, yet never insulting to her. Perennially amused but rarely showing genuine humor. The deep, quiet way he spoke to her that felt almost tender.

"If only that were true," she whispered. "If only that were true."

A raucous laugh sounded from a nearby table as the people there rose to leave. She prepared to do the same when one of the men clapped another's shoulders.

"Same time tomorrow, Martinus?"

"Why not?" A stocky man with an impressive beard helped himself to a wheel of cheese.

She froze. *Martinus.* The vigile who'd burned her records. *Hairy as a northerner*, the archivist had said. The man before her would be at home in Arsamea.

Without further thought, she sat at his table. "Vigile Martinus? Do you have a moment?"

"*Former* vigile," he said genially, then took one look at her robes and bowed low, brushing crumbs off his tunic. "Petitor Sarai, a pleasure."

She knotted her shaking fingers. "I had a few questions on a case before Tetrarch Kadra's time. The Sealed Records archivist recommended you."

His chest puffed up. "That's kind of him. What can I help you with?"

"What do you know of the Sidran Tower Girl?"

He sighed. "Ah, the investigation that cost me my career. I heard you weren't from Edessa. She's a legend here." He dropped his voice. "You're this Quarter's Petitor, so you may as well know, but she isn't a dead one either."

Sarai tensed. "Hold on. You knew—" She stopped before she could give herself away. "The Sidran Tower Girl's alive?"

"Only a few vigiles and healers knew back then. Everyone else got the same story for procedural reasons."

"You couldn't have her assailant know she was alive."

He looked pleased. "Exactly. Thing is, she couldn't remember how it happened, and Tetrarch Othus forbade a Probe."

Because he knew Kadra was there that night. "Wouldn't searching her memories have been the easiest way to find the culprit?"

He shook his head. "Tetrarch Othus, Elsar bless him, was never one to reveal the workings behind his orders. Few days later, he told us she was a pleasure worker and to cease investigation." Martinus sat back in his chair. "He'd just lost his Petitor, so I figured it was the grief talking, but then he asked for her records. I brought them over, and he up and threw them into his fireplace and blamed me for it."

"Why . . ." She struggled to speak past the ache in her throat. "Why close the case?"

Martinus shrugged. "It's a classic tale. Working girl sleeps with some wealthy scion, gets jilted, and goes to the extreme in a display of petulance. It happens. I'm not saying that made it right. But he had his reasons. That case was cursed."

"How?"

"Every healer that touched that girl and all the vigiles who questioned her vanished the day before he closed it."

Fear swallowed her whole. She undid her suddenly tight collar. "They died?"

"Fled the city. Not so much as a parting letter. It was eerie enough that I didn't object when he wanted to stop investigating. But I became the only one who knew she was alive." Martinus stared at his plate. "Next day, Othus was gone too. And I bundled the girl off."

"How did Othus die?"

He winced. "Bludgeoned to death in an alley. The damage was extensive. Hands in pieces. The Lugens couldn't begin to guess at what happened."

I can. Chilled, she swallowed. "I heard rumors that . . . Tetrarch Kadra could have been involved."

To her surprise, he laughed. "I doubt it. He didn't get along with his old man, but he was furious at his death."

"There weren't any suspects?"

"Tetrarch Othus was too powerful for a mere criminal to have taken him down. A foreign spy was our best guess, but there's practically no catching those." He hesitated. "Petitor Sarai, I don't know what Othus was hiding or why he used me as a scapegoat. I didn't want to damage his name, so I accepted the blame. But I will say, there was something odd. He made every person in the know swear not to tell Tetrarch Kadra that the Sidran Tower Girl had survived. Refused to include him in the investigation."

Slowly, as if manipulated by some magic, her head swiveled to Martinus. *That can't be right.* But the words crescendoed in her head, ripping through her nerves. Because there was only one reason why Othus would have kept the truth from Kadra. Only one person who couldn't know that she had survived the Fall.

The man who'd pushed her.

"No." It came out as a croak.

"Oh yes. Elsar only know why, but Othus was never kind to Kadra. Great Tetrarch but not much of a father." He gave her a stern look. "Don't you go telling Tetrarch Kadra either."

"I won't." Her voice was strung tight, inches from unraveling. "Thank you for your time, Martinus. And for what it's worth, I don't think Tetrarch Othus deserved your loyalty."

Insisting on paying for his meal, she kept up a serene facade until she left the tavern. Then, she emptied her stomach on the grass.

Tetrarch Othus made every person in the know swear not to tell Kadra. Spitting onto the ground, she braced herself against a tree. *He wouldn't have harmed a fourteen-year-old girl.* But hadn't she heard his voice while bleeding out? Hadn't she seen ample proof of his sadism? *He's a monster. That's what monsters do.* Cisuré had been right.

"Damn you," she spat, pressing the heels of her hands into her eyes. In the distance, the citadel housing the Academiae rose high, Aoran Tower a dark cudgel in the west. "You manipulative, violent bastard."

She didn't know how long she stood there, hunched over, until approaching voices made her retreat to where she'd tied Caelum.

The Tetrarchy approached the tavern in full regalia. Cassandane smiled weakly at something Tullus said, the deep shadows under her eyes saying that she'd prefer to be anywhere else. Aelius inclined his head graciously at passersby and took a few hands when people sidled up to greet him. And there *he* was at the back of the group. The Tetrarchy's black sheep. The statues of former monarchs on Edessa's city walls showed more expression.

A deep, slow-burning anger burgeoned until it eroded her numbness. She yearned to plow her fist into his face until that aristocratic nose shattered. But there were better ways to hurt him. Mounting Caelum, she dug in her heels and sped off. Steps from the front gates of Aoran Tower, she dismounted, breathing hard.

Think. Look at the facts. Kadra had known she was alive when he'd ordered for her to be given a new face. Why had Othus lied to him about her death?

Because he knew Kadra did it. She laughed bitterly. To spare him jail, he'd destroyed the records and turned her into a dead prostitute, rather than have his homicidal foster son learn of her survival. He'd most likely bribed the healers and vigiles into leaving and keeping her survival a secret. An edict they'd all have kept after he and his Petitor had died. And as for Martinus, who seemed incorruptible and obedient to his Tetrarch, Othus had simply ruined his career. And she'd passed into legend.

Then why would Kadra kill Othus and his Petitor despite those efforts?

She didn't care. He'd ruined her life. She'd destroy his. Sarai stared at Aoran Tower, trying to find the strength to storm in and ransack it. Bile hit her tongue again as the smooth fabric of Kadra's robes slid across her skin. Undoing the buttons, she threw them on the ground and pulled out her key.

"Petitor Sarai." A figure detached itself from the shadows on the cobblestone path. She brandished the key in front of her, a poor weapon.

Gaius raised his hands in surrender. "I apologize for intruding." He sighed. "This is the last thing Tetrarch Kadra would want, but I can't sit by. Do you really believe that he's behind the Petitor deaths? Does what you've seen of him match with that?"

Fear spiked fast. "Were you listening to Martinus and me? Have you been following me?"

"Not intentionally, alright? I heard Othus's name and figured you were asking about the rumors. And you're clearly upset so—"

"Why are you watching me?"

He looked uncomfortable. "Tetrarch Kadra's orders, but it's to keep you safe!" he added hurriedly when her hands formed fists. "Helvus has you in his sights. Half the men in that tavern were Metals Guildsmen, and you were isolated. If you die—"

"Kadra gets blamed," she finished. "You want to know what sort of man I've seen? I—" She swallowed, close to tears.

You've always been strong, Cisuré had once said ruefully. *Perhaps too strong.* But that wasn't true. She wasn't strong so much as capable of numbing herself to the worst and watching every blow land with wry fatalism. She'd buried the parts of herself that hurt and raged, turning wary and self-contained. It had worked for years. Until *him*.

She'd disliked him, even while reluctantly admiring his knifelike mind, tightly leashed control, and the way his every movement was imbued with the unconscious grace of a man accustomed to violence. Part of her had taken quiet pride in the moments he called her *his* Petitor, in their silent agreement on the law's malevolence. And now she only had herself to blame for having fallen too deep.

"I can't tell how much of him is real and how much is a façade that's duped everyone into fawning over him," she bit out, on the outermost edge of her restraint.

"Has he ever sought out public goodwill?" Gaius demanded. "I've worked with him since he was a fledgling iudex, mind like a steel trap even then. But I've never seen him do something purely because it would make someone like him. Have you?"

Stricken, she halted. She'd associated goodwill with his actions because it had drawn her to him. But killing the Guildsmen guarding the debt-slaves instead of jailing them, covering up her Probing of Helvus, none of that would look good for him if it came to light.

"He's one man, Petitor Sarai. He has the sharpest mind I'll ever have the privilege to know, but he is just one man. Why do you keep acting like he's Deceit himself?"

Because if he were simply a man of preternatural cunning and not an evil manipulator, then she would have no shield against *everything* she felt for him. If she allowed herself to trust in his potential innocence in the Fall and she ended up being wrong, it would destroy her.

Whatever was on her face made Gaius hurriedly take a step back and apologize for upsetting her further. After he left, she walked along the path, trying to set her head to rights. A splash of scarlet caught her attention. A statue stood at the edge of the path. She drew closer and paused in awe.

Madness etched into marble, Lord Wrath rose before her, sword aloft and pointed at an unseen enemy. Fury twisted his features into a snarl. His burnished armor shone in the moonlight, a crimson swath staining his shield.

There wasn't a more fitting guardian for Aoran Tower. Reviled and revered, Wrath held a controversial position in the High Elsar. Most saw no use for the god's favor in a civilized world. Of course, those people rarely saw how thin the veneer of civilization was. She felt a strange kinship with that otherworldly face. In the silence between midnight and dawn where truth yearned to leap off the tongue, she knelt before the statue, desperate for a confidant.

"Help me," Sarai whispered. "I . . . care for a monster. I haven't condemned him when I know that the Tetrarchy is desperate for a chink in his armor. I don't even know if my memories can be trusted"—her voice cracked—"or if I'm so angry that I've twisted everything."

His mad eyes seemed to ask if there was anything wrong with anger.

"Most would say that there is. It swallows you whole if you stare too long at it."

Righter of Wrongs. The thought abruptly entered her mind. One of Wrath's oldest titles, it stemmed from a tale in the Codices that posited him as once being Lord Justice. Having given humanity laws to aid them in serving each other, he'd grown bitter and disillusioned when they used them to fashion wars and approve atrocities. After tens of millennia, Justice had gone mad, birthing Wrath. Only one of his former appellations remained. Righter of Wrongs. Where Justice had failed, Wrath would rectify what the law lacked courage to do.

Anger but with courage and restraint. The words slid into her head. She took an unsteady breath, tears rolling down her cheeks. The gods had never spoken to her. Not the grand ways they apparently did to clerics. But as she bowed low before the god of anger, quiet erasing her turmoil, she thought that perhaps they hadn't forsaken her entirely.

CHAPTER SIXTEEN

A hard rap on the door propelled her to wakefulness.

Stumbling from bed, Sarai briefly glanced at the window. *He's early.* The moons had barely reached the night sky's summit. Her eyes were swollen, turmoil still fresh. She had *nihumb* and *zosta* active before drawing the bolt.

Kadra's gaze fell on her and lingered.

"Are we starting early?" She addressed the far wall.

A beat of silence. "Did someone hurt you?" She raised her head in surprise, and his eyes narrowed. "Tullus's Petitor again?"

Sarai debated on directing him to a mirror. "What do you need me for?" She stilled upon taking stock of the scorch marks on his robes. "Was there a strike?"

Something flickered across his face. "A Guildmaster's home."

"I'll be right down."

He looked hesitant for a moment, as though he wanted to say more. Grim lines tightened on either side of his mouth. Then, he left.

Numb, she hurried through her ablutions and joined him, their horses kicking up mud as they wove through the streets. Unless a Petitor also possessed some talent for lightning or fire, they couldn't do much post-stormfall save assisting vigiles with rescue efforts. *It must be bad if he needs me there.*

She smelt the carnage before she saw it.

The air grew thick and bitter, smoke veiling homes like low-hanging mist. The radius indicated a catastrophe worse than the one on the outskirts nine days ago. Halfway up a street, Kadra dismounted and secured their mounts, indicating that they'd walk from there. Covering her nose and mouth with her sleeve, she followed, peering through the wall of smoke. The air shifted. Her heart sank.

The ruins of a magnificent home lay before them. Flames roared across every storey despite chains of vigiles atop the roofs of neighboring domii tossing buckets of water and sand at them. Gold leaf floated in a sea of floating sparks. A column from an upper floor teetered, then crashed through two floors to shatter on the ground, opulence crumbling.

A soot-covered vigile let out a groan of relief upon seeing Kadra. "He's here!" he roared above the crackling flames.

The others scrambled off the roofs, away from the domus. Kadra placed an arm in front of her, guiding her to stand behind him.

"Don't breathe too deeply," he warned.

He raised a palm, features taut. The flames on the upper storeys faltered, their wispy tips leaning toward him. He did the same with his other hand, the blaze on the ground floor hungrily licking in his direction. Slowly, meticulously, he closed each outstretched palm, pulling them toward him as he did. The fire followed, racing over wood and upholstery to rise before him in a wall as high as the domus.

Her breath unfurled in bursts. A few vigiles staggered back in fear when the air warped into black poison. Kadra didn't flinch. Only the tight set of his jaw revealed how difficult it was. He pressed down and out until the wall of flame split into several red columns, weaker in temperature. Hands steepled and steady, he turned to his vigiles and tilted his head. Looking as awestruck as she probably did, they stumbled back to their buckets, water sloshing as they tackled the stacks of flame. She did the same, scrunching her eyes against the ensuing smoke. The air screeched and sizzled. Within minutes, all was extinguished.

Kadra dropped his hands. "Watch for embers in the upper storeys," he reminded his vigiles before turning to her.

Blood roared in her ears. "I see why you're a Tetrarch," she said without thinking.

His eyebrows rose. "You didn't before?"

"That was . . ." She trailed off. "You're terrifying. Whose domus is this?"

"Grains Guildmaster Admia."

She froze, recalling the sharp-faced woman at Aelius's convivium. Had she been inside when the strike occurred? "This fire must have been raging for hours. Why did no one call us here earlier?"

Something slithered in Kadra's eyes. Before he could respond, a vigile called to him to indicate a patch of wood about to flare up on an upper floor. She picked her way across the thick fulgurites scattered in the debris to where a gray-cloaked healer crouched, features contemplative.

"Have you found any victims?" she called.

Their expression cleared upon recognizing her robes. "Just him." They indicated a black shape at their feet.

Wisdom and Wrath. She flinched.

Tearing a strip of cloth from their bandaging supplies, the healer dampened it and passed it to her. "Wrap it over your nose and mouth. Best defense we have against esophageal burns. This strike's a bad one."

"We were only told an hour ago."

The healer snorted. "Probably because everyone from the neighbors to their servants thought it served them right. Admia and her husband"—they cast a meaningful glance at the corpse at their feet—"weren't well liked. I mean, you'd be lucky to get a crop out of her during a bad harvest. She ate well, even if it meant that the rest of Ur Dinyé didn't."

And she was paying the price now. With great difficulty, Sarai drew her eyes from Admia's husband, mouth drawn open in a terrified wail. *Just like Ennius.* "Where's Admia?"

"Haven't found her." The healer gripped the dead man's rigid outstretched arms and dragged him to a pallet, uncaring of how his flesh snagged against debris. "To think that with everything she got from the gods, she still didn't have faith! It's a wonder her home wasn't struck earlier."

Sarai bit her tongue before she said what she thought of that explanation. Circling the debris, she helped Kadra's vigiles search for its owner. Eyes stinging from the smoke, she glimpsed the glint of metal. *A scutum.* Drawing closer, she stared. Admia's fulgur scutum had burst open, molten steel trailing down the sides. Some sort of mass lay within the rod, sparks still sizzling within. She jerked away right as a sweat-drenched Gaius rounded the corner.

"And here's the last one," he muttered upon sighting the rod. "All four exploded. Great." Lifting a thick fulgurite, he gingerly prodded the scutum with it, cursing at a shower of sparks. "Wrath and cursed Ruin, of all the places for a bolt to strike, why on the rods?"

"Lightning struck the scuta? Not the house?" She spotted a twisted scrap of iron that looked to be the remnants of a steeple. "Not even the steeple?"

"That's what eyewitnesses are saying." He indicated a cluster of spectators.

Going over, she found an exhausted vigile trying to prevent an elderly man from scavenging in the rubble. Promising the man an aureus for his information, she steered him away.

"Did you witness the strike?"

"*Certo,*" he quavered. "There was a flash. A few seconds later, her house exploded. Lord Fortune spoke loudly today. The bolt targeted her. Good riddance."

"What did the flash look like? Did it hit her house?"

"No, struck all four scuta outside." He looked incredulous. "What little faith did they have for not even one scutum to shield them?"

Why hadn't lightning gone for the steeple? "Did you see Admia?"

He chuckled. "*Certo.* Screamed down the street to all and sundry that she was going to rip Helvus a new pair of holes."

Her suspicions coalesced. Helvus, the scuta, and his comment the night he'd framed Jovian's death as a suicide. *Anything that threatens the scuta threatens us and threatens our clients.*

Pressing an aureus into the old man's hands, she returned to Admia's scuta. Each one was warped, the rod's flat heads burst open to reveal a powder within. It was one thing to melt under the heat, but these scuta had combusted.

The scutum before her tilted, thudding to the ground. She stilled as the powder spilled out. Reddish-brown, it sparked in the air, and her heart dropped. *That's iron dust.* A full-body shiver reduced her legs to cotton wool. Almost everyone in Arsamea kept a little iron dust on hand when their wood got too damp or for celebratory bonfires. Because it was highly combustible.

The gods hadn't been behind this strike. Helvus had.

More dust spilled from the fallen scutum, grains picked up by the wind. Sarai shrank back. If any of it hit the smallest ember, the whole domus would go up in flames again. She didn't pause to think. Racing around the back, she pulled the cloth from her nose and mouth.

"Get out! You all need to leave!" she yelled, running to where Kadra was speaking with the healer. "You need to evacuate everyone," she wheezed, the back of her throat raw. Her collar was a manacle, her robes too much in the oppressive heat. "This place might explode again."

"Show me."

"We don't have time! There's iron dust in the scuta! It could ignite any second!"

He didn't miss a beat, voice cutting through the hubbub like an executioner's axe. "Leave the area. I want everyone three domii away," he ordered.

The healer snapped to attention, dragging Admia's husband's body toward the closest horse. Vigiles herded onlookers away, making a last sweep of the rubble.

Kadra turned to her, features pulling tight. "Sarai–"

"I need to get to Helvus," she said without preamble. "Every scutum here was stuffed to the brim with iron dust. Everyone kept talking about faith and how Admia must've been taunting the gods to deserve this, but the scuta were faulty!" Even saying it knocked the breath from her lungs. "Helvus is in danger. Admia's just lost her husband. That's motive, and she's had plenty of time for opportunity."

"I can't leave while there's a hazard here. Helvus is likely dead." He listed his head to one side, a sinister gleam in his eyes. "It's better for you that he's dead."

The words multiplied a thousandfold in her head. For an ugly second, she thought of letting it go. Helvus was no loss to the world.

"It doesn't matter." Sweat trickled into her eyes. "If he dies, every evil he's committed goes unknown and unpunished."

"So you'll save him to doom him." A glimmer of amusement crossed his face. "As you wish. He lives four streets north. But"—he had never looked grimmer—"you're on your own."

"I know."

There was a tension in him, the same hesitation she'd seen that morning. She fidgeted, knowing he was about to ignite Admia's home and contain the explosions while the iron dust burnt itself out.

She didn't meet his eyes. "Be careful."

For a moment, Kadra looked as though he'd say what seemed to be pressing on his tongue. Then, he nodded tightly. Sarai got on Caelum and, with a look at the dispersing vigiles and the madman standing before a house of death, rode north as if all ten hells were chasing her.

She counted the streets. *Please let me be in time.* A woman's bloodcurdling shriek reached her right as she turned onto the fourth. She didn't have to guess at Helvus's home. The domus rivaled Aelius's tower for size, and Helvus had seen fit to gilt-edge everything down to the doors, turning it into an overlarge gold brick.

Kadra's vigiles were already at the locked gates, slamming axes into the bars. *How'd they arrive so quickly?* The question became immaterial when another scream sounded, male this time, along with what sounded like an explosion. The gate parted after several blows. She raced inside the home, and froze when a familiar stench burned its way up her nostrils. *Blood.*

Helvus lay in a corner of the atrium, a pool of scarlet widening around him. Whatever had pierced him had obliterated the left half of his torso, remnants of his innards spilling out. She grew cold. A healer could repair crushed organs, but they couldn't regrow obliterated ones. Admia had gotten her revenge.

She turned her head at another scream. A soot-covered woman, burns lacing half her torso, struggled against Kadra's vigiles as they restrained her. Sarai's heart sank. *Admia.*

"Petitor Sarai." A gray-cloaked healer motioned her over. "She's somewhat conscious if you're ready to Probe her for the events leading to this. I can't guarantee that she'll stay awake once I start."

"Of course, I . . ." She trailed off, with a glance at Helvus's body.

Admia had committed *homicidium* today. And Helvus, for all his crimes, was a victim. Yet, if he'd known that Admia's scuta were faulty, or worse, if her scuta weren't the only faulty ones, then others could be in danger.

Sweat trailed down Sarai's temples. This was a terrible idea. She'd already Probed him once and barely gotten away with it. *But if he dies, then no one will know the truth.*

Wisdom help me. She knelt beside Helvus. "Is he conscious?"

The healer looked taken aback. "Well . . . yes, but he won't hold on for long."

She drew a deep breath. The scent of warm iron was everywhere, tugging at memories only too eager to intrude. Helvus's eyes flickered open, glazed with pain.

He glowered weakly at her. "Will . . . I . . . die?" he gurgled, blood leaking from his chest.

Swallowing, she wiped a bleeding thumb over *herar.* "I'm really am sorry," she whispered, gripping his head. And plunged in.

The world went crimson. The library of Helvus's mind was in chaos. Books and pages hung in the air, fragmenting images that trembled at her touch. She searched through the tangle until she saw an image of a scutum. All dissolved when she touched it.

"The rod will have two parts. A steel sleeve and core." Helvus announced to the hundreds of Metals Guildspeople assembled before him. *"You'll produce the sleeve, and for the Elsar's sakes, etch the runes right. I've a different group producing the core in Kirtule."*

A wiry man raised a hand. "Begging pardon, Guildmaster, but wouldn't it be faster if we make and assemble both parts here?"

He crossed the floor toward the fellow. "I pay you to work, not think." Readying to slap him, he thought better of it—damned man was too tall—and he punched him in the gut. The man doubled over with a satisfying squeak, and the others shifted nervously.

Iron dust was so much cheaper than steel. His Guild would do as told. Everyone in the south would buy his scuta without knowing about the dust core, and those two would take care of the rest.

Sarai wrenched herself out of Helvus's mind with a gasp. His breath rattled, blood spurting from the hole in his side. She didn't care.

How could you? She swallowed the scream, her shock melting into a single, terrible realization. The iron dust had transformed every lightning shield into a lightning rod. And Helvus had profited for it.

This was what Jovian and Livia, and likely even Othus and his Petitor, had died for. They'd found the truth and must have tried to warn consumers of the danger. And now, Helvus was going to take everything to the grave.

Anguish swamped her. When a Petitor Probed, only they saw the memories in question. That left the door open for people to argue that she was lying if she spoke out. The south was too eager to cite the gods for everything, and she still didn't know who Helvus's clients were. Materialization was a power reserved only for trial, but surely procedure was beyond the point here. Everyone had to know.

Removing her sweat-sodden robes, she moved on trembling legs to where Kadra's vigiles held a still-screaming Admia down. She knelt, seized by the knowledge that she was on the precipice she'd sensed during Helvus's raid at Decimus's, and, this time, she was about to irreversibly go over. Her blood sank into *astomand*. She gripped Admia's head, where the most recent page of a ledger of memories was only too easy to grasp. Sarai pulled it into the open.

Smoky figures formed in Helvus's atrium. The vigiles started, as a transparent Admia strode toward an equally see-through Helvus.

"Admia, what a surprise." Helvus sounded annoyed. *"Any reason you look dreadful?"*

"Your scutum!" Admia screamed. *"It exploded! I know iron dust when I see it. You've been lying to everyone!"*

"Don't play the innocent. No one forced you to buy one."

"My husband is dead because of you! Don't you fear the gods?"

"Why should I?" Helvus's grin held malice.

In a movement too fast to follow, he unsheathed and threw a dagger that embedded itself in Admia's gut. A croak left her as she stared at the hilt protruding from her, then her eyes hardened. One hand snuck to her pocket. As Helvus laughed, she tossed a pouch into the fireplace behind him.

He raised an eyebrow. "Really—"

The fireplace exploded. Blood and organs splattered the walls, Helvus's scream echoing through the atrium. "You—" His roar emerged as a gurgle when Admia crouched over him.

She spat on his head. "There's the rest of your iron dust."

Sarai braced herself against the ground, gasping from the effort of pulling it out. Several yards away, a rattle left Helvus, his jaw slack in horror. His eyes fluttered once, twice. Then shut.

Eyes darted from her to Helvus in a dizzying dance. She willed herself to get up, to explain, just as a roar shattered the graveyard silence.

"What the fuck?"

She stumbled to her feet and found Tullus behind her, Harion in tow. "Tetrarch Tullus, I can explain—"

His hand cracked across her face, knocking the breath from her. She staggered back, winded, as she clutched her burning cheek.

"How dare you?" Tullus spat, craggy features mottled with rage. Behind him, Harion looked delighted. "Who gave you the right to Materialize memories?"

"Enough, Tullus." Aelius appeared in the entryway, a pale-faced Cisuré in tow. Without looking at Sarai, he snapped his fingers at those tending to Admia. "Stop. Toss her in prison."

She sucked in a panicked breath. "Wait, Tetrarch Aelius, please. Admia is absolutely guilty of *homicidium*, but Helvus has committed an awful crime—" The words died when he glanced at her.

Gone was the affable Tetrarch. This was a stony-faced man in ivory robes who looked like he'd enjoy throttling her.

"Petitor Sarai, you just violated every oath you took at the Robing and humiliated a dying man in his own domus by airing out the delusions of a murderer." He looked bitterly disappointed. "I was wondering at your lack of cooperation. I see Kadra got to you."

She blanched, speaking so fast the words tumbled over each other. "Helvus warped your invention. He added iron dust to the core because that made them cheaper to produce. I *saw* the dust at Admia's home. Helvus—"

"That's *Guildmaster* Helvus to you," Tullus interjected, eyes glittering. "We've never heard of a single complaint with the scuta. What you saw was a plot to damage his reputation, and instead of punishing the perpetrator, you joined her." His voice dripped with scorn. "Evidently, an untrained Petitor can be worse than none at all. Future Robings will feel the consequences of your actions."

Terror swallowed her. "Tetrarch Tullus, I swear on all the High Elsar—"

"Another word, and I'll charge you with *calumnia*."

Blood fled from her cheeks, pooling in nerveless hands that shook hard enough to rattle her. The charge punished officials for malicious

226

prosecution with a thousand lashes. Certain death. She stared from one hard-faced Tetrarch to the other, and the bottom fell out of her stomach. They didn't believe her.

"Probe me if you must," she whispered. "Even now, hundreds of thousands of scuta are—"

Tullus's hand wrapped around her neck and slammed her against a bloodstained marble column. She choked, chest going concave.

"You still don't understand your place," he growled. "I'll fucking show you."

His fingers tightened. She could feel her windpipe closing. Spots danced in her eyes. Scrabbling, she tried to pry herself free. Cisuré made a plaintive sound of distress and stepped forward, but Tullus halted her with a furious look.

This can't be happening. She'd expected censure, would have accepted it. But not once had she foreseen such merciless disbelief. Her legs gave out, Tullus's death grip on her neck preventing her from sinking to the floor. Her lungs screamed. She fought, vaguely aware of footsteps ringing across the atrium, a figure at the edge of her dimming vision.

"Let her go." Kadra's voice was forbidding. "Now."

With a derisive laugh, Tullus released her. Slipping on the blood below, she struggled for balance and air and was about to lose both battles, when Kadra gripped her shoulders. She sucked in harsh breaths, rubbing the raw circumference of her neck.

"Like Tetrarch, like Petitor," Tullus snarled. "*Tibi gratias ago* for the summons, though this wasn't the sight I expected. Sending her to do your dirty work, Kadra?"

It was on the tip of her tongue to say that she had damn well made her own decisions when Kadra squeezed her shoulder.

"No less dirty than what your friend's been up to," he said mildly, with a glance at Helvus's corpse being moved to a pallet.

Tullus's eyes flashed. "There's no authority on which to believe those accusations. Your *girl* is deluded."

"Then you'll have no complaint if I seek authority by cutting open a scutum to see if the accusations hold true."

"Producing scuta will be slower than ever now, and you want to chop them up? You would deprive people of a shield for your ego?"

"This is *my* Quarter." Kadra's voice was soft. "Mine is the only authority here. If your friend wanted to market lightning rods as shields, he should have conned people on your land. Seeing as you don't seem to mind."

Sarai's pulse thudded at the gimlet stare Aelius leveled on Kadra.

"Let's put the issue to trial then," he said coldly. "You have a month to bring anything to support your suppositions. If you fail, the appropriate decision will be rendered."

Tullus's eyes filled with disgust when they found her. "As to the matter of *your* actions, there will be charges. When the Metals Guild files a petition, we will act on it in accordance with the law." His eyes said, *As you should have.*

A buzzing rang in her ears as both Tetrarchs stormed out. Sarai could barely bring herself to look at Cisuré. The other girl looked like she'd aged a year, new hollows under her eyes.

I'm sorry, Sarai mouthed. Cisuré's expression hardened before she left as well.

A slight movement of Kadra's head, and Helvus was unceremoniously dragged out of his home. The ridges of his spinal column peeked through the hole Admia had blown.

Four years ago, hers had probably looked similar, broken in so many places that the healers had groused that she was more work than she was worth. She realized that Kadra's hands were still on her shoulders. Withdrawing, she steadied herself against a wall, following it out of the house perfumed with blood.

She'd known that the law served the needs of the powerful. Truth and fairness were only raised for crimes by regular folk. When the wealthy butchered their way through life, the only words used were "necessary" and "profit." Justice was a game of who could tell the better story in court and pay off iudices and vigiles. But she'd hoped that the Tetrarchy was different. Because if their leaders were different heads of the same monster, then this was a land without hope.

She could still feel Tullus's fingers on her throat. A room crowded with Tetrarchs and Petitors, and only Kadra had stopped him.

A weight draped over her shoulders. Black and gold robes slid across her skin. *Speak of the Wretched and they appear.*

"Thank you for stopping him," she said hoarsely.

Something that looked oddly like conflict twisted Kadra's face and vanished. "You may regret saying that."

"Because I'm in more trouble now that you can shield me from? You're right. Perhaps it would've been better if Tullus snapped my neck." She blinked back tears. "It's ludicrous. Everyone was too scared to question Helvus, too fixated on the gods to search for a tangible explanation, or too eager to believe that everything he said was true. And despite Helvus admitting *everything* in what I Materialized, the Tetrarchy cares more about me procuring evidence illegally than what the evidence says."

Wrath save me, I'm going to be on trial. A month from now, her life could be over.

"If only Aelius and Tullus hadn't arrived, I—" She halted as Tullus's comment returned to her. *Tibi gratias ago for the summons, though this wasn't the sight I expected.*

Her blood went cold, eyes rising to the silent man across her. "Did Aelius and Tullus get here so quickly because you *asked* for them?"

Kadra watched her for a long moment. "I did."

"Why?" She didn't care that her voice had gone thin with dread.

He raised an eyebrow, silently asking her if she really didn't know. She stepped back, wanting him to speak, to banish the horrible conclusion she'd reached, but he was motionless, gaze half-calculation, half-emptiness, and all power.

"You let me come here alone on purpose," she whispered.

"I did."

Truth. There were no coincidences with Kadra. He hadn't sent any summons while riding with her or in the midst of the chaos at Admia's domus, meaning he'd sent for Aelius and Tullus beforehand. But for Kadra to have warned them to get to Helvus, meant he'd known the Guildmaster was in danger, and that could only mean . . .

"You knew," she said in dawning horror. "You knew about the iron dust in the scuta before I found out. But you needed proof." The conclusion crystallized and stabbed deep. "So you sent me off, knowing that I'd be angry and foolish enough to fish it out of Helvus's or Admia's head for you—" She stopped before her voice cracked. "You godsdamned manipulator."

Kadra's features were devoid of emotion. "Predicting how you'll act isn't manipulation."

Her blood boiled. She couldn't even blame him. She'd done it all herself. "So this was your plan. To rid yourself of Helvus and a Petitor you didn't want."

"To see if you'd let him die a victim or a villain."

"Then *ask!*" She'd thought they'd built enough of a relationship for that. "Why the fuck would you drag out two other Tetrarchs and get me strangled? Was this some sort of test—" She froze, thinking back to the vigiles and healers who'd already been waiting outside Helvus's in time for her arrival. How no one had been surprised at Aelius's and Tullus's appearance.

No. "Was this a test?" she whispered.

The cruel edge to his smile was all the answer she needed. And her control shattered.

She didn't notice herself pushing away from the wall or closing the distance between them. She barely felt her hands fist in his robes, uncaring of his vigiles' wide-eyed stares. All she saw was the arrogant face above her.

"You godsdamned bastard," she snarled. "I've given you no cause to suspect my loyalty. From the Robing to every bazaar we've adjudicated in, have I not *consistently* held to my duties as your Petitor?" She wanted to scream that she'd had every chance to rat him out to Aelius and chosen not to, but he wouldn't care. She'd only been a tool to him. Today had proven it.

Kadra tipped his head down at her. "Doing your duty before a crowd is simple. Today, you went against half the Tetrarchy."

Sarai lost what little breath she had left. "This was about your game of choosing you over the Tetrarchy? You had me earn the ire of two Tetrarchs for *that*?"

"Would you have let Helvus die as a victim if it meant keeping their goodwill?" he asked softly.

She knew he could see the answer on her face. Her hands ached with the desire to hurt him, to make him feel as small and foolish as he had her.

Releasing his robes, she laughed. Short, bitter, as ugly as his. "You think you're better than the rest of the Tetrarchy? You aren't. To them, everyone is expendable to law and procedure. And everyone is expendable to you, period. If the law deserves to be torn down, then so do you for treating your *allies* like puppets."

He'd stilled when she called herself his ally, but she broke in as his lips parted.

"Still, I'm a quick study, Tetrarch Kadra. So rest assured I've understood everything you sought to impart." Another half-step forward and they were a breath apart. "The law of this land is wrong. Its lawmakers are even worse. Tullus is a violent bastard." She checked each lesson off on her fingers before balling up the robes he'd draped over her and throwing them to the ground. "And you're the worst of them all, you *havïd* sadist."

Shaking with hurt and fury, she mounted Caelum. But as she pivoted, the man watching her with what looked like pride did the strangest thing.

He smiled.

CHAPTER
SEVENTEEN

She wandered the city. Thinking, trying not to think. Life outside a Petitor's strict schedule seemed a busy, beautiful thing. Coin to be earned, a thousand ways to spend it, all manner of books, clothes, foods, and lands that seemed close under a sunset that made everything feel possible.

Perhaps she could run away. Leave behind vengeance and people who saw her as a tool. Before the thought would have felt like a betrayal of her younger self, but she was so horribly tired. Perhaps the Fall didn't matter, and she should have moved on with her life as Cisuré had said. Maybe then, she wouldn't be facing charges for abusing her power.

Her head hurt. She wished she could down Telmar's entire supply of *ibez*.

Hours after an unsuccessful attempt at eating, she squinted at a Tower Gate. The letters etched at the top swam in her watery vision.

"This is the Favran Tower Gate," one of the magi standing guard finally muttered in exasperation when she rose on her toes to decipher the lettering.

Cassandane's tower. Entering, she walked beside Caelum, kicking a pebble across the cobblestone path. Ahead, Favran Tower was at least a hundred and sixty-five yards high. Vines and flowers curled possessively over the orange-red limestone surface exterior. Wine red, they perfumed the night breeze with traces of cherry and mint. The petals were an exact match for Cassandane's crimson robes.

At the sound of hooves behind her, she turned to find the Tetrarch herself, dark hair tumbling loose about her shoulders. Looking surprised upon sighting her, Cassandane dismounted.

"Petitor Sarai." A dimple flashed her cheek when she smiled. "What brings you to my tower?"

Sarai bowed. "I was admiring the flowers."

"Naiya's Orchids. Hardy little things." Cassandane plucked a low-hanging bloom and handed it to her. "I've tried a few varieties, but nothing grows as well as these beauties."

"They're lovely." Sarai traced the soft petals with wonder. Arsamea hadn't had much in the way of flowering plants. "Is there a reason for the name?"

Cassandane's eyes brightened. "It's an old tale. Centuries ago, when matters were quite sour between Ur Dinyé and the island nation of Kashyal, there was an Kashyalin debt-slave, Naiya." She leaned against a column bracketing the entryway to her tower. "Now, Naiya understandably has little interest in being a slave and escapes one night. But as the gods would have it, she's mistaken as the subject of an ancient prophecy, a heavens-sent demon master, and captured by a bounty hunter."

Sarai whistled. "And does she escape the hunter?"

"Unfortunately not. And she discovers that our hunter is the demon himself. He knows that the nation that controls Naiya will turn him into a tool of war and he wants none of it. So he resolves to kill her."

"But she isn't the demon master."

"Ah, but he doesn't believe that."

"So he kills her, and these orchids bloom from her blood?" Sarai guessed.

Cassandane gave her a reproving look. "They fall in love."

She winced. "So it's *that* kind of story."

"And the first flowers he brought her were these," Cassandane continued, undeterred. "Hence the name."

Sarai held Caelum back from attempting to eat the orchids. "What happened with the prophecy?"

"That's a much longer story." The Tetrarch laughed, before casually adding, "I've been wanting to meet you."

"I'm honored, Tetrarch Cassandane."

"More specifically, I wanted to meet the Petitor the Metals Guild has just put an internal bounty on."

The ease of their conversation gave way to a sudden, thrumming tension, the laughing storyteller vanishing in favor of a steely-eyed Tetrarch, who looked just as ruthless as the rest of the Tetrarchy.

"What do you mean?" Sarai whispered.

"Any Guildsman who separates your head from your body will be rewarded for it."

Sarai's legs would have given out if she wasn't holding Caelum's reins. "I see." Her voice didn't shake. Her nerves had been cauterized. "I broke the law. There's always a price."

"I won't comment on whether you should have Materialized that memory or not, but the fact remains that the law won't protect you now." Cassandane's gaze dropped to the bruises Tullus had left on Sarai's neck, and her face closed. "But I can."

"I don't understand."

"There's a Tribune in Kirtule who's searching for a scribe. I can smuggle you out of the city tonight. No one would find you. Outside Edessa, the Metals Guild doesn't know what you look like. You're in dangerous waters, and I don't want to see you drown. You showed strength at the Robing, standing up to Kadra."

"I haven't had an inch of peace since." Sarai's shoulders slumped. "He got what he wanted. He'll be rid of me one way or the other now."

"If Kadra wanted to be rid of you, he had every chance at the Robing," Cassandane said matter-of-factly. "But he's gone to extraordinary lengths to keep you close, and I'm not the only one who's noticed."

"I made myself useful, and I've served my purpose."

"You live with him. He barely lets you out of his sight. Word in his Quarter is that he dotes on you. Those aren't the actions of a man who doesn't want you here. You may very well know him better than I do, because throughout our careers, I've never seen him show any hint of partiality. Not until you."

I can't hear this. "Trust me, Tetrarch Cassandane. He doesn't care."

Moonlight struck Cassandane's face and sank into the tense lines of her forehead. "Petitor Sarai, last night, during the Tetrarchy's triweekly meeting, Helvus visited us to discuss you. He complained of being Probed without consent." Cassandane looked weary when Sarai flinched. "Don't tell me if that's true or not. The gist of our resolution was that an investigation would be opened into your abuse of power. Helvus is a powerful businessman. You would have been pulled before the four of us and Probed by one of your colleagues. If you were guilty, you'd not only be dismissed from the position but also be barred from Edessa with at least a year in the mines," she finished grimly. "Then, in a few hours, Helvus is dead."

Sarai's breath seized as the implication slammed into her. "But Admia killed Helvus."

"Stormfall had ended hours ago. There wasn't a cloud in the sky. But my people report that a lightning bolt, just one, came out of nowhere and blasted Admia's home to embers."

She went cold, recalling Kadra's raw power. *Of course.* That would explain why the bolt had targeted Admia's scuta. He'd known they would explode, and known that Admia would go after Helvus. *He knew there was iron dust in there from the start.* Had he hidden it from the public because he didn't know who Helvus's clients were?

Cassandane sighed. "Admia was unpopular, but that doesn't change that she was a woman with dreams and a husband she loved deeply. And now she faces a Summoning."

"I tried." Sarai's voice was hoarse. "I wanted to get to Helvus in time to stop her." She realized that Kadra had given Admia a head start. "I didn't know until it was too late."

"Petitor Sarai, you don't belong here," Cassandane said gently. "I knew it when I saw you balk at burning that man at the Robing. You'll lose pieces of yourself the longer you stay. Kadra's playing a dangerous game, and for some reason, he's placed you at the center. Save yourself. The Metals Guild's furor will die without a target."

Stricken, Sarai stared at the ground. *She isn't wrong.* To stay here in the face of charges for abuse of power was foolishness, and she'd partaken too much of that fruit already.

She'd never believed herself capable of cowardice. But right now, she wanted nothing more than to leave the Sidran Tower Girl in the past, abandon Ur Dinyé's south to scuta that would kill them, and toss aside a man who had only sought to use her.

At her silence, Cassandane's features grew pinched. "Take the chance. I'd prefer not see another Petitor die."

There it is. Every time she wanted to leave, there it was. "Are you . . ." She took a deep breath. "Tetrarch Cassandane, are you saying the Petitor deaths haven't been suicides?"

Something remarkably like fear passed over the Tetrarch's face. "There's nothing keeping you here."

"You're right." Tears blurred her vision. "But I can't sit back when I *know* that someone's about to be hurt. I wish I could ignore and focus on myself and be as practical as you are. My life would be the smoother for it. But I don't know *how*. Thousands of lives have been and will be ruined by the Metals Guild. I can't let that keep happening. If there's a chance I can win this trial, I have to try."

"There's no chance, Petitor Sarai." A bleak edge underlay the observation. "Not with these people. Only death."

She nodded. "I'm familiar with those odds, Tetrarch Cassandane."

"Then if they ever appear too great, come to me." The older woman looked grim. "The offer stays open."

If she did go, then all was truly lost. "Thank you."

CHAPTER
EIGHTEEN

Sarai woke to a note from Kadra asking her to meet him in his office at the vigile station and to Gaius waiting outside Aoran Tower's wards to accompany her.

Dismounting at the station, she ignored the vigiles' whispers, everyone apparently aware of the bounty. Rather than have the grace to look abashed, a group in her path took her dour glare as an invitation to swarm her. Most were familiar faces that had ignored her for a month and a half, that had watched Tullus strangle her as though it were a spectacle.

Sarai crossed her arms. "Yes?"

Gaius looked nervous at the scowl in her voice. "Let me take you to—"

"Not bad yesterday," a woman said. "I thought you'd be corrupt."

"A month and a half of trials wasn't enough to prove the opposite?"

She shrugged. "We had to see what you were made of. Plenty have tried to get into Tetrarch Kadra's good graces to spy on him."

Sarai didn't mention that she'd agreed to do the same. "So watching Tullus strangle me was the best way of determining if I was a spy?"

The woman looked like she'd swallowed a lemon.

"My apologies." Gaius gave Sarai a pacifying smile. "We should head to Tetrarch—"

"Still, Tetrarch Kadra must trust you now to install you here permanently," another vigile interjected.

Her eyes narrowed. "Permanently?"

"To work in his office on occasion, as he does. We were wondering why he kept trotting you out to marketplaces every day."

A muscle worked in Sarai's jaw. "Trotting me out," she repeated evenly.

"You've gone through six months of cases in six weeks," the vigile blithely continued. "It's quite something."

The smile Sarai gave Gaius was all teeth. "That *certo* is."

Gaius hurriedly steered her into the station. Leading her down a marble-tiled hallway bordering a courtyard, he indicated the door at the very end.

"That's Tetrarch's Kadra's office. We'll need to knock down a few walls to build yours. Until you're safe, you'll be working mostly in there."

"How did he work before me?"

"After trials, he'd sequester himself to record judgments into the evening. He barely slept." Gaius shook his head. "I don't know how he did it."

She didn't either. His work ethic was inhuman. She tipped her head to one side. "You've known Kadra eight years?"

"More or less. Why?"

"Good. You can clear this up. How many more throttlings lie in my future?"

He blanched. "Petitor Sarai, Tetrarch Kadra would not have intended for Tetrarch T—"

"Tullus aside, I haven't forgotten Ennius," she cut in, and he quieted. "When I became a Petitor, it wasn't with the understanding that I'd be burning a man alive. Or that I'd be completing six *months* of trials in six weeks. Is there a reason Kadra's trying to kill me?"

"I'm sure he's ensuring that you gain experience in a variety of—"

"Throttlings? Tutorials on how to torture a man?"

Gaius wisely refrained from saying anything else. He drew her through a network of corridors, pointing out the bunks the vigiles used between shifts, a well-stocked pantry, and casks of wine that looked like they saw regular use. Slicing a few strips of smoked meat, he kept up a dizzying stream of chatter on everything from the state of affairs in Kadra's Quarter—generally calm—to more of Helvus's misdeeds.

"You've done a lot of good," he assured her. "We tried to put Helvus away for years, but Tetrarch Tullus kept springing him out. His reputation's finally gotten a hit because you Materialized that memory." He gave her an approving look. "Even Tetrarch Tullus can't waive a charge of *homicidium* after that."

She accepted a slice of meat. "Tullus waives *homicidium* charges?"

"Oh yes. Manufactures some extenuating circumstance and the wealthy scion's free to go. There isn't anyone with coin who doesn't aspire to his patronage." He frowned. "Didn't Tetrarch Kadra tell you?"

"He didn't," she said slowly. "Does Kadra have his favorites?"

"Never. Bit of a closed book, except perhaps where you're concerned."

She paused mid-bite. "What's that supposed to mean?"

Gaius widened his eyes. "You live in Aoran Tower."

"There's nothing exciting about my being privy to the interior of his tower."

"The forbidden has always held an allure," he insisted. "None of us ever imagined the Tetrarch would show interest in—"

"I'm honestly sick of how much you all gossip." She fixed him with a glare. "Six months' worth of trials in six weeks, and you think I've the time to fuck him."

Sheepish, he raised his hands in surrender. "We assumed—"

"You assumed wrong." None of it meant anything. Kadra had proven it yesterday.

Gaius turned the corner into a familiar hallway, and she realized they were back where they had started. The water clock by the pillars dripped slow. Dawn was still an afterthought in the inkblot sky.

A frisson of unease snaked through her. The door to Kadra's office loomed large at the end of the hallway, the shuttered jaws of a wolf. She swallowed, recalling the less-than-flattering epithets she'd flung at him at Helvus's. Gods, she'd called him a *havïd* sadist.

Wholly unaware of her turmoil, Gaius grinned. "So are we forgiven for yesterday?"

It took a moment for his question to penetrate, but when it did, she shot Gaius a glower that had him stumbling back. Tugging down her collar, she presented the mottled violet lines circling her neck from Tullus's grip.

Red painted Gaius's cheekbones. He stared at the courtyard, then at the tiled floor, as though either could tell him what to say.

"Games, tests, your Tetrarch might think highly of them, but I don't." Her voice was icy. "Human life, human *dignity*, shouldn't be toyed with."

She left him there, the beginnings of something apologetic on his lips. Dread filled her as she closed the distance to Kadra's office. Her knock sounded too loud in the hallway's silence.

"Enter." His voice sliced across her brittle confidence.

Boots clicking on the tiles, she closed the door behind her. Behind the desk, Kadra raised his head. His office was even simpler than his study in Aoran Tower. Rolls of parchment nestled in cramped shelves along the walls. Light filtered in from a floor-to-ceiling window, occupying the left side of his room. She glimpsed the mouth of the hallway from it and realized he'd seen her conversation with Gaius.

She avoided his eyes. "I know about the bounty. I gather I'm to hide here until Admia's trial and the trial on the scuta are heard?"

He inclined his head. "If you'd like."

"I wouldn't." She couldn't work in this cramped space with him, where he could see too deep and hurt her more. "I'd prefer to work in the Hall of Records."

His cavernous gaze sought hers. She examined the floor with single-minded determination.

"Why?" he finally asked.

"Decimus and the archivist at the Hall of Records kept saying that Jovian spent almost every night in there. He was searching for something, and seeing as he was killed for knowing about the scuta being defective, he must have found out through less-illegal methods than I did."

"And his evidence would prove your case at trial." Kadra looked thoughtful. "Unless it's gone."

"Unlikely. Jovian knew he was going to die. He took the trouble to return home just to paint *modrai* over the walls, and wrote letters in Urdish when barely anyone in the south can still speak it let alone read it. He would have secreted his evidence away. I'll find it."

"Good work," Kadra said approvingly, and she stamped out a spark of pleasure. "But you still haven't told me why."

"Why I don't want to work here with you?" She pretended to think. "I'd like to keep my neck *on* my shoulders."

A faint tightening of his temples. "Is this about my being a '*havïd* sadist'?"

Her breath caught at the way he elevated the filthy curse into something dark and elegant.

"Can I work out of the Hall of Records or not?" She leaned forward, hands on his desk, before realizing her mistake. *Too close.*

Kadra's eyes narrowed, fastening on a point below her jaw and she realized she hadn't tugged her collar back up. A vein in his temple rose to prominence as he studied the bruises.

"I'll charge him with assault." Every word was a chip of granite.

Truth. She snorted. "Why? You called Tullus there. You—" She broke off before she cursed him again. "You knew he was violent."

Kadra's shoulders tensed. "He wasn't supposed to touch you."

"And does everything always go as you plan, Tetrarch Kadra?" Satisfaction filled her when his jaw clenched. "So don't bother when this wouldn't have happened if you'd—"

"I won't always be here." Kadra's features were remote. "In this job, you'll encounter hundreds like Tullus, down to diplomatic officials who'll expect you to service them to keep the peace. I can shield you from the very worst, but I won't be there every time."

"I'm aware, damn it! I know you caused the strike yesterday. You've more than kept your end of our bargain. I'm not angry because you didn't *rescue* me from Tullus!"

"Then?"

Damn him, he wasn't even denying that he'd just engineered the deaths of two Guildmasters. "How am I to work with you when you give me *nothing*?"

The tautness of his face slackened like she'd said something bewildering.

"Yesterday, if you'd told me that Aelius and Tullus were on their way, I'd have done the *same* thing, but I'd have been faster or better prepared with a scutum from Admia's home as proof. You hide, and you obfuscate, and you play *everyone* like puppets and you don't understand why I can't work with you? Kadra, you only see me as a tool."

"Never," he grit out, and she stilled. The icy intensity of the word told her that he'd tried to relegate her to that role. That he'd failed.

"Not once," he repeated.

Truth. She suddenly felt buoyant. "I see," she stammered. She didn't. She'd never been more confused.

Kadra's eyes dropped to her neck. Muttering something that sounded suspiciously like a curse, he took the material of her collar and gently drew it over the bruises.

"Work at the Hall of Records if you must, but see that a healer looks at that." His voice lowered to a rough growl. "Yes?"

"Yes," she whispered, and he nodded, fingertips brushing across her jaw.

Hunger unfurled her in with the speed of a striking snake, nearly clawing out of her skin. Flushing, she gripped the door handle for balance. His hand dropped to the desk, a disturbing intensity in his eyes as they searched her features.

She looked away. "I'll be off. There's no need for an assault charge. Try not to ignite a civil war in the Tetrarchy while I'm gone."

"Very well," he said quietly.

Twisting the handle, she ran out of his office, halting at the station's stables to drag slow, calming breaths. Yearning rippled through her at the echo of his fingertips grazing her jaw and his visible anger at her bruises. He'd killed two Guildmasters to protect her.

Gods help me. Perhaps it wasn't that he didn't care. Perhaps, just perhaps, in their equally closed-off ways, they both cared too much.

CHAPTER
NINETEEN

News of Helvus's death and Admia's imprisonment spread across Edessa like wildfire over the next few days. The particulars of both, however, didn't make the grapevine's cut. All people knew was that Admia had killed Helvus and that Sarai had Materialized his last moments and ruined his reputation. Depending on how much the owner cared for Helvus, Sarai got varying reactions at taverns. One had served her a double helping of chicken stew. She'd gotten a plate of shit in another.

Reports of the scuta being faulty were quickly dismissed as nonsense. Coupled with the fact that Aelius hadn't officially set the matter down for trial, and scutum manufacturing was paused as the Metals Guild regrouped, demand was sky-high.

She'd found out the hard way.

Making rounds throughout Kadra's Quarter, she and Gaius had stopped at homes with more than one scutum and politely requested if they could purchase it from them. She'd tottered out of the first domus soon afterward, ears ringing after a thousand bellowed curses that their lives were worth more than any amount of coin. She'd barely gotten a word in with anyone else.

"You northern folk really think you're something." A woman had beaten at her laundry like she wished it was Sarai's face. "Wait in line for your own."

"Do you know how many times these scuta have saved me?" Another had gesticulated wildly with a kitchen knife. "Who do you think you are?"

Another put it more succinctly. "Get lost, northern whore," he snarled. She quickly abandoned the idea.

"I'm starting to see why Helvus fooled everyone so easily," she groused to Gaius upon returning, dejected, to the Hall of Records.

"Stormfall is a terrifying thing to endure regularly," he explained. "For four years, the scuta have represented hope. No one likes to have that taken away. Even Tetrarch Kadra can't legally force anyone to give one up."

"At least we've Admia," she said wearily. "She saw the iron dust too. They'll have to believe it when I Materialize the evidence."

Gaius's wince said he wasn't so sure.

Days blended into a week at the Hall of Records. She scoured the Archives Jovian had frequented most, going through indexes he'd consulted and books he'd borrowed, all to no avail. Gaius hovered at her elbow in case Metals Guildsmen were hiding between the shelving, and Kadra's vigiles discreetly patrolled the entire area. Every night she emerged empty-handed.

Almost a week after Helvus's death, she snapped another of Jovian's favorite books—*The History of the Sidran Tower Girl*—shut in the Hall of Records. *This is useless.* She needed concrete proof to pair with Admia's testimony.

Just four pieces of evidence would prove everything. Something that linked the Petitor deaths together as murders, something that linked the murders to the scuta, something that proved the scuta were faulty, and something that showed Helvus's clients were behind it all. Any less and she'd reveal only part of the truth.

Mulling over what Decimus had mentioned on their first visit, she frowned, recalling that Jovian had been investigated for treason prior to his death.

Heading to the Sealed Records archive, she made her request of the archivist only for him to gape.

"Petitor Jovian's criminal record?" He looked at her like she'd gone mad. "Why would he have one?"

It was her turn to stare. "I was told that Tetrarch Aelius had sealed it after his death."

"Absolutely not." The archivist withdrew a massive index covered in spidery writing and thumbed through it. He flipped the book to show her all the entries on the month of Jovian's death. "We didn't seal anything pertaining to him."

Then why had Aelius told Decimus that he had?

"Were there any other archives Jovian frequented most?" She'd combed through the ones for missing persons, family trees, and Urd Guilds.

"I do recall seeing him in Homicidium often. He was always digging into death, whether the Sidran Tower Girl or all those poor Petitors." The Sealed Records archivist gave her a pitying glance. "I suppose he was as worried as you are about the job."

The Archive of Homicidium. Of course! Jovian had loved a good mystery. He'd probably suspected foul play in the other Petitors' deaths.

Racing to the archive, a bewildered Gaius in tow, she pulled out the indexes covering suicides in Edessa over the past five years. He positioned himself by the door, whittling away at a bit of wood as she sat in the cramped space between the shelves and gingerly opened a book. The spine gave a creaky groan, then settled into place. She began reading.

Sunlight shafted in through the archive's sole window and climbed across the wall as morning drew to a close. She squinted at Aelius's spidery writing and Tullus's scratches on older records, making note of every Petitor who had committed suicide: their method of death and where they were found.

Several hours later, she sat back, tapping her overworked ink pen against her case summaries, and tried to make sense of everything.

In addition to Othus, his Petitor, Jovian, and Livia, there had been five dead Petitors since her Fall. As predicted, the bodies had been pulverized and the deaths marked as suicides. From being trampled by horses to flattened by granite slabs, Helvus had come up with increasingly ingenious ways of camouflaging how they'd died. That part didn't trouble her. What did was the common thread tying the victims.

Each one had started acting strangely in the weeks leading up to their death. Their families and relatives had reported paranoia. Writing wills. Muttering about dreading stormfall. Whatever they knew had to be more than just the scuta. Despite knowing they were faulty, and having a bounty on her head, Sarai hadn't experienced anything close to the terror these Petitors had.

Her hands trembled. *I need more to tie the deaths together.*

She had to investigate Sidran Tower.

If these records were right, then her Fall had occurred before the first Petitor death. She was the first victim. After entering Edessa, she'd been invited to a convivium at the Academiae by *someone* who'd let her know of the passage into Sidran Tower so she could avoid the Tower Gates. While attending the party, she'd discovered *something* and been drugged by someone before being tossed off Sidran Tower. *But who did I meet? What did I see?* And how had ten people—that she knew of so far—been thrown off Sidran Tower without any witnesses? Her Fall had occurred in the midst of stormfall, but Jovian's . . . she clapped a hand to her mouth in realization.

Jovian's fall had happened during the same. *They're using stormfall to cover the falls.* And what was it Helvus had said to reassure his Guildsmen?

"We're fine. They'll ensure it."

Whoever Helvus's clients were, they were wealthy lightning magi who'd had access to the convivium that night. Which could be at least half the partygoers.

She slammed the records book shut in frustration and blanched when the spine cracked. Staring at the two halves of the leather-covered boards, she resigned herself to paying the archivist a hefty fine. Gently lifting the carnage, she paused at the sight of a folded piece of parchment stuck to the endbands. Tugging it free, she unfolded it and froze at the lines of Urdish in a different hand than Jovian's scrawl.

My dear Jovian,

If I could, I'd wipe last night's events from memory. I've thought about it all night, and my conclusion doesn't change. I saw that scutum explode. Cassandane looked worried when I brought it up. She said I was stressed and to ignore it. But how is a Petitor to hide from her mind?

Will you help me? Meet me at the courtyard behind Homicidium and Materialize that night for me, so I can put this to rest. By Wisdom, I hope I saw wrong.

Your faithful friend,
Livia

Below Livia's letter, a different hand had responded.

I'll be there.

1: Next one's the first floater.

Sarai reverently folded the letter and tucked it in her robes before muffling a squeak of excitement in her hands. She'd be willing to bet that there were more such letters here. She took in the thousands of books in archive with grim anticipation. *Three weeks to search them all.*

"Fancy seeing you here, barmaid," a serpentine voice murmured too close to her ear.

Sarai whirled around to find Harion. *Havïd.* She reached for her armilla, readying for trouble. "What do you want?"

He shrugged innocently. "I'm just here to laugh."

"Of course you are. Just focus on keeping my hundred aurei safe, lecher." While Harion shook with laughter, she returned to the sharp-eyed Homicidium archivist and sheepishly paid two aurei for the broken spine, vowing that she'd be more careful with the books.

Harion followed her as she left the archive and ducked into a nearby courtyard in search of Gaius. "You don't seriously think you'll win our bet, after being strangled by Tullus! How was that, by the way? Learned your lesson?" He tugged the collar hiding her fading bruises, chuckling when she flinched away.

"You two must get along well seeing as you both assault women."

"Putting an uppity barmaid in her place is 'assault' now? I must deserve a prison cell."

"That can be arranged." Finding Gaius, she relaxed. "Petitor Harion of Dídtan, have you had your laughs? Ready to leave me alone now?"

"Do you even know where Dídtan is?" Before she could speak, he nodded. "Of course not. It's a military port to the west. Distinguishing yourself in a place like that is hell." His forearms strained, hands balling into fists. "Everyone wants a way out."

"I know the feeling."

"Do you? You paid nothing to get here but the costs of your travel from that mountain. You didn't invest sacks of coin or years of education sucking up to instructors you care nothing for. You just waltzed in and got where we *worked* to be, and you don't even respect the job."

"What do you want me to say?" She threw up her hands. "Yes, I got a leg up. And I respect the job *too much* to allow wealthy bastards like Helvus to walk all over the people we protect and stifle us when—"

"Stifle?" Harion said incredulously. "Do you think Anek, Cisuré, and I keep our opinions to ourselves because we feel *stifled*? You think you're the only one here with a conscience?" His voice rose. "We keep our heads down because we know the consequences of acting out. As you're learning."

The fissure of anger he'd broken open widened. "Are you saying you knew about the scuta?"

"No, and I'm still getting one. It could turn me green for all I care, but if Tetrarch Tullus says it doesn't, then it doesn't. Join the real world, barmaid." He tapped her forehead with a finger with a pitying look before sauntering off.

Her hands clenched around the letter in her pocket.

CHAPTER
TWENTY

Days slipped through her fingers as Sarai and Gaius scoured the *homicidium* archive, lying to the bewildered archivist about researching for a highly secret case of Kadra's.

Jovian and Livia had been adept at tucking the letters into the gaps in the spines, secured with a dab of bone glue to prevent anyone else from finding them—not that anyone could have understood the language even if they did. Each contained a reference to the book in which the next could be found for the other person, with both Petitors taking great delight in confounding each other with the most obscure references.

Unable to read Urdish, Gaius relied on Sarai's translations during the search.

"Next one's the first floater." He quoted from the letter she'd found and wryly held up the first records of murder by drowning in Edessa, a letter secreted in the spine. "Clever."

Some letters contained records of daily amusements and commiserations on the job's hardships. Those, she read with a pang at the picture they painted of their bright-eyed writers, who couldn't have guessed that their words would be all that was left in a future they'd vanished from too soon. In the months before their deaths, the letters had grown bleaker, harder to find. She translated the newest one to Gaius.

My dear Jovian,

I think I saw something I shouldn't have.

I know you've told me not to think of it ever since you Materialized it out of my head. But I was at Archive of Lands Sold and Purchased for a deed and happened to see the name of that insula on the same page. I only glanced at it. It was sold the week after the strike.

Jovian, the Metals Guildmaster bought it. Just like he did the other patch of land you spoke of after the strike. I wanted it to be a coincidence, so I looked at a plot that was struck months ago. He bought it too.

You needn't worry. I won't say anything. Will you distract me, though? Tell me what you've found, even if it's about the STG (Elsar hold her soul). I'll try to forget this.

Your frightened friend,

Livia

As always, Jovian had responded with the location of his answer.

Forget it all. More on the STG in pre-Tetrarch walls.

"STG?" Gaius frowned.

"Sidran Tower Girl." Sarai folded the letter, placing it in chronological order to the others she'd found. "His answer might be in another archive. I can't see anything on walls here."

"I'll check the Architectural Archive." Gaius straightened with a groan.

She thumbed through their collection of letters in the interim. It was nowhere near enough. Helvus having bought land that had been devalued after a strike was helpful but wasn't determinative proof of his scuta being faulty. *If only I could get my hands on a scutum.*

Sighing, she didn't notice the figure at the edge of her vision until Cisuré tapped her shoulder. Sarai started. The other girl looked exhausted, eyes bloodshot and pale hair stringy.

"Are you alright?" Sarai asked worriedly.

"I should be asking you that," Cisuré whispered. "I just heard about the Metals Guild's bounty from Tetrarch Aelius. By the Elsar, this is everything I feared."

Sarai shifted so the other girl could sit beside her. "Don't panic just yet. This'll all be sorted out at trial. I'm handling it."

"Like you handled Tullus at Helvus's? Do you know how difficult it was for me to see that?"

Sarai voiced the question she'd pondered for nights afterward. "Why didn't you or Aelius do anything?"

"*Tetrarch* Aelius. And how could we? After what you pulled . . ."

The pit in her stomach yawned, swallowing the rest of Cisuré's response. If Tullus hadn't stopped, would Cisuré have just stood there as Sarai had the life choked from her?

"We can still smooth this over," the other girl said firmly. "Tetrarch Aelius hasn't announced that there's going to be a trial yet to give you time to rectify your mistake. I've spoken to him. Just retract these bizarre allegations, and this'll blow over."

Flummoxed, Sarai ran the entire rush of words once more through her head. "Retract?"

"What's done is done. Admia killed a man, and she'll pay for it. There's no reason to have a separate trial on the basis of her accusations. Just let Helvus be put to rest."

"Those aren't just *her* accusations. They're mine! I saw—"

"You were confused." Steel lined Cisuré's voice. "Helvus was dying, and you were exhausted. Admia believed what she wanted to believe, and you pulled it out."

"Not you too! Please don't act like I'm mad. I saw the exploded scutum outside her home! There was iron dust in the core!"

"That doesn't mean that Helvus did it on purpose or that every scutum is defective! The Guildsman manufacturing Admia's must have made a mistake."

"I Probed Helvus," Sarai blurted. Cisuré stilled. "I had to know the truth."

"I can't hear this." The other girl rose, her face bloodless with panic. "What have you done? You violated the head of a *dying man!*"

"None of it made sense to begin with! How can faith power a metal rod against a lightning strike?"

"How can other countries control ice or glass? Why do only certain magical abilities flow in our veins? Runes are the tongue our power speaks and responds to! And if it can call down lightning and mask scars, then who's to say that they cannot tie us to the gods?"

"But I had a chance to learn the truth about those inner workings and save lives! That's why I looked in Helvus's head!"

"Enough!" Cisuré said shrilly, causing the archivist to stare. "The scuta have saved hundreds of thousands. Faith is believing without seeing. Some people just aren't capable of that." She stared at Sarai as if she'd never truly seen her. "As Petitors, our duty is to *follow* the law, not rewrite it. You've damaged our profession."

Sarai's nails cut into her palms to stop herself from screaming. "The law isn't infallible, otherwise it wouldn't require me to willfully ignore evidence because Helvus is rich!"

Cisuré gripped her shoulders. "Don't you *dare* speak like Kadra. Anything he's said, no matter how enticing, is a lie. This city is a hotbed of corruption because of *him*. You're in the palm of a seasoned manipulator, and you don't care!"

"Because my decisions aren't based on him!" Sarai snapped and immediately wished she hadn't when Cisuré's face crumpled.

"You could be sent to the mines! Do you even have any physical proof that Helvus tampered with the scuta?" A tear rolled down Cisuré's cheek at Sarai's silence. "The harder you cling to this, the more it looks like you've something against Helvus, and that's fodder for a *calumnia* charge on top of your abuse of power. Please just drop it. Pin everything on Admia's delusions, and you'll be safe. The public will believe anything about a madwoman."

Anguish stuck in Sarai's throat. She spoke past the lump. "They *certo* will."

Cisuré flinched. "*Don't* draw that parallel. Admia is a criminal, and you were fourteen! Gods, why can't you be rational? Why are you choosing *him*?"

"I'm choosing myself!" She pulled free of Cisuré's grip. "Every day, I choose *that* girl whom everyone failed. So why won't *you* choose her?"

Sarai hunched forward, breathing hard. Several breaths later, Cisuré took her hands, their delicate structure standing out in stark relief against Sarai's trembling fingers.

"I can't tell you not to choose her," Cisuré said quietly. "But you're going about it the wrong way. Violating laws, accusing a dead man who can't defend himself—that's revenge, not justice, and it kills the soul. It's why you're always *angry*. Tetrarch Aelius says—"

Sarai's jaw clenched. "I think I'd rather not hear what Aelius has to say."

Cisuré closed her eyes. "I only want what's best for you." When she opened them, hard resolve filled the brown depths. "I won't apologize for that."

"I know."

Discomfort lingered between them, seeping into every crevice of their silence. Spotting Gaius in conversation with another vigile outside, Sarai sighed.

"I need to head out. Thank you for looking out for me. I didn't mean to upset you."

"It's *tibi gratias ago*." Cisuré looked wan and fragile. "No commoner speak, remember?"

Hand on the door, Sarai forced a nod. "Of course."

As she left, her smile vanished.

You're in the palm of a seasoned manipulator, and you don't care. Cisuré's accusation haunted Sarai for days. The manipulator in question continued to hold court without her while she and Gaius scoured the Hall of Records for the rest of Jovian's and Livia's letters to no avail.

They'd practically ransacked every archive pertaining to architecture, limestone, and old palaces to determine what Jovian had meant by "pre-Tetrarch walls" and found nothing. The two had either taken great pains to hide their last ones before death, or destroyed them, in which case Sarai was doomed.

Worse, the coming Month of Flowers was notorious for stormfall during the transition between winter and summer. If she'd had even a fraction of a chance to obtain a scutum, it was gone now.

Two weeks from trial, she gave up on the Hall of Records and marched all the way to Sidran Tower before she could change her mind. Her Fall was the only lead she had left. A knot of fear formed in her stomach when the tower's grim spire entered her vision. Gaius looked askance at her when she stopped.

"I hate to say this, Petitor Sarai, but you won't find much. Many magi and students searched for clues afterward to no avail." He followed her gaze to the tower's uppermost balcony. "That girl fell from the worst possible place. Right onto cobblestone. Any other tower and she'd have lived."

Clarity hit her with sudden, devastating force. Sarai turned to Gaius. "Say that again."

"None of the other towers would have resulted in a fall that bad."

Chills prickled at the back of her neck. "Why?"

"The balconies are largely too low. Most have grass below them."

Gaius watched in bemusement as she paled and sank to the ground, pieces swimming in her head. Kadra ignoring the Petitor deaths, then suddenly investigating them after she became his Petitor. *One.* She ripped a flower from the ground. Kadra pronouncing that Jovian had fallen to his death. *Two.* Kadra looking unsurprised when she'd related seeing Helvus stage Jovian's death at Sidran Tower. He'd known that there was nowhere else the Petitors could have been thrown from. *Three.* And he'd long known that the scuta were lightning rods. Her skin crawled.

Every second of their investigation, he'd been a step ahead.

"Petitor Sarai, are you going to pull out all the flowers, because I don't think the agromagi maintaining them will be pleased," Gaius said nervously.

She stared at her clenched fists, holding mounds of daisies.

She had to ask. She couldn't keep spinning wheels in her head. "I need to talk to Kadra."

"But we just—" Gaius stared at the sky, brow furrowed. "Petitor Sarai, get inside!"

A blinding flash illuminated their surroundings as a seething mass of steel-gray cloud rolled overhead. She and Gaius joined everyone racing pell-mell across the ground to squeeze into the closest instructional hall. Inside, she watched as lightning took the sky from sunset to day. Wind rattled the windows, and a few magi-in-training swallowed, eyes huge in their young faces.

An hour passed in desperate prayer to all the Elsar that there wasn't a scutum in their vicinity. When the lightning finally dwindled and the rain pattered to a stop, there was a collective sigh of relief.

No one would have seen Jovian and the others die in a storm like that, she thought grimly. Helvus's clients had known what they were doing.

Outside, Gaius fidgeted nervously until she finally asked him what was wrong.

"Could I return to the station?" he mumbled. "It's just . . . my partner was on the city battlements today. Can you return on your own?"

It was on the tip of her tongue to deny it, but she understood his worry. "Of course. Go to them."

Alone, she oriented herself toward Aoran Tower, selecting one of the westward paths and wishing she'd brought Caelum with her. She plodded along until hoofbeats sounded behind her. Moving off the path to give the rider room, she paused when the horse stopped.

"Petitor Sarai, what a surprise."

Every one of her muscles locked in place. Inch by inch, she turned to meet Tullus's smirk, and fear gripped her. This man was not here to talk.

Her throat worked. "Good evening, Tetrarch Tullus."

"I see your shadow is absent." He dismounted, eyes fixed on her chest. "Surely, Kadra knows it isn't wise to leave you alone these days."

SHIT. A glance around revealed only grass and a few trees, the air thick from the storm. Her breath came fast. They were alone.

"How can I help you?" she whispered, inching to the right, toward his horse.

"You could have two weeks ago." Tullus tsked. "We even gave you time to withdraw everything. Yet, here we are, with a good businessman's name ruined and a nuisance of a trial."

Must get to his horse. "I thought–"

"The Tetrarchy does the thinking, Petitor Sarai, because commoners are incapable of *thought*." He arched an eyebrow. "Two months and you're wrapped tight around Kadra's fingers. And probably his–"

"I've antagonized him at every turn." Fire rose up her throat. "I agreed to spy on him for you." And despite it all, Kadra hadn't harmed a hair on her head. "I saw the exploded scutum–"

"Now *that* really won't do." Tullus had been circling her, radiating menace, but now he prowled closer. "You haven't learned anything in the past two weeks, Sarai. It's time you do."

Her stomach curdled at the heated look on his lined face. And suddenly, *everything* tumbled into place.

Panic took over. She sprang toward Tullus's horse, barely getting a foot in the stirrup before stubby fingers seized her braid and wrenched her off. She hit the rocky path, pain shooting through her.

Elsar save me, she thought just as his fist connected with her skull.

She opened her eyes to silence. Every bone ached. Memory surged back in a rush, and she shot to her feet only to find herself bound to a chair. It tipped with the force of her struggles, sending her crashing to the ground with a stifled scream. He'd gagged her.

Again, a buried part of her whispered.

She closed her eyes. *Of course.* It had been him four years ago too.

Fighting panic, she tried to make out her surroundings. A lit sconce vaguely illuminated the polished floor of a ballroom.

"Ah, she's awake. Take that thing off her mouth," a voice ordered. Cool, authoritative. *Familiar.* She'd been right.

She shrank back to no avail as he approached. Her chair was righted, the cloth around her mouth wrenched free.

"Of all people, I didn't expect you to be involved in this," she rasped. "Tetrarch Aelius."

A chuckle sounded from the shadows before Aelius's ivory robes came into clear view.

"Well done, Petitor Sarai. I did say you were bright." He spread his hands. "This is quite unfortunate."

"Why are you doing this?"

"Because you have no foresight." He crouched before her with a rueful smile. "As a result, I'm going to have to oversee Admia's trial instead of Kadra."

"You can't do that," she said hoarsely. "The murder happened in Tetrarch Kadra's Quarter. Only he and I can—"

"Do nothing." Drawing a scroll from his robes, he snapped the seal and unrolled it before her. She recoiled at the first two words, every thought morphing into a sustained scream. Surely, she'd made a mistake. Had somehow inverted those precise letters into the wrong words like a child. But the longer she stared, the more every word solidified.

Arrest Warrant.

Sarai of Arsamea, Petitor to Tetrarch Drenevan bu Kadra, is hereby charged with calumnia for her malicious Probing of Helvus of Edessa. Her charges will be heard at the Aequitas along with her accusations of faulty scuta . . .

The world blurred as though she were looking at it from the bottom of a frozen pond, suffocating under ice and water and more terror than she'd known she could hold. *Calumnia*. A thousand lashes. A punishment no one could survive.

"You can't say that you didn't illegally Probe him. *Twice* at that. And you can't say that it wasn't out of malice." Aelius genuinely looked disappointed. "The Metals Guild will testify against your claims of defects in the scuta. And you'll be guilty of perjury too. At this point, the trial is a formality."

"The scuta were a sham from the start, weren't they?" she spat. "Faulty or not, they would never have worked, but Helvus wanted to buy up devalued land so he took things further. Did you three enjoy watching people buy up worthless steel and blame each other when they died? How dare you call yourselves godly—"

Tullus slammed a fist into her jaw. The chair fell, knocking her head so hard against the ground that she nearly passed out. Blood filled her mouth.

"Well, we're the most powerful men in all Ur Dinyé." Aelius cupped her cheek. Her flesh screamed at his touch. "If the gods gave a damn about you or those who've found out before you, they'd have struck me down. But they've only given me more. There's nothing wrong with making coin, and I've brought them more devotees." He considered her and chuckled. "You commoners all hate the wealthy, but fantasize of joining us. I gave you a chance to do so. You chose transgression. I'd normally give you over to Tullus to use you and kill you but . . ." He trailed off with a crooked smile when she began struggling at her bonds in a panic. "You're in a rather favorable position, so let's try this again."

His thumb halted at her jugular, digging in.

"You're going to search Kadra's tower and bring me anything that I can frame him with," Aelius said amiably. "Or I'll file the warrant. You'll be found guilty, whipped until your blood glues you to the post, and die a pariah."

Her eyes were hot with fury. "If Cisuré knew who you really were—" Her words were lost in an onset of laughter as Aelius doubled over, clutching his thighs. Even Tullus chortled.

"My dear girl." Aelius wiped a tear, tapping her cheek with the scroll. "Who do you think signed your warrant?"

Her heart stopped.

It shattered when he jabbed a finger at the signature beside his.

"Bless her, I think she believes she's helping you." He tutted. "Here's how this will work. We'll hear your silly little accusations in—how long did I give them, Tullus?"

"They've two more weeks." The other Tetrarch leered.

"Splendid. At the trial, I'll initiate a no-confidence vote to have Kadra unseated as Tetrarch. You will bring me everything in Aoran Tower to support this vote. Ruin Kadra, and I'll destroy this warrant. Turn on us, and I'll destroy you." Aelius's grin was all the more terrifying for its lack of malice. He truly thought he was being reasonable. "This is truly fortuitous. He's given you all the rope to hang himself with by letting you in his home. Every Tetrarch and Petitor must be in unanimous agreement for a Tetrarch to be removed from office. And in two weeks, we will be, won't we?"

I must have lived through this before. What choice had they given her then?

At her silence, Tullus moved in. Fire winked at his fingertips, wrenching her from her shock-induced haze as agony seared its way across her skin.

"I won't—" She screamed when Tullus seized her throat in a grip of molten iron. Smoke rose from her clavicles.

"One word and you can walk away." Aelius's voice was whisper soft. "I don't want to hurt you. Just give us Kadra."

Her flesh sizzled. Blood ran down her neck, pain and terror blinding her to all thought. Her pulse battered against her eardrums.

"Yes! Yes!" she heard herself scream from far away.

Tullus tore his fingers from her skin, sending spots across her vision. He rubbed his fingertips, burnt shavings of her skin littering the floor.

"Excellent." Aelius looked relieved. "Report to me through Cisuré."

When she found her voice again, it was a croak. "You can't believe the gods condone this. You assaulted–"

"Ah, but I haven't touched you, Petitor Sarai. Tullus got carried away, but that's his peace to make with the gods." He shot Tullus an irritated glance. "Arrange for a large donation to the Temple to atone, and toss her back outside."

Tullus scratched a grizzled cheek. "The students might say something if they see her outside Sidran Tower."

She was *in* Sidran Tower? Her eyes darted around the room until they found the outline of a balcony. *The balcony.* Darkness seeped across her sight like fog. She strained at her bonds, vaguely hearing Aelius ask Tullus what was wrong with her.

"Theatrics." Tullus sounded bored. "Are you sure I can't fuck her a little?"

"I said no." Aelius crouched beside her. "We aren't the villains here, Petitor Sarai. This wouldn't have happened if you'd behaved. So, you see, this is really your own fault."

She tumbled into unconsciousness with those words ringing in her ears.

CHAPTER
TWENTY-ONE

Sarai woke to the cold stone floor of an alcove, remnants of rain dripping down the walls. Her neck throbbed relentlessly. Weakly raising a trembling hand, she shuddered at the five whorls embedded into her shoulder, sinking through skin into muscle.

He would have melted me. Had she kept refusing, they would have thrown her off Sidran Tower for the second time. Her broken body would have ended up atop some Lugen's examination table. Another dead Petitor.

She couldn't feel anything. Pushing herself up on one knee, then the other, she swiped a finger through the mess of blood on her neck, using her last dregs of magic to clot some of the burns. She didn't even know if she could heal them. Forcing one foot before the other, she stumbled forward, a single inescapable truth reverberating with every step.

You're going to have to choose.

Kadra had been right.

After an eternity of walking, Aoran Tower drew in sight. Her hands left bloody trails on the gate when she unlocked it. Around her, the world slumbered, soundless but for the night creatures going about their tasks. At least she wouldn't have to face Kadra. He was probably in his office, unaware and uncaring of what she'd faced.

This close to sanctuary, the tears that had choked her throughout the walk rose unimpeded. She should have learned her lesson four years ago. Justice was a mirage, a game of lies and platitudes played by politicians who ensured they weren't held to the same standards as the populace. And no friendship was immune to that game.

"Bless her, I think she believes she's rescuing you," Aelius had said. The worst part was that Sarai believed it too.

She shuffled toward Kadra's tablinum and paused at the line of light snaking out from under the door. Had Cato left a candle burning? As she stared, the light blurred. Legs giving out, she collapsed against the door, agony flaring across her neck at the impact. Wetness trickled from her barely closed burns.

She dimly recognized that her body had gone as far as it could. But she wasn't safe yet. Not until she was sequestered in her room and the Sidran Tower Girl could sob her heart out.

Clawing at the jamb, she dragged herself to her feet and tottered into the study, only to freeze at the man blocking her path, eyes boring into hers.

"Kadra," she whispered a second before she pitched forward.

His hands closed around her shoulders, halting her fall. A whimper left her when his fingers swept over her burns, and he stilled. Brushing her ruined braid aside, his gaze went from her ravaged neck to her face before turning murderous.

"Who?" The word was as cold and hard as ice.

"Tullus." The world grew unfocused.

Fingers tipped her chin. "Sarai, can you see me?" Kadra asked grimly.

She tried to focus on his face, but her eyes wouldn't hold still, circling from the travel dust on his robes to the clenched set of his jaw.

The door thudded open, startling her back to clarity. Cato strode in with a cheerful smile, cup of tea in hand, and went stock-still.

"What the—"

Kadra plucked her off the floor and deposited her onto a couch as Cato hurried to her side.

"What happened? Drenevan, don't tell me you—" He cut himself off with a shake before turning to her. "Let's get you to a healer."

"No," she whispered, but Cato was having none of it. "Wait, I can't—"

"She asked you to wait." Kadra's voice sliced through the tablinum, and the older man shot him a glare only to falter when Sarai nodded weakly. "Then . . . ?"

"I can heal it," she lied. She couldn't have a healer seeing her scars. Drawing upon her precariously stretched reserves of magic, she poorly clotted one burn and hoped it would satisfy them. Both men blinked.

Cato still looked worried. "Was it the Guild?"

"Tullus." Kadra looked close to breathing fire. "See to the wards. And inform Gaius that I want his head."

Cato departed with a nod.

Kadra crouched by her, the sleeves of his tunic rolled to his elbows. "I'll help you upstairs."

"No." She'd had too much time to think on the walk back to Aoran Tower. Enough to realize that he must have known who Helvus's clients were all along. He'd stayed quiet because he'd known he couldn't take on Aelius and Tullus and had used her instead. This was the result.

Her thoughts must have shown, because his face smoothed into a hard-eyed mask.

"Did you know this would happen?" She was proud of how the words came out. Empty, indifferent.

He studied her like she would bite if he turned his back. "Gaius was supposed to watch you."

"To protect me from the Metals Guild, I'm sure. If he'd known he was guarding me from two Tetrarchs, he wouldn't have left tonight." Despite the cotton wool lining her throat, she laughed. "Imagine that. You keep your secrets, and I pay the price."

A muscle jumped in his jaw, but he extended a hand to help her up.

She jerked away. "Don't act like you care. The deeper you drag me into the filth of this country, the worse it gets. Two months and I've been nearly drowned, choked, and burned to death. Why me? Why open my eyes to all this?"

A flash of bleakness in his eyes. "You needed to know who your enemies were."

"My enemies? You mean yours!" she hissed. "You're going to get me killed, aren't you, Kadra? You'll be the hero who revealed Aelius's and Tullus's duplicity, and I'll be the Petitor who lost her life in the process. Tell me, how many innocents have died because you valued your damned goals over their lives?"

An ugly harshness tightened his face, warning her she was treading on thin ice. *Good.* If he only understood violence, then she would be violent.

"Then leave." His words were knives. "If you find it so difficult, then consider yourself released as my Petitor. Perhaps your friend over at Aelius's will have you." His eyes turned cruel at her stricken look. "I have no interest in keeping you here against your will."

Tears warped her vision. She wanted to scream that he was wrong, that even Cisuré had thrown her to the wolves. But all that left her was a bitter, choked laugh.

"Do I really have no right to be angry?" She blinked to keep the tears at bay. "For a man who wants me to choose him, you've taken great pains to rip me apart. Since the Robing, it's only been burnings and blood and bodies in everyone's closets, and six fucking months of cases in six weeks." Her voice cracked. "If you've been trying to show me my enemies, you're one of them. Did you spare one thought for me in all this? Was I not innocent in your eyes?"

Something nameless twisted in his gaze.

"You knew it all but told me *nothing*. I had no idea who was coming for me. And you don't think I've a right to be angry?" Her voice broke. "Gods know why, but I expected better of you."

The spark of fire that had sustained her winked out. Kadra's unreadable silence was punctuated by the sluggish beat of her pulse. Crimson flashed at the edge of her vision from her armilla, and her heart stuttered at the warning that she'd drained her reserves of magic. Following her gaze, Kadra went dangerously still. Before she could hide her armilla, his hand clamped around her wrist like a vise, sliding it loose. One look at *nihumb*, and raw anger unlike anything she'd seen tautened his face.

Fortune save me. She didn't have to guess his thoughts. An illusion rune in his tower. It all added up to only one conclusion: a spy.

"Kadra, wait!" She jumped when the entire tower shuddered. Her plea collapsed into a petrified gasp as sparks snapped into life around them, threatening to set the tablinum on fire. The fury smoldering in his eyes chilled her to the core.

"Explain." The order held a threat of imminent violence if disobeyed.

"It isn't what you think—" She froze as he casually drew a wicked-looking blade from his robes, candlelight glinting off the edge.

What was left of her heart after Cisuré's betrayal broke apart at his seething menace. As though they hadn't spent two months as partners, as though he hadn't told her under that tree in the midst of that storm that she was *safe* with him.

The knife brushed her throat. "I asked you to explain." His voice was clipped and hard.

She raised her head without fear. Part of her wanted to let him kill her. It was a path out of all this. The violence, the *pain*, the blades they kept pointing at each other. But the Sidran Tower Girl who'd refused to die wouldn't allow it.

She dropped the illusion.

Kadra stilled, shock entering a face that could have been carved from iron.

"Here you go," she said bitterly. "This is why. If someone touches me, they'll feel the scars, so I don't let anyone but—" *Cisuré.* She couldn't say it. "I wasn't out to deceive you. I just hated how people stared—" Her voice broke, control crumbling. "Are you happy now? Is that everything you wanted? Is—"

It was too much.

Choking on ragged sobs, she hunched over, surrendering to the panic attack and pleading with all the gods and Saints for unconsciousness. She couldn't breathe. A vicious curse sounded far away.

"Sarai, open your eyes."

She instinctively obeyed, her head lolling back with dizziness. Warm hands cupped her face. She met Kadra's coal-black stare.

"Blink slowly." His palms were rough. "Good. Now, breathe." His face tightened when she struggled to inhale. "Damn it, keep going."

A hideous rattle filled the air, and she almost laughed at the realization that it was her.

"Again," Kadra urged when she wheezed a breath. "That's it."

Shaking like an aspen, she drew ragged breath after breath until the agony in her chest loosened. When the flood passed, she simply lay there, hollowed out, barely cognizant of the man wiping her tears.

She wished she hadn't run into him. She'd only wanted to heal.

A rough sigh grazed her face, and she dimly noted that she'd said it aloud. The floor tilted on its axis as Kadra lifted her, striding upstairs to sit them both on her bed, with her on his lap. Her teeth chattered, shock taking panic's place. Wrapping a blanket over them both, he held her as she shook. He smelled of oranges and wine and the blood she was getting on him, and, gods, she was going to be so utterly humiliated tomorrow when she had the strength to give a damn. But for now, she waited, wondering who would speak first.

Long moments later, he angled his head to study her with unflinching intensity. "You're still bleeding."

"I don't have the magic to clot it."

A breath and his hand circled her wrist around her armilla. Heat flared from his fingertips, and she realized he was pooling some of his magic in her.

Gritting her teeth, she pricked a finger and wiped it over *beshaz*. The rush of power was familiar, as was the way her vision sharpened behind her closed eyelids, sinking internally, to survey the damage. Hovering her shaking hands above the oozing mess of burns circling her neck, she tried to rebuild the first layer of tissue. Unable to handle the flow of power, her fingers pressed hard into the burn, reopening it. She swallowed a scream and tried again, fighting tears, when Kadra's hands gripped hers, steadying her fingers.

Gently leading them to each burn, he held her knuckles straight, allowing her to focus. Power slowly leaked into her skin, and she could have cried as she painstakingly rebuilt each layer of tissue, using her magic to push her body into repairing itself much faster than it could on its own. Long moments later, new skin stretched uncomfortably tight over the area.

Kadra watched the process in silence. He had to have questions, but he wasn't the only one who could leave people in the dark.

"Thank you," she muttered. "I haven't been able to do that for . . . years."

"Sarai."

She refused to look at him. An easy task, despite her ear currently lying over his heart.

"I apologize."

For a moment, she was too stunned to speak, then a weak laugh burst out. "The mighty Kadra is sorry."

"When he's wrong."

Her eyes burned. "Can't imagine that happens often."

"No." His voice was quiet.

"At least you didn't roast my neck," she said bitterly. "Or would you have sliced it?"

Kadra paused before heaving the sigh of a man who knew that his next words wouldn't please their listener. "I have roasted many necks. But I wouldn't have touched yours. Earlier." He tucked a strand of hair behind her ear as if to soften his words. "The knife was a threat."

"So I humiliated myself for nothing." The only person besides Cisuré who'd seen her scars, and it had been under duress.

"Sarai—"

"I should have realized that you wouldn't. The optics of having your Petitor turn corpse and all that." A sardonic laugh wedged in her throat. "I'm surprised you aren't gloating."

In response, Kadra slid a finger under her chin. She gave into the unspoken request and raised her head for his perusal. Cavernous eyes traveled her face, lingering on her scars. His jaw ticked, features settling into something quiet and bitter that looked oddly like regret.

"My hands are the worst of it." She extended them, matching her palm to his larger one. "That's why my writing looks the way it does."

He went rigid at her touch. His gaze didn't leave her as he took her hand and explored it clinically, measuring each misshapen finger, each crooked joint, the scars webbing across the backs of her palms, the evidence of the shattered mess of her digits.

"This was done to you?"

She nodded, unable to think of a lie and certain that he'd see through one. "I'd rather not speak of it."

He acquiesced, tracing her skin with the callused hands of a swordsman. She braced herself for him to wince, to shudder as so many had. Surrounded as she was by him, she'd feel it.

He didn't. Instead, he asked no further questions, offered no condolences, merely interlocked their fingers and pulled her closer to hold her more securely. A motion that placed her face barely inches from his. Her breath caught when he looked down.

"If anyone should be humiliated here, it's me," he admitted, tight lines bracketing his lips. "You have nothing to be ashamed of."

Speech failed her. At the apology. At the fact that he was holding her in a way that defied explanation.

Kadra frowned at her expression. "Are you still in pain?"

"I don't know." Her head was so jumbled that she could barely sort pain from everything else. "Are you still kicking me out?"

"No," he said softly. "Unless you want to leave."

"And join Aelius? He had me branded with Tullus's palmprint."

His eyes narrowed. She started when he moved the blanket off her shoulders to survey the holes in her robes where burnt fabric had melded with her skin. When his fingers brushed her collar, she stilled at the silent question in his eyes. Heart in her throat, she nodded.

Silence itself seemed to hold still as he undid the first button. The pads of his fingers brushed her skin, moving down her neck to stop between her breasts. His hands lingered on her exposed skin, and she held her breath as his jaw turned to granite, before he returned to her wound with ruthless efficiency. Her pulse tripled as he peeled the material from her shoulders, only to halt when he brought out the same knife he'd threatened her with.

At her flinch, Kadra followed her gaze and cursed. "I'll find another—"

Sarai gripped his wrist. "Do it."

Looking grim, in a deft motion, he cut off the sooty fabric, revealing the handprint seared into her skin. Something lethal flared in Kadra's eyes, jaw clenching so hard she swore she could hear the scrape of his back teeth.

"It'll heal." She tried to sound offhand.

"Will it?" The low gravel of his voice said he wasn't referring only to the wound.

"Will tonight happen again?"

"No part of it ever will." Every word was a vow. He took her chin between his forefinger and thumb. "You're safe here. Forgive me for breaking my word to you."

She blinked away the heat pricking her eyes. "Two apologies in a night. I must have some use as a Petitor."

"You're an excellent one."

"Kadra, you have no basis of comparison for that."

"I've seen at least a dozen come and go."

Torn between horror and amusement, she sputtered. "You call that a frame of reference?"

His lips lifted faintly as though he was pleased at having made her laugh.

"What do you really want from me?" she dared ask. "Why let me in here and lead me through all this?"

"Because you're strong."

She almost rammed her head into his chin. When his eyes found hers, they burned with the same strange tenderness she'd seen at Aelius's convivium.

"You don't bend. You'd rather break, but this land needs strength like yours. I've waited for it for years."

Her heart caved under a catastrophic flood of emotion, crumbling to ash when Kadra soothingly traced a line down her spine.

"I . . ." Her eyes watered. She glanced everywhere but him. "By all the Saints, if you'd said this that first night here, I'd have chosen you without question."

"Would you really?" He sounded intrigued.

"No, I'd have tried to get you arrested."

A semblance of a laugh from him.

"Aelius and Tullus"—she took a deep breath—"they came after me tonight so I'd ruin you. They've been asking me to do it since my first day. I agreed initially, but I gave them nothing."

"Why not?" Kadra looked amused, confirming her guess that he'd known. "The debt-slave ring would have been a good time."

She flushed. "You're mad, but . . . you aren't without honor. I had to agree tonight because Tullus would've burned me alive if I didn't."

"I'll kill him." Sounding terrifyingly sincere, he traced the swelling below her right eye, the bruises on her cheeks. "I'll eviscerate him muscle by muscle, if you'd like."

Awestruck, she grasped for words. "There's no need to commit treason," she muttered. "Thank you, though."

The ruthless look on his face told her he disagreed. "What's Aelius using against you?"

"*Calumnia.* Apparently, he's taken both of us off Admia's trial." She deflated when Kadra nodded in confirmation. "He has a warrant and a list of witnesses from the Metals Guild that he's bribed into testifying for Helvus." She cursed. "I'll steal a scutum if I have to, if it means tearing them down."

Adjusting herself on his lap—Elsar help her—she winced when her battered arms protested the motion. Kadra's brow creased. He gently lifted and settled her under the covers.

With a glance at the dwindling night outside, he eased off the bed. "I'll leave you to rest. Stay here tomorrow and heal."

Eyeing the loosening line of his shoulders, she had the vague feeling that they'd passed some crucial threshold but was too exhausted to pinpoint what that was.

"Goodnight, Kadra."

He watched her for a long moment. "Goodnight, Sarai," he said softly.

And for once, that night, she didn't dream of that Fall, but only of how close he'd held her.

CHAPTER
TWENTY-TWO

Sarai woke to a pounding head and the unfamiliar tightness of new skin around her neck.

Awareness brought with it bone-deep fury. Cursing Aelius and Tullus to the worst of the ten hells, she took in the noonday sun with surprise. She'd slept for over a day.

Momentarily thrown by the very visible dent on the chair by her bed, she touched the leather and was surprised by its warmth. A drowsy memory surfaced of a hand stroking her hair in the early hours of the morning, and she flushed. *Impossible.* Kadra had better things to do. Still, the prospect of facing him was nerve-wracking in a way that spoke of long-stifled hungers having received too much ammunition. There was no forgetting his arms around her or how beautiful he was up close in that stern, severe way.

Nothing has changed, she reminded herself throughout her bath. With *calumnia* hovering over her head, she had to focus on taking the teeth out of Aelius's threat. There was no reason to keep dwelling on the way Kadra's gaze had seemed to memorize her features, or . . . Realizing she'd paused halfway down the staircase with a stupid grin, she hurried all the way down, vowing never to think of it again.

Her newfound resolution lasted the few seconds it took to descend the stairs and spot the couch she'd had a panic attack on. She cringed.

She was surprised to find Kadra's tablinum empty. A quick search of the atrium revealed no one. She listened for any creak, any footfall that would indicate his presence.

"Cato?" she called, his name reverberating through the atrium. "Kadra?"

The tower yawned before her, whispering of tantalizing possibilities, buried secrets, and answers on Sidran Tower. She couldn't refuse the dare. If there was anywhere that Kadra hid his skeletons, it was in here. This wasn't for Aelius. It was for her, finally being able to probe Kadra's depths.

She proceeded to scour every inch of the tower, knocking on the walls to search for hidden chambers and testing the flooring for movable tiles. She came away empty-handed. The uppermost floors, above the mezzanine holding Kadra's bedroom and hers, yielded Cato's cozily furnished room and a vast library. Even the cellar—accessible via a trapdoor set into Kadra's study—only contained cask after cask of wine.

She hesitated in front of his bedroom, plagued by embarrassment at going through his inner sanctum. Gingerly pushing the door open, she peered in, headfirst.

Done in the black and gold that adorned his robes, his seal, and gods only knew what else, Kadra's bedroom contained the usual items found in such places: a bed, wardrobe, various instruments of torture . . . Sarai blinked.

The serrated metal instruments on a chest were as meticulously clean as every corner of the house had been. Hesitantly, Sarai examined the tip of a wicked-looking knife, and paused, seized by an awful truth. She could take these blades to Aelius. Granted, Kadra would be framed for some awful crime or the other, tossed out as Tetrarch, and forced to face a Summoning in the Aequitas.

But I'd be safe. Aelius and Tullus would reward her. Her sphere of existence could remain unperturbed.

Setting the knife down, she smiled wryly. *The Elsar and their irony.* Once, she would have done anything for this chance. Now, she couldn't take it.

Turning from the blades with a hard swallow, she squinted at a threadbare ribbon nailed to his wardrobe. Likely once white, it had since yellowed with age. She touched the soft material with a frown. Below it were two words in Kadra's script.

Never forget.

It sounded like the ribbon's owner was dead, or far away at the very least. Her heart sank like a stone, something unpleasant and hot snaking around it. Whose was this? The words below the ribbon spoke of attachment. Regret. Was this the reason for Kadra's celibacy? A long-lost lover?

Suddenly ice-cold, she looked away, wishing she hadn't seen it. Forcing herself to complete her search, she went through Kadra's wardrobe, patting at his folded tunics and trousers, before crawling under his bed. *Nothing.*

Returning to the tablinum, she leaned against one of Kadra's wall-to-ceiling bookcases with a sigh and nearly jumped out of her skin when it clicked. Inching away from it, she paused. *That sounded like a lock.*

Upon closer inspection, an imperceptible horizontal handle jutted out of one of the shelves. She pushed, and the entire bookcase swung open. Sarai stepped outside to what had to be the orange grove she kept smelling around his home. Four rows of trees greeted her, their boughs laden. Woven baskets had been arranged at the base to catch any premature fruit drop.

She shook her head with a laugh. So these were Aoran Tower's secrets. An unsettling ribbon, some tools of torture, and a few orange trees. *Aelius and Tullus would be apoplectic if they knew.*

Circling back to the metal gates marking the start of Kadra's wards, she found Cato sitting outside, cup of tea in hand.

He looked up at her, concerned. "Sarai, how are you feeling?"

She tensed even as she reminded herself that he couldn't have heard her searching the tower. "Much better. Where's Kadra?"

"At the Grand Elsarian Temple. Something about questioning the Master Cleric."

Why had Kadra suddenly decided to interrogate Ur Dinyé's highest religious official? "I'll head out too."

"Are you sure you're well enough?"

She nodded reassuringly. "We've two Tetrarchs to ruin."

Cato hid an odd smile in his tea. And as she left to saddle Caleum, she could have sworn she heard him chuckle that Kadra wasn't going to know what hit him.

Ur Dinyé's largest house of worship to the Elsar was a mile past the Favran Tower Gate, steps from the Aequitas. Carved from the same ascetic white limestone as the courthouse, the Grand Elsarian Temple's cluster of domes rose almost as high as Aelius's statue. Oak doors barred entry into the temple. Her breath caught at the black-robed figure before them.

Remember, nothing has changed.

Surprise lit Kadra's eyes. He caught her reins as she dismounted. "You should be resting."

"I'm feeling better." The words left as a croak, and she cleared her throat. "Much better."

Like Cato, he didn't seem convinced. "You don't look it."

"Lovely—" Before she could finish being affronted, he clasped her wrist and placed two broad fingers against her pulse, eyes narrowed in calculation.

Havïd. She willed her pulse to cooperate.

A notch appeared between his eyebrows. "Your pulse is fast," Kadra pronounced grimly. "You should be in bed."

Torn between horrified amusement and sinking to the ground in humiliation, she settled for a strangled smile. "I'm fine."

He studied her for a moment before releasing her hand. As he did, his thumb brushed an absent stroke across her wrist. She quelled the rising heat in her. *Nothing has changed.*

She gestured at the Temple. "Why the Master Cleric?"

In response, he withdrew the letter of Livia's that had confounded them from his saddlebag. "Gaius told me you were searching for 'pre-Tetrarch walls.'"

It hit her. "He was referring to the Temple?"

"Oldest walls in Edessa." Kadra's lips rose a fraction when she rubbed her hands in excitement. "And it has a library."

Of course. "They were looking into whether the scuta actually called on the gods for protection," she realized.

The doors creaked open. A young cleric-in-training bowed. "Master Cleric Linus will see you soon. Please wait within," he stammered and fled at Kadra's nod.

"Will Linus give us anything?" she wondered, following him in. "I imagine the temples must be benefiting from the story around the scuta."

"I'm sure we can make him talk."

Sarai almost felt sorry for Linus. She watched with slitted eyes as Kadra crossed the temple's threshold. Catching her perusal, he raised an eyebrow.

"They say evil can't pass the High Elsar's doors." She shrugged. "I was expecting you to burst into flames."

"Expecting?" He gave her a dark smile. "Or hoping?"

"I'd have saved you." She tilted her head meaningfully to a nearby fountain and the devastating grin she'd witnessed only twice made a return.

"I thought I was a *havïd* sadist."

"You still are." She strode past him, one hand over her racing heart. His huff of laughter followed her inside.

The Grand Elsarian Temple was an excellent distraction. Meticulously hewn from white limestone with the floor worked in red porphyry, it boasted statues of the High Elsar and several Saints from the minor pantheon of the Naaduir. She bowed before Lady Radiance and jumped when Kadra's voice brushed her ears.

"I didn't take you as devout."

Sarai scowled. "A little respect won't doom the country, Kadra. In fact . . ." Trailing off, she indicated a statue of Lord Wrath. Unlike the Academiae's figure, this sculptor had given the god hair flowing to his waist, and a longsword, but there was no doubt in her mind as to whom those cruel features resembled. Kadra eyed it before giving her a droll look.

"Unlike Aelius, you'll never have to commission a marble tribute to yourself." She gave him a bland smile.

Faint lines crinkled at the corners of his dark eyes. "I'm Wrath?"

She nodded.

"Shouldn't you be cowering? Pleading to serve me?"

"You mean, *kneeling* and requesting to service you—I mean *serve* you. *Serve!*" Biting her tongue as a predatory look crossed his features, she resolved never to speak again.

"Service?" His wine-rough voice turned the word even filthier. "The gods have it good."

Her resolve vanished. "Damn it, Kadra!"

A rusty laugh filled the air. Not the ugly, sardonic thing he made on occasion, but genuine, unguarded. The sound curled up in her chest, and she stumbled, nearly careening into one of the statues. Kadra smoothly caught and righted her.

He watched her thoughtfully. "Why believe in the gods at all?" His thumb skimmed over an invisible scar. "You've every reason not to."

"I didn't for a while after . . . it happened. Recovery was difficult, and I had no one," she admitted. "But I did recover, and I found purpose. That was enough."

"I expected a miracle," he said dryly.

"I think this *is* the miracle," she mused. "A northern barmaid, here, beside Ur Dinyé's maddest Tetrarch, scars and all." She met his eyes with complete sincerity. "Thank you for not minding them."

"There's nothing to mind."

True. Bereft of words, she squeezed his hands in thanks. The doors leading into the priests' chambers snapped open. A white-haired man in beige robes strode into the temple, stately features irritated.

"The temple is closed for rest," the Master Cleric haughtily informed them.

"I wasn't aware the gods needed rest." Kadra ignored Linus's sputter of displeasure. "My Petitor will need access to your library henceforth. As you did with Jovian and Livia."

Linus's jaw tensed. "You need to leave."

Sighting the danger in Kadra's too-pleasant smile, she considered the temple's opulent furnishings and recalled Aelius's order to Tullus.

"Perhaps people should know how you're funded," she mused.

"What do you—"

"You received a substantial donation last night, didn't you?" Satisfaction filled her when he paled. "Tullus pays you for absolution. The dates of the donations are kept here, I imagine? I wonder what I'd find if I looked into what Tullus did on those days. I'm sure your congregation would be keen to know."

Linus turned ruddy. "You can't threaten me in a house of the gods!"

Kadra chuckled. "They aren't exactly stopping her. What'll it be?"

The Master Cleric's face was a map of indecision, fear warring with loyalty. "Fine. But I don't know why you're bothering. Even Tetrarch Aelius's current Petitor scoured the place after Petitor Jovian's death and found nothing."

Sarai's eyebrow drew together. "Cisuré wasn't acquainted with Aelius then."

"She wasn't?" Linus snorted, and a strange sick premonition rose in her as she thought back to haltingly answered questions and the odd hints of history between Aelius and her oldest friend. "Four years ago, he brought her here and vowed before the Elsar to make her his Petitor." He shuddered. "And here we are. Like he knew that the previous three would die."

She staggered in shock. "They knew each other before the Robing?"

He looked at her like she was dim. "That girl has been trailing after him for years now, from the temple to his vigile station. I wouldn't be surprised if she was a regular in his bed—"

"Enough!" she interrupted sharply. "I asked for facts, not defamation."

Relishing his dropped jaw, she took a steadying breath, ordering the gaping hole in her stomach to close. She would make sense of everything later, from Cisuré signing the warrant to why she'd lied to her. Right now, she had a job to do.

"Besides the scuta, have you heard of any runes or magic that require faith to work?"

"A Summoning could qualify," Linus muttered. "But that depends primarily on the summoner's will, though that can be intertwined with faith."

So there's no precedent for Aelius's supposed ancient runes. Another strike in her favor. "Our magic isn't infinite. It gets depleted and needs recovery like any other muscle. So why do you think the scuta work every second of the day?"

"Faith doesn't tire," Linus mumbled. "I don't understand what you two want. Jovian asked the same questions. Not a lot of faith in him either and look at where it got him."

Exchanging a glance with Kadra, she thanked the disgruntled Master Cleric and left with his reluctant promise to let her rummage in the Temple's library.

An ever-increasing din greeted her outside. Just past the gate fencing the Temple, thousands descended upon the Aequitas, elbowing each other for entrance.

Admia's trial. Her shoulders sagged. Aelius had wasted no time in rushing the conviction. All the evidence on iron dust that she'd been hoping to Materialize from Admia's head was going to be lost upon her death.

"He's charged her with treason for offing Helvus. She'll be subjected to a Summoning," Kadra murmured behind her. "Only two events command this high a turnout. The Robing. Or a god."

She cursed. "How did no one question the scuta? Why pay for and plant something outside their homes without knowing how it worked?"

"Some questions are dangerous," Kadra said softly. "The scuta are a culmination of every ounce of the people's faith in the Guilds, the

Tetrarchy, and the gods. Unknotting that tangle means daring to question all of it. Few ever start."

"You did."

A grave sigh left him. "And it changed nothing."

"It brought me here," she said and sensed him turn to her. She watched the crowd surging into the Aequitas. "I should go see it, shouldn't I?"

His gaze ranged from her clenched hands to the pulse throbbing at the base of her throat. "Aelius is presiding over it."

She raised her chin, mounting Caelum. "I'll have to contend with him at some point."

"Your friend will be there too."

"I—" Her voice cracked. "I know."

He watched her for a moment. Then, moving to Caelum's side, he reached up and gently cupped her cheek.

"Come outside when it's over. I'll accompany you home."

"I'll be fine. I've dealt with worse."

"I can tell." His voice went even softer. "But you aren't alone anymore."

He turned abruptly and mounted his horse, veering toward his Quarter in a blur of black and gold. Spreading her fingers over the warm impression of his hand, Sarai decided that they'd both gone mad. *Everything has changed.*

When not involved in a trial, Petitors held the best seats in the Aequitas: in the first row, to the right of the dais where the presiding Tetrarch sat, and directly before the defendant.

Admia was a wreck of blood. It trailed from lacerations in her flesh, dampening her tunic as Aelius's vigiles gave her a few choice prods across the stage. A month ago, she'd swanned about Aelius's convivium. Now, she raised her head at his command, battered features emanating loathing.

Sarai's palms grew clammy. *That could be me.*

Beside her, Anek's expression was unreadable. Harion was surprisingly quiet as well, a bruise on his cheek. She wondered if it was Tullus. A man like that didn't conserve his violence for women alone.

She drowned out Aelius's lengthy speech on the evils of social chaos, focusing only when Cisuré stepped forward at the end, sunset and firelight painting her golden. Sarai could scarcely recognize her.

Who was this girl with confidence in the line of her spine, directing a sneer to Admia as though she were garbage? When had her friend vanished?

"Admia of Edessa, you have forsaken Urd law and the law of the Elsar by taking a life so vital to this country that its extinguishing amounts to treason. Now you must beg the gods' mercy." Cisuré's voice was frosty. "Whom will you Summon?"

"Lord Death." Admia spat the name of the Elsar who would likely be her doom.

A nod from Cisuré, and Admia was unbound. She collapsed, dripping blood onto the stage.

This was all wrong. But no one seemed to care that Admia had been sent straight to execution without any recounting of the events leading to the murder. It was a spectacle to the crowd. They applauded when Admia daubed her fingers with blood from her wounds, and jeered when she faltered.

"Pitiful," Harion muttered under his breath when Admia tottered at one point.

Anek's eyes were chips of slate as Admia completed the first rune, *safsher* for "sword." The air quivered with anticipation. Something cold and panicky roiled inside her with each stroke of blood over marble.

Admia completed her rune after rune. The Aequitas pulsed with magic, a painful buzz building with each symbol. Sarai recognized some; Anek filled in the others. *Safsher, yaris, riukhen, naiya, khon, frazam, layk,* and *modrai.* Sword, flame, strength, heart, blood, end, unity, and, finally, the rune for Death himself that Jovian had fearfully painted across his study.

Tendrils of black mist rose from the symbol. Before completing the last stroke, Admia looked up, turning pleading eyes to Cisuré and Aelius. Bile crept across Sarai's tongue at their near-identical expressions of serenity. Admia closed her eyes and drew the final line.

A falling pin could have been heard in the subsequent resounding silence. Even the wind seemed to hold its breath.

Then the Aequitas trembled with a strident crack as black fire flared from the runes, rapidly growing high. The agonized screech of a voice broken beyond straining filled the air as Admia bent backward at the waist, radiating—*no*—being *drained* of power.

The crowd gasped as Admia was lifted from the ground by an unseen force. Her eyes bugged out of their sockets, filling with blood as she shrieked her throat raw.

Sarai's white-knuckled grip on the railing tightened, and Anek shot her a concerned look when her teeth clacked together audibly. But she couldn't explain the horrible twisting in her chest, an awful mix of dread and dark familiarity.

Bright crimson ran in a stream from Admia's nostrils, her wails like nails on slate as she rose and rose until she was a beetle-sized figure at the very top of the Aequitas.

"She can't hold on." There was no emotion in Anek's voice. "She's done."

"Lord Death," Aelius's voice boomed. "Is this woman worthy of pardon?"

The flames rising from the runes across the stage winked out of existence. Admia jerked, limbs splayed wide as the force that had anchored her to the air vanished.

And Sarai knew what was going to happen.

Look away. Don't watch. But she couldn't move as Admia dropped like a stone, hurtling to the ground, gaining speed with every second.

Look away—

Admia slammed into the marble floor of the stage with a crack, neck snapping in two. Staring at the exposed mess of her vertebrae, at her splintered skull, and at the fragments of her hands, Sarai blinked once. Twice. Three times.

Then, she collapsed.

Anek caught her arm, sitting her down. Around them, the crowd booed their disappointment.

Aelius didn't bat an eye. "Lord Death has provided his judgment."

"As the Elsar will it," the onlookers chorused, starting to file out of the Aequitas.

Nausea rose hard and fast. Muttering a brief thanks to Anek, Sarai raced out of the Aequitas and vomited onto the grass. She leaned against the wall, attempting to steady her breathing when a hand tapped her shoulder.

"Sarai, are you alright?"

She turned, every movement stilted. Slow. "Should I be?"

Cisuré swallowed. She took a step back, sucking her lower lip between her teeth. "You've heard about the warrant."

"The one where I die on a whipping post? *Certo.*" Sarai couldn't hide her bewilderment and hurt. "What I want to know is *why.*"

"One of us had to make the right choice." Cisuré's eyes welled. "You're headed for disaster, and I *won't* see you go there. You weren't going to stop. I *had* to!"

It took Sarai several minutes to hoist her dropped jaw. "Please don't discredit your intelligence and mine. You can't expect me to believe your only option was signing off on that warrant and having Tullus roast my throat!"

Cisuré's eyes widened. She pulled Sarai to a deserted patch of grass. "What do you mean?"

It poured out: Aelius, Tullus, the burning. Throughout her explanation, Cisuré's face grew increasingly baffled until it was a mask of horror.

"He hurt you?" The other girl wrenched down the collar of Sarai's tunic and paused. "I don't see anything."

"I healed it, but he almost went through my jugular," Sarai whispered. "I thought I was going to die."

Cisuré bit her lip. "Are you sure?"

Sarai froze. "What?"

"I'm not doubting you!" Cisuré said quickly. "I only mean that Tullus hurt your neck at Helvus's, didn't he? Perhaps he accidentally inflicted the burns, and you didn't notice. You were both troubled at the time, so it's understandable."

Sarai wondered if she was dreaming. She had to be, because none of it made sense.

"Cisuré, I'm not lying."

"I'm not saying you're lying! But it's been so difficult for you. You're confused."

"I'm not *confused*! I felt him searing my skin on your Tetrarch's command!"

Impatience rippled across Cisuré's face. "Tetrarch Aelius had no reason to do that. You were going to agree to search Kadra's tower anyway." At Sarai's silence, her eyes narrowed. "Weren't you?"

"Why should I after what Aelius—"

"*Tetrarch* Aelius!" Cisuré glanced skyward, searching for patience. "If anyone burns people alive, it's Kadra. He could have done this to you and tricked you into thinking that it was Tullus."

Sarai stared at her oldest friend, something bitter building in her but refusing to bubble over. Because that would prove Cisuré right.

"You don't believe me," she finally said. "You can dress it however you want, but the truth is that you'd rather believe that monster you serve over me."

Cisuré paled at the eerie calm of her voice. "I'm being objective. And let's not point fingers at who really serves a monster."

"Right." Tears pricked at Sarai's eyelids. "The thing is, I didn't *choose* mine." Cisuré tensed. "I didn't go into the Grand Elsarian Temple and vow to be some smooth-talking snake's Petitor and *lie* to my stupid, scarred friend thousands of miles away about it every single day for *four years*." Her voice escalated until each word was a snarl. A few vigiles some distance away cast a wary eye at them.

Cisuré blanched. "Who told you?"

"It should have been *you*!"

"I didn't want you to feel bad!" the other girl yelled back. "You were broken. Ruined. How could I tell you I was doing better than you ever could?"

The breath vanished from Sarai's lungs. "You thought I'd resent you?"

"Haven't you always?" Cisuré's voice cracked. "All you talk about is poverty and disparity—"

"Because that was my life and still is! I just got beaten and *burned*—"

"This is what I mean!" Cisuré's eyes were hot with anger. "You're *unbearable*! Even when Marus beat me and forced me into being the most-talented daughter anyone could ask the gods for, you still *hated* that you didn't have my life, didn't you? But now that you're here, can't you see why you got so much less? You have no regard for centuries of established law or social order. These are the consequences! I never believed in your silly visions of tearing everything down, and I never will. I hoped for you to grow past it, but you're still stuck playing the victim."

"So that's what you think of me." Sarai's voice was tight with pain. "Well, I'm glad you've finally let it out. It must have been difficult letting it fester all these years. And you say *I* hold on to anger."

Cisuré jerked back as though she'd been slapped. "I—" She seemed to have finally realized what she'd said. "Sarai, I—"

"I'll let the scuta go." The lie came from the deep well of her long-held rage, and as it emerged, Sarai didn't feel guilty. "I don't want to fight. Tell Aelius I'll have something for him before the trial."

A shocked smile formed on Cisuré's face. "By Wisdom, you've finally seen reason." She hugged her tight. "Sarai, I'm so happy you came around. All it took was a little quarrel." Releasing her with a watery chuckle, Cisuré fixed her gaze at a point behind her and turned murderous. "Watch out, here comes the monster. I'll see you soon, then?"

Staring at the other girl's excited grin, Sarai wondered how Kadra did it. No lovers. No lies. No weaknesses. Right now, she would give anything for the same.

"Of course," she said listlessly. Her body didn't feel like her own. At least Cisuré would convince Aelius and Tullus that she'd been cowed.

She carefully composed her expression before walking over to Kadra and their mounts, but his piercing eyes missed nothing. They cut to Cisuré, ice forming in their depths. Before he could walk over, and undoubtedly shred the other girl to the bone, she stepped into his path.

"I'm ready to head home." As she said it, she realized she'd never referred to Aoran Tower as "home" before.

The violence on Kadra's face faded. "Of course."

In a blink, she found herself lifted and deposited atop Caelum. He smoothly swung up on his horse. Maneuvering past the crowd, they left the Aequitas, reaching Aoran Tower in silence. Accepting Kadra's hand to dismount, she joined him in brushing down their horses, trying not to flinch whenever Cisuré's angry epithets resurfaced to haunt her.

"You'll have to tell me how you do it," she said, after a moment. "Limiting who's allowed in your tower. Refusing to work your way through every pleasure house in Ur Dinyé. All that."

He didn't balk at the question. "Lovers are a liability. Everyone has a price." Moving behind her, he assisted her with brushing Caelum. "It's easier to take care of my needs myself than foist them on others."

Her brush halted in her horse's mane, suddenly assaulted by images of him half-naked in a dressing robe, working himself in his bedroom, sweat gliding down his neck as he—

"Most people don't mind a bit of foisting," she stammered.

"They're welcome to it." He sounded unconcerned.

"Aelius could frame you even without the act. The person could just . . . use their imagination." Her cheeks could fry an egg with how hot they were.

"Ah, the gods have blessed me with a very noticeable birthmark. It's an easy charge to disprove, even if it means showing the audience my—"

"You—" She spun to face him, horribly aware that she was crimson. She scowled at the laugh he was barely suppressing. "You aren't supposed to have a sense of humor." It came out as accusation. "You're all blood and terror."

He flashed her a wry grin that threw her even further. "I sound unbearable."

She nearly said it. That he was. Then Cisuré's words resurfaced. *You're unbearable.* Her smile drooped. The stone in her heart sank deeper.

"Goodnight, Kadra."

Watching her carefully, he nodded and followed her into Aoran Tower. A sliver of moonlight dappled their path, laying their shadows out beside them. Side by side.

Any other day, she would have been catatonic at the knowledge that her only friend thought so little of her. But for now, she took refuge in the fact that there was at least one person in Ur Dinyé who didn't think her easily confused or eternally angry. Who saw her as strong, deferred to her judgment, and saw power in her rage.

"Thank you," she whispered to the man beside her.

And if she wiped her eyes a few times too many, he said nothing of it.

CHAPTER
TWENTY-THREE

Rain slammed into the ground under Silun's bluish glow, turning the landscape outside Aoran Tower into a blur of midnight and thunder.

Her hurt at Cisuré's barbs tangled with a thousand worries. Aelius's warrant, the trial . . . Kadra. Sarai glanced at the window, knowing he was out there, soaked to the skin and throwing lightning back to the sky. She wondered how often he'd brushed fingers with Death, if he'd ever seen a bolt tunnel down to earth, and wondered if he would fail in altering its path.

He knew Aelius and Tullus wanted his head, but she hadn't told him of the choice they'd given her between removing him as Tetrarch or being whipped to death. At first, it was because she'd barely been able to think straight that night. But afterward, she hadn't wanted him to know. He'd already killed two Guildmasters to prevent her from going to the mines, at complete consequence to him. Against a more imminent threat, she had no doubt he'd do worse and bear the blame for it.

She needed something so irrefutable that it would strip the teeth off Aelius and Tullus before they could even begin to accuse her of *calumnia*. If only she knew what that was.

She barely tasted her breakfast, and her mood didn't improve a whit upon finding Kadra absent from his study hours later, despite the storm having faded to a dull pattering.

"He was on the city battlements," Cato explained. "The storm was a bad one, so he'll need to recover. Gaius will accompany you to the Temple instead."

It felt wrong to think of Kadra ever needing rest. "He always seems relentless."

Cato gave her an appraising look over his cup of tea. "He's been alone too long to know much else."

It was on the tip of her tongue to ask whether the owner of the ribbon in his room had been the reason for that solitude, but she forced it down. Casting a worried glance at Kadra's bedroom door, she left for the Grand Elsarian Temple with Gaius.

Master Cleric Linus greeted them at the doors, glower in full bloom, and huffed all the way to the library. She exchanged a weary look with Gaius at the books squeezed into every corner of the octagonal room.

"I'll take the left wall," she said resignedly. And they began.

It took them three days to find the first letter. Gaius fussed about, bringing plump pastries into the library, much to Linus's outrage. He'd apologized at least fifty times for having left her vulnerable to Tullus's abduction and seemed keen to boost the count to triple digits by the end of the week. They worked through the shelves, day after day, squinting in the dim light, and pacing the room to keep awake when nighttime fell.

Five days before the trial, she'd gathered a list of other scuta that Jovian and Livia had witnessed bursting along with the land parcels that the Metals Guild had then bought up post-disaster. While Livia's notes had grown terse, Jovian had redoubled his efforts to amass proof. He'd been a meticulous researcher with the sort of dogged resilience that Sarai wished she could have known in person. He'd dug into her fall, suspecting that Othus had purposefully destroyed the records. But his line of deduction hadn't taken him to Kadra.

> *I don't know why everyone thinks our STG was a jilted pleasure worker. I doubt a noble would bring one to Aelius's conviviums. Aelius would have a fit.*
>
> *But even if they slipped one past, the theory still falls apart. No seasoned pleasure worker, especially one*

accompanying a powerful, well-paying noble, would throw their life away over something as inconsequential as feelings. It's insulting that the theory's lasted this long.

But you won't believe who went to that function four years ago. Helvus! It was around this time that his star started to rise, after finding that iron mine. That convivium has to be when he was contracted by Aelius to manufacture scuta. None of this looks good at all.

He hasn't suspected anything yet. He thinks I'm praying away at the Temple, but there are moments when he looks at me, and I could swear on all the Wretched that he knows.

I think we should leave. I'm as lost as you are.

Yours,

Jovian

Sarai buried her head in her heads, blinking back tears. *Elsar rest their souls.* Searching for Livia's reply, she lost track of the hours, only realizing that it was near four in the morning and that Gaius was fast asleep when she accidentally dropped a book.

Groggy-eyed, he left her at Aoran Tower, promising to be back at it in a few hours. She fished out the key from around her neck. A quiet footfall sounded behind her. She stilled at the soft snick of metal sliding against metal.

Pretending to be unaware, she reached for her armilla and got *beshaz* active, just as her late-night visitor reached her. Then, she struck. Sarai seized a muscular arm, her magic reaching through their skin to locate the closest tendon and sever it. Their hand went limp, the dagger falling to the ground.

"Next time, be quieter," she hissed.

"Bitch!" Her completely unfamiliar assailant yanked her by the braid, slamming her head against the barrier of Kadra's wards.

Why is it always the hair? Reaching behind her to the hand on her head, she snapped three of his knuckles. Hair-Yanker let her go with a high-pitched howl. Gripping her key, she prepared to flee into the security of Aoran Tower when the whisper of a blade leaving its sheath sounded unnaturally loud in the night. The edge kissed her neck. A sliver of pain followed in its wake. *Shit, two men.*

"I think I've had more than enough of men mauling my neck," she muttered.

"It's the only part we need," The second Guildsman's eyes were greedy. "It's worth five thousand aurei."

What? "That's more than my salary." She didn't know whether to be pleased or offended.

The men shrugged. The knife rose. She jerked back, inserting a hand between the dagger and her neck as he plunged it downward. The soft flesh between her thumb and index finger split, the point of the blade emerging through her palm. Cursing, she wrenched the dagger loose, and drove it into his shoulder.

A roar of fury rent the night. Evading both men, she palmed the head of her key, debating on how to distract them so she could run inside when another voice cut in.

"Sarai?" Anek looked mildly confused, glancing at both Guildsmen. "Well, this is something."

Hair-Yanker nudged Dagger-Shoulder. "The neutralis is here too."

"Two heads." Dagger-Shoulder looked gleeful. "Eight thousand aurei."

Sarai did the math. "Wait, why is their head worth less?" She ducked when Hair-Yanker attempted his signature technique again and let him shove her to the ground.

Closing her eyes, she reached with her magic, found a tendon and sliced it. His screams told her she was on the right track. She continued, ripping into muscle, metal clashing in the background as Anek handled Dagger-Shoulder.

At a piteous squeal, she opened her eyes and peered past a now-wailing Hair-Yanker to where Dagger-Shoulder had gotten another dagger through his hand and was now fleeing. She let go of Hair-Yanker to allow him to do the same, and he quickly followed.

"Ruin's tits." Anek plopped down beside her on the grass. "You've been busy."

Sarai nodded, harsh breaths sawing from her. "So have you. How do you have a bounty too? You're the quintessential Petitor."

They heaved a sigh. "You first. That's a dangerous skill you've got."

"Don't tell Harion."

"That you could have healed his nose? Never." Anek toyed with the scarlet hilt of their dagger. "Have you heard of a Petitor named Livia?"

Her head jerked up. "Yes." She eyed Anek warily. "Why?"

"I was looking into her." They returned Sarai's start of surprise with a speaking look. "She was my predecessor after all."

"Did you find anything?"

"I wish I hadn't." They passed Sarai a familiar square of parchment. "This was in the spine of the last volume she ever requested from the Hall of Records. She died the next day."

Sarai curled her fingers around the letter. "Have you read it?"

"My Urdish is rudimentary, but I got the gist. I spoke to Livia's mother and heard you'd been by. When you started practically living in the Hall of Records, I figured you were looking for what I'd found."

Unfolding the letter, Sarai steeled her nerve at Livia's shaky writing.

My dear Jovian,

I'm going. I can't ask you to come, but if all goes well, we'll be at the center of Edessa's most explosive case tomorrow. I just need a scutum to prove it.

I overheard a few of the Metals Guild's guards saying that they'll be drinking on their shift tonight. I can sneak past. A scutum isn't that heavy. I'll be in and out before they notice. If we crash a trial at the Aequitas and reveal it all, no one can hurt us with the whole city watching.

I'm leaving at midnight. If you're coming, I'll be by the side doors into the forges.

Your fearless friend,
Livia

Sarai returned the letter to Anek. They both knew what had happened next. Livia hadn't made it out of the Metals Guild that night. Jovian had died two weeks later.

Anek stretched out on the grass. "I went to the Guild and asked about how a young woman could possibly fall into a vat of molten metal. The openings for those are narrow to keep the metal from cooling. The Guildsmen didn't like that. Hence the bounty."

"When was this?"

"Right about when you caused all that trouble with Helvus."

Sarai winced. "Bad timing." She healed the stab wound in her palm. "Stop looking into this. You have your family, people you can lose. I don't."

"Believe me, I'd rather leave it to you and Kadra." They squinted. "Does Cisuré know?"

She stiffened. "She doesn't believe me."

Anek sucked air in through their teeth. "She'll learn. Just because these gods-obsessed men created the rules, doesn't mean they should be above them. Especially if Helvus and our Saintly Head Tetrarch have been running a dangerous con for years."

"Don't forget our Violent Senior Lecher Tetrarch."

Anek let out a bark of laughter. "He couldn't look a woman in the face if it killed him. It's right down to the tits." They tossed their dagger in the air and caught it. "But we all play the game."

"You sound like Telmar. He's been telling me to keep my head down from the start."

"Never discount what Telmar's seen. He's been a magus for decades." Anek withdrew a crimson handkerchief and handed it to her. "I also came by to give you this. Cassandane says that her offer to leave still stands. If you're ever in need of her assistance, place that somewhere visible."

"That's kind of her." Sarai sighed. "She knows everything too, doesn't she?"

"She's the fulcrum," Anek mused. "Not powerful enough to support Kadra without causing a civil war, and too weak to whittle at Aelius and Tullus like Kadra does. If he falls, then Aelius and Tullus will stand uncontested."

"He won't fall," she said firmly.

"Perhaps not. But he's been acting uncharacteristically reckless. Bringing that strike on Admia's home was a bad move. I've seen him change only once before and that wasn't for the better." At her confused look, they explained. "He went a little mad with the bloodshed when he first ascended to Tetrarch after Othus was killed. I thought it was because he cared for Othus in his own way, even if Othus wasn't particularly kind to him. But, sometimes, I wonder if there was something else that changed him four years ago. Just like you seem to be the catalyst now."

Four years ago. That number kept cropping up.

Anek raked a hand through their curls. Getting to their feet, they stretched out a hand to help her up, then stopped. "Sorry, forgot you don't like being touched." They laughed at her shock. "Did you really think you were being unobtrusive, flinching sky-high whenever Harion prodded at you?"

This city was going to pry all her secrets from her. "It's just . . . men," she muttered and accepted their hand up. "You're fine."

Grinning, they slapped her shoulder, then cleared their throat. "You don't seem as uncomfortable with Kadra, though." Her eyes narrowed, and Anek winked. "Now, don't tense up. It isn't just me. Every vigile across Edessa was probably assigned to watch you two at the start."

"Care to share what you discovered?"

"Some other day." They chuckled at her unamused stare. "Hold Kadra back. Cassandane's convinced that he's up to something. Keep him on his throne. And Sarai"—their face turned serious—"be very, very afraid of Aelius and Tullus."

Shoulders slumping, she watched their departing figure grow smaller in the distance. "I am afraid. That's the problem."

Perhaps this was why Telmar drank. There was nothing sweeter than oblivion in a world this ugly. But as she fell asleep in Aoran Tower for what could be her fifth last night, she prayed to a silent sky that she wouldn't see that oblivion soon.

CHAPTER
TWENTY-FOUR

"I think that's it." Three days before the trial that would determine her fate, Gaius leaned back with a groan. "That's every book in here."

Sarai slumped against the wall. She had written records of Petitor deaths matching with dates of stormfall, family statements of a common theme of paranoia before their deaths, registers of the Metals Guild buying plots of land after they'd been struck by lightning, and she'd soon be requesting the certificates Jovian had mentioned of Helvus's ownership of the iron mine from which he'd produced the scuta.

But she had no direct evidence.

Heading to the Hall of Records, she tried to convince herself that she could survive a thousand lashes, while Gaius kept up a steady stream of chatter to boost her spirits. She'd always expected to starve in Arsamea, not be whipped before a crowd.

"Sometimes, I think you're more terrifying than Tetrarch Kadra," Gaius went on cheerfully. "Scarier when you can use their mind against them, instead of mutilating or burning or torturing the truth out of men and women—" Finally seeming to realize that he wasn't doing Kadra's character any credit, he pressed his lips shut.

"So Tetrarch Kadra tortures women?" she asked wearily.

"They commit crimes too, you know!"

"Right," she muttered. "What if it was a girl? Say, fourteen."

Gaius's brow furrowed. "Tetrarch Kadra doesn't harm young people. Sends them to the mines in rare cases. But he tends to give them a chance."

At least there was that.

She had the Hall of Records memorized at this point. Seeking out the dull gray limestone building that housed the Mining Archives, she requested the records for iron mines found over four years ago. The archivist's eyebrows jumped to the ceiling.

"It's good to have someone come looking for these." He handed her a set of tomes. "Haven't had anyone read those since Telmar."

Her fingers stilled on the first page. "Magus Telmar?"

"You know, the drunk." The archivist chuckled. "How he hasn't stabbed himself during a swordsmanship lesson is beyond everyone. The man has a liver of stone."

Odd. She thanked him and promised to return the records in a few days. After the trial. Part of her hoped that making the promise would ensure that it came true.

"So that's it?" Gaius looked worried at the blank way she kept staring at the records. "Nothing else Jovian or Livia left behind?"

"This is it." She zipped Aoran Tower's key back and forth on the cord around her neck. "If we could get our hands on a scutum, it would change everything, but . . ."

"What about Livia's mother or Decimus? Did they have any?"

"No. Livia got rid of all her scuta before her death, and Decimus—"

She froze. Decimus had attempted to give her a scutum in thanks after she'd dispatched Helvus. Then, there'd been his tearful remarks the first night they'd visited. *She even helped pay for our scutum when he was short on coin*, he'd said.

But Livia and Jovian had both known the scuta were flawed.

Livia had died two weeks before Jovian. He'd moved in with Decimus. And brought a scutum with him, saying Livia had helped him purchase it.

Dumping her books on Gaius, she dug in her pockets for the leather pouch in which she'd been storing all the letters. She thrust Livia's last letter under Gaius's nose.

"That night she went to the Metals Guild, he came with her!" she said triumphantly. "She died, but he was able to lug out a scutum."

No wonder Jovian had gone half-mad toward the end. He must have blamed himself.

"Gaius, Decimus has that scutum!" She beamed. "He tried to give it to me a month ago! I didn't remember—I refused back then because I didn't know, but—we have proof for the trial!"

"Elsar be praised!" Arms full of books, he grinned from ear to ear. "I'll inform Tetrarch Kadra to assign Decimus a guard right away."

Bubbling with excitement, she nearly skipped out of the Hall of Records.

"This calls for celebration," Gaius said thoughtfully.

"We can't very well throw a convivium." She laughed.

"What about something equally exuberant that Aelius won't suspect?"

"Like what?"

He smiled mysteriously, eyes faintly cunning. "You'll see."

Sarai set her pen down, eyes swimming. Her collation of written evidence for the trial twisted in the flickering light from the hearth in Kadra's office.

Everything's ready. In three days' time, all of Ur Dinyé would know.

The door swung open. Kadra stalked in and paused to find her bracing her head against his desk.

His eyebrows snapped together. "You need to rest."

"I agree wholeheartedly." She organized the parchment spread over the desk's surface.

"Petitor Sarai, will you be coming?" Gaius's head popped out from behind Kadra's frame.

"Where to?" she asked absently.

"The pleasure house! To celebrate! We're all going. Tetrarch Aelius won't suspect anything."

She was suddenly, completely, utterly awake. Something hot and bitter squirmed in her chest. She turned to Gaius, studiously ignoring Kadra. Her words were slow and precise.

"Anek mentioned that it was a tradition." She forced her face into something resembling amusement.

"Good way to release the pressure." Gaius winked. "It's been too long since our last outing. We curtailed it on account of your arrival, but you're one of us now." He patted her shoulder. "Should I saddle your horse?"

"Yes," she said at the same time that Kadra said "No."

She didn't look as Kadra's gaze bored a hole into her profile.

"You're tired," he said as though that was the end of the matter.

"I'm awake." She reached for her birrus, stomach churning. "You aren't the only one who's been under pressure."

Gaius shifted awkwardly as she awarded him a bright smile.

"Are we going as a group?" She wrapped her birrus around her.

Glancing at Kadra, who was radiating visible menace, Gaius muttered something about having to confirm that and raced out of the office.

The door shut, leaving a strange, uncomfortable intimacy in the room. Acid frothed in her gut, dread snaking under her ribs to squeeze tight. She shoved it aside, shaken.

It's not like we're anything to each other. This shouldn't matter. Kadra had gone to pleasure houses before and likely seen all manner of exhibitionism. She slapped the scrolls containing her summaries of evidence on his desk with unnecessary force, all too conscious of him watching her. *Stop, you're being ridiculous.* Pulling herself together, she retreated behind a placid mask. Neither of them said a word. By the time Gaius returned, the tension in the room was thick enough to slice. Looking terrified, he eked out that their horses were saddled and fled once more.

Kadra finally moved from his position by the fireplace. "Do you really want to come?"

Her eyes jumped to his. His coal-black gaze glittered, something turbulent within. At least, she wasn't the only one seething.

"Might as well see what the fuss is about." It was past time that she cauterized this madness. What if Kadra met someone in the future? Or if the owner of that accursed ribbon resurfaced? That panic was welling in her even now at both possibilities didn't bode well.

Kadra's jaw tensed. "If you'd like."

"I would."

Their black moods persisted until they reached the stables, where Kadra's vigiles, who'd been chatting excitedly, suddenly found themselves quite occupied with the sky, the grass, or the buttons of their tunics. She put on an outward show of interest in "Where the Cocks Crow" as the pleasure house was called.

"Do they have anything similar in the north?" a woman asked with interest.

"It was just affairs in Arsamea, with each other or the rare outsider." A new female arrival in town sparked as much of a hunt as for deer in the winter. "The closest pleasure house was all the way in Sal Flumen."

The vigile gave her a pitying glance. "You haven't lived much then."

"Life was survival."

"Isn't it always?" The woman sighed.

It wasn't long before their motley group of at least twenty vigiles drew up outside a pleasant-looking inn. Only the jaunty sign perched on an over-large weather vane at the top gave its identity away. As Sarai read it, her lips twitched. Someone had seen fit to convert a "C" to a "G."

"'Where the Cocks Grow,'" she read. But a laugh wouldn't come.

The clammy feeling in her chest twisted with every step to the front gate and she was flooded with dread when a stunning woman met them there.

"Tetrarch Kadra's party?" Her strikingly pale eyes seemed to glow as she smiled. "Right this way."

Inside, the pleasure house wasn't like any of the raucous, wine-soaked xanns she'd slept at on her journey to Edessa, or as opulent and high-priced as a xann she'd briefly spotted in Kirtule. This place embodied comfort and easy amusement.

An array of plump couches and cushions decorated the atrium's tiled courtyard with a fountain of wine at the center. Artfully placed candlesticks illuminated a wide staircase that led to two floors of private rooms, scantily-clad pleasure workers at every corner. By the fountain, a troupe of musicians roared bawdy songs to a growing crowd, dancing in the nude.

Groupings of all orientations and numbers lounged about, clothed, unclothed, deep in conversation or fondling each other on couches, blowing clouds of blazeleaf into the air. The vigiles scattered in every direction with uproarious cheers. And, suddenly, she was alone in a world she'd only ever read of. She hung her birrus over her wrist, skin tingling at the moans coming from the patrons and drifting down from the second floor.

Off-kilter, she nearly didn't notice the quick glances from vigiles at every corner, even as they selected their partners. Eyes swerved toward her and then several steps to the left where Kadra was heading to the bar. Trying to escape them, she ducked into the ebb and flow of people dancing by the musicians and accidentally inhaled a lungful of blazeleaf. She tottered, a languorous heat spreading through her.

Across the room, Kadra inspected a bottle of wine. Glowering at the cork for a long moment under the barkeep's nervous gaze, he uncorked it, poured some in a glass, and stared at it some more before practically downing the entire bottle. She stared as he pointed out another bottle and performed the same ritual. He didn't turn to her once.

He never engages, Anek had said, but perhaps, deep down, she'd secretly hoped that she would prove the exception. A foolish wish that had cost her. *I shouldn't have come.* Perhaps this was why he'd tried to stop her. Because he'd known how lost she would be here. Swallowing, she ignored the heat behind her eyes. At least she hadn't given any outward indication of what she felt for him. Tetrarchs and Petitors were bound for life. One foolish confession and she'd have condemned them to horrendous awkwardness. She debated slinking away when a beautiful neutralis stepped in her path.

"Petitor Sarai." They smiled, all dark eyes and riotous golden curls. "I'm Tavlis. Your first time, I gather?"

She nodded in admiration at how unselfconscious they were by their nudity. "I'm still taking it all in."

"*Certo*," they said easily. "Would you like to know where to start?"

Catching a glance from a vigile who'd never cared much for her until recently, she stilled at the pity in his eyes. Turning back to Tavlis, she nodded. This foolish pining would only get her hurt.

"I . . ." She stared at the floor. "I don't really know what to do. Should we talk first?"

"Would you like us to talk or would you like me to start slowly?" Tavlis asked gently. "You can halt whenever you'd like."

She'd never seen a smile as mesmerizing as theirs. But she felt nothing. "Slowly," she stammered.

They leaned toward her, looping an arm around her waist to pull her close. Her palms went damp with something that felt like panic.

"Buttons or do you want my mouth?" they whispered, inches from her.

A weight squeezed her chest. "Buttons," she made herself say.

Gentle fingers caressed her jaw, another hand working at her collar. The first button slipped free, then the next. Cool air brushed her exposed skin, and all she could think about was when Kadra had done the same after Tullus had burned her.

Pressing her against a pillar, Tavlis stroked the exposed skin of her collarbone and stilled, looking thoughtfully at her skin.

The scars. "Could you," she stammered, and tried again. "Could we finish the buttons first? And can we keep . . . everything on?"

Tavlis smiled softly. "Absolutely."

They resumed their downward path. Feeling close to tears, she glanced back at the bar. Kadra's fist choked the stem of his wineglass as he tipped it upward, taking a hard swallow. His mouth drew into a hard line like the burn of alcohol wouldn't soothe him. Looking terrified, the barkeep refilled his glass.

Is something wrong?

Lips brushed her shoulder, and she jumped.

"Is something wrong?" Tavlis asked carefully.

"No."

Tavlis tilted their head to one side. "It's darker on this side of the pillar. If you'd prefer the privacy."

A few feet away, the vigile who'd teased her about not having lived enough enthusiastically slid onto her partner and waved at Sarai.

She immediately shifted over to the other side of the pillar. "That's helpful, thank you."

Tavlis pressed another kiss against her collarbone. She tried to make her body respond to the soft whisper of hands into her open tunic, but it all felt wrong. Yet, if she left, there would be pitying glances tomorrow as the vigiles gossiped that their Tetrarch truly did feel nothing for her. She had to prove that she was equally unconcerned. Because, at some point between her distrust and this powerful, unyielding man calling her "strong," she'd wanted the rumors everyone had been parroting to be true.

She didn't pull her gaze away fast enough when Kadra looked up from his drink, and he unerringly found her across the room. The look in his eyes knocked all breath from her. Heat tangled with something sour. She only realized that she'd gone motionless when Tavlis raised their head.

"Are you alright? Is this what you want?" Cupping her cheek, they pressed an openmouthed kiss to her jaw.

And something splintered, echoing like the crack of a whip across the room.

She sprang back. The pleasure house barely paused for an instant before resuming its business. It took her only a moment to find the source of the sound. Fragments of Kadra's shattered glass dug into his hand, wine leaking into the wounds. He stared at it, the anger in his eyes looking strangely like it was directed inward.

I can't do this.

Sarai turned to Tavlis. "I'm so sorry. You're absolutely lovely. I just . . . I thought I could, but I can't."

When she managed to meet their eyes, there was a hint of a smile on their face.

"Of course, Petitor Sarai. Perhaps another time."

Insisting on paying them, she hastily half-buttoned-up her uniform and strode to the door. She'd just have to absorb what the other vigiles had to say tomorrow. Easing out of the crush, she walked right into Kadra.

"Leaving already?" He pried a shard of glass from his hands. Something infinitely wild seethed under his now too-calm demeanor.

She swallowed. "You were right. I'm tired."

A muscle bunched in his jaw, eyes flinty. "Does my presence bother you?"

"In general?"

"Now."

Her heart beat at a breakneck speed. "You mean am I not indulging tonight because you're looming over my shoulder like one of the Wretched?"

The muscle in his jaw looked liable to snap. "Yes."

Fascinated, she stared at it. "No." Throwing caution to the wind, she stepped closer. "You aren't the only one who manages their needs," she murmured.

Kadra went rigid. A breath and his eyes closed. "Fuck."

A violent shudder rippled through her when his eyes traced the open column of her throat as though he were searching for words in the gait of her pulse.

A patron squeezed past them, pushing them together against the door. Kadra braced himself with a palm right as she clutched at his robes to steady herself. The muscles under her palm tensed. She expected him to step back. He didn't.

"Is that the only reason why you're leaving?" Wine scented the air between them. "I saw you. Earlier."

"People expect celibacy of you. I'd be the odd one out if I didn't indulge."

"Then why stop?"

"Because I feel *nothing*," she grit out. "And when you"—she snapped her fingers in front of her face to signify his glass shattering and her corresponding snap of realization—"I had enough of forcing myself to try. I *can't* so—"

"Neither can I."

She was suddenly afire. She looked up, her lips parting at how close his mouth was to hers.

"Because everyone's a liability?"

"Yes." Kadra slipped a hand on the back of her neck, tilting her head up with his thumb. "And because I shouldn't."

"Why?" she whispered.

"I *shouldn't*." His voice was hoarse. His palm circled her throat. The faintest hint of pressure, and she instinctively tilted her chin to give him better access.

"Because?" It was almost a plea.

His thumb moved to her jaw, eyes holding a world of conflict. That halted her. *Not like this. Not if you'll regret it.* She grabbed his hand before he could lean in. He looked as dazed as she felt. They stared at each other, before their hands fell.

After a long moment, he spoke. "This way." He led her past the crush of bodies and to a side door that led out of the building.

Outside, she drew several deep breaths, the sweet smoky scent of blazeleaf, alcohol, and sex fading in favor of unpleasant reason. When she finally looked at Kadra, he was getting their horses ready, movements jerkier than she'd ever seen them.

"I . . . hope you don't regret leaving," she mumbled.

He turned, face back to its implacable set. "I never stay long enough for them to actually poison the wine."

Her jaw dropped. "You terrified that barkeep for no reason!"

A hint of the wildness she'd seen earlier returned to his features. "You were watching."

Flushing, she cleared her throat. "Your hand."

He looked like he'd long forgotten that it was bleeding. Taking it, she held herself back from pressing into him when he curled his fingers around hers, holding them still as she quickly mended the cuts.

Kadra gave her a dark smile, helping her onto Caelum. "Home?"

Wisdom save me. Aoran Tower wasn't her home. She was long overdue to find her own domus. She took the reins, searching for common sense and finding none.

"Home," she agreed.

CHAPTER
TWENTY-FIVE

Praefa was a thin crescent in the night sky, barely lighting the now-familiar paved ribbon to Decimus's home on which Sarai rode beside Kadra.

With a day and a half before trial, they'd decided to transport the scutum to Aoran Tower. Cato had warily made space for it in the wine cellar, with Kadra dryly assuring him that it wouldn't explode while he was home.

I'm so close. The scutum would be exposed as fraudulent, and Aelius and Tullus would have no further hold over her. Granted, she had nothing yet to prove they were behind the dead Petitors and Othus's murder, but it was a solid start to destabilizing them.

The air hung damp and chilly, winter giving way to the wet month of spring. Sarai glanced at Kadra. Posture impeccable as ever, he appeared lost in thought.

"What'll you do when this is over?" she asked.

The question seemed to throw him. It was a moment before he answered. "I'll have peace." A bitter edge underscored the words.

He'd been like Jovian and Livia, too, she realized. Trapped by knowledge he couldn't act on and waiting for enough allies so he could bring Aelius and Tullus to justice. For all her fear of the trial, she was glad that he'd seen an ally in her.

Dismounting by Decimus's haphazardly repaired front door, she squinted at the lack of light within. Even the windows had been boarded up.

"Your vigiles must be exhausted after last night." Sarai secured Caelum. "I thought they'd be on watch and alert for—"

Kadra raised a finger to his lips, gliding off his horse with the fluidity of a predator. He examined the domus for a long moment before he cursed in a manner far different than he had at the pleasure house. Before she could ask why, he gripped her hand and steered her back to her horse, pressing a dagger into her palm.

"Ride back a quarter mile, and you'll find Gaius. He'll accompany you home."

She stared at him like he'd sprouted two heads. "Why in *havïd* would I do that?"

There was a grim tension to him, harder and colder than she'd seen yet.

"Kadra." She blanched, stock-still. "What aren't you telling me?"

Grasping her shoulders, he turned her to face him, staring beyond her to something at the front of the house. Something she wasn't seeing.

Sarai tried to turn.

"Don't," he said softly, but she stepped away.

She had to know. Trembling, she walked to the front door, pushed it open, and staggered back.

The air reeked. An ugly brown painted the interior, a mass of limbs scattered about the narrow entryway, with a few toes ghoulishly stuck in the doorframe. A dark object rolled out of the shadows, its path no longer impeded by the door. The head came to a rest by her feet, bloated with death, eyes staring blankly at the ground.

Decimus. Or what was left of him.

As if manipulated by some magic outside of her body, her head swiveled toward the windows, where Kadra had been looking. She'd thought they were boards. They weren't. Kadra's vigiles had stuck to their duty after all. They watched through the window even now.

Blood trickling from her throat. Her face hitting the ground. Sarai slammed a hand against the doorjamb.

"He's dead." She stared at Decimus's slack face, as though there was a possibility the man could come back to life. "He's dead," she repeated. And she already knew that the scutum was gone.

She should be panicking, but she couldn't feel anything.

Kadra took her by the shoulders, turning her away from the carnage. At the quick pace of her breath, he tipped her chin up to him.

"Come out of there." He took a step back, encouraging her to do the same. "Breathe."

She was shaking so badly she knew she'd collapse if he let her go. "If I hadn't sought him out—"

He cut the thought off at its legs. "He's been dead for a while." He tightened his grip when she tried to turn again. "Look at me, Sarai. He's been dead for at least three weeks, if not longer. The Metals Guild got to him a while ago."

"Because I illegally Probed Helvus—"

"Because Decimus made accusations at a tavern." His voice was glacial, meant to slice through her panic.

Decimus had been polite to her even when she'd just been Kadra's mouthy Petitor. She'd intended to give his brother justice. She'd wanted him to be there. She didn't realize that she was saying it all out loud until Kadra nodded.

"I know."

"Your vigiles—" She couldn't breathe.

"Aelius stationed people here to kill them if they came looking."

He exuded nothing in the way of grief, only fierce detachment. She'd have thought that he felt nothing and that his vigiles were assets at his disposal were it not for how his eyes had iced over. Right now, Kadra wasn't a politician, he was a general at war, whose people had suffered heavy casualties. He was already preparing for how the other side would pay.

And then and there, her resolve solidified. *They won't take him.* No matter what happened at trial, even if she was tied to the Aequitas's whipping post, she wouldn't allow them to topple Kadra. It wasn't just because he was a good man, or because she respected—*loved*—every mad inch of him. The land needed him. And he cared for it just as deeply. The knowledge sank to her bones, mingled with her grief.

"Give me a moment." Balling her hands into fists, she allowed the tears to fall silently, too numb to scream or sob. "One moment. Then I'll think of something too."

A fissure appeared in Kadra's hard mask at that. Snatches of emotion waged a war on his face. Conflict. Ferocity. Bleakness. And then, he visibly gave up. The hands on her shoulders moved to the back of her head, and he pulled her into him, arms like bands of steel around her.

"I'll make them pay," she bit out, and he stroked her hair, echoing the same fierce vow.

"*We* will."

Pressure tightened her chest. Sleep hadn't come. Every movement felt difficult, unnecessary, when she could simply lie in bed. Kind, grieving Decimus had been murdered. She had no hope of finding another scutum in a little over a day, and she couldn't ruin Kadra.

She slipped out of Aoran Tower to pace the Academiae's tangled walkways, seeking clarity, aid, anything that would save her from Jovian's and Livia's paths. The sky had no answer. She walked back.

Unlocking Aoran Tower's gate, Sarai noted Kadra's mount outside. He'd left for the vigile station after bringing her back several hours ago. She couldn't imagine having to let the others know their colleagues were dead.

Padding into the atrium, she paused at the raised voices coming from Kadra's study. Peering through the keyhole, she found Cato by one of the couches, furious. Kadra was less visible, but she could make out his face and the grim resolution in his eyes.

"How could you be so reckless?"

Unconcerned, Kadra brought a wineglass to his lips. "Everything's ready."

"*Drenevan!*" Sarai jumped at the roar. "She isn't ready. She's been worn down enough!"

"There's no other way."

She stilled at the finality in Kadra's tone.

"Times like this, I see why Othus called you a monster," Cato spat.

Kadra smiled sardonically. "And look at where he is and where I am."

Cato slammed a fist onto the table. Sarai raced toward the front door just as he stormed out of the tablinum. Pretending that she'd just returned, she released the doorknob.

"Is something wrong?"

"Just . . ." Cato struggled to compose himself. "Please make sure he's alright," he finally muttered, before leaving the tower.

She warily eyed the door to the tablinum, pausing at the series of rough curses coming from within, each one filthier than the last. Flushing, she considered the merits of sleeping in the atrium when the door parted a little wider, and she caught sight of Kadra.

He was covered in blood.

Sarai's breath stuttered as he shrugged off his tunic with another curse. Powerful muscles rippled at the motion, a few pale scars at his waist catching the firelight, but that wasn't what held her attention.

A series of deep gashes stretched across both collarbones, looping around his shoulder to curve down his back. More nasty gouges spanned his chest, his upper abdominal muscles practically shredded. Sweat-dampened hair hung over his forehead as he grimly surveyed the extent of the damage. How had he spoken so evenly to Cato? She'd have been screaming. What in *havïd* had happened in the hours since they'd returned from Decimus's home?

Tearing a strip from a roll of bandages, Kadra blotted the blood, then attempted to wrap another strip around his shoulder, grimacing when it slipped, digging into his wounds. Twisting around, he paused upon sighting her in the doorway.

Sarai's eyes followed the trail of blood dripping down his body, to the puddled tunic leaking scarlet onto his spotless tiles. There was far too much blood for all of it to be his.

"How many did you kill?" Her question hung in the iron-scented air, a gauntlet.

"Twelve." He knotted the bandage across one of his wounds, somehow managing to look immaculate despite the crimson rivulets charting a path down his tattered chest.

Any sane woman would run. She took a shaky step toward him.

"You should see a healer," she said hoarsely.

"And inform Aelius and Tullus that I'm injured?" The gravelly undertone to his voice hinted he was in pain. "I may as well open my gates and undo the wards while I'm at it."

"You took that risk with me." She closed the rest of the distance between them, the potent scents of wine, sweat, and iron overpowering. "I could have let anyone into your home."

"You despised me." One side of his mouth rose. "But at the Robing, you risked yourself so a man who was vermin would receive a fair trial. That was enough." Her breath hitched when he tucked a blood-covered knuckle under her chin. Kadra tilted his head down at her. "To hope you'd choose me."

Her pulse doubled. A drop of blood trailed down his arm, dripping off a fingertip to splatter on the floor. Those gouges would scar him for life, his muscles would never repair. He had to know it.

She spoke quickly. "I could heal that."

He halted his binding.

"Only if you want me to," she muttered.

A gleam lit his eyes before he unwrapped one of the bandages. And waited. She dropped her illusion and ran a pricked finger over *beshaz*. She held out her hands, and as he'd done when she'd tried to heal herself, he held her fingers still, pressing them to the golden skin of his stomach. Slowly, tentatively, she traced the jagged edges of one of the wounds and closed her eyes, searching deep. The cuts were a ragged mess, but there was nothing embedded in his skin. Scarlet coated her hands as power flowed from her fingertips, binding broken tissue, rebuilding torn arteries and muscle. She knew it burned, but he sat through it like stone.

Many moments later, she opened her eyes to his unblemished abdomen and Kadra regarded her for a moment before undoing the rest of his makeshift bandages. Without a word, she started on the worst of the wounds, the one that had all but shredded his chest.

Silence stretched between them, loaded with the questions he wasn't asking and the rabid hunger unfurling through her with every stroke of her hands across his flesh.

She broke first. "Growing up, I wanted to be a healer." She moved on to another gash, avoiding his eyes as he tried to catch hers. "Cisuré was gifted and wealthy enough for the Academiae. I wasn't, so I learned as much healing as I could on my own." She smiled bitterly. "I worked really hard."

"You always do."

She smiled sadly. "But Arsamea's healer didn't want an urchin as an apprentice. So, when I was fourteen, I left for Edessa to join Cisuré."

"And challenge the entrance exams," he said matter-of-factly.

She nodded. "I was here for a little over three days before I had to return."

"Why?"

"You've seen the scars. Cisuré brought me back to Arsamea after I was healed. I was in no condition to do anything. All I knew was that I was missing all memory of what happened here and that I could never be a healer again. I can still hurt people. There's no precision required to that, but handling serious damage is impossible on my own. As you can see"– she took a deep breath–"my hands are ruined."

Black rage dawned in his eyes. "The person who hurt you was here?"

"Yes."

"Who?" It was an order.

"I don't know."

She thought back to Kadra standing over her, cavalierly ordering a new face, a furious Othus beside him. All those years hungering for the truth, and now, part of her wanted nothing more than for it to stay buried, to stay assured that whatever he had done hadn't been to hurt her.

Once the final wound sealed, Sarai drew away, staring at the blood coating her fingers.

"That isn't what you'd do, though, is it, Kadra?" she asked softly. "You wouldn't maim an innocent so badly that they wished they were dead."

"No." The word was guttural. Taking her hands, he wiped the blood from each finger with a clean bandage. "Are you alright? After Decimus."

"I'll pull myself together. I've a little over a day left. Can't let them win."

His gaze turned molten. She shoved down the aching warmth humming in her, the painful desire to reach out and touch him just once more. Instead, she gestured at his chest.

"New skin usually itches for a day or two. Goodnight, Kadra."

"Why?" he asked as she made to head upstairs.

She didn't pretend to misunderstand his meaning. "Because you're wrong," she said, her heart racing a mile a minute. "I never despised you. Even when I wanted to."

At his silence, she looked up to find him watching her with an emotion that defied description. She didn't protest when he took her hand. For an aching, electrifying moment, she thought he would pull her to him.

Holding her gaze, Kadra bent and pressed his mouth to the inside of her wrist, lingering against her skin. "Goodnight, Sarai."

When he let go, she wobbled to her room and leaned against the door. There was no going back from that. No hiding from what she'd seen in those black eyes.

Hunger.

CHAPTER
TWENTY-SIX

One more day. Sarai eyed the white column of Cobhran Tower to the east with grim resolution. She had no doubt that Cisuré would seek her out tonight.

She had the curious sensation of being perched on an executioner's axe, watching as it tore sinew from bone in a shoddy stroke. It seemed that her friendship with Cisuré needed only one more blow to sever it. And while she would have held on for as long as it took, she doubted Cisuré would be as willing. Not when she had repeatedly brought the axe down herself.

A somber Gaius waited for her outside Aoran Tower, and she was hit by a wave of guilt so deep that she nearly dropped to her knees.

"I'm so sorry about the others." She met his eyes without cowering. "If I hadn't brought all of this on—"

"Forgive me, but I must stop you." Gaius shook his head, holding up a hand. "We've lost many people to Tetrarchs Aelius and Tullus. Including Tetrarch Othus, as we've only just discovered. Some may blame you. But the only people at fault here are those doing the killing. The rest of us are only guilty of not keeping our heads down when trying to do the right thing."

She halted at the familiarity of his response. Just like Telmar's odd pronouncements the day he'd given her Kadra's invitation to Aoran Tower.

"Gaius, I have an idea," she breathed. "Where do the instructors live here?"

He looked unnerved at her change of subject. "Petitor Sarai, if you're unwell—"

"I need to see Telmar."

Raising his eyes to the sky, Gaius muttered something about Kadra's Petitor being as mad as he was. "Oh, alright then."

She'd expected a magus's offices to be grand, but Telmar's abode, stashed in a corner of the Academiae's Safsher Hall, was barely bigger than her bedroom. Though that likely had to do with the bottles littered across the floor.

She'd knocked at first, then pushed the door open when he hadn't responded. Plumes of dust wafted about his cramped office, clinging to heavy curtains that only let slivers of light through. The shelves, laden with books on posture and technique, looked like they hadn't been touched in decades, but the crates of *ibez* scattered around the room were spotless. Gaius took one look at the mess and indicated that he'd rather stand guard outside.

She pointedly cleared her throat. The figure dozing in his chair, wrapped in his cloak, didn't budge. Grabbing the closest bottle, she uncorked and held it under his nose.

Telmar jackknifed to his feet, grabbing at the bottle. She held it out of reach, waiting as his eyes adjusted to the dim lighting.

"I know about the scuta," she said without preamble.

He halted mid-yawn. All color bled from his face.

"So, that's it," she said. "That's why you drink."

"I've said nothing—*nothing* to you," he stammered, collapsing into his chair. "Get out! Don't drag me down with you."

"I'm not going to involve you." She sat across him. "But I need evidence. You were honest with me from the start, and I never understood why."

"Should have listened, barmaid." He grabbed the bottle from her.

"How long have you known?" She held up a placating hand when he shook his head furiously. "It doesn't matter. My word is useless without evidence, and I'm set for trial tomorrow. Your secrets will die with me."

He took a gulp of wine before speaking. "Three years ago, I earned tenure as an instructor here." His eyes glazed over as he returned to those days. "I had everything I wanted. Never so much as heard a word of reprimand."

"But?" she prompted when he trailed off.

"There was a storm. I saw one of those *things* explode and down a block of insulae." His face tightened. "There was so much screaming. And the fire . . . it burnt out of control before we could do a thing. Forty-two dead. A younger magus with me saw it, too, and asked afterward, about why the scuta had exploded." Telmar swallowed. "Tullus's vigiles pulled her body from an alley days later. And I knew. And I couldn't stop knowing."

"Aelius and Tullus are shadow owners in that iron mine, aren't they?" she asked wearily.

He nodded. "There used to be a few records. Transfers from Aelius's coffers that matched investment receipts in the mine. But they got rid of them after that magus's questions. I snuck a look beforehand but it didn't matter. No court would have touched them." His bloodshot eyes met hers. "I'm sorry. I don't have anything for you."

She watched him, let the silence unravel until he started nervously glancing at every corner of the room.

"Where's your scutum?"

He turned white. "Get out."

"I'll pay you anything if you give it to me." When he attempted to move past her to leave his office, she blocked his path with a hand, wincing at the contact.

"I won't die, Petitor Sarai. Not after all I've endured!" he cried, wine sloshing over his floor as he gesticulated wildly. "Don't you think I'd have done something if I could?"

"But you *have*," she reminded him urgently. "You kept one of them, didn't you? Just in case your life was ever in peril or someone in the future could do this for you. Telmar, you wouldn't have to hide from your thoughts anymore."

His face crumpled. "Please leave." He fell to his knees. "Please just leave."

Her throat worked, eyes burning. "This is my only chance too. Tomorrow at the Aequitas, it all ends for me without that scutum."

He said nothing. She could force him now. Snap every bone in his wrist until he conceded. But if he was right about Aelius's eyes everywhere and he died for this as Decimus had, then she'd never forgive herself.

"I have until tomorrow." Her voice was hoarse. "So do you."

She left.

Sarai's spirits deflated when she spotted the pale-haired figure waiting for her at the Aoran Tower Gate. She'd imagined this conversation a thousand times since Admia's Summoning, and delayed it to the last moment possible. She had the awful sense that it wasn't going to hurt any less. Assuring Gaius that she could handle herself from there, she dismounted and pasted on a smile.

"I was about to head in your direction."

Cisuré beamed, shooting a wary glance at Gaius. She tilted her head toward a garden folly not too far away. They walked, the sky deepening to indigo above. Both moons were slivers in the east. She felt miles from the determined young woman she'd been two and a half months ago.

"Well?" Cisuré whispered once they'd reached the garden folly. "Did you search his tower?"

She took a steadying breath. "I did."

Cisuré clutched her, eyes wide with excitement. "And?"

"He has an orange grove, a massive number of books, and a great deal of wine," she explained, as Cisuré looked increasingly baffled. "I searched every inch, but there's nothing Tetrarch Aelius would find nefarious."

Cisuré's brown eyes held hers for a moment, emotion bleeding from them.

When she spoke, each word was devoid of inflection. "So you're telling me that Kadra is this protective of an *empty* home."

It took everything in Sarai to remain expressionless. "It's his home. He values his privacy."

"But that isn't true, is it?" The other girl's voice held a hard edge. "Because he brought you there."

"Only until I find a house of my own—"

In a blur of movement, Cisuré shoved her against the folly wall. She pulled back her sleeve with a sneer. "*Liar.*"

Sarai went stock-still at the sight of *zosta* gleaming on Cisuré's armilla. She'd been Examining her.

"I've spent weeks hearing about how he watches you like a wolf, and your little fascination with him is so *obvious.*" Cisuré's words came faster and faster until each one was a hiss. "I was hoping I could trust you, but he's gotten to you. What did you find in his tower?"

"I honestly found nothing relevant."

A weaker woman would have quailed at the disgusted look Cisuré shot her. "That isn't for you to decide. What. Did. You. Find?" At her silence, the other girl's grip tightened on her shoulders. "Are you really going to be this foolish? Losing everything for a man?"

"I would have done the same for you!"

"And you can't do that if the Metals Guild kills you!" Cisuré yelled, and, for a moment, her friend of old seemed to resurface past the ice-cold woman before her. "Just stop! You could escape Kadra's thumb and advocate to Tetrarch Aelius. Shape the law the way you've always wanted. You'll be safe—"

"Safe from who?" Sarai snapped. "Aelius and Tullus knew the rods were faulty! How much do you know, Cisuré? Are they powerful madmen I should follow at every cost? Or wise, benevolent rulers who can do no wrong? Have you even decided? I've doubted Kadra over and over. But have you ever doubted Aelius?"

Cisuré went white. A gravid silence hovered between them, the gulf yawning wider with each breath. There was no bridging it.

"He's my Tetrarch," Cisuré finally said. "He's only ever been good to me."

She stared at the sky to halt the flow of tears. "I need you to believe me. Aelius's former Petitor was pulverized to death like I nearly was. Several

Petitors realized that the scuta were a lie and that Aelius and Tullus were likely behind it. Then, they were suddenly dead. *Havïd*, even Othus died the same way."

Cisuré's pupils quivered. Bewilderment passed over her face, before morphing into anger. "You promised me you wouldn't dig into Sidran Tower," she whispered.

Sarai blinked. "You knew Othus was connected to my Fall?"

"You broke your promise." Cisuré looked like she couldn't believe it, like Sarai had somehow done her a grave wrong. "You *lied* to me. I thought the gods had taught you better than to dash headlong into things after your Fall. But you'll never stop."

Sarai's last tether to sanity snapped.

"Don't turn what happened to me into some moralistic lesson," she snarled. "I was fourteen, Cisuré. What were the gods punishing me for?"

"They probably didn't want you to turn out as you have." Tears welled in the other girl's eyes. She wiped at her face. "But you'll see the truth soon. I'll make you see it if I have to."

Cisuré departed without a backward glance. Only once her silhouette had vanished did Sarai release the sobs building in her chest. Turning in the direction of the journeying moons, she counted her paces back to Aoran Tower. Each one a shattered fragment of a friendship that had run its course.

CHAPTER
TWENTY-SEVEN

Sarai trudged inside Aoran Tower, noting the darkness underneath the door to Kadra's study. Just as well that he wasn't home. Having him see her break again was just embarrassing at this point. She'd spent years without a single tear, and now she had a fountain of them.

To think that an eternity ago, when she'd first entered this study, it had been with the intention of ruining Kadra. It felt ridiculous now.

Dropping the illusion, she watched her joints shift, those hated scars crawling over her fingers like white vines. A strangled sound left her throat, part sob, part scream. She slid down the length of the door, tucking her chin to her chest, and wept into her knees, drawing in painful drags of air.

Memories flitted behind her closed eyes of her and Cisuré sneaking out bottles of Cretus's wine, giggling together and planning the future they'd intended to seek in Edessa. She stared at the new void in her life with incomprehension and mounting anger. Years of friendship shattered, and for what?

After what felt like hours, her eyes ran dry. She got up, sapped of strength.

The stairs were a vaguely formed blur in the dark. With her luck, she'd likely lose her footing and tumble down. She padded to one of Kadra's couches instead. Sinking onto it, she jumped upon encountering a muscular thigh beneath her own. A hand clamped around her mouth, smothering her half-formed scream.

"Your night vision is surprisingly poor," the hand's owner informed her before letting go.

Clutching her chest, Sarai glowered. "Kadra, light a candle! You almost took ten years off my life!"

How long had he been sitting there? She hadn't heard anyone coming downstairs, and she'd been crying against the door. Which meant he must have been here all along. The dark closed around them, concealing her scars and swollen eyes. Her air filled with wine and the clean scent of his soap, warm skin and velvety fabric under her fingers.

She was also sitting on his lap.

"I'm sorry." She stumbled off him, almost falling over a side table. "Goodnight."

"Come back." The quiet order seemed to caress her. He extended a hand into the suddenly electric space between them.

A heartbeat. Two. Her breath came fast. In the quiet of his tablinum, as the world slumbered beyond Kadra's tower, all boundaries seemed to vanish. Her restraint broke. Reaching out in the dark, she took his palm in hers.

Between one breath and the next, his arm wrapped across her shoulders. Another fit into the crook of her knees, pulling her on top of him. He threaded a rough hand through her hair and drew her head onto his shoulder.

"Breathe," he ordered.

Without thinking, she did just that.

"Good." His lips teased her forehead. "Slowly now."

The tension drained from her immediately. Turning into his neck, she sighed at his warmth, exhaling so slowly she felt like she was floating. His thighs tensed under her. He held himself rigidly as if he didn't know what to do now. Perhaps he didn't. She didn't even know why he'd done it.

"I don't usually break down every few seconds," she whispered into his skin.

"I know." His arms tightened around her.

A lock loosened from her ragged braid, and he brushed it aside, the gesture seemingly cursory. She wondered if it was purposeful—if they were both waiting for the other to say something first. In the weak moonlight shafting through the curtains, he was as pristine as ever—dark hair grazing his neck, robes unwrinkled. But he looked exhausted. The hollows under his cheekbones were more pronounced and there was a weary tension to his stubbled jaw.

He tilted his head toward her. "Cassandane mentioned that she made you an offer some time ago."

"She did," Sarai murmured. "It was a good offer. She said you had me in dangerous waters."

Kadra's gaze shuttered. "And?"

"She isn't wrong."

"I see," he said in that same resigned, too-soft voice. "Will you be leaving tonight." It was a statement.

Throwing caution to the wind, she brought her hands to rest on his chest. "I won't."

Kadra blinked, and she had the extraordinary pleasure of seeing him momentarily thrown. His shoulders relaxed in slow increments as though he still couldn't believe that she wasn't fleeing.

"Why not?"

"Like I told Cassandane, it's a character flaw." She managed a small smile. "I can't predict how tomorrow's trial will go, but I'll give it everything."

"If nothing works, throw this on me." Sliding a finger under her chin, he tilted her head up, eyes locking with hers. "I'll shield you."

Her eyes burned at his sincerity. *You don't even know that they're readying to dethrone you.* This wasn't a simple bit of public censure. They'd destroy him.

"I'd rather have Aelius's head," she muttered. "I'd Probe the truth right out of him."

Something flashed in his eyes. "You may have a chance."

"Don't you ever get tired of all this? The violence, the games."

"At times."

"What do you do when you're tired?"

"I drink," he said dryly.

Sarai paused, recalling all the times she'd found him with a wineglass. He smelled like wine tonight too. She squinted at the dark shape on the table that looked like a bottle.

Him and Telmar. One used it to escape and the other used it to keep going. She wondered if those who thought Kadra unfeeling knew that he drank in the dark because he felt the weight of what he did.

"Why go against Aelius and Tullus at all?" she asked. When he remained silent, she guessed. "Is it because of Othus?"

If possible, Kadra grew even more rigid. By Temperance, he didn't bend easily, but perhaps if she gave a little, he'd be willing to reciprocate.

She took a steadying breath. "I broke ties with Cisuré tonight. She's so far under Aelius's influence that I fear there's no pulling her loose." Her voice dropped to a thread. "But, in truth, we were probably doomed even before then."

Amusement filled his eyes, and she elbowed his chest, earning her a grunt.

"Try not to gloat, damn it. She was all I had. Becoming your Petitor didn't help our friendship a whit either."

"I imagine not." He didn't sound troubled by that, and she frowned.

"Why do the two of you hate each other so much?" A thought occurred to her so terrifying that she stopped in her tracks. "Were you *involved*—"

"No," he growled, sounding disgusted.

Unsure of what to do with the relief swamping her, she switched tacks. "Your turn. How did you become a Tetrarch?"

He refilled his wineglass. "You've heard of the supposition that I killed Othus."

She nodded, wondering how he could remain so unfazed over the rumors. "I heard your relationship was . . . strained. But you were his successor."

"No." Wine swirled in the glass as he tilted the stem. "Another man was slated to top the election."

"Dare I ask what happened to him?"

A predatory light entered his eyes. "Augustus was a little too indiscreet about his proclivities. Involving children. Aelius was heavily involved in covering it up. Took a few counts of blackmail." Kadra shrugged. "Some larceny to free the children."

"And a bit of torture?" Sarai finished.

And just like that, the would-be-Tetrarch would have vanished from the ballot, leaving a surefire win for the most popular iudex in Othus's former Quarter.

She shook her head in disbelief. "You absolute madman."

"No diatribe?" He dipped his head dangerously close to hers. "Two and a half months ago, you'd have given me an earful."

"And you wouldn't have believed a word of it," she mused. "We've always seen right through each other, haven't we?"

A slow, fascinating smile curved his mouth. "It bothered you to no end at first."

"Because you thought I was a fool!"

"Never." The low tenor of his response sent a surge of hunger through her. "Not once."

Seeking a distraction, she seized his wine bottle and took a sip. And promptly gagged.

"Gods, that's *vile.*" Cretus's infamous Violet Snowgrape Delight, bottled in the Month of Seas, Year 548 of the Tetrarchy, had a new contender for sheer acridity. Desperately wishing for a glass of water, she swallowed and shuddered as the aftertaste reared its head again. "You drink this willingly?"

He looking thoroughly amused. "A connoisseur, I see."

"A connoisseur, you are not! Seven years as a barmaid and I've *never* had anything this awful." She wiped her lips with the back of her hand. "Has the mighty Kadra of Edessa never tasted good wine?"

Watching her shove both the glass and the bottle out of his reach, something extraordinarily playful unfolded on his face. "Drenevan," he said softly.

She stilled, night concealing her scarlet flush. Blood thrummed in her fingertips. He'd given her his name that very first night too, in the garden folly. By the look in his eyes, he remembered it.

"I couldn't. It's strange enough calling you Kadra, when everyone else puts such respect into their Tetrarch's titles."

"We're only people," he said with a wry smile. "With far too much power."

Sarai laughed. "I'd drink to that if your wine wasn't poison." She tentatively took the hand that wasn't around her shoulders. He gave her an inquiring look when she squeezed it. "The next time you feel the need to drink, I'll join you."

Rough fingers closed over hers. "Why?"

"Because I'd like to think we're . . . friends," she said hoarsely.

"Friends." He sounded unused to the thought.

"You can't tell me you've never had a friend, Kadra. That's ridiculous." For all his cruelty, he was no loner, well loved by much of the public, and respected by his vigiles.

"I have people I speak to."

Damned man. "To be friends is to not betray each other even when you have the power to. That's what you've been asking of me this whole while, isn't it? To choose you."

"Yes," he said starkly.

At long last, it all made sense, why he'd wanted her on his side, why he'd ordered her to his tower. She'd resided in hell for a long time, but this man had entrenched himself in its frozen depths.

"Then we're friends," she vowed.

He smiled softly. "Is that a declaration of allegiance?"

She tsked. "It's determination to save you from blood poisoning, that's what. I can't have you dying when I've earned the enmity of half the Tetrarchy. Shield me, damn it."

With a rough chuckle, Kadra leaned back on the couch, pulling her with him.

"I don't know if I should thank you or stab you," she muttered. "But I would've made the same decisions even if you weren't here. Though the consequences would have been much worse if Aelius or Tullus had been my Tetrarch."

All sardonicism vanished from his eyes. "Don't thank me, Sarai."

"Don't play the monster, Kadra."

He looked thoughtful. "I've never played at it."

"You're an infuriating man, Kadra." She took a deep breath. "But I don't think you're an evil one."

She knew evil. Had seen it in the crevices of many a soul. But it wasn't the sum of the man holding her, who looked startled by the prospect that he *wasn't* evil.

"And when did you decide that?" he asked softly.

Barely a handspan away, his cavernous eyes were even more all-consuming up close, but the perennial cruelty inhabiting them had vanished in favor of unadulterated hunger. Temples tightening, he stared down at her, and she ached to close the distance, to step closer to the abyss.

Her breath hitched. "After Helvus died."

"The day I became a *havïd* sadist."

"I took issue with how you went about it. Not why you did it. And now . . . I can't even bring myself to loathe the former."

"Why?"

Sarai wet her lips. The answer he sought hovered on her tongue and she would have given it were it not for the grim set of his features. There was hunger there, but heavily walled behind gates he seemed to have no intention of opening.

"You know why," she said quietly. "You know me."

"I do." A strange bleakness laced the words. "From the second you stared up at me at the Robing."

A ragged breath left her. "I should head upstairs," she said after a moment.

"Stay." It wasn't a demand. He slipped a hand beneath her hair. Tilting her head up, he pressed his thumb against a knot at her neck, easing it in a slow stroke.

A fierce fondness rose above her yearning. "Bribing a Petitor, Kadra?"

With a droll glance, he worked into her shoulder, and she admitted defeat.

"I suppose I can," she muttered, and his teeth flashed in a warm smile.

Unsure of where to rest, she awkwardly leaned against his shoulder. He cradled the back of her head and brought her into the curve of his neck. His arms tightened, secure as iron. And for the second time in as far as she could remember, she finally felt safe. Cared for. She closed her eyes against the burn of tears and slipped her arms around his chest. This was enough for now. This soft peace would sustain her another day.

As the seconds passed, she felt him relax in slow increments, his heartbeat dwindling to a sedate pace that her pulse unconsciously followed. The cares of the city beyond their walls faded.

As her eyes drooped, she felt him stroke her hair. A hoarse breath sawed out of him when she curled into his neck. Between one breath and the next, the world faded to midnight.

CHAPTER
TWENTY-EIGHT

What roused her wasn't the twitter of songbirds or the crick in her neck, but the ray of evening sun piercing through the curtains to arrow into her eye. Scowling, Sarai shifted against the blanket wrapped around her and froze as the *blanket* moved as well.

Flushing to the roots of her hair, she disentangled herself from the crook of Kadra's shoulder. At some point in the night, he had slightly slumped to the left, still holding her across his lap, a muscled forearm locked around her waist.

He looked younger, features relaxed in sleep. Stubble laced his jaw and cheeks and her heart gave way at the picture he made, painted in the sun.

"Drenevan." She tested the syllables out loud.

His mouth curved. She jumped back as Kadra opened an eye and cocked an eyebrow at her.

"Good morning." His voice was a low burr, even more spectacular when rough from sleep.

"Good morning," she stammered, looking left, then right, then left again in the vain hope of finding anything that could assuage her embarrassment. That quest proving futile, she jackknifed to her feet and swallowed at his completely undone robe in the daylight. A valley of tanned skin freckled with curling hair trailing past his abdomen lay open for her perusal. She immediately fled from his study to the rough music of his laughter.

Hiding until he'd left for work, she paced his study, formulating and reformulating until a maneuver with a chance of success began to coalesce.

If she cast enough doubt on the testimony of Aelius's witnesses, then she could extricate herself from the *calumnia* charge and preempt Aelius's no-confidence vote. It was all she had if Telmar didn't show.

Hours passed, and he didn't. The weight on her chest grew heavier.

As the day drew to a close, she quietly gave up. There was no point thinking about what his refusal to show meant for her. Dressing, she paid meticulous heed to her appearance. Polishing her boots and weaving her hair into a sleek braid, she eyed her grim-faced reflection.

I won't be whipped to death, she tried to convince herself. *I'll be back here tonight. This isn't the end.*

But when she left Aoran Tower at sunset, it was with a thousand fervent prayers to the uncaring gods above.

Dusk was still new to the sky above the Aequitas. The audience buzzed, crammed into every nook of the court, roars of excitement rising when she entered the stage to mark the beginning of the trial.

Sarai bowed low. Just as many had shown up today as for the Robing. It wasn't every day that a Petitor had to prove their decisions at the land's highest court.

On the opposite end of the stage, the Tetrarchy assembled on the long dais to thunderous applause. Kadra seemed unperturbed, but a pale-faced Cassandane wet her lips, hands clenched on the arms of her seat. Aelius and Tullus were the image of composed serenity.

When Aelius raised a hand for silence, Sarai grit her teeth at the familiar scroll in his hand. *The warrant.* That he hadn't filed it yet indicated he was giving her until the end to recant on the scuta and ruin Kadra.

"Many of you are aware of this case," Aelius noted. "A month ago, Metals Guildmaster Helvus was murdered by former Guildmaster Admia. However, rather than be given justice, he was humiliated in his domus as he died and accused of purposefully manufacturing faulty scuta by the Petitor before us."

The onlookers had never sounded more divided. Jeering originated from some seats, the occupants sporting the colorful robes and crests of

Guildmasters. Yet there were just as many raucous cheers from those of Edessa's social classes who had little love for the Metals Guild.

She prepared to defend herself when Aelius's smile turned sly.

"Seeing as Tetrarch Kadra and his Petitor"–his weighted pause had many heads swiveling toward her–"will be occupied with proving these accusations, my own Petitor has stepped in to resolve the matter with fairness."

Sarai's heart plummeted as Cisuré emerged from the side entrance to the Aequitas, eyes hard. Whatever was on the other girl's mind didn't seem to include fairness.

Aelius steepled his fingers. "Bring in the witnesses."

Wisdom and Wrath help me. Courage nearly deserted Sarai as Aelius's vigiles opened the double doors that marked the witnesses' entrance. She waited for a stream of Guildspeople to emerge, but a lone vigile ran up the dais instead to whisper into Aelius's ear. The Tetrarch's features went slack with fury.

She wiped her sweaty palms against her tunic as a figure emerged, his gait awkward. The first thing she noticed were the burns dotting his skin. Her next glance identified him as the first name on Aelius's list.

Aelius spoke through clenched teeth. "It seems that a strike hit the Metals Guild a night ago."

Goosebumps pebbled Sarai's skin. Cisuré clapped a hand over her mouth in horror. The injured Guildsman's bloodshot eyes roved across the dais before alighting on Sarai. Racing over, he dropped to his knees. A stream of hoarse words left his throat, barely audible.

She flinched, crouching beside him. "I'm sorry," she whispered. "I don't understand."

Shaking, he pulled a crumpled roll of parchment from his robes, and thrust it at Cisuré, who quickly unrolled it and, at a nod from Aelius, began to read.

"'We, of the Metals Guild, out of gratitude to Tetrarch Kadra for his assistance in rescuing us from a strike, hereby–'" Cisuré broke off, eyes bulging with fury. "'Recant and admit that we've no knowledge of the manufacture of a scutum's metal core. Our work was limited to a steel shell. We sought to preserve the reputation of our Guildmaster but have been punished for our lies. We repent sincerely to the gods and the people,'" she spat.

Time stood still, the world paling to a dull gray, then a blinding white. The audience's exclamations of horror and anger faded to a tinny ringing as the Guildsman's statement registered.

Hereby recant. Aelius had nothing by which to argue that her accusations were false or malicious. He couldn't charge her with *calumnia*. His warrant was useless.

She wasn't going to be whipped to death.

Resisting the urge to bury her head in her hands and sob, she drew a rattling breath. *Gods be praised, I'm safe.*

"This is preposterous!" Tullus roared, vying with Aelius for who could turn the deeper shade of puce. Both ignored the crowd, which had risen to their feet roaring for answers on the scuta. "So Tetrarch Kadra happened to be on hand to assist during this strike, did he?"

She froze, eyes flying to the man who was watching the proceedings with customary amusement.

You didn't, she asked silently.

The cruel-eyed god who ruled her heart gave her a slow smile, and she nearly fell to her knees. Kadra, Wretched Prince of Punishment, indeed. He'd meted out justice the way he always did: in blood. And in doing so, he'd doomed himself. One strike was a coincidence. Two weren't. The matter had his stamp all over it. If she saw it, others would too. Whispers were already rustling throughout the crowd of the Aequitas. She caught several raised eyebrows and suspicious glances in Kadra's direction.

"Probe the Guildsman." Tullus barked the order to Cisuré even though she wasn't his Petitor. "Let's see what actually happened."

Manic fervor returned to Cisuré's face. She took a step toward the man when he stumbled back, turning beseeching eyes to Kadra, of all people. The crowd issued a collective gasp. Tullus's knuckles strained in his clenched fists.

"You would really have this man relive a traumatic memory to satisfy your curiosity?" Disapproval laced Kadra's voice. "The Guild has admitted their error. Leave him his dignity."

"We're merely marveling at how conveniently he lost it," Aelius responded evenly.

This is bad. The more people thought about it, the clearer it would become that the only people with anything to gain from the Guild's recanting were her and Kadra, seeing as they'd made the initial accusations. It was all the fodder Aelius needed to bring up a no-confidence vote to kick Kadra out. Judging by the tight set of Cassandane's features, she knew it too.

He's been acting uncharacteristically reckless, Anek had said. *How could you be so reckless?* Cato had argued that night she'd healed Kadra.

Kadra, what are you doing?

On the dais, his smile was pure ice. "I was nearby. It turned out that my assistance was necessary."

True. She was torn between horror and amazement at how he'd framed it. Inches from being booted out as a Tetrarch and he still wasn't lying.

"Are there any witnesses to your heroism, Tetrarch Kadra?" Aelius's smile grew. "Or should we pull the truth from *your* head instead?"

"Am I on trial, Tetrarch Aelius?" Kadra sounded intrigued. "If so, your vigiles appear to have misplaced the warrant they should have served me with."

"That won't be necessary." Aelius rose, ivory robes aglow. "It seems the second matter for which we gathered today has arrived early. I do not doubt the intelligence of my fellow Urds, and I believe they see what I have noted from the start of Tetrarch Kadra's appointment."

This wasn't how it was supposed to go. She'd intended on preventing the trial from reaching this point. She sought out Kadra's gaze, but he shook his head, something that looked bewilderingly like resignation in his eyes.

"Despite being tasked with the administration of justice, Tetrarch Kadra has used this court as his personal dungeon." Aelius's voice cracked through the hubbub like a cane. "He has killed, burned, executed, and dismembered within these very walls. I have let it pass only because he was supposedly doing so in the name of justice. But I cannot let it go any longer. A grave miscarriage of justice has occurred today. Over a hundred witnesses, who should have set a good man's name to rights, now recant. I know I speak for us all when I say that we know they were tortured into it by *him*." He jabbed a finger in Kadra's direction.

Tullus added his piece. "I have no confidence in Tetrarch Kadra's ability to lead Ur Dinyé. As such, I formally call for the Tetrarchy and its Petitors to vote on this matter. The punishment for a Tetrarch's abuse of power has always been clear and we will not deviate from it now. If found guilty, Tetrarch Kadra will be dismissed from his position."

The bottom fell out of her stomach. The crowd was chaos, yells of outrage—though she couldn't tell whether it was at Kadra or on his behalf—mixed with questions on the scuta.

A storm brewed in Kadra's eyes and the air crackled dangerously around the stage, sparks of lightning flaring into and out of sight amid the angry yells and boos of the crowd.

Aelius sniffed disdainfully. "I'll thank you not to bring the Aequitas down to avoid your charges. Though this display is enough to convince me that you're guilty. The Tetrarchy will now vote. And this is my word." His features held triumph. "Guilty."

This can't be happening. She saw the line of Kadra's back loosen as though he'd been waiting for this. His head remained unbowed. He was allowing himself to be dethroned. But why would he . . . She halted, and took in the sparks still sizzling in the Aequitas.

He's charging up the air.

"Guilty," Tullus echoed with equal malice.

He's going for another strike.

"Guilty," Cisuré crowed.

Kadra's hard mask splintered for a fraction of a second, but it was enough. She spotted the vicious, bitter look he slanted in Aelius's direction, and everything slotted in at once.

I'd rather have Aelius's head. I'd Probe the truth right out of him, she'd said last night.

And he was about to give it to her.

Features drained of color, Cassandane shook her head and stayed silent, indicating that she was abstaining. Anek did the same.

The second Kadra was dethroned, he'd strike before Aelius could so much as utter a word of victory, and give him to her to fish the truth from his head. But Aelius was the Magus Supreme, the most powerful magus in the land. Add Tullus to that and ... *they'll kill each other*, she realized in horror.

"Guilty," Harion murmured after a confirmatory glance at Tullus.

The weight of almost every stare in the Aequitas struck Sarai at once, but she only had eyes for the man she loved, who was about to lose everything. He gave her an imperceptible shake of his head. Asking her to doom him.

Why is this your solution?

Her lips parted, as she tried to think of a way out, and a glint of metal caught her attention at the side entrance to the Aequitas.

Steel rolled out of the doorway, a flash of violet robes vanishing down the hallway. Relief and elation engulfed her. She could have wept. *Thank you, Telmar.*

A broad smile bloomed on Aelius's lips as he took her silence for abstention. Beside her, Cisuré's eyes welled with tears.

"I knew you could do it." She gripped Sarai's hands. "I'm so proud of you."

"The Tetrarchy speaks with one voice!" Aelius roared exultantly. "Drenevan bu Kadra is hereby found guilty of abusing his power and—"

Shaking off Cisuré's hold, Sarai ran to the side entrance.

"Petitor Sarai?"

She ignored the knife-sharp warning in Aelius's voice and ran faster. Ducking under the arm of one of Aelius's vigiles, she crouched to grab the scutum and hugged it to her chest. *Fuck, yes.*

She didn't think. Racing to the center of the stage, she held Kadra's gaze and ascended the steps to the dais purposefully. One step away from him, she rested a foot on the uppermost stair, inclined her head, and fanned the material of her robes back. And she knelt before Kadra, scutum in hand.

Her voice rang across the court. "Innocent."

Then, for a long, glorious moment, she watched as Kadra was struck wordless. His features went slack, shock flaring in his midnight eyes.

Aelius roared something in the background.

Rising smoothly, she smiled placidly in his direction. "I understand your concern, Tetrarch Aelius," she announced as the cacophony from the audience grew. "But there has been no miscarriage of justice. Tetrarch Kadra was injured that night. I can testify to his condition. He's blameless here. I can't say that for most things." That gained her a ripple of laughter from the crowd. "But I can say it for this."

She turned to the spectators before Aelius could speak, keeping her every movement graceful. Showing them someone they would want to believe.

"Citizens of Edessa, you came here for a trial on the crucial matter of the scuta you rely on." Turning back to the dais, she snuck a glance at Kadra, who looked torn between pride and homicide. "I say that we examine the basis for my accusations. I have an ordinary scutum here, and I don't have the skill to have engineered or warped one for this trial. Every Petitor here knows I speak the truth, and like Tetrarch Aelius, I don't underestimate your intelligence."

Striding center stage, she placed the rod there. "And as a show of faith, I'll stand here, if one of the Tetrarchy would be so kind as to bring forth lightning."

"Petitor Sarai." Tullus shot to his feet, incandescent with rage. "You cannot dare test the gods with such little faith."

"Tetrarch Tullus, I have more faith than I know what to do with. After all, my life is in their hands." As murmurs spread through the crowd, she spread her hands wide. "I'm all yours. I also have a collation of evidence by two former Petitors on numerous scuta blowing up during strikes, as well as the Metals Guild's purchase of lands after they're struck by lightning. If that isn't enough, I will submit to a Probe here so *everyone* can see what I witnessed at former Metals Guildmaster Helvus's and Grains Guildmaster Admia's residences."

Cisuré looked stricken, eyes darting to Aelius, whose jaw looked liable to snap if he kept clenching it that hard.

Sarai bit back a chuckle. *You can't do it, can you? Or everything you did in that domus will air out as well.* She turned back to the crowd, who cheered their agreement. "The people want the truth." She smiled innocently. "I am happy to provide it."

Silence fell over the dais, Kadra looking as though he was fighting a laugh while debating on dragging Sarai away from the scutum. Aelius and Tullus seethed. Cassandane eyed the men on either side of her with a wide grin, letting the silence lengthen until it was clear that there was only one way forward.

"Very well." Cassandane raised a hand. Silver sparks lit the air. Kadra's features tautened a second before layers upon layers of a familiar gold shield flared around her.

The Aequitas erupted with the sounds of people getting to their feet, craning to get a better look. She held herself still, not covering her ears so as not to be accused of a lack of faith or anything else that would invalidate her test.

The air throbbed, a low hum building. Cassandane flicked her wrist and lightning scissored down from the sky. A deafening crack followed. The scutum exploded.

Metal warped, spitting fire and iron dust into the air. Propelled to her knees by the force of the blast, she hunched over. Above her, three of Kadra's shields had vaporized. The remaining two held with fierce control. Rising, she grinned at him. *It's done!*

Raw emotion burned in his eyes. He looked relieved. And furious.

A roar of anger and horror swelled across the Aequitas, several people climbing over railings to get a better look at the warped, sizzling metal. The Metals Guildsman still standing there looked uneasy.

"I believe that's all the evidence we need," Cassandane said wryly. "The Guild has admitted the truth as well, so it seems that Petitor Sarai and Tetrarch Kadra's concerns weren't unfounded." She gave Sarai a grateful glance. "The Metals Guild and Helvus's estate will work out the appropriate compensation for those still owning a scutum. I encourage any who know of deaths caused by scuta to bring their petitions. Tetrarch Aelius, Tetrarch Tullus? Do you agree?"

Aelius pressed his lips tight, forcing each word past them. "The matter will be dealt with as such. The Tetrarchy has spoken."

For the second time in her life, Sarai crumpled to the Aequitas's stage in relief, taking in the devastation and rage coming from every corner of the audience. She couldn't imagine how many had lost people to a strike, or shouldered the blame for a death due to a lack of faith. She didn't envy the Metals Guild right now. Four years of greed and death ended. She wished Jovian and Livia had lived to see it.

Eschewing its tradition of descending center stage for a final bow, the Tetrarchy parted. Kadra and Cassandane headed one way, and Aelius and Tullus stormed off in the other. Sarai ducked into the corridor leading outside to Aelius's massive statue when Cisuré blocked her path.

"We need to talk."

"No, we don't." Sarai tried to edge past when the other girl caught her arm.

"I won't let you carry on like this." The light in her eyes sent a strange chill down Sarai's spine. "You're going to pack your things and leave that *sadist's* tower. Now."

"By all the High Elsar, if you dare try to coerce me to lick Aelius's feet one more time, I'm burning his tower to the ground."

"You—"

"Cisuré, stop," Anek interjected, a hand on her shoulder. "You and your Tetrarch had your say in court. You lost. Live with it."

Cisuré looked close to screaming, hands forming fists before she stormed off. Sarai let out a pained breath. Outside the Aequitas, Kadra crossed his arms, Cassandane beside him, her dark head bowed close to his. The tempest in Sarai coiled tighter at the sight of the older woman's beautiful features, at the familiar way she caught Kadra's elbow, apparently irritated.

Cassandane has no interest in men, she reminded herself, calming the irrational impulse to ride Caelum right between the two of them.

Following her gaze, Anek's lips twitched. "She's chewing him out. Deservedly, too, given that he just announced his weakness to all of Ur Dinyé." At her pause, they tilted their head to the Academiae. "Ride with me."

She followed with a parting glance at Kadra, noting with worry that he still seemed vaguely out of sorts. The sky was well into moonrise by the time she and Anek managed to make their way through the crowd, find their mounts, and leave the Aequitas.

"Four years ago," Anek's features were drawn tight in contemplation, "a body was found at the base of Sidran Tower. Smashed like a pumpkin."

Starting at the sudden mention of the Sidran Tower Girl, Sarai winced. "I've heard."

"I became a Petitor because of her," Anek said. "If Harion had been found dead, then the vigiles would have cared. But this was a girl no older than I was. A stranger to the city. So she was dressed in rumors, swathed in apathy, and buried like so much garbage."

Sarai's throat burned.

"I realized that these people would do the same to me. They'd probably peer at my corpse and laugh, saying they knew my sex now." A humorless sound left them. "But things changed upon Kadra's election. He was vicious, but always fair." Anek studied her. "You lied. Kadra was behind the strike, wasn't he?" At Sarai's silence, they smiled. "This is why people love him. He's mad, but he doesn't sit back and watch as people are buried."

"Sometimes I don't know if it's because he cares, or because he finds their loyalty useful in this war he's waging," she admitted.

"Both," Anek said readily. "Everyone with a brain saw that he did this to protect you. Just as they're all putting two and two together at Aelius and Tullus freezing when you pulled out a scutum." Tension returned to the neutralis's features. "But Kadra has survived for so long because he has had *no* weaknesses. He's been as immutable as stormfall. Yet, over the past two and a half months, everyone's seen him watching you like he'd like to—pardon the expression—throw you against a wall and have you."

Her cheeks heated. "There really is nothing. We haven't—" She stopped as Anek raised a hand.

"Gods, please don't. That's a picture I don't need." They steered their mount toward Favran Tower. "I'd watched you two the first few days on the job, you know." At Sarai's start of surprise, they nodded. "You and Kadra butted heads more often than you drew air, but I saw respect. An ability to consider the good and flaws in each other's approaches. On the other hand, Cisuré might as well have been an extension of Aelius."

Sarai groaned. "Gods, I don't know what's happened to her."

"She's a fool." Anek gave her a speaking look. "She'll rationalize everything she does as reasonable if it means saving her skin. Is it incumbent on us to allow her to ruin lives while she figures out that the world isn't all gods and roses? Do the elites give the lower classes that kind of concession?"

Impressed, she whistled. "Careful. Best not let Aelius or Tullus hear you saying that."

"At least until they're toppled." The neutralis laughed, reaching across their mounts to grip Sarai's shoulder. "Protect that Tetrarch of yours. There's something strange about what he's up to. The Kadra of old would never have gone with so many blatant strikes." Anek looked puzzled. "For someone who's always been excellent in subtle manipulation, it's reckless beyond belief."

Reckless. Everyone kept using that word.

"Thank you," she said, realizing she hadn't acknowledged how much Anek had risked in giving her Livia's letter. "I couldn't have done this without you."

They cleared their throat, looking awkward. "Yes, well. Didn't want to see anyone dying. We've done well so far, yes? Lasted nearly three months." They paused before bursting into laughter. "By the Elsar, you're two weeks from winning that wager with Harion!"

Sarai counted the months and snorted. "Care to bet if he'll be a gracious loser?"

"I'm not betting anything against you. Your luck's far too good."

Her smile wavered. That only meant it was bound to run out.

Yet, as Anek waved goodbye upon reaching their Tetrarch's abode, Sarai turned determined eyes toward Aoran Tower.

Perhaps she could push her luck one more time.

CHAPTER
TWENTY-NINE

The trail of wet footsteps into the tablinum was her first clue that Kadra was home. Sarai eyed the thin line of light under the door to his study, anxious at facing him.

She'd knelt before him, her heart in her eyes. *But what if he doesn't acknowledge it?*

She wiped her sweaty palms on her tunic, pulse thundering in her ears, reminding herself that she'd faced down Aelius and Tullus today. Whatever his response was, she could take it. Striding to the study door, she pushed it open before she could talk herself out of it.

Seated behind his desk, Kadra looked up, robe half-undone as usual, damp hair falling rakishly over the hard planes of his face. But his usual composure was gone, replaced by the same unfettered wildness she'd seen at the pleasure house.

"You nearly blew yourself up," he said without preamble.

She took a steadying breath and rounded his desk. "It was the only way to save your head. You matter, Kadra. This country needs you to hold those two mass murderers back. I don't know what you were thinking today in serving yourself up to them, but I won't stand for it."

"You fought for me." His voice was hoarse.

"I chose you." Flushing, she glanced at the wine bottle he was gripping as though his life depended on it. "I thought we agreed that I'd drink with you in the future."

"Then drink." He rose, trapping her in the space between his seat and his desk. Placing the bottle to his lips, he took a swallow.

She stilled when he brought it to her mouth, circling her lips and seeking entry. It felt carnal. Her lips parted and she took a sip, warmth slipping down her throat as it had on the night of their first meeting in this study. Need streaked through her, coiling tight.

Her eyes were level with his chest, catching its rapid rise and fall. "Are you angry with me?" she whispered.

"No." His thumb replaced the wine bottle, tracing the curve of her lower lip. "You knelt before me."

Air came slowly. She nodded.

"Why?"

"Because I wanted to."

His thumb eased its pressure on her lips, sliding past her jaw to halt at her wildly beating pulse. "Why did you want to?"

He was so close that every breath tasted of him. "Gods, Kadra."

He didn't relent, tilting her chin to face him when she tried to turn away. "Why?"

"You know why," she breathed, molten desire pooling in her when he stroked her throat. At his silence, she closed her eyes, defenses gone. "Because I've wanted you ever since you tipped that damn wineglass in my direction that first night here. I wanted you when I wanted to ruin you. And now—" She broke off, hope and fear choking her. "There's nothing I wouldn't do for—"

With a rough curse, he gripped the back of her head and pulled her mouth to his, devouring her like a man possessed. The world vanished and there was nothing but the taste of him under her tongue, the rough scrape of his teeth against her lips. The stern line of his mouth parted, bit, sucked her lower lip, teasing her with forays of his tongue.

The wine bottle fell, shattering, as he pulled her onto his desk, dragging her ankles up until they locked around his waist. Pressed against him, liquid fire streaked through her.

"You want me," she accused.

"Always," he bit out. Blood rushed in her ears as he gripped the back of her neck.

"Then take me," she whispered, elation giving her the boldness to run a hand through his damp hair. A harsh sound tore from his throat when she gripped his shoulders and ground against his cock. A tremor ran through the arms holding her.

"Tell me not to do this," he demanded hoarsely. "You'll despise me later."

"Never." She gave him back his words. "Not once."

"Sarai, I am not a good man." His teeth scraped her earlobe to punctuate the statement. "I have done things that will horrify you."

Pulling back to frame his face between her hands, she met that cruel gaze without fear and smiled. "I know."

And he came undone.

He feasted on her mouth, breathing her in, as if it would never be enough. His fingers speared her hair, one hand going to the column of her throat as he trailed kisses down the heated skin of her jaw, and sucked a mark into her neck. Something fell off his table. She didn't care. She was on fire.

Gripping her thighs, he rocked her against him. She moaned.

"Is this what you want?" He nuzzled the question into the shell of her ear, his voice a sinful croon. "To be taken?" He squeezed a sigh from her throat.

Knotting her fingers in his hair, she fused her mouth to his, fumbling at the tie to his dressing robe in answer. A groan shuddered through him, legendary control eroded to dust as he lifted her with ease. Taking the stairs two at a time, he kicked open his door and tossed her on his bed.

"Your fucking chest." Crawling over the covers to him, she gripped the sides of his waist, parting his robes and tasting his skin, moving quickly downward. "It's been driving me mad since that first night."

Kadra choked out a laugh. "I know. You couldn't tear your eyes away fast eno—"

He bit out a curse when her mouth slid over the glistening length of him. She pulled back and stared up at him, licking her lips.

His voice went guttural. "Again."

Obediently, she dragged her tongue over the head, and in seconds she was flat on her back, her mouth reclaimed, his hands snatching at the tie to her bathrobe. The cold air on her newly bared skin cut through the haze of her arousal.

She stared at the scars running down her breasts and hips, the raised lines misshapen, ugly. Her throat closed. She couldn't look at him.

"I–"

"Fuck." Red stained Kadra's high cheekbones as he stared down at her. "Fuck, I knew you'd be beautiful."

Her eyes smarted and she blinked furiously to keep the tears at bay as he leaned over her to press a tender kiss to her mouth, her collarbone, her chest. He lavished attention on her breasts, his lips tracing the lines of her scars, as he slipped a hand between her legs, breath going choppy.

Her back bowed as his fingers plunged deep. She'd done this before on her own, but it was nothing, *nothing*, like this. He was as all-consuming as she'd hoped and feared, drawing out her pleasure until she begged him for mercy.

"Look at me," he demanded as she neared her peak. "Eyes on me. I want to watch you."

His fingers worked faster, deeper, and she flew apart, the orgasm rushing through her with brutal intensity, lighting up every nerve in her body. He pressed kisses against her forehead, her nose, her upturned lips, breath coming in harsh bursts.

"Like lightning," he whispered.

And he was the storm itself. Her muscles were limp, but she wanted more. She reached between them to grip his length, stroking it from root to tip. He uttered a rough moan of pleasure, watching the motion as though it held his salvation. Her thumb brushed over the wet head, and she heard his teeth grind seconds before he captured her arms and pinned them above her head. But instead of entering her, he stilled, pupils blown so wide, she couldn't see anything of his irises.

"Sarai," he whispered hoarsely. "I've wanted you for so long." Sweat trailed down his neck, but he waited, silently asking her one last time if she was sure.

She arched herself against him, notching his cock to her entrance. "*Please.*" She pressed against him again just as he pushed inside her.

Kadra captured her hiss of pain, whispering an apology against her lips, waiting for her to get used to the feel of him, before moving gently, tenderly, letting her find her rhythm, watching her as if he'd die if he didn't. Electricity sizzled down her spine, centering between them, growing with every hard thrust, every snap of his hips. She gasped his name, and lust suffused his face.

"What do you need?"

"You," she whimpered as he moved deep. "More."

"Shit," he shuddered, before giving up on reining himself in. "Fuck, Sarai."

He began to take her in earnest and she cried out, her wetness seeping down her thighs. Her body moving of its own will, she ground against him, meeting him viciously with lips, tongue, and teeth as he caressed her with soft, filthy words of praise, his voice driving her closer to the brink.

"That's it," he growled against her mouth. "Gods, you're so fucking beautiful."

He drank in her pleas and cries, taking her with frenzied intensity, every inch the demanding lover she'd known he would be.

Her body tightened in impending ecstasy, and their eyes locked just as she erupted. Pure bliss slammed into her, through her, around her, only his name on her lips. He groaned. His hips shifted, thrust deep, and a harsh growl left Kadra's throat. He clutched her to him, body shuddering against her as they fell against the mattress, utterly spent.

"I belong to you," he whispered against her hair. "I will always belong to you."

And she felt the truth of it without any magic.

CHAPTER
THIRTY

Sarai woke to hands in her hair and a stubbled jaw nuzzling a path down her neck. Her cheeks heated as Kadra gave her a wicked smile.

Gods. How did one usually handle this sort of thing?

"Good morning," she tried, and his smile widened.

His eyes were soft as he kissed her, the hard planes of his face relaxed. For a man who exuded murder most hours of the day, he was luminous.

Pulling her on top of him, he searched her face. "Regrets?"

She swatted him with a pillow. "Of course not."

"Good girl."

She flushed at the reminder of the last time he'd said that. Sunset streamed through the window, dappling their bodies as she drew up on her elbows to survey his room.

He eyed her, raising an amused eyebrow. "I thought you'd seen your fill when you searched it."

She hadn't thought it possible to blush even more. "How did you know?"

"You tucked my bedspread in."

She dropped her head to his chest. "*Havïd.*"

"What did you tell Aelius afterward?"

"That you're all oranges and wine." She ran a hand through his hair, reveling in the fact that she'd made the immaculate Tetrarch Kadra so disheveled. "And an absolutely stunning voice."

The knowing look he gave her was a reminder of how easily she had succumbed to what that voice had whispered in the night. Grinning when she went red, he rose, reaching an arm to pull her up just as there were several frantic knocks on his bedroom door.

"Drenevan, she's missing! Sarai's gone!" Cato yelled outside the door. "Aelius might have her! By all the Elsar, this is my fault. I should have noticed she wasn't in her room."

The missing woman in question groaned, head in her hands, as Kadra laughed.

There was silence on the other side of the door.

"Drenevan," Cato said evenly. "She isn't missing, is she?"

"She isn't," Kadra pronounced gravely.

"In that case, I'm leaving. Take all the time you need."

She buried her face in the sheets as Cato's footsteps faded. Slipping on his robe, Kadra smiled at her.

"The day awaits. Come, Petitor," he ordered imperiously, and she laughed.

"I've done a great deal of that."

"Evidently not enough." Sweeping her up, he carried her to the bathing room, where she was immediately and immensely thankful that Cato had left the tower.

By the time they reached the vigile station, midnight had long since become dawn, and Gaius was impatiently pacing by Kadra's office. Spotting them, he let out a sigh of relief.

"Thank the Elsar, I thought you'd been kidnapped after that trial, or—" He broke off, turning from her flushed cheeks to Kadra's too-even features. A broad grin split his features. He rubbed his hands with glee. "Three hundred aurei to me. Betting's finally over!"

"Betting?" Sarai asked as Gaius shoved the day's worth of cases into their hands.

"On when he'd do the deed." Gaius winked and stiffened as Kadra's gaze turned deadly. "Congratulations!" he squeaked before fleeing, possibly to collect his winnings.

Sarai and Kadra turned to each other with matching scowls.

"Nothing better to do," she pronounced.

"Far too much time on their hands," he agreed.

But a smile played on their lips for the rest of the evening.

If she'd thought that becoming Kadra's lover would somehow affect their work, those worries vanished quickly. They settled back into their rhythm, and as morning came, the scrolls before them dwindled: Kadra heading out on occasion to interview witnesses where a case's particulars were lacking.

She'd darted glances at him while he worked, and grown fascinated by a particular muscle ticking in his jaw that she'd come to realize meant that he was inches from fucking her. She realized it when he pinned her to the wall of his office and ordered her to keep quiet, then dropped to his knees and tongued her before taking her once more.

Only Gaius had eyed them suspiciously when they emerged.

Afternoon became evening. Rolling up an account of a particularly grisly murder, Sarai paused as her armilla slid out from under her sleeve at the motion. *Nihumb* glowed a dull scarlet, an unwelcome reminder of the secret she was still keeping from Kadra. *The Sidran Tower Girl.*

Perhaps the time for asking should have been much earlier, before she'd allowed him into her heart. But, as it had been that night she'd healed him, part of her still didn't want to know.

I'm being foolish. He wasn't involved. She only had to ask. Perhaps she'd do it when he returned—Sarai jumped when Gaius burst into the room.

"Petitor Cisuré to see you." Looking uneasy, he indicated the figure wringing her hands behind him.

Sarai set aside her the scroll. "I'll see her."

She indicated a chair as Cisuré shuffled in, eyes red rimmed and swollen.

"Please," the other girl whispered. "Just hear me out first."

"Sit." Sarai massaged her temples. "You look exhausted."

Cisuré eyed the chair but made no move toward it. "You were right," she blurted out. "About Aelius, the scuta, all of it." Her face crumpled.

Pity swelled in her. "I know he means a great deal to you—"

"No, there's—" Cisuré's voice dropped to a whisper. "Sarai, they have Anek."

The lazy warmth of the past few hours shattered. Sarai bolted upright. "What do you mean?"

"The Metals Guild has a bounty on Anek, and . . . I—I noticed it kept defending you so I mentioned it to Tetrarch Aelius, and now, Anek's gone! Cassandane's frantic! Her vigiles are here now to ask for help."

The floor-to-ceiling window on one side of Kadra's office revealed a group of crimson-robed vigiles speaking to Gaius.

Sarai slumped against the desk. "Damn it, Cisuré."

"Please, you have to help me." Cisuré wiped her eyes. "I have to set this right! I can't do this alone!"

"I will. I promise. Do you know where they took Anek?"

"I think so." More tears leaked past Cisuré's fingers. "Will you come with me?"

Sarai hesitated, glancing at Kadra's empty chair.

Catching her glance, Cisuré shook her head. "We don't have time! It's already been hours since they went missing. Gods, I don't even know if they're dead!"

She swallowed. If another Petitor died after everything she and Kadra had tried to do, then everything had been for nothing. Making her decision, she rummaged about Kadra's desk for a bit of parchment.

"I'll come. Where are we headed?"

"Anek was in Edessa, then they just vanished. There's a path I just learned about that leads into the Academiae from Edessa. Bypasses the vigiles and Tower Gates. I think that's what Aelius might have used to abduct them and bring them back to Sidran Tower."

Sarai paused in the process of leaving Kadra a note, black ink forming a drop at the tip of her pen.

"We're going to Sidran Tower?" she asked hoarsely.

"Will you be alright?"

She set her jaw even as her fingers shook worse than ever. "I have to be." She wouldn't let Anek die.

Finishing the note to Kadra, she followed Cisuré out of the station and saddled Caelum, Cisuré mounting her own dapple-gray mare. Resolve mingled with fear in her chest as she turned toward the Academiae.

"Lead the way."

Night reigned supreme over Edessa, clouds veiling the moons as Sarai wound through the narrow streets behind Cisuré. A few raedae clattered mournfully about them, coachmen half-asleep while the horses plodded on.

She followed Cisuré down a ribbon-thin dirt road until they turned into an alley, barely wide enough for them to stand side by side. A silver ring was set into one of the paving stones, practically undetectable.

Cisuré pulled and the stone rose, part of a trapdoor set into the alley. Steps yawned before them, leading into a pitch-black passage. Sarai swallowed, breath flaring out in a pale cloud.

"This way." Cisuré ducked her head in. "There're seventeen steps."

There are seventeen steps to the bottom.

A flash of white-hot pain nearly blinded Sarai and she reeled, clutching her head—*sunshine, a handwritten note.*

The sliver of recollection dissipated as quickly as it had appeared, leaving her frozen.

What was that?

The trapdoor grated shut, plunging them into darkness. She stumbled, would have fallen down the stairs had Cisuré not gripped her hand.

"Watch out." The other girl's whisper echoed about them.

Taking a deep gulp of the passage's musty air, Sarai carefully descended step by step. Pressure built in her head, memories winking into and out of her mind.

Cold. Tired. Clutching her satchel as she gingerly counted each step.

A sick, clammy fear gripped her. Jovian was right. This was how she'd gotten into the Academiae four years ago.

Following the sound of Cisuré's footsteps, she wished she had Kadra's talent with lightning to illuminate the path ahead. But her body seemed to know precisely where they were going, treading sure-footedly despite her mounting panic. They trekked in silence, until the tunnel sloped up, and Cisuré stubbed her toe on the first of the seventeen steps that would take them back to the surface.

Wood creaked as the trapdoor slid open, revealing a broom closet, dimly lit by sconce-light filtering in from the keyhole. The same one Helvus had taken Jovian into, smuggling him out the other way. Sarai twisted the handle and peered into the hallway. Nothing stirred in the shadows.

"Students only live on the first three floors." Cisuré stepped out of the closet. "Everything above it is . . . Aelius's domain."

Sarai cast her a sidelong glance, relieved that she'd already dispensed with Aelius's title.

Cisuré motioned to the tower's wide spiral staircase. "I think they're at the top."

"Probably. That's where Tullus and Aelius took me when they were holding that warrant over my head."

Sarai's skin crawled as they ascended past each landing, stopping at the last. An eerie familiarity shook her as memory merged with reality for the briefest of seconds, the fifth floor of Sidran Tower stretching before her past and present selves. A lengthy row of paintings extended in both directions down the corridor.

Without thinking, she found herself walking toward the portrait of a red-haired woman, posed imperiously.

"Magus Supreme Caelina. She headed the Academiae before Tetrarch Aelius," a familiar voice whispered in the recesses of her head. *Cisuré's voice.*

Sarai stilled, hearing her past self laugh in response. Turning from the portrait, she found Cisuré watching her with an inscrutable look.

"How did you know it was this one?" the other girl asked carefully.

Why do I remember you telling me it was this one? Sarai's breath came fast, every fiber of her being screaming at her to race out of the tower and examine each new piece of information before proceeding further.

She tamped down her fear. Anek was in danger. They could be—*No, don't think that.*

"Looks recent," she muttered.

Cisuré bit her lip before removing the painting from its nail, revealing a shallow depression. The wall parted when she pushed it, displaying a massive room that could easily have been its own domus. Squinting in the inky darkness, Sarai vaguely made out a staircase leading to a second level. Cisuré paused with a hand to her lips, listening carefully before deflating.

"No one's here," she whispered.

"Check upstairs," Sarai strove to keep her tone hopeful. "When they had me here, they tossed me in an alcove afterward. We might spot them from above."

"This way." Cisuré maneuvered across the room with ease, beckoning to Sarai, who picked her away past opulent hangings, furniture, and sculptures.

The staircase opened up to an eerily familiar ballroom. Every bone in her body turned to stone at the memory of Tullus burning her here.

"Sarai?" Cisuré's voice broke in.

She hadn't realized that she was gasping. Clutching her chest, she propped herself against the wall. "Give me a moment," she croaked. "It's the proximity—"

"It's coming back to you, isn't it?" At the other end of the room, Cisuré's eyes were stark.

"Just look around for anything that'll help us find them." Clutching her chest, Sarai peered about the ballroom, finding only chairs and the vague outlines of other sconces. Was it her imagination or had she heard a door closing?

She cast a wary glance at the stairs. With only one way up and one way out, they were sitting ducks here. "We can't stay here for long."

"Actually, we will." Cisuré swallowed, turning to face her.

Sarai struggled to inhale. "Did you find something?"

"I'm sorry, Sarai. But you left me no choice."

The hairs on the back of her neck barely had time to stand before footsteps sounded, coming up the stairs, slow and measured.

Her blood chilled. "What have you done?" she gasped. Staggering across the room, she fisted Cisuré's robes, shaking her. "What the fuck have you done?"

"What I had to do. For your sake," Cisuré spat. "So don't worry. *You'll* be safe."

Anek's and Cassandane's warnings returned to her. *I've never seen him show any hint of partiality. Not until you. He just announced his weakness to all of Ur Dinyé.*

Not pausing to think, she wrenched Cisuré's dagger from its sheath and cut her hand, dripping the blood over every rune in her armilla. Her magic flared hot and fast as she turned to face the man who'd reached the landing.

Tullus. Her heart plummeted.

"Look at that. You're here again, Petitor Sarai," he sneered.

"If either of you touch me, you'll regret it." Sarai gripped the dagger, maneuvering to keep both Tullus and Cisuré in sight, while trying to gauge the distance to the stairs.

"I've kept my word." Cisuré addressed Tullus. "Don't hurt her. Keep her restrained until Kadra comes."

Sarai dashed toward the stairs when Tullus blocked her path.

"Let's stop being difficult, yes?" he said lazily.

Her heart hammered in her chest. She knew little of Tullus's magical strengths beyond fire and had almost nothing in the way of offensive magic.

She tried not to betray her burgeoning terror. "Quite upstanding of you, resorting to kidnap to bring down a political rival. I'm sure the gods are *delighted.*"

"Sarai, you're brainwashed," Cisuré pleaded. "But you'll see clearly once Kadra's gone."

"Says the woman who's been seeing out of Aelius's ass for the past four years!" Sarai roared, still unable to believe what the other girl had done. "How could you deliver me to *them*?"

"Not you! Just *him*!" Cisuré shot back, and Sarai laughed scornfully.

"Gods, I almost hope they kill me, just so you can see how wrong you were." She darted behind Cisuré, going for the stairs again.

Tullus smiled and raised a hand. Ropes of fire burst to life, wrapping her wrists and ankles to pin her spread-eagled to the wall. Blinding pain seared her, wrenching a scream from her throat as the restraints burnt through skin. Air fled her lungs, smoke taking its place as she thrashed in agony.

"You were saying?" Tullus called over her shrieks.

"You said you wouldn't hurt her!" Cisuré screamed. "Stop!"

Looking bored, Tullus backhanded her with enough force to throw her to the ground.

Gasping, Cisuré clutched her cheek. "Tetrarch Aelius will hear of this!"

Tullus laughed. "Yes, I'm sure. But until he arrives, try not to test my patience."

Walking to where Sarai fruitlessly struggled, he traced a line down her jaw. "Gods only know what Kadra sees in this. Has he had you yet?"

She spat in his face.

His eyes turned ugly. "So be it."

He fastened a hand around her throat. Terror emptied her mind, the scent of her burning flesh tunneling up her nostrils as her bonds scorched deeper. She twisted from side to side, searching for a weapon, for anything—

"Don't you dare!"

Tullus's weight vanished as Cisuré grappled him to the ground. Gripping her hair, he slammed her face-first into the ground. Bone cracked, and she wailed, clutching her nose.

Sarai recoiled as Tullus turned to her.

As he approached, she used the only weapon she had left. She dropped the illusion.

One second. Two. The scars winding across her face were reflected in Tullus's dark pupils. He tottered back. The fiery ropes holding her vanished for the briefest of seconds.

And Sarai sprung into action.

Shoving the agony of her wounds to one corner of her mind, she sidestepped him to pick up Cisuré's dagger, and immediately sliced through his left hamstring from her crouched vantage point. He crumpled with a scream. Stretching out a hand, he ground his teeth, attempting the fiery ropes once more.

"Like hell you will," she spat.

Matching her palm to his, it took her less than a second to reach beneath his skin, to tunnel into the intricate mass of capillaries beneath. And to shred every one of them.

Tullus screamed as Sarai did the same to his other hand.

Panting, she forced the magic through her exhausted limbs. *Just a little farther.*

Hands locked around her shoulders, dragging her from Tullus to shove her across the room. Sarai couldn't halt a scream when Cisuré purposefully slammed a heel into her injured ankles.

"You can't leave." Blood dripped from Cisuré's broken nose. "Hate me if you must, but this is for your own good."

Footsteps sounded hard and fast up the staircase, a familiar roar of rage vibrating through the ballroom. Cisuré shoved Sarai's face into a curtain, suffocating her with the fabric. She flailed wildly, vision going multicolored and hazy. Elbowing her face, she grappled with Cisuré, colliding with a door.

It burst open, throwing them onto the balcony. She barely had time to register the horribly familiar view before Cisuré gripped her head.

"I'm keeping you safe," she pronounced. And slammed Sarai's skull into unconsciousness.

CHAPTER
THIRTY-ONE

Sarai opened her eyes to agony. Hers. And someone else's. The blood on her hands hadn't begun to dry. She'd only been unconscious for minutes.

A tormented scream cut through her stupor, and she turned her neck to see Kadra, blade aloft, the very picture of one of the Wretched from legend. Her eyes followed the arc of his sword as he sliced through Tullus's wrist, cleaving it straight off to join his other severed hand.

A weak sound of shock left her, but he didn't seem to hear it.

"I think I'll make you a torso," he said hoarsely.

He was completely undone. Eyes incandescent, he brought the point down and through Tullus's kneecap. Cisuré whimpered, curled up against a wall as Kadra gripped the Tetrarch's remaining limb and did the same.

He placed a boot over the now-limbless Tetrarch's mouth. "You should never have touched her." His voice was hoarse. "She was *mine*, and you—"

Rearing back, he plunged his blade into Tullus's chest with a sickening crack that made Sarai flinch in shock. Leaving it in to prolong Tullus's suffering, he leveled malevolent eyes on Cisuré, just as footsteps came up the staircase for the third time that night.

But this time, it wasn't just one person. Aelius and his vigiles stormed the room, half of them freezing at the tableau before them.

"Tetrarch Aelius!" Cisuré sobbed, rushing to cling to his ivory robes. "Oh gods, he's killed Tetrarch Tullus!"

"Killing," Kadra snarled. "He isn't dead yet."

As Aelius's vigiles surrounded him, Kadra gripped the hilt of the half-buried sword, and wrenched it free with a twist.

A wretched scream rent the air before Tullus stopped moving, eyes empty.

"Now, he's dead." Tossing the blade to the ground, Kadra's smile was a madman's. "I've been wanting to do that for years."

"Was it worth it?" Aelius sounded genuinely curious as he mildly surveyed the limbs littering the tower floor. "You're guilty of murder now. I won't lack for witnesses."

"He killed my Petitor!" Kadra roared. Sparks flared to life in the ballroom. "I won't lack for motive."

Aelius gaped, then burst into vicious peals of laughter. "The Petitor who's staring up at us?"

Kadra's head whipped toward her, features suddenly ashen. A malicious smile curved Aelius's lips, and before Sarai could gasp a warning, he struck.

One moment, Kadra was sprinting to her. The next, he was flying back to slam into the wall, a thousand thin bolts of lightning binding him. He ground his teeth against the same excruciating pain she had known.

"No!" she screamed, trying to struggle to her feet, to do *something*, but her wrists and ankles were a wretched mass of burns.

Aelius shook his head. "Really, Kadra. I know she looks worse than usual, but she wasn't *dead*."

She expected Kadra to break free, to bring out the fearsome power she'd witnessed, but he only watched her, relief in his eyes.

"You weren't breathing," he whispered. "I waited. You had no pulse."

Burning, suffocation, and head trauma. She couldn't speak.

Color returned to Cisuré's face as she laughed, high-pitched and hysterical. "The invincible Kadra. Bound. I've waited years for this." She stalked to where Kadra was pinned to the wall and spat in his face. "Now, Kadra. Did you ever tell Sarai about the Sidran Tower Girl?"

Bile and foreboding rose in Sarai's throat. Meeting Kadra's eyes, she shook her head.

"I don't want to know," Sarai croaked, and almost laughed at the irony of it. Four years chasing after answers and now she would do anything not to hear them.

Torment lined Cisuré's face. "You see, Sarai, four years ago, this man came across the Sidran Tower Girl. She was alive then, but bleeding out. He had enough time to seek a healer, to find help. But he didn't, did you, Kadra? What did you do instead?"

When he stayed silent, a glint appeared in Cisuré's eyes that chilled Sarai to her core.

Taking his fallen sword, Cisuré drove the point into his shoulder. "I asked you what you did to her!" she screamed.

Sarai flinched as Kadra's eyes closed and he let out a hiss of pain. Still, he said nothing.

"Very well." Wrenching the blade free, Cisuré strode to Sarai and held it to her throat. "Will you say it now?"

"Don't touch her!" Kadra snarled.

She laughed in victory. "Then say it." She pressed the blade against Sarai's neck. "Just say it."

He met Sarai's gaze, his face pale with anguish.

"Don't," she managed. "Please."

"What did you do to that girl, Kadra?" Cisuré shrieked.

He searched Sarai's eyes for a long moment, a thousand emotions in his night-black gaze. Then, he bowed his head, grating out each word.

"I killed her."

The world went deathly still. For a moment, she wondered if Time had made an exception for her and condemned everyone else to live on. Refusing to acknowledge his words, she looked away from the face that she loved. The mouth she'd mapped with hers only a night ago.

A door buried at the bottom of her consciousness, weighed down by horror too deep for utterance, suddenly snapped open.

And Sarai screamed.

CHAPTER THIRTY-TWO

Four years ago

Sarai wandered the bazaar, newly purchased reed pens and parchment in hand, though she was pretty sure the merchant had fleeced her for the goods.

She grimaced at her threadbare tunic and trousers. At least half her hair had escaped its braid, a white ribbon precariously hanging on to the remainder. She needed a comb. And a proper pair of shoes.

Nothing I can do about that. How to get to the Academiae was the question.

Debating on whom to ask, her gaze fell on a tall figure in iudex regalia striding through the bazaar. She hadn't expected iudices to be young. He looked only a few years older than her, although there was a severity to his features that suggested the job had hardened him early.

Hushed voices followed his path. The wary side-glances thrown his way became disapproving whispers when he stopped before a wine vendor, purchased a bottle, and proceeded to down at least half its contents. He didn't seem to care. Holding a few gazes, he inclined his head and toasted them. Buying a second bottle, he tucked it under his arm and stalked out of the crowded market. She followed. Perhaps someone like this, who flouted social convention, would be willing to help her.

Stopping some paces behind the fence he'd used as a hitching rail, she worked up the courage to speak while he stuffed the uncorked bottle into his saddlebag. Then, two men in opulent robes approached him on horseback.

"Iudex Kadra?" an ivory-robed man asked, dismounting.

The man he'd called Kadra looked irritated. "Tetrarch Aelius."

Tetrarch? She hid behind a post, peering at the iudex. He had the most beautiful voice she'd ever heard.

The other man beside Tetrarch Aelius regarded Kadra grimly, eyes going from the half-empty bottle under his arm to the one in his saddlebag with an expression of habitual distaste.

Aelius smiled pleasantly at Kadra. "What a surprise to see you here."

"Indeed. Especially given how well known it is that I frequent this bazaar," Kadra said dryly.

Sarai stifled a laugh.

"I'll keep this brief," Aelius said coolly. "I'd like to request your presence tonight at Sidran Tower."

"For what purpose?"

"Dinner. A few Guildmasters and noblemen are eager to meet the brightest star of Edessa's judiciary."

Kadra's smirk showed what he thought of that, but he shrugged. "I'll be there. Anything else?"

"Straight to the point." Aelius's eyes seemed to harden. "Do try not to be late."

The Tetrarch mounted his horse and left in a flurry of dust. His friend watched his figure diminish in the distance, then turned to Iudex Kadra, eyes icy.

"What do you have to say for yourself?" he demanded.

"I have twelve more trials to sit through."

"And enough wine to ensure that you're sloshed through them all." The man's lips thinned. "The assaults in Aelius's Quarter last night. Was that you?"

"If they were missing a few limbs, then yes."

Assaults? Limbs? Sarai shrank against the fence post. People leaving the market eyed her with disapproval.

"Didn't I warn you to cease targeting his people?" Aelius's friend argued.

"Then they shouldn't brand children."

"That last one. He'll be disfigured for life!"

"Hopefully. I held the brand on his face for at least a quarter hour."

"You—" The other man raised his hand, and she saw Kadra hold still, waiting for the blow to strike. Gritting his teeth, the man whirled away, spitting on the ground.

"Well done, Father." The word held a wealth of mockery. "After all, we're in public."

She winced.

"Why do you think Aelius invited you tonight? I warned you that targeting his men would get you in trouble. When you go tonight, go expecting death."

"And a few Guildmasters and noblemen will be witnesses. And you, of course. Tell me, what will you do when Aelius drives his blade home? Fawn at his feet? Or will you finally grow a spine?" Kadra didn't sound like he cared either way.

His father's jaw visibly clenched. "You think the bloodshed you unleash is 'growing a spine'? What of the people who watch that, the *children* who'll grow to believe that emulating your violence is right? You're only spreading hurt and violence, and you're corrupting them all."

"I am." Kadra shrugged. "Don't you have duties to attend to?"

"You—"

Sarai couldn't hold her tongue. "I wonder," she broke in, peering over the fence. "Is it really right to coddle a child and assure them that the world is theirs for the taking, only for reality to push them into despair later on? Wouldn't it be kinder to equip them with the tools to navigate reality from the outset, even if that means opening their eyes to its grimness?"

Kadra whirled around.

"Who's this?" His father jerked a finger at her.

She faltered under Kadra's stare. He had the sharpest eyes she'd ever seen. "I'm sorry, I didn't mean to be rude." What did one do with upper-class folk? She dived to the ground, prostrating herself.

"An outsider." Kadra's father sighed. With a sound of frustration, he swung onto his mount and rode off.

"You can stand up now," Kadra informed her.

She climbed to her feet, grimacing at the mud along the hem and knees of her trousers.

Kadra's gaze narrowed. "Have you eaten?" he asked brusquely.

"Not for some time, to be honest."

"Give me your hands." When she stared, he took them anyway. Fishing several aurei from a pocket, he closed her fingers around them. "Have—"

"*Tibi gratias ago*, but I cannot accept this." She shoved the coins back into his hands. "If you insist on charity, a few denarii is enough."

"You'll hurt yourself if you go on like this," he informed her.

She drew herself up to full height, affronted, and he appeared mildly taken aback. "I know how I look, but that's only because I just arrived here, and it's been a rough journey. I'm not entirely without coin."

"Where from?"

"The north."

His eyebrows rose. "That's a difficult journey for a child to make on her own."

"I'm fourteen," she said indignantly.

"Why here?"

"The Academiae." She beamed. "I'm going to challenge the entrance exams."

"Hmm. It won't be easy," he warned her. "They aren't kind to charity students. Or northerners."

"I know, but I've nothing else to hope for."

He paused. "You don't sound afraid."

"Gods, I'm terrified," she admitted. "But I can do this. I've trained myself for years. Which brings me to why I was . . . listening. I would like your help," she said politely. "I can't figure out how to get into the Academiae. Is it true that only students are allowed in?"

He looked bemused. "Why sneak in?"

"I don't have anywhere to stay until the exams begin."

"You won't find anywhere to stay in the Academiae either."

"I've a friend there. We grew up together. She'll let me stay with her."

He thought for a moment and nodded. "I'll help you."

Excitement shot through her. She paused. "Why?"

"So suspicion rears its head now?"

"Talking is one thing. Helping is another."

"And if I've a favor I require in return?"

As long as it isn't anything physical. She nodded, hesitant. "Then you have a bargain. How do I get inside?"

"Don't take any of the gates. The magi will refuse you entrance. There's a dirt road between Lisran Tower and Aoran Tower going down the citadel. Follow it to a trapdoor within an alley. Hardly anyone knows of it, and it leads to a tunnel underneath the gates and into the Academiae. It'll be difficult," he warned her. "It's pitch black in there, but you'll evade the vigiles."

"Hold on a moment." She rummaged in her worn satchel, pulling out a reed pen, ink, and a roll of parchment to record his directions.

Kadra's brow furrowed. "Don't." He placed a hand on her arm. "There's no need to waste your supplies."

Pulling out a warped metal ink pen and a crumpled bit of parchment from his saddlebag, he wrote out his instructions. "Dirt road. Tunnel," he repeated. "There are seventeen steps to the bottom. The ground will slope up as you get close, and you'll reach a staircase. Seventeen steps to the top. Open the door and you'll be inside a broom closet within Sidran Tower."

"Really?" She beamed.

He smiled faintly. "Really."

"Thank you!" She took the parchment from him reverently. "Gods, thank you! And what would you want from me in return?"

He was silent.

She sighed. "I've heard it all, really. Tell me."

Kadra studied her. "Only this. No matter what the other students do to you, hold on. Understood?"

She stilled as the request registered.

"I asked if you understand me."

Blinking away tears, she nodded. "I do."

"Good." He mounted his horse, looking for all the world like a Tetrarch. Powerful, unyielding. Perhaps someday, she could aspire to such a position.

"Wait! Sir." She grasped his reins. "When I complete my training, in a few years, do you suppose I could thank you?"

A smile lifted his lips, almost making him look human. "I suppose."

Wisdom and Radiance, she didn't have a single token to give him. Inspiration struck, and she pulled the ribbon from her hair.

"Here. I'll come back for that. And then you'll know it's me."

. . .

"Sarai!" Cisuré's eyes were huge. "I don't understand. How are you here?"

"There's a tunnel that avoids the Tower Gates!" Sarai smiled ear to ear. "A man I met told me of it. You said you lived in Lisran Tower, remember?"

"By Wisdom, what sort of strange men have you been meeting?" Cisuré laughed, but there was an odd strain to her eyes. "Why did you come?"

Sarai faltered. "I sent you a letter two months ago." At Cisuré's baffled expression, she swallowed. "That I was coming?"

"Oh, *that*. I didn't think you'd—" Cisuré broke off. "I've only been here five months, things have been so busy . . . I'm so sorry, I meant to reply. Where are you staying?"

"Well . . . can I stay with you for a few days while I get an appointment to challenge the exams?" Sarai rushed on as Cisuré tensed. "Just to rest and bathe. Even just bathe. I'll leave for the rest of the day. I know it's an imposition, but these magi are prejudiced, and maybe if I'm well groomed, they'll think better of me?"

"But you'll have to wait months! It isn't easy to get an audience with the instructors."

Months? Her heart dropped. "I thought you said that it was only a few days' wait."

"That was—" Cisuré twisted the fabric of her robes. "They changed it soon after I arrived. It's a lengthy process now, and I can't hide you for that long!"

Shame sunk beneath Sarai's skin. The sole denarius left of her savings seemed to burn through her pocket. She shouldn't have spent so much on those writing supplies. She swallowed. *There'll be a tavern that needs help.* She'd think about it after she left.

"I'm sorry. I didn't mean to trouble you." Her voice was a sliver of sound. "I'll go."

Cisuré sighed. "Didn't you research this before coming here?"

"I just believed you." Sarai didn't mean for the reply be so caustic, but the other girl flinched, staring at the ground for a long moment before taking Sarai's hand.

"There's a party tonight. A number of influential people will be there, including Head Tetrarch Aelius. If we tidy you up in time, I can bring you as a trader's daughter. That might be enough to get the process going faster. They could even test you then and there."

Glorious relief swept over her. She decided not to mention that she'd seen Aelius earlier with Iudex Kadra. "I'll do anything. I won't let you down."

"I know." Cisuré's smile was finally genuine. "Tetrarch Aelius is an exceptional man. He's the Magus Supreme, too, you know, Head of the Academiae. He'll be fair with you." She looked Sarai up and down, grimacing at her travel-worn tunic. "Now, let's get you dressed up."

. . .

"A hidden room?" Sarai gaped as Cisuré removed the portrait to reveal the door set in the wall.

"You're a trader's daughter tonight," the other girl reminded her. "Don't stare all wide-eyed and unsophisticated."

Sarai nodded, feeling opulent in the navy robes Cisuré had lent her with her hair braided in an intricate knot.

Cisuré pushed the door open, and a glittering new world unfurled ahead. She stepped into a brightly lit ballroom with frescoes tiling the walls, sweeping up to the cavernous ceiling. Jewels dripped from the party's wealthy attendees, winking from ears, necks, and rings. Platters of meat occupied a long table at the center of the room, people popping a few morsels into their mouths as they sized up their peers.

"That's Tetrarch Tullus." Cisuré tilted her head toward a stately man in indigo and navy robes. "I'll introduce you. Tetrarch Aelius is occupied."

Sarai was impressed. "How do you know him?"

The other girl flushed. "Well, Tetrarch Aelius noticed me when I attended the Grand Elsarian Temple for worship. He's a great leader, you know. Kind, and caring"—she turned red—"and he practices what he preaches. This is a real honor. You're meeting the most powerful people in all Ur Dinyé, so don't embarrass me."

"I won't. I promise." Sarai put on a glowing smile as Tullus approached.

Cisuré bowed low. "Tetrarch Tullus, if you'll please forgive the intrusion, this is my friend. She's a trader's daughter come to challenge the exams. I believe she could be extremely helpful to you. She's brilliant at healing."

"Well then." Tullus looked fascinated. "What are you called?"

"Sarai," she said, bowing until she nearly split in two. "I'm so honored to meet you, Tetrarch Tullus."

"Talent is always worth nurturing, Sera." She almost corrected him but Cisuré shook her head slightly. He turned to Cisuré. "Why don't you take a turn about the room? I'll take care of your friend."

Cisuré beamed. "*Tibi gratias ago*, Tetrarch Tullus."

Throwing Sarai a meaningful glance, she strode toward the dinner table.

Tullus smiled. "Would you like to see the ballroom upstairs?"

. . .

Tullus chuckled, bringing her to a balcony at the top. Edessa spread out below them.

"Well, Sera, I can allow you into the Academiae if you pass a test of skill. My tests aren't easy, but I'm confident that anyone Cisuré recommends will succeed. Tetrarch Aelius vouches highly for her."

Sarai's chest swelled. "Name it and I will."

"It'll be toward the end of this gathering, I'm afraid. We're getting storm-fall soon." His eyes went to a point beyond her shoulder, and he sighed ruefully. "Ah, but here comes Cisuré to take you away. If you'd prefer to do this another time . . ."

"No! I'm happy to wait. I'll let her know!"

Excusing herself with a smile, Sarai raced to where Cisuré waited. "He's asked me to stay until the end for a test! If I pass, he'll let me in."

"Gods, you're going to join me!" Cisuré squeaked. "This is *wonderful!*"

Sarai gripped the other girl's shoulder in delight. "It's all thanks to you. And to Tetrarch Aelius, although I haven't seen him yet."

"Anything for you," Cisuré said affectionately. "Don't worry, he's just mingling with a few Guildmasters. He's a busy man." She dropped her voice. "Just watch out. I hear Tetrarch Aelius is expecting some high-flying iudex to make an appearance tonight. He's notorious for his violence, but the people love him."

I wonder if it's Kadra. "I'll watch for him." She really did owe him.

Cisuré squeezed her hands. "I need to go assist Tetrarch Aelius, but come find me when you're done and tell me all about it."

"I will." She accepted a glass from Tetrarch Tullus, who'd reappeared at her elbow, and took a sip. It tasted as if it had gone a bit off. "I promise."

. . .

She shrank back as a door creaked open. Footsteps entered the room, a group of men judging by their voices. One approached the closet, purposeful strides ticking like seconds on a water clock. He stopped before the doors.

Gods save me.

The man leaned against the door of her pitch-black prison. "—doesn't matter," another familiar, cultured voice said. *Aelius.* She must've passed out only a few minutes after she met him. "They'll all buy it up. It's almost a pity how gullible they are, but it's profitable."

She grew cold. The man she'd spoken with hadn't sounded so patronizing.

"You're sure they won't find out?" an unfamiliar male voice asked.

"That the miracle shield I've discovered doesn't actually run on faith? No, Helvus, they won't. The public isn't known for their critical thinking."

"Should have seen the hick girl I had to chaperone the whole evening. All acquiescence and nothing in the way of intellect."

Tullus. She bit down her rage.

"So we pretend it's some sort of miracle from the gods, hide our stakes in the mine, Helvus manufacturers it and everyone snatches it up." Tullus whistled. "We'll be rolling in aurei."

"And if a few hundred homes blow up, then they'll only curse themselves. The Guild gets the land." Aelius laughed. "Foolproof."

Petrified, she crouched by the door, hoping they'd leave. *Stay quiet,* her instincts told her. *Wait for them to leave, then break your hands and ankles, whatever it takes to get the restraints off and the door open.*

Something skittered past her leg. She heard it again, a clacking in the same space as her. The narrow slit of light between the hinges illuminated a many-legged insect preparing to crawl up her leg.

She involuntarily shrieked. The sound, muffled by her gag, cut through the conversation outside.

The men fell silent. Aelius's weight shifted away from the closet.

What have I done?

Whatever had secured the closet's handles hit the ground with a thump, and the door opened. She stared up at Aelius, tears streaming down her face.

His features turned ugly. "Tullus," he hissed. "You have some explaining to do."

. . .

She was going to die.

Tullus had beaten her before trying to strip her. Then he had beaten her some more when she'd resisted. And now Aelius was going to throw her off Sidran Tower.

The monstrous gods had stayed quiet.

Tullus dragged her onto the balcony. Her body wove a path through fragments of the vase he'd smashed over her head.

"You're disgusting," she whispered to Aelius with the last of her strength. "You think you're clever. But someone will notice. They'll wonder why I died."

He didn't care.

She drifted in and out of consciousness in brief bursts, struggling as she did. Tullus swore when she elbowed his side. He kicked her feet out from under her, plowing her head into the ground. Her vision blurred, growing dark with each slam.

"Useless bitch," he snarled.

Dazed, she raked her nails into his face when he bent over her. He manacled her wrists in a grip of steel and delivered a final, resounding blow to her face. Blood filled her mouth, along with shards of her teeth.

"What a shame." Aelius eyed her dispassionately. "This is what happens when you aspire too high above your station, Sera. You fall."

Sarai wanted to scream that she'd only wanted to study, but her mouth was in too much pain. Blood dripped into her eyes, tinting her vision crimson.

"I'm going to enjoy this show." Tullus slit her palm with a blade, and her hand burned as skin parted. Dipping the fingers of her other hand in the blood, he drew a rune she didn't recognize. "Where's that pet of yours, Aelius? What'll you say when she comes looking for her little friend?"

Through the veil of red coating her vision, she saw Aelius shrug. "I sent her off earlier. By the way, I invited Kadra tonight. Bastard's late. But if he does show, he'll be just in time for a good framing."

For some reason, Tullus and Aelius found that hilarious. They maneuvered her body, puppeteering her to draw rune after rune.

Something twisted in her chest as they finished the first few, the limbs of her body growing taut, fighting as an invisible force began to pull the life from her. *What are they doing to me?*

"You . . ." Her voice was little more than a croak. "The gods will burn you for this."

Tullus cuffed her ear hard, slamming her head against the balcony's railing.

"The gods sanction everything we do," he said. "Or they would have stopped us."

A deep rumble sounded in the distance.

Aelius frowned. "Hurry with the Summoning. The storm's almost here."

Her blood ran cold. Blinding white split the sky, followed by another drumroll of sound. Tullus drew the last rune. *Modrai.* This one she recognized.

"And here we are, Sera," Aelius mused. "If there's a life after this one, ask them to make you a little less foolish."

Sarai, she thought as magic drained from her. *My name is Sarai.*

The two men hurried back inside, leaving her lying in a mess of blood.

A heartbeat. The spatter of a raindrop on her cheek. Then, a pale blue fire roared to life around her. An agony unlike anything she'd ever experienced burned through every limb. Her mouth fell open in a scream to the storm-laden sky as an invisible force reached through her ribs to wrench at the weak heart beating beneath.

Rain lashed her face, stole her pleas. She rose above the balcony, above the tower, a marionette to invisible forces. Pressure squeezed her head in a vise until rich iron choked her throat, and she couldn't even scream anymore.

Help me! she pleaded to the Elsar, to anyone. *Please make it stop!*

And, suddenly, it did. Charged air thrummed in her ears as she hovered, a speck above Sidran Tower.

Then, she fell.

Air rushed past her in an eerie wail.

Was this the sum of her life? Of her foolish dreams?

Poor Cisuré. She wouldn't be seeing her after—

. . .

Someone crouched by her, seemingly uncaring of the raging storm. Fingers brushed the end of her braid, followed by a rough intake of breath.

"Fuck!" Anger laced a beautiful, familiar voice. She tried and failed to place it. "Damn it to the ten hells. Why is she here?" He felt for her pulse and cursed, and she knew that she wasn't going to survive.

Her good eye blinked, squinted, trying to make out his face. Several yards behind the man—she still couldn't remember his name—she saw Cisuré staring at her, petrified. Her mouth opened in what looked like a sob.

Then, she ran away.

Sarai slipped back into oblivion. When she reemerged, another man had joined the first one.

"Drenevan, this is unforgivable!" The man sounded horrified. "What have you done? Her face is gone."

"Get her another."

"You surely don't think she can be rebuilt after this? Anyone who sees her—"

"Can be bought."

"This is the last time I'll cover for you. Never again!"

A bitter chuckle. The scrape of boots. "If only that were true. Leave her, she's gone."

"She's still alive!" the other man roared. "She might live if we take her to a healer."

"She won't." His voice held no doubt. "And she doesn't matter, so long as I get to Aelius."

Shoes ground against stone, and she knew the man with the beautiful voice had vanished, and though she didn't understand why, something inside of her split at the sound of his fading footsteps.

CHAPTER THIRTY-THREE

Her wrists and ankles were a mess of blackened flesh. The cell stank of blood, rot, and bodily fluids. But Sarai couldn't bring herself to care. She finally knew the truth.

She doesn't matter, so long as I get to Aelius.

She leaned against the bars and listened for movement in the adjoining cell. He was there, but he hadn't said a word since they'd been thrown in here. She drew her knees tighter against her chest, only vaguely able to recall the chaos that had ensued after Kadra's revelation.

Aelius laughing. Kadra hoarsely begging her to breathe. Cisuré dropping the blade, a triumphant gleam in her eyes. It had abruptly winked out at Aelius's next words.

"Lock them up."

Oh, how Cisuré's jaw had dropped then. The pleas had begun. Hadn't she brought Kadra to him, as promised? Had he agreed that Sarai would be spared?

Divorced from her body, Sarai had dispassionately watched Aelius shrug ruefully.

"I'm sorry, my dear. But she's as much a part of this as he is."

And then, for the sheer amusement of it, he'd beaten Kadra bloody before his vigiles carted Sarai away.

She eyed the flickering candle stub by their cells, dreading what would happen when it went out and left them at the rodents' mercy.

She'd considered escape for the first minute of her imprisonment, before spotting the thin ropes of lightning crossing the arched entryway into their cellblock. That avenue closed, she steadied her fingers against the brick wall, pouring magic into the lesions around her wrists and ankles. Some healed. Some didn't.

Drained of energy and magic, she cast a glance at the wall between their cells. He still hadn't made a sound.

She took a deep breath. "Why did you do it?"

A long silence. Then the sound of shifting. "At the time, I thought the girl was too far gone. Getting Aelius seemed the better choice." Kadra inhaled roughly. "But he was already gone when I reached his ballroom."

The confirmation cut her, but she couldn't help the tears that sprung to her eyes at his voice. So strained, as though even breathing was difficult for him.

"Afterward, I went back. Just in case." His words were slurred, speech evidently painful. "She and Othus were gone." He made a hoarse sound. "He said she'd died moments after I left."

Sarai closed her eyes. "He thought you did it."

"Didn't I?" His voice was bitter. "Either way, it gave Aelius all the leverage he needed over Othus. Not that he was ever good at following orders. Hence, his death."

And you felt responsible for it all.

She'd hoped that he'd been her savior. A man who'd ordered her to be patched up after the Fall, however callously. *But if Othus hadn't been there I'd be dead.*

"You could have saved her," she whispered hoarsely. "And you didn't."

"I know." There was a world of grief and self-loathing in his words. "I crossed that line knowingly. And I can never forget."

She remembered the words below the ribbon in his bedroom. *Her* ribbon.

He didn't ask for absolution, and it hurt even worse than if he had, knowing that he had kept that ribbon for four years. Reliving that night every time he saw it.

"Gods!" she choked, crawling to the wall as if she could somehow reach through it and touch him.

She heard him do the same, a groan tearing from him as he settled against it.

"I couldn't attack Aelius and Tullus." He coughed, an ugly gurgle. "Not directly. They would have won. So I waited for years. For someone to emerge. Someone with whom at least a fraction of the land would be safe."

She couldn't comprehend any of it.

"They'll try me for murder tomorrow," he said quietly. "You know what that means."

She hadn't thought of the future. Hadn't been able to conceive it. "You're powerful. They can't force you into a Summoning—"

"I expected it," he admitted, eerily calm. "I've done my damned best to ensure it."

Reckless, Anek and Cassandane had said. *Uncharacteristically reckless.*

"What are you saying?" she demanded hoarsely.

"I've killed one." He coughed again, the rattle in his chest terrifying her. "Tomorrow, during the Summoning, I'll take the other with me. And everyone involved in her death will be gone."

She rose in a rush. "That's enough. This isn't like you."

He didn't seem to hear her. "My seat will be yours."

Realization struck like lightning. It had all been for the Sidran Tower Girl. He'd broken his code and gone to war for her, fighting them all out of guilt and rage for four years. Risked his life, his career, for the unnamed girl he'd left dying. And he didn't know it, but he was attempting to give that same girl his legacy.

She buried her head in her hands and sobbed brokenly for the years they'd both wasted.

"My Sarai," he whispered as she wept. "I never wanted to hurt you."

A door clicked shut in the distance and she involuntarily tensed as light footsteps approached. She knew who it was even before golden hair caught the candlelight.

"I've convinced Tetrarch Aelius to pardon you," Cisuré said without preamble. "Just pin it all on *him* tomorrow and you'll walk free."

Sarai stared at the wall.

"I warned you this would end badly," Cisuré bit out. "For once in your life, just do as you're told, and you'll be saved."

Sarai wiped her wet cheeks, pondering the ends of her ruined braid.

Cisuré kicked the bars. "Say something!"

"I'm surprised you're still fawning over him." Sarai refused to turn to her. "He didn't think twice about breaking his word to you. You don't know what he's done."

"You know what Kadra's done." Cisuré's voice was venom. "Are you as gormless as the people of his Quarter to forgive it?"

"His people aren't brainwashed." Sarai faced her. "They're relieved. Because life is hard, and cruel, and they have a Tetrarch who will fight for them. I'm not surprised that you don't understand that."

"The victim returns." Cisuré sneered. "I've done everything I can for you!"

"Someday, you'll realize that love isn't possession!" Sarai snapped back. "It isn't bowing someone to your will and perspective. It's—" She swallowed at the memory of her first week working with Kadra. "It's disagreeing with them but trying to find a way forward because you care. It's understanding them . . . even if I would never have done what he did at Sidran Tower."

On the other side of the wall, she heard a sharp intake of breath.

"You're pathetic," Cisuré spat.

"And you lied to me for four years, you bitch!" Sarai pushed her face against the bars and dropped her voice so Kadra couldn't hear her. "I remember *everything*. I saw you at the end. I saw you *run away*. You've hated Kadra all this time, but you left me for dead just as he did." Cisuré paled with each furious word. "He's never hurt a hair on my head, but you?" She touched the wounds on her forehead. "You have committed almost *every* violence against me."

Cisuré averted her eyes. "You're wrong—"

"If you ever had any regard for me, find Anek and give them this." Sarai thrust Cassandane's red handkerchief between the bars. "You owe me that much."

"Only if you swear not to throw your life away for him."

"I have no intention of dying."

Cisuré opened her mouth, then pressed her lips together before storming from the jail.

"Do as she says." Kadra's voice seemed to have deteriorated even further in the scant minutes that had passed. "Don't risk yourself for me."

"Ordering me around, even in prison." She tried for levity and was rewarded with a rusty chuckle.

I won't let them ruin either of us any further. If Cassandane would help, then there was a chance for them to survive. It was a slim ray of hope, but she was the Sidran Tower Girl. She had clung to less.

Settling against her shared wall with Kadra, she kept her gaze on the wavering candle stub. And waited for dawn.

CHAPTER
THIRTY-FOUR

It was a fair morning for death.

Edessans swarmed the Aequitas under a cloudless sky, having woken to the horrifying announcement that one of their Tetrarchs had killed another and was to be tried immediately for treason. On top of the insidious scutum conspiracy, it was enough to cause widespread panic.

Shackled in a prison raeda outside the Aequitas, Sarai listened to the furor through the windows, noting with grim pleasure that most people seemed to think there was more to the matter than they had been told. She made sure her illusion was firmly in place. Only Tullus had seen her scars last night, and she needed it to stay that way for now.

The horn sounded with a sonorous boom. Aelius's ivory-liveried vigiles dragged her out of the carriage, shoving her through the prisoners' entrance. She kept her features blank, praying that Kadra would be there, too. They'd pulled him out of his cell at least an hour before her, and she dreaded to think of what they could have done in the interim. Killed him, perhaps, with the goal of holding a sham posthumous trial . . . *Stop*, she ordered herself. *Aelius wouldn't miss a chance to crow over him in public.*

The thought brought little comfort.

She kept her eyes on the ground until they reached the doors that would bring them onto the stage. Raising her head, she sighed in relief at the tattered black and gold robes of the man in front of her. Deep cuts marred Kadra's broad back but all that mattered was that he was alive.

The double doors into the Aequitas parted, giving her a view of the chaos as people raced to any available space to witness what would be the trial of the century. Never before had the Tetrarchy shattered from within. She swallowed. An hour or less from now, it would all be over. Who would the people hail as victor? Whose corpses would litter the Aequitas's stage?

"Bring in the accused," Aelius intoned.

It was time.

She knew the second Kadra moved that something was wrong. His head lolled forward; the vigiles she'd assumed were immobilizing him, were actually dragging him.

She scarcely heard the crowd's tumult as she and Kadra were forced on their knees at the center of the stage. She let out a broken gasp as she finally caught sight of his face.

They'd all but turned it to meat.

Judging by the way he hunched over, bracing himself against the ground, the rest of him hadn't fared much better.

The Summoning, she realized in horror. If there was anyone who could pull one off, it was Kadra. *So they weakened him.*

On the dais, Aelius radiated satisfaction. Cassandane seemed on the verge of hyperventilation. Anek placed a hand on their Tetrarch's shoulder, meeting Sarai's gaze with careful blankness. Her heart dropped. Had Cisuré been so spiteful as to not deliver the handkerchief?

"People of Edessa." Aelius raised a hand for silence, smile slipping when people continued to gasp in horror at Kadra's condition. "We gather today for the worst of reasons. The worst of all crimes. In the early hours of this morning, I and many of my men witnessed a horrific sight at Sidran Tower, where the man before you murdered Tetrarch Tullus in cold blood."

The crowd tittered in disbelief. Some rose to their feet, screaming in outrage. Black-robed vigiles formed an inkblot among the masses, Kadra's people watching him with anguish.

Behind Aelius, Cisuré watched her with cold eyes, head raised in determination. Sarai met her gaze and the other girl stiffened before nodding once.

A wave of relief washed over her. *Anek knows.*

Aelius looked irritated as the spectators continued to roar their opinions. "The charge is provable." He turned to Cisuré.

Striding from the dais, she selected one of Aelius's vigiles and placed a hand on his head. Within seconds, a transparent Kadra and Tullus materialized on the stage.

The audience went still as Kadra wrenched the blade from Tullus's chest with a twist. Aelius's smile grew as even Kadra's most fervent supporters quieted.

Sarai turned to Kadra, wincing at the ragged pulp of his face. But despite being partially swollen shut, those black eyes remained as clear as ever, meeting her with calm acceptance. She trembled. They both knew what would come next. Because Cisuré wouldn't bother with showing the Aequitas *why* Kadra had done it.

As expected, the memory ended immediately after Tullus's death, showing nothing of what preceded it.

Aelius rose. "This man is known for violence. Celebrated for it—it is the reason many of you voted him into power. Are you surprised that he would commit a crime this heinous?" His eyes went hard. "You are all equally to blame for his sins."

The drop of a pin could echo in the Aequitas's silence, the air itself immobile.

"Is this man still your hero?" Aelius roared. "Do you still doubt his guilt?"

She held her breath as the audience sank back into their seats. With only two Tetrarchs left of four and Cassandane staying silent, there was no contesting this trial. Not with the evidence Cisuré had put forth.

Aelius masked his jubilation with his customary serenity. "Drenevan bu Kadra, you have forsaken all law and morality as ordained by the gods.

And now you must beg for their mercy." He nodded to Cisuré, who strode to Kadra, eyes alight with a terrible joy.

"Whom will you summon?" she hissed.

The crowd waited with bated breath as Kadra raised his battered head.

And Sarai spoke. "What of the rest of his crimes?"

Kadra went still.

"Sarai of Arsamea." Aelius glowered at her before turning to Cisuré, who watched him with pleading eyes. "I'm prepared to pardon your complicity in luring Tetrarch Tullus to—"

"Tetrarch Tullus isn't the only person who was murdered at Sidran Tower," Sarai announced to the Aequitas. "There was another, four years ago. A girl who dropped to her death. You have all heard of her. Tetrarch Kadra also stands accused of killing her. Will you not give her justice?"

There were sounds of shock, followed by a collective murmuring that swept through the crowd. *Yes.* They remembered the Sidran Tower Girl.

Aelius looked pleased now. "Unfortunately, owing to a lack of witnesses, we can't—"

"I witnessed it," Sarai yelled. "I saw him standing over her body."

A flurry of gasps ran through the crowd, swelling to a roar of shock. And Kadra, who had barely moved the whole time, swiveled to face her.

"Tetrarch Aelius, one look in my head will tell you if I'm lying." Sarai risked a glance at Anek, who was watching her intently. "I was here four years ago. I saw *everything.*"

The louder the crowd roared, the more annoyed Aelius looked. He glanced at her, and she saw his disbelief. He thought she was stalling.

"Probe her and Materialize it," he finally ordered.

As Cisuré approached, Sarai addressed the Aequitas. "Four years ago, I came to Edessa. I was only fourteen. Utterly unsophisticated. Naïve. Innocent. Perhaps because of this, I was badly hurt one night." Aelius's brows drew together in suspicion. She swallowed, and went on, "I've had to wear an illusion ever since. But today, for honesty's sake, I'll show you my scars. To prove the truth of what I've just told you."

And then, Sarai dropped the illusion.

Cassandane's gasps echoed through the Aequitas as scars unraveled across Sarai's features, laced her arms, crawled down her neck. She looked at Kadra and saw something shatter in his black gaze. He'd nearly pieced it together. But it was Aelius's reaction she needed. She needed him to balk, to put his foot in his mouth while his credibility was still weak from the scutum trial.

Turning to the dais where Aelius stared blankly at her, she raised her chin. "I'm ready, if Petitor Cisuré wishes to begin."

The other girl eagerly approached and raised a hand to Sarai's forehead.

"Stop!" Aelius's command was a roar. He hurriedly masked his features in calm, but there was a wildness in his eyes.

Sarai smiled. He hadn't bothered to confirm that she was dead that night. *Everything has a price.*

"Tetrarch Aelius?" Cisuré looked bewildered.

"Step away." For the first time, he looked shaken. There was a pale sheen to his skin. "There's no need for a Probe. She's lying."

Cisuré dropped her hand. "I don't understand."

Neither did the crowd, by their muttering. *Good.*

"Let us see it!" one brave soul shouted.

Aelius's nostrils flared. "People of Edessa. This is a cheap trick. She and Kadra are *involved*." His voice dripped with scorn. "She's buying time—"

"For what? We're both clearly incapable of escape," Sarai pointed out. A few people hooted.

"Enough!" Aelius roared, turning to Cisuré. "We start with his Summoning." His voice brooked no disobedience. "Then hers."

Cisuré's face collapsed in horror. She raced up the dais. Her pleas were met with Aelius's stony stare.

Fighting to stay calm, Sarai turned to Anek and widened her eyes. *Please. I won't ask more of you than this.*

Grim-faced, Anek nudged Cassandane, who swallowed thickly. "I'll allow it."

"You'll do nothing of the sort!" Aelius yelled.

Cassandane's chin rose. "As one of two remaining Tetrarchs, I have every right to see the testimony of a witness."

"Tetrarch Cassandane, do not try my patience."

"Tetrarch Aelius, you agreed that your Petitor would Probe her. Why have you suddenly changed your mind?"

The crowd looked on, shocked at the sight of their leaders in utter disarray. One dead, one bound, two at war with each other. Aelius had lost his initial hold on those present, and he knew it.

Now show them who you really are, Aelius.

He swiveled back toward Sarai, eerily calm. Then, he struck. A thousand thin strands of lightning shot from his hands toward her. A latticed shield enclosed her just as swiftly, sparks arcing across the surface as it absorbed the attack.

Breathless, she turned to the only person who could have done it: Kadra, coughing blood, his hand flung in her direction, holding the dome steady. He struggled to turn his head toward her.

Was it you? his eyes asked.

She nodded, fighting back tears, and had the horror of seeing him crumple, head bowed.

Look up, she wanted to plead. *This is not the vengeance I wanted.*

The Aequitas was utter chaos. The crowd's outraged protests, Cassandane shielding herself from Aelius's barrage of attacks. Amid it all, Anek darted from the dais.

With a strained groan, Kadra widened his shield, creating an opening. Anek slipped in and gripped Sarai's head.

"Materialize it," she whispered. "Let them see all of it."

Over Aelius's roar, Anek plunged into her mind, brow creasing with strain as they sifted through Sarai's memories until they found the newly recovered threads from the night of the convivium.

Cisuré's and Tullus's figures formed onstage, the transparent contours of memory untouched by Aelius's attacks. The crowd barely breathed as they beheld the ballroom. They roared their outrage when Tullus drugged her, and fell silent hearing the scheme she'd witnessed in the closet. As the Fall played out. And as the man who'd ordered that she be given a new face came and went.

There was utter silence when the silhouettes vanished.

Then, a wave of people rose, screaming, howling, cursing as they surged over the railings onto the lower tiers, thousands descending from all corners of the Aequitas. The crowds stormed the stage, heading for a frozen Aelius, whose vigiles fought them off. White-faced, Anek let go of Sarai's head, looking close to retching. On the dais, Cisuré stared at Aelius as if she'd never seen him before.

For a moment, Sarai almost pitied her, in spite of all the damage she had done. But it was only for a moment. Steeling herself, she glanced to her left and saw Kadra staring at the ground, eyes blank. Her lips parted, though she could barely conceive of what to say, when metal crashed to the ground behind her. She jumped aside as another broken railing hit the ground. Several enraged citizens hefted it, throwing it into the wall of Aelius's vigiles. Edessa was baying for his blood.

Kadra's head whipped up. He bit back a curse seconds before the shield around Sarai flared to extend across the mob in a stunning sweep of gold, right as Aelius seemed to recover. Then everything happened at once.

Cisuré screamed Aelius's name. Cassandane yelled for her vigiles to assist her. Aelius's hands dropped to the sword at his hip while he shot forth a bolt of lightning at Sarai, nearly searing her vision. And she knew what was going to happen before it did.

"Kadra!"

Aelius's second bolt snapped against the shield in a burst of light, seconds before his blade buried itself in Kadra's chest.

The shield quivered as she dropped to her knees. It trembled as a sound of raw agony left Kadra's throat. But it held until Aelius's attack was absorbed before vanishing, leaving only the man on his knees before her. Head bowed. A blade through his chest.

No. She shook her head. *This isn't happening.*

"Sarai, we need to get out of here." Anek had recovered their composure. "Come! Before Aelius strikes again!"

The man in question folded his arms as horrified silence fell in the Aequitas.

"Looks like your champion is dead." Wiping a trail of sweat from his brow, Aelius cast an inquiring glance at the people who'd so eagerly mobbed the stage and now cowered away from him. "Really, what harm did I do to you in asking you to trust the gods? If anything, I enriched your lives. I deserve to be formalized as a Saint for that alone."

"Aelius," Cassandane began, only for a serrated blade of lightning to slam into her shoulder. The older Tetrarch gritted her teeth in pain, but a translucent shield of crimson lightning flared to life with a flick of her wrist, encircling Sarai, Anek, and the crowd. "That's enough."

Aelius gave her a dismissive glance. "You can't take me, Cassandane." He looked out at the crowd. "Wipe out the lot of them, blame Kadra, and life goes on."

They were going to die. Like Tullus and K—

No. He's just injured. Nothing you can't heal.

Uncaring of what was happening around her, she crouched before him and stroked his cheek.

"I healed you once. I can do it again." She felt for his pulse. Waiting. Waiting.

Can't feel his pulse if you're shaking, she reminded herself. "I'll have to remove the blade first. So—"

"Sarai, stop." Hands gripped her shoulders, gently pulling her away. She struggled against the hold, but it only tightened.

"Don't do this to yourself." Anek's voice trembled, features tormented. "He's gone."

"He's *not* gone! He needs a healer. I can help!"

"Look at him," Anek said quietly. "*Look* at him and tell me what you see."

Frustrated, Sarai turned to Kadra, swallowing at his pulpy face, at the burns Aelius had inflicted. His robes hung in tatters, bisected at his chest where the hilt of Aelius's sword jutted out. And he wasn't moving.

Her heart cracked. "No, I don't accept that . . ." She knelt before the man who'd protected her only moments ago and shook him by the shoulders. "He wouldn't just go without a word!"

Anek pulled her into a tight hug. "Sarai, I'm so sorry."

Aelius shrugged. "Not to worry. You're all about to head where he did."

He stretched out a hand, lightning forming within, and she numbly waited for it to strike her, the panic in Cassandane's eyes indicating that even she didn't know if her shield could withstand Aelius.

A red streak appeared across Aelius's cheek and the fire winked out as the dagger hit the ground behind him. He touched the cut, and turned slowly, looking strangely hurt, before his features hardened.

Cisuré's eyes were unseeing, glazed, a blonde marionette whose strings had just been severed, arm still outstretched from the throw.

"Not you too." The fire winked back to life in his palm as he gripped Cisuré's neck. "Not after all these years." Cisuré's lips parted in a scream just as Cassandane lurched to her feet, freeing her sword from its baldric.

"Stand down," she snarled.

Aelius glowered at both women, webs of fire building around him.

It's all gone to hell. Sarai numbly gripped Kadra's cold hands. "You can't be gone. You—you said you belonged to me." Her voice broke.

Anek looked close to tears. "Sarai, please let him go—"

A manic laugh left her at that. "He didn't let me go! And I hunted him—hated him for so long. We both had it wrong and ruined our lives over what *he* did." She pointed at Aelius, who was now dueling with Cassandane and Cisuré. "And now the gods do *this*?"

The gods. A single thought separated from her grief with complete, piercing conviction. She tore free of Anek's grip, pulling their dagger from its sheath as she did.

"Whatever you're thinking of doing, don't," they bit out with a glance at where Cisuré had escaped the fracas to flee down the dais toward them.

"Sarai, I'm so sorry," she sobbed, then paused at the dagger in Sarai's hand. "What are you doing?"

"This is *my* decision." The words were steel. Sarai held Anek's gaze. "Don't you dare take this from me."

With a grim nod, Anek stepped away, pulling Cisuré with them when she tried to grab Sarai.

"You've done enough," they hissed.

Sarai didn't look at what was happening on the dais as she sliced her hand open from palm to elbow. She needed blood for this.

The runes from Admia's Summoning two weeks ago returned to her with absolute clarity. Daubing a finger in her blood, she drew the first one. *Sword.* A hysterical laugh slipped from her at the knowledge that each one was far too apropos for the violence of the last hour.

Flame, strength, heart, blood, end. She painted each one onto the Aequitas's floor with the dim shape of Cisuré screaming in the background and Aelius battling Cassandane—none of whom she could be bothered with at the moment.

With every stroke, her chest tightened as it had four years ago, breath growing painful as magic drained from her in waves. But pain was an old friend now, and she paid it no heed.

Unity was the second-to-last rune. Then, *modrai.* The invisible band around her chest constricted as black flames flared across the Aequitas's stage. For the third time in her life, Sarai sat in a mess of her own blood.

And waited for Death to come.

CHAPTER
THIRTY-FIVE

A bolt of agony stiffened her spine, an all-too-familiar pressure wrapping thorny fingers around her heart and trying to tug it from her chest.

Sarai didn't fight it, not as she had four years ago. Closing her eyes, she surrendered to the torment, letting it pull her off the ground and toward the too-bright sky. The world shrank to the screeching whistle of wind around her as every ounce of power was wrenched from her without mercy.

But she didn't break. She couldn't. She was the Sidran Tower Girl and the Petitor to the maddest man in all Edessa. Nothing could break her. So she didn't scream, and breathed through the pain.

Then something flickered at the edge of her sight.

Black fire flared high in a wall around her, coalescing until it settled into a figure at least twice her height. Her mouth fell open.

The gold patterned cowl and burnished armor were unmistakable, as was the balance hanging from his cloak for the weighing of souls. Swords of every make and metal were sheathed in a hundred scabbards strapped to him. But what transfixed her were his pitiless eyes, dark and red as blood, in an ageless, gray face. Eyes she'd seen once before.

Moments passed in silence before Death raised a pale eyebrow. "Well?"

The word held all the chill of the frozen north, and all the pleading shrieks of every dying soul. She would have fallen to her knees in piety, if not for the fact that they were floating halfway above the Aequitas.

"Lord Death." Her voice was a rusty creak. "I seek a favor."

Death drew near, touching her hand with an ice-cold finger. His face held mild interest at the scars, but his eyes were utterly, inhumanly blank.

"I didn't let you go four years ago for you to arrive here again." He tilted his head to their surroundings and gave her a speaking look. "You court disaster."

Her awe shattered at his detachment.

"Disaster *found* me," she bit out, pointing down to Aelius's ivory-robed figure. "That man used your names to tyrannize this city, but you did *nothing* to dissuade him. Does that weigh so little on you?"

Death looked curious. "Why should it? We did not cause those deaths."

She bit her tongue before she could offend the god whose aid she sought. "Will you grant my favor or not?"

Faint amusement crossed his iron-gray visage. "I haven't heard it."

"There's a man who just . . . died," she whispered, tears burning her throat. "I want him back. Whole and hardy and in no less condition."

Death inclined his head before taking a black book from somewhere within his robes. "Name?" he inquired.

"Drenevan." Her voice broke. "Drenevan bu Kadra."

The god flipped through a few pages before his brow formed the faintest crease. "Him?" Death sounded vaguely disgusted. "He who has sent two hundred and fifty-nine people to me over the past four years alone?"

Sarai closed her eyes, torn between pain and horrified laughter. *Gods, did he kill someone every week?*

"You ask me to unleash a murderer back into the world." Death's scarlet eyes were without mercy. "And for the basest of reasons."

She set her jaw. "All who perform a Summoning are granted a favor by the gods."

"We do not grant *every* favor," Death said softly. "Not where doing so could cause harm."

"Since when has it been the task of Death to preserve life?" she shot back. "I'm not claiming that he's a good man. But none of those he killed were innocents. They would have caused further tragedy if left unchecked."

Death was silent. Terror built in her with each passing second. Because if the gods themselves wouldn't aid her, then he was really, truly *gone*.

Tears spilled down her cheeks. *I can't even remember the last thing I said to him.*

"Then is this the end?" she whispered.

Death's features were inscrutable. "Twice now, we have crossed paths without consequence," he noted, the edges of his figure already starting to blur. "Do try to prevent a third meeting."

"Wait! I beg of you, please at least tell him that I—"

The black flames winked out of sight, leaving Sarai with nothing but the ground as she slowly fell to meet it, and an anguish too deep for words.

CHAPTER
THIRTY-SIX

As her heels touched the Aequitas's stage, the first thing Sarai noticed was that someone had pulled the sword free of Kadra's chest. It lay on the ground, gleaming scarlet.

Hefting the blade, she searched for its owner. The crowd parted, aghast, evidently having witnessed the otherworldly figure conversing with her. She would have laughed at the fact that Aelius had been scant yards from a god and missed it. But there was no laughter in her.

On the dais, the object of her pursuit easily fended off attacks from Cassandane's and Kadra's vigiles, many of whom lay dead with charred necks. Anek had abandoned Cisuré in favor of supporting their Tetrarch, who sported several ugly wounds in addition to the hole in her shoulder.

Tossing away another body, Aelius fought a black-robed vigile Sarai recognized as Gaius. She tested the blade, recalling her offhand remark to Kadra months ago.

Every snowgrape harvester learns to throw a knife.

"I'm the Magus Supreme." He shot a bolt that Gaius narrowly missed. Sarai raised her arm, narrowing in on Aelius with single-minded hatred. "You could never—"

An ugly squelch filled the air. The wet sound of a stake sinking into mud, of a knife severing a vine. Aelius froze, looking down at the blade that had slammed through one side of his ribcage to emerge from the other. His mouth worked even as his knees buckled, and he fell headfirst down the stairs to rest in a crumpled heap.

Sarai watched the tremulous rise and fall of his chest for a moment, then turned to the crowd.

"We'll start with a single log."

For a moment, no one moved.

Then, Gaius, eyes wet with tears, staggered down the steps toward the log pile that was always to the far right of the stage.

Several vigiles fisted Aelius's white robes, dragging him to the post at the center of the stage where they bound him. His fingers twitched, only able to summon a few sparks of lightning in his weakness. Kadra had been stronger.

Gaius placed the log by Aelius's feet and then turned to her, bowing low. Crouching beside it, Sarai drew *yaris* and stepped back as flame swept over the wood. Aelius shook his head groggily, the sword bisecting his body still embedded.

"Aelius of Edessa, you stand here accused of the *homicidium* of too many people to count, including past Petitors. Your crimes are *ambitus*, *calumnia*, torture, attempted *homicidium*, bribery, corruption, and almost every unsavory act an elected official can commit," Sarai said softly. "How do you plead?"

Alarm sparked to life in his gaze as the fire moved toward his feet.

Sarai turned to Gaius. "Another log."

Someone pressed a log in her hand. She turned to find another of Kadra's vigiles, eyes red. Several of his people waited, all carrying wood. She gripped the vigile's shoulder in silent grief before placing the tinder at Aelius's feet.

He yelped as the log cracked, sending a shower of sparks over his feet.

"How do you plead?" Sarai asked again, too numb for spite.

Blood ran from his mouth as he opened it, trying to speak.

She tilted her head. "Another log."

One by one, they gave them to her, and she placed each one at the feet of the man who had ruined so many lives for coin.

She didn't have to wait long for the heat to bite his heels, for it to wrap around his ankles to the discordant music of his screams. Expelling a long breath, she sat on the stage, drawing her knees to her chest as Tetrarch Aelius of Edessa, Magus Supreme, burned to death with his own blade in him. Tendrils of fire ran up his cheeks as people cursed his name, and vigiles vindictively added logs to his pyre in the name of the man whose life he had taken.

And she couldn't tell if it was smoke or anguish behind her silent tears.

So this was vengeance, Sarai thought numbly. A broken, empty blankness where joy should be, devoid of pomp and celebration. *And why would there be any?* In less than a day, the Tetrarchy had been whittled to a single Tetrarch. And the man she loved was dead.

"Sarai." Cisuré staggered toward her, sounding as though she was in shock. "You—"

"Leave me alone." She was the last person Sarai wanted to see.

"Turn around, you need to—"

She shot Cisuré a glower so fierce the other girl retreated a few steps. But there were whispers growing behind them. Frantic. Awed. Sarai stilled as she heard boots approaching her from behind. At the other end of the stage, Gaius turned deathly pale. And someone sat beside her.

She didn't move. Didn't turn to face her companion. She'd deluded herself once already. If she did it again, she might never be able to stop.

"He looks better charred," a beautiful voice murmured. "But I thought you disapproved of burning."

Her lower lip trembled.

"You have no obligation to ever forgive me," the voice continued. "You owe me nothing. But I must ask."

She steadfastly stared straight ahead as his voice grew the slightest bit hoarse.

"I seem to be missing a hole in my chest. You wouldn't happen to know anything about that, would you?"

She exploded. "Of all the *havïd* things to joke about—" Swiveling toward him, she halted.

With knives for eyes and a cruel edge to his smile, Drenevan bu Kadra, scourge of her heart, sat beside her, utterly intact.

I never said I would deny you his return, an ice-cold voice whispered in her head, and if she could move, she would have crumpled and sobbed in relief.

Kadra's gaze traced her features, dropping to the arm she'd nearly cut in half. With a rough curse, he reached for it but froze as his hands met her skin, the weight of the past settling between them.

Conscious of all the eyes on them, she wearily rose, throwing her good hand toward Kadra.

"The gods have answered," she announced to the crowd, and only faintly winced when they roared in jubilation. She had no words after that.

Cassandane took over, clutching her wounded shoulder. "There will be much to do in the upcoming days. To record what happened here, and construct safeguards to prevent it from happening again. But those are concerns for the future. Today, we rest and heal. We will convene again four days from now," she said, voice weak, and was met with more cheers.

The spectators in the Aequitas began to disperse. On the dais, Anek shook their head, looking stunned, before indicating that they and Cassandane would be leaving. Factionless, Cisuré blankly watched as the crowd thinned, then she quietly filed out. Gaius turned to them, bowing low before dragging Aelius's charred corpse from the stage so it bumped every step.

Then it was just her and Kadra. And the truth between them.

In the intervening minutes, his features had closed, eyes carefully blank when she turned to face him. In an attempt to disrupt that rigid calm, she threw down a gauntlet.

"I see you took good care of my ribbon," she began, and watched an almost imperceptible flinch run through him. He expected recriminations and judgment; she knew that much.

"I was told that you were dead," he said simply.

"Othus truly thought you were guilty. He had me healed, given a new face, then carted back to Arsamea." She drew a deep breath. "I spent four years hating you."

Kadra inclined his head, distant and unreadable. "Understandable."

"I didn't remember much, but I recognized your voice at the Robing. Even when I agreed to stay in Aoran Tower, it was with the intent to destroy you."

His features tightened. "So why save me?" He looked from her bleeding arm to her runes on the stage. "Why risk your life for me?"

"You did the same."

"Fourteen, and I left you to die," he ground out. "I owe you *everything*. You owed me nothing."

"Your debt is paid."

He shook his head. "Don't be so quick to forgive me. There will be days when this will resurface between us. And you will despise me for it."

"You keep saying that. That I'll hate you or regret being with you. But if I did, I wouldn't have Summoned Death to beg for you!" she snapped. "Gods, I love you, Kadra, but you're the biggest fool in all Edessa."

He blinked, and she laughed.

"I spent the past few months forgiving you," she said, drawing closer. "Disliking you, doubting you, admiring you—reluctantly. I've gone through every stage between grief and acceptance already. And that was when I still wondered if you had thrown me off Sidran Tower."

"I left—"

"Me for Death? Yes." She shrugged. "But you ran there right after me in a four-year-long apology. Cisuré didn't even try."

Something bleak crossed his face.

One more step and she was inches from him. "Like it or not, I've already forgiven you. So if you'd just hurry up and kiss me, I'd appreciate—"

With a raw groan, he lifted her against him, one hand gripping the back of her head. His stubble scraped her skin as he pressed kisses against her wet cheeks, her jaw, her throat, whispering that he was sorry, that he loved her. She reveled in the feel of him. He was here. Alive.

Long moments later, he stroked her hair. "We need to have an election."

"Plotting already?"

He chucked her under the chin. "Can I convince you to take up a position? You were magnificent. Especially today."

She shuddered, arms wrapped around his waist. "Absolutely not. I'm happy where I am."

He gave a wry sigh. "Cato said you might say that." He searched her eyes. "You've done well. Better than your younger self dreamed." He exhaled roughly. "That was the worst part of it. Seeing the dreams in your eyes, then seeing you on the ground—" He broke off.

"That makes two of us." She swallowed, clutching him close. "Still, you were very kind back then, telling me how to get to the Academiae."

"Led you straight to your doom. But you always did see the best in me." His lips curved. "Trying to make me better?"

She snorted. "I think you've made me worse. I set Aelius on fire."

"I saw." Interlocking their hands, he kissed her fingers. "Tell me, what do you want from here on out?"

She raised a brow. "Anything?"

"Name it and it's yours."

Footsteps alerted her that Kadra's vigiles had decided that he and his Petitor had had enough time together.

She rose on her toes to whisper it into his ear. "Then be happy with me."

A slow smile formed on his face. "My beautiful Petitor." He swung her into his arms to the shock of them all. "That will be the easiest of feats."

CHAPTER THIRTY-SEVEN

Two months later

Sarai spun a dagger in one hand, keeping her eyes on the weasel before her.

"I'm not here to bargain," she reminded him. "The law's been revised. You can't make your Guildspeople work for longer than twelve hours under the table."

Stones Guildmaster Albanus arranged flowers within an elaborate vase for the umpteenth time. "You know, this is Errigal porcelain." He indicated the sleek finish. "Estimated at six thousand aurei. It could be yours."

"No, thank you." The Guildspeople who kept "passing by" the open window of his office looked relieved at her rejection. One man, who seemed to think he was well concealed in a corner outside, raised his eyebrows. "Two people are already dead of overwork. I'm here as a courtesy. Next time, it'll be with a warrant."

Albanus sat up at that. "You lot think you can waltz in and ruin our businesses. We employ this city. We're worth far more and you pander to *them*?"

"Worth far more," she repeated. Her dagger ceased its spinning. "Worth far more?"

Past the window, the eavesdropping Guildsman smiled faintly.

She rose. "For the last time, I'm not here to negotiate. If Tetrarch Kadra or I hear of any violation, your quarries will be taken from you."

He smiled nastily. "Try, and I'll send both of you right back to Death's door—"

Her dagger shot out of her hand. Light flashed on porcelain and Albanus shrieked as the vase crashed to the ground, shattering.

"Six thousand aurei!" He clutched the pieces, trying to gather as many as possible.

Selecting several, she stalked out of his office and flung them in a nearby bush, nodding to the ill-concealed Guildsman.

"Try a different corner," she advised dryly.

A slow, strangely familiar smile rose to his lips. "Interesting. It didn't take."

His voice was . . . incredible. Soothing, yet sheathed in menace. A slow glide into icy waters. That was when it clicked. He reminded her of Kadra.

Sunlight hit his features as she backed away. Eyes widening, she opened her mouth when he placed a finger over it.

"You never saw me today. And you won't notice me again unless I give you permission." Nausea swamped her, vision blurring as he bent to whisper in her ear. "I'll see you soon, Death-Summoner."

She blinked, and wondered why she'd halted in the Guild's empty courtyard for no reason. Shaking her head, she headed outside and found Anek waiting by Caelum, looking mildly alarmed at the screams now coming from Albanus's office.

"Should I ask?"

"I wasted a good hour talking to him when I should've just done that earlier." Sarai sheathed her dagger. "What brings you here?"

"She's leaving," Anek said quietly. "I thought you'd want to know."

Sarai halted. "I see."

"I thought all four of us might go see her off." They mounted their horse.

Climbing into the saddle, Sarai followed and was halfway down the street when she frowned.

"Hold on, did you say all *four* of us?"

Gold arced across a rosy sky. Summer had come to Edessa last month, and was just as beautiful as Sarai had imagined. Carpets of sun cups and desert marigolds spread across the Academiae, peering through cracks in the cobblestone. Telmar, slowly coming off *ibez*, had taken to painting them, while Gaius studiously refused to go outside as the pollen left his eyes streaming. As a result, she got to gallivant off and perform all manner of tasks: handling some of the rainwater drainage efforts post-stormfall and, on occasion, journeying to other cities to handle cases there. Some wondered at her presence, but she enjoyed seeing the country at its different levels, learning more of its intricacies and people.

She and Anek dismounted at the city gates, at the mouth of the entrance to Kadra's Quarter. The two figures standing there turned at their approach.

Cisuré hesitantly raised a hand in greeting, buckling an overstuffed saddlebag onto her horse. Beside her, Harion tilted his nose down at them.

"Well, I wish you the best," he said shortly, stalking past them in a cloud of navy robes.

"Off so soon, Harion?" Sarai inquired politely and saw him scowl.

"That's *Tetrarch Harion*, to you, barmaid," he snapped.

"You still owe me a hundred aurei, *Tetrarch* Harion," she said sweetly, and laughed when he muttered something about giving her the coin later.

Anek shook their head as he rode off. "He'll never do it. Up to his eyes in debt with all the nobles and Guildmasters he paid off to get elected."

"It's fun to hang it over his head, though," Sarai mused. "See him get that panicked light in his eyes."

Anek snorted, clapping Cisuré's shoulders. "I hope your new post treats you well. In Kirtule, is it?"

Cisuré nodded. "At a military outpost. I hear it's strict, but . . . it might do me some good."

"Glad to hear it."

Cisuré turned to Sarai next and paused, eyes dropping to the ground. In the days after what the public had deemed the Great Unraveling, they had scarcely seen each other as elections were called, nominees were announced, and Harion had bought himself a position. And when they had met, nothing had been the same.

It never would be. But she owed it to herself to see this ending through.

Sarai turned to the girl who had once been her sister, who had seen her every trial and sorrow for so many years. "Goodbye," she said quietly. It was a poor word to express everything.

Cisuré's throat worked. She stepped away. "Perhaps you'll come visit. All of you."

Sarai couldn't answer. With a glance at her, Anek took over. "*Tetrarch* Harion as well?" they scoffed. "No, he's too busy for us. But who knows what the future'll bring?"

Downcast, Cisuré mounted her laden horse. "I'll see you then."

She exhaled shakily, eyes pausing on Sarai. And for an instant the girl she'd known in Arsamea, before Aelius, before all of this, seemed to reappear. Sarai's heart clenched, broke.

Cisuré smiled through her tears. "Goodbye."

Without further words, she steered her mount around and set off on the winding road out of Edessa, past small towns and a curving river, to a place that might be the start of her journey.

Sarai wiped at the tear that ran down her cheek as Cisuré's figure shrank to a dot in the distance. Robes shifted behind her as the vigiles guarding the gate stiffened, and she knew who approached even before his roughened hand wrapped around hers.

"What's this I hear about six thousand aurei?" Kadra inquired gravely to Anek's loud guffaw.

"That's my cue to leave." They inclined their head at Kadra. "She's as bad as you these days."

He looked amused. "So I hear."

Shaking their head, Anek departed as the sun sank low on the horizon, Cisuré long having passed out of their sight. Something sat on the tip of her tongue, the blurred outline of a figure at the Stones Guild, and the warped shadow several paces from her. A breath and the thought winked out.

"Election results for the final Tetrarch should be out soon." Kadra's thumb stroked her wrist. "The Guildmasters' pick is leading."

Sarai sighed. "It'll never end, will it?"

"No," he said softly. "There will always be someone to fight against, great or small."

She tilted her face up to his, resolute. "Then we'll keep at it. You and I."

The last rays of the sun illuminated his tired features, black eyes full of so much love that she couldn't help but twine her arms around his waist.

"You and I," he agreed with a wicked grin.

With quiet joy, Sarai kissed Ur Dinyé's most vicious Tetrarch under a sky like blood and knew she had finally found her place in the land they would shape.

And the Sidran Tower Girl smiled.

THE END

RUNES IN URDISH

ASTOMAND: A rune meaning "Materialization." This rune can only be used by Petitors to pull out memories for public view from the minds of those they are Probing. Attempts by magi who do not possess this magic won't work. *Astomand*, *herar*, and *zosta* are colloquially known as the "Petitor's Trio."

BESHAZ: A rune meaning "heal." This rune can only be used by healers to reach into another's body and perform muscle-deep repairs, a talent that requires great precision. Contrary to the rune's literal meaning, it can also be used by healers to perform destruction to the body, shredding muscles and bone from within.

FRAZAM: The rune for "end." Used to cease or destroy something, by a magus with the appropriate bloodline. Powerful Urdish magi use it to dissipate lightning. Those of other countries can use it for halting mudslides or even quelling tornadoes.

HERAR: A rune meaning "Probe." This rune can only be used by Petitors to reach into another's mind and view the archive of their memories. Attempts by magi who do not possess this magic won't work. *Astomand*, *herar*, and *zosta* are colloquially known as the "Petitor's Trio."

KHON: The rune for "blood." Any invocation of this rune does not bode well. Across lands and cultures, it has traditionally been used for sacrifice and dark rituals.

LAYK: The rune for "unity." Largely used when combining elements or runes into a greater whole.

MODRAI: A rune meaning "death" and the very last rune used in every sequence of Summoning runes. Ur Dinyé's draconian laws require a Summoning as punishment for certain crimes, which has given the rune a reputation as a criminal's mark.

NAIYA: The rune for "heart." The rune's original name faded into obscurity some eight centuries ago after people colloquially began referring to it as the "Naiya" rune after the former Kashyalin debt-slave. Now, the latter term reigns.

NIHUMB: The rune for "concealment." A minor illusion used by Sarai to hide her scars.

RIUKHEN: The rune for "strength." As with *naiya*, the rune's original name was lost to time in favor of being titled after Naiya's powerful husband.

SAFSHER: A rune meaning "sword." The rune has little practical use for Urds, but is useful in the southern land of Ysāññe, whose populace can manipulate metal as the Urds do lightning.

YARIS: The rune for "fire."

ZOSTA: A rune meaning "Examination." This rune can only be used Petitors to read when someone is lying. Attempts by magi who do not possess this magic won't work. *Astomand*, *herar*, and *zosta* are colloquially known as the "Petitor's Trio."

GLOSSARY

ANCIENT TONGUE: The language of Ur Dinyé's long-dead monarchs and scribes that persists in use across academia and the upper class.

ASSARIUS (*pl:* assarii): A bronze coin of Ur Dinyé. The head of the coin is engraved with approximations of the many Saints or their emblems. The tail sports the seal of the Metals Guild, verifying the coin to be authentic.

AUREUS (*pl:* aurei): A gold coin of Ur Dinyé. The head of the coin is engraved with approximations of the seven Elsar or their emblems. The tail sports the seal of the Metals Guild, verifying the coin to be authentic. An aureus is equivalent to ten denarii or a hundred assarii.

BIRRUS: A woolen half-cloak of sorts worn over the head and shoulders.

THE CODICES: The eighty-three manuscripts depicting and detailing the workings of the seven High Elsar, seven Dark Elsar, and two ambiguous Elsar. A collection of firsthand and secondhand events, The Codices are sacred to Elsarians, those who worship the Elsar.

CORPUS JURIS TOTUS: The collated volumes of Ur Dinyé's body of law and legal procedure.

DAMNATIO AD METALLA: A phrase meaning "Damned to the mines" in the ancient tongue. The severity of the punishment depends on the mine and its Minewarden.

DENARIUS (*pl:* denarii): A silver coin of Ur Dinyé. The head of the coin is engraved with approximations of the seven Elsar or their emblems. The tail sports the seal of the Metals Guild, verifying the coin to be authentic. A denarius is equivalent to ten assarii.

THE ELSAR: The pantheon of gods worshipped in the Elsarian religion. They are divided into High Elsar (Charity, Harvest, Radiance, Temperance, Truth, Wisdom), Dark Elsar (Avarice, Discord, Famine, Indolence, Pestilence, Ruin, Deceit), and Ambiguous Elsar (Wrath, Death, Time). The gods are considered benevolent, malignant, and mercurial, depending on who is asked.

INSULA (*pl*: insulae): Apartment-style buildings occupied by lower-income Urds.

IUDEX (*pl*: iudices): An Urd judge.

LUGENS: Healers whose specialty it is to examine the dead and autopsy their bodies.

THE NAADUIR: The minor pantheon of gods, comprised of humans who achieved deification through devotion to the Elsar. The Naaduir are divided into Saints and the Wretched, who are presumed to respectively serve the High Elsar and the Dark Elsar.

NEUTRALIS: An individual whose gender identity and/or gender expression expands outside the traditional gender binary.

ACKNOWLEDGMENTS

One August, a manipulative judge and his wary prosecutor strolled into my head and altered the course of my life. Over the following years, these two and their slow-burn dance around each other occupied my every free hour. I grew as they did and learned so much from them. It feels surreal now that they will be known by others and that this story of my heart will have a life beyond my laptop.

This journey would never have been possible without so many wonderful people. I'm endlessly grateful to Molly Jamieson and Ginger Clark, my rock star agents, for giving me the chance of a lifetime and helping to strengthen this book while championing it from both sides of the Atlantic. You've both been such a steadying presence, and your enthusiasm and love for *This Monster of Mine* means the world. I couldn't ask for better partners! And to my extraordinary editors, Calah Singleton and Mahalaleel M. Clinton, thank you both for being an utter dream to work with. You're brilliant, incisive, and genuinely understood Sarai and Kadra so well that I knew they were safe in your hands. Thank you for taking a chance on *TMOM*, for seeing everything it could be, and for working tirelessly to make it shine.

I'm deeply indebted to the amazing, talented publishing teams at Union Square & Co. and Hodderscape. Thank you so much for adding me to your incredible roster of authors. I'm honored to work with you and so grateful to Christina Stambaugh, Alison Skrabek, Sandy Noman, Kevin Ullrich, Jared Oriel, Patrick Sullivan, and Lisa Forde at UNSQ and to Molly Powell, Sophie Judge, Natalie Chen, Juliette Winter, Kate Keehan, Laura Bartholomew, and Carrie Hutchison at Hodderscape. A massive thanks to my copy editors for polishing this book and the cover illustrators for capturing its essence so stunningly.

ACKNOWLEDGMENTS

To my critique partners, Kimberly Mann, the first person who believed that I could write; Katie Lindskog, who read *TMOM*'s zero draft twice; Carrie Ann, who assured me that this book wasn't hopeless; Mariet Kay, who taught me the importance of tacking a horse; A. M. Crafton and Julia Sung, who pointed out every plot thread I dropped; and the wickedly talented Isabella Ford, whom I am constantly pointing at for the universe to send big things, I love you all! A huge shout-out to the AMAZING community of authors and readers I've met since the start of this publishing journey. I remain in awe of all your talent, marketing ability, and generosity of spirit.

And finally, my biggest, deepest, most soul-deep gratitude to the people of my heart. To J.R.R. Tolkien, Peter Jackson, and the creatives involved in *The Lord of the Rings* and *The Hobbit* trilogies as well as The Rings of Power series, annon allen, mellyn nin for expanding the boundaries of my imagination so brilliantly, beautifully, and evocatively. Middle-earth will always be my preferred universe.

To Ji Sung, whose characters have kept me going for a decade now, it's no exaggeration to say that your work transformed my life. Thank you for your cheekbones and for giving the world both Cha Yohan and Kang Yohan. 감사합니다 그리고 항상 응원합니다!

To my family, to the man who hears my every deranged idea with utter patience and who never doubted that this book would be published even when I was inches from giving up, I love you, Demille. To Andrea, for coming armed with cats and food and using her precious days off to chill with me, you're the best sister ever (yes, I'll stop being mushy now). To my very overworked mom, who didn't bat an eye even as I walked away from my legal career and who supported me wholeheartedly as I wrote on the couch all day, I know how lucky I am, but you're going to think I'm very weird when you read this book!

And to God, we really did make it. I owe you everything. I can't wait to touch that horizon.